HELEN CAREY

Lavender Road

First published in Great Britain 1994 by Orion Books Ltd
This edition published in 2017 by Cambria Publishing.

ISBN 978-1-9997416-3-1

In memory of my parents

Prologue

'Sorry about squashing you when I died, Jen,' Dodie Miles whispered. 'I slipped.'

'It's all right,' Jennifer Carter muttered irritably, her eyes on the stage, green and intent. 'It didn't hurt. Look, go on, quick, it's your turn. Miss Dobson is waving at you.'

Left alone in the wings, Jennifer Carter flexed her bruised knee under the crumpled white velvet skirt and listened to the applause as Dodie Miles took her bow. Dodie had made quite a good, if somewhat buxom, Paris, delivering her lines forcefully straight to the back of the hall as they had been taught. Better than Gillian Price whose dumpy, excitable Romeo spoke his lines the same way Gillian used the new class typewriter, in eager erratic bursts, forgetting to use the space bar.

Jennifer looked across the stage to the opposite wings where Gillian stood waiting behind Miss Dobson's raised arm. She caught her eye and they smiled at each other briefly, nervously, hero and heroine, tragic lovers, Romeo and Juliet, alive again, waiting to face their audience for the last time. Waiting to take their bow.

Seeing Gillian grimace and point exaggeratedly to the back of her head, Jen realised that some of her hair had escaped from her plait in the dramatic death scene. There wasn't time to retie it. Abruptly she yanked off the ribbon and shook out the plait, letting the thick rust-red waves flare out over her slender shoulders.

Miss Dobson dropped her arm and the two girls walked out, Gillian, smiling broadly, rather Humpty-Dumpty-like in the short navy jacket and plus-fours and Jen, in the dusty white dress, pale skinned and wild haired like a gypsy bride.

At once, the rhythm of the applause changed, became stronger, more insistent, more genuine.

As arranged, the rest of the cast divided to let them through. And as she met Gillian centre stage and turned to the front, Jen's heart swelled with pride. She knew the audience was clapping for her. She knew she had moved them. Had made them hang on her words. She'd even heard someone sniffling when she died. She squinted over the makeshift footlights and saw

1

them smiling. Smiling at her.

She could see Katy Parsons at the back, smiling and coughing in her excitement. She could see the enthusiastic adoring faces of the fourth and fifth forms. She could see the rows of proud parents and relatives clapping and murmuring to each other. Not hers of course, hers hadn't bothered to come. Shakespeare wasn't their cup of tea, not even when their daughter had the biggest and the best part.

None of her family had come, none of her brothers, not even Angie, her younger sister. For a second, as she sank into her graceful, well-practised curtsey, Jen wished at least one of them had come. Just one to tell them at home that she could do it, that she was good, that the audience went on clapping and clapping.

But then as she straightened, she shrugged it off. She didn't care. She squared her shoulders and lifted her chin. Their opinion didn't matter. What did they know anyway?

She knew. She knew she could do it. Wasn't the smiling, clapping audience telling her just that?

Suddenly she smiled back and to her surprise the applause surged again. It was a wonderful moment. A powerful moment. More than just a small success in a school play. It was the confirmation of her hopes and dreams. Confirmation of her talent. Confirmation of her ambition.

She was going to be an actress. She was going to escape from the mundane life of a South London street preparing for war. She wasn't going to shove gunpowder into shells all day long at the munitions factory in Croydon like so many of the girls, she wasn't going to break her nails on a typewriter, she wasn't going to learn nursing like bossy, bosomy Dodie.

No, she was going to be a star, a bright shining star, and nobody was going to stop her: not her family, not the government, not Adolf Hitler, nobody.

Chapter One

1 September 1939

Joyce Carter thrust her hand into the flour jar and swore as a cloud of flour puffed out of the top, whitening the ragged sleeve of her cardigan. Then her probing fingers met something cold and hard and she grunted in grim satisfaction and withdrew her hand.

Rinsing under the tap at the sink revealed a gold chain-link bracelet held at the ends with a delicate safety chain and a heart-shaped clasp.

For a moment Joyce stared at it gleaming wetly in the rough palm of her hand. If it was real gold, as Stanley said, then it might just be worth the ten pound they wanted for bail. But if it wasn't, then that sharp old bastard Lorenz wouldn't give her more than ten bob for it. And then there would be all hell to pay with Stanley. It would be her fault if Lorenz said it wasn't gold, of course, not Stanley's. Nothing was ever Stanley's fault. Not even getting nicked for falling blind drunk off the getaway truck.

As she turned her head, she caught sight of her reflection in the spotted mirror that hung on the back of the kitchen door and quickly looked away again. She didn't much like what she saw there at the best of times. With her straight mouth and wide chin, she'd never been a beauty, and time had taken its toll on the soft skin round her eyes. But today her face reflected rather more than care-worn middle age: it reflected the fist of her husband. She lifted a hand to her swollen cheek and winced. It was never worth annoying Stanley. She turned abruptly back to the flour jar. There should be a diamond ring left in there. The last one.

She laid the bracelet on the draining boards, dried her hand on her skirt and made the decision.

She'd have to take the ring to Lorenz as well. In case the bracelet wasn't enough. Though what the hell they'd live on if Stanley was put away, God only knew. What with Bob already inside and Jen full of twaddle about becoming an actress and refusing to take a factory job, young Pete was the only one earning. And he only brought home thirty bob a week.

Joyce shook her head. With the younger three evacuated she'd probably just about cope. But what if the war was over in a couple of weeks like everyone said? What if Hitler's bombs didn't fall after all and they weren't all

3

gassed to death? What if the kids wouldn't stay in the country and came back?

She sighed. That ring was her fallback, her security. She'd hate to see it go.

But when she once again eased her hand into the soft cool flour, she couldn't find it. Carefully she probed every inch of the jar. No ring. Nothing. She blinked. Numb.

For a second's frozen horror she wondered if she could possibly have cooked it. But she hadn't made pastry for weeks. Bread and jam and fish and chips was all the kids would eat these days.

Suddenly she felt a cold welling fury. A fury born of desperate frustration. Stanley must have taken it. Without telling her. The bastard. The utter bastard. She wished suddenly she had cooked the ring, diamonds and all, in a steak and kidney pie. It would have served that selfish bugger right if he'd broken his bloody teeth on it.

Two doors along, Pam Nelson pulled the lavatory chain, opened the door, ducked under the washing line and bumped her knee on the mangle. Walking back into the kitchen, she rinsed her hands under the tap, sat down at the table and burst into tears.

She had been so certain. So sure. Sure that this time it was for real. Even her body felt different. She hadn't suffered the usual cramping stomach aches and her breasts had felt more tight than tender. She had even felt a bit sick in the mornings and the secret smile on her lips had brightened her eyes and brought a bloom to her creamy complexion.

She reached over for a tea towel and held it to her eyes as another wave of misery overtook her. Thirty-three years old, childless and tired. Tired of making do on Alan's meagre wages and what the lodger brought in. Tired of the dull repetitive meals she cooked for them, tired of her broom and duster, tired of the poky house and the shabby street, and, she hated to admit it, tired of Alan.

Alan, for whose steady devotion and shy smile she had given up her other suitors and a good secretarial job in the London County Council five years ago. The LCC didn't employ married women, and anyway Alan had wanted her to make a home, ready for their children.

Blessed with so much, looks, brains and a ready smile, she now suddenly seemed to have so little.

Tonight Alan would ask, as he did every twenty-ninth day, if she had any 'news' for him. And she would say her curse had come as it always did, regular as clockwork, and his face would fall and he would turn away to hide his disappointment, the inadequacy she knew he felt even though it wasn't necessarily his fault. And then later he would pat her on the arm and smile a thin faded version of his old heart-stopping smile and say, 'Well, never mind.

It's fun trying, isn't it?'

And she would smile back and nod, but they both knew it wasn't true anymore. It wasn't fun anymore. Not like the early days of their marriage when they had found extraordinary pleasure in each other's bodies. Nowadays their coupling was strained and tense and silent and limited to the few days in the month which the doctor said was the 'best time'.

Pam's shoulders slumped and then suddenly stiffened as she heard a step on the stairs. Alan?

She glanced wildly at the clock through swimming eyes. Ten o'clock. Certainly not Alan. He'd gone hours ago. Her heart jumped and her whole body tensed. It must be Mr Byrne, the lodger. Frantically dabbing her eyes with the tea towel, Pam prayed he would go straight out of the front door.

But he didn't.

She heard steps on the hall lino and then the kitchen door swung open. Clutching the tea towel, more embarrassed than she had ever been in her entire life, Pam leaped to her feet.

She had never wanted a lodger. It had been Alan's idea. Why, oh why, when Alan had come home saying he'd heard of someone, a Mr Burn, needing a room, had she ever agreed to it? Because they needed the money, that's why. And because deep down she had thought it might give her something new to think about.

Alan had been at work when the lodger arrived. So he had missed the awkward moment when Mr John Burn turned out to be Mr Sean Byrne, considerably younger than Pam had expected, and very Irish.

What's more, the Irishman had seen her dismay at once and his sharp blue eyes had narrowed slightly. 'Is it my handsome face you'll be objecting to, Mrs Nelson, or my nationality?'

And Pam had at once flushed with embarrassment and backed inside, forcing herself not to think of the terrible Irish bomb that had gone off in Coventry only last week killing five innocent people. One of them a schoolboy of fifteen.

'Neither, Mr Byrne,' she had mumbled unconvincingly. 'You're most welcome, of course.'

'I'll be no trouble to you, Mrs Nelson,' he had said, his soft lilting voice mocking her as he lifted his suitcase and followed her into the hall. 'A pillow for my head and a bit of food for my stomach is all I'll be asking for.'

And he had been no trouble. He kept to himself, coming down promptly for breakfast, leaving straight after for his work in Croydon, reappearing for his tea at six, going out again in the evening and letting himself in quietly at ten thirty.

In the four weeks they'd had him, he'd paid the rent promptly and in full. As Alan said, he was the perfect lodger. He was clean, he was quiet and he

5

coughed up.

It wasn't Sean Byrne's fault that Pam found his perfection annoying, found herself acting uncharacteristically cold and brisk with him, avoiding his watchful blue gaze, ignoring his wry smile.

And now, just when she least wanted to see him, he'd appeared in her kitchen in the middle of the morning and caught her with bloodshot eyes and a red nose, sobbing unhygienically into a tea towel.

Wishing she could pretend she'd been peeling onions, she swallowed hard and glared at him. 'Mr Byrne. Shouldn't you be at work by now? Why are you still here?'

Sean Byrne's eyebrows rose slightly at her tone: 'Mrs Nelson. Shouldn't you be down on your knees scrubbing the floor by now? Why are you crying?'

Pam felt herself flush, irritated by his cheek, by his mocking imitation, by the faint smile on his lips. She glared at him but before she could think of a quelling response, he shook his head.

'No, to be sure, you don't have to tell me. It's easy enough to guess.' He caught her nervous glance and held it steadily.

'You're bored, Mrs Nelson. You're driving yourself to tears of boredom cleaning and cooking all the day long.' He shrugged. 'I don't blame you. It'd bore me to death too, that's for certain.' He grinned at her suddenly. 'Not that I'm all that much of a cook, of course, not like yourself.'

Pam dropped her eyes quickly from the charm of that smile, hating him for his accurate assessment, but suddenly craving reassurance none the less. 'Other women don't seem to mind,' she muttered.

'Other women have children to occupy them,' he said and Pam tensed. She could feel his shrewd eyes on her and dreaded what he might say next. What he might ask. But he merely leaned back against the door jamb and lit a cigarette without offering her one.

'Things are about to change, Mrs Nelson,' he went on blandly, his eyes narrowed against the smoke. 'War's coming. Adolf Hitler will take Poland any day now. He intends to have Europe and as much of the rest of the world as he can. And he doesn't care too much how he goes about getting it.'

'He'll have the British forces to contend with first,' Pam said stoutly, irritated by his abrasive unconcern, 'and the Commonwealth countries too. And the French.'

Sean smiled. 'I'm not blessed with the blind faith and patriotism of the English, Mrs Nelson. All I'm saying is while the men are away defending their nation's honour, the women will have to go out to work.'

His blue eyes met hers with a faint challenge as he drew on his cigarette. 'A fine, intelligent woman like yourself, Mrs Nelson, will have no trouble in finding something useful to do.'

Pam shook her head crossly. It was easy for him to say. A nice-looking, employable, single man. 'Nobody wants married women,' she said crossly.

'Is that right?' Sean laughed softly, pushing himself off the door jamb to flick ash into the sink. 'Oh, now and I wouldn't be too sure of that either if I was you, Mrs Nelson.'

Pam's eyes widened. Then blinked. Surely he didn't mean? She saw the glint of amusement in his eyes and tried to pull herself together. Tried to think of some way of squashing his damn cheek, of preventing the hot colour staining her skin.

But before she could find the words to break the silence that suddenly seemed to envelop the kitchen, someone knocked on the front door.

Pam was along the passage with her hand on the latch before she remembered her earlier tears. She would hate for anyone to know she'd been crying.

She took a quick step back from the door and faced herself in the hall mirror. She looked odd about the eyes and annoyingly pink, but not tearful any more.

The caller knocked again. Pam hesitated. Her heart was pounding and she badly needed to powder her nose, to get rid of that embarrassing flush.

She heard a movement and turned to see Sean Byrne watching her lazily from the kitchen door.

'You look fine,' he said. 'Sparkling. Nobody would know.'

Damn him for reading her thoughts. Damn him for his sauce. Abruptly she turned back to the door.

A car stood in the road, with a driver waiting. A smartly dressed woman stood on the step. Tall, almost governessy, with her hair parted at the centre, waved over her ears and pinned in a flat chignon at the back, she closely resembled the elegant Mrs Wallis Simpson, Duchess of Windsor, and although this woman was unlikely to run off with the King, she had the same way of appearing to frown down her aristocratic nose.

Pam recognised Mrs Rutherford at once. Mrs Celia Rutherford, wife of Mr Rutherford of Rutherford & Berry, owners of the local brewery where Alan worked as an accounts clerk.

Along with the brewery, half a dozen pubs and a car, the Rutherfords also owned the big white house at the top end of Lavender Road, the posh end, overlooking the common. Pam's yard backed on to their large garden. From the upstairs windows Pam had occasionally seen Mrs Rutherford pruning her roses, or with a drink in her hand showing guests the colourful flowerbeds that bordered the garden.

'Mrs Nelson?'

Pam nodded, squinting slightly against the bright morning sun, surprised the other woman even knew her name. Mrs Rutherford had never come calling before. Pam hoped to God Sean Byrne would have the sense to keep out of sight.

'I'm Mrs Rutherford from Cedars House.'

Pam nodded nervously. Was it something to do with Alan? An accident? Pam had a sudden vision of Alan flinging himself in despair into a vat of hops.

But the older woman was smiling pleasantly. 'I'm in something of a predicament, Mrs Nelson. My housemaid is threatening to return to the country if war breaks out and I was given your name as someone who might be prepared to help me out with a bit of cleaning.'

Pam blinked. It was a moment before she realised she was being offered a job. A chance to earn some money. Blasted Sean Byrne's prediction was coming true rather sooner than she had expected. She imagined him, smiling smugly in the kitchen behind her and almost smiled herself. She glanced over her shoulder, then quickly pulled the door to in case Mrs Rutherford caught sight of him down the passage.

But cleaning? Her heart quailed suddenly at the thought of more scrubbing, more dusting, more polishing. If she really was thinking of finding a job surely she could find something a bit more interesting than cleaning. Couldn't she? Presumably she'd still be able to type at least. Even after five years.

'You'll want to ask your husband, of course,' Mrs Rutherford was saying, 'but I was thinking of two or three days a week.'

Pam shook her head. She didn't need to ask Alan. She had already made her decision. 'I'm sorry, Mrs Rutherford, but I think I'd rather find something a bit more useful, if you don't mind. An office job or some war work, maybe.'

Mrs Rutherford obviously did mind. 'Jobs like that aren't very easy to find,' she said stiffly. 'Not for married women.'

Pam lifted her chin. 'If all our men and boys get called up to fight, the government will need all the women workers they can get, married or not.'

Then as Mrs Rutherford paled, Pam suddenly remembered that she had teenage sons. She had seen them in the garden during the summer, and heard them over the wall, two handsome boys arguing in their bland public school voices over the relative military strengths of England and Germany, the merits of Spitfires over Messerschmidts, over the test cricket score. 'I'm sure it won't come to that though,' she added lamely.

'I hope not.' Mrs Rutherford spoke firmly, with a hint of disapproval. 'My husband thinks Hitler will turn tail as soon as he finds we mean business.' She adjusted her handbag on her arm and took a pace back. 'Well, Mrs Nelson. I'm sorry to disturb you.'

'That's all right.' Pam felt herself colouring uneasily. 'I'm sorry I can't help. I suppose you could try Mrs Carter, down the road,' she added doubtfully. 'She might be glad of the money.'

Closing the door, Pam walked reluctantly back down the passage. Sean Byrne was still in the kitchen and had clearly heard every word. He slowly stubbed out his cigarette in the enamelled sink and smiled knowingly.

'You learn fast, Mrs Nelson. That's a quality I admire in a woman.' His blue eyes were glinting suggestively. 'Your husband is a lucky man.'

Pam felt a faint tightening in her throat and swallowed. 'Mr Byrne, I think …'

He held up a hand. 'I know what you're thinking, Mrs Nelson. You're wishing I would go off to my work. And you're right. I'm late as the devil already and I've disturbed you enough for one day as it is.'

Once again he was right. She did want him gone and quickly.

But once he had gone she found herself staring at the twisted cigarette butt in the sink and wondering with an unwelcome shiver of anticipation how often her lodger would be late getting off to work.

Joyce Carter had two favourite routes over to the street market in Northcote Road where Lorenz, the pawnbroker, had his shop. She either walked up to the top of Lavender Road and then diagonally across Clapham Common and down Lakehurst Road, or she went down Lavender Road, along Lavender Hill, left at Adding & Hobbs department store and up past the shops in St John's Road.

Today she chose the route over the common. Mainly because she would have to call at the police station on Lavender Hill with the bail on the way back, but also because it was a sunny day and sometimes the stroll across the common lifted her spirit.

Lavender Road was quiet today, Joyce thought, as she closed her front gate and turned left up towards the common. Not that it ever buzzed exactly. Other than the pub and the school there was little to draw anyone to the shabby Victorian terraced street. But this morning, apart from two parked cars and a sleeping cat, it was deserted, and silent. There was no noise from the school, of course, not now the children had been evacuated, and for once old peg-legged Malcolm Parsons wasn't clanking his beer barrels about outside the. Flag and Garter.

Joyce looked up the narrow street ahead of her, one of hundreds similar slotted into the area between the river and Clapham Common. Funny to think that in the old days this whole hillside had been market gardens serving London on the other side of the Thames, growing the lavender that now remained only in some of the local place names. Like Lavender Road.

It wasn't a bad road. There was no lavender any more but it had the odd tree, and the terraced houses, three up, two down, with the sash windows in the white painted bays and neat slate roofs over the red brick, had probably been quite sought after when they'd first been built at the turn of the century.

Now, of course, the paint was peeling off the bays, the sashes had stuck and the red brick was lost behind layers of London grime. And when those black roof slates slipped in a gale it was a devil of a job to find the leak. Joyce had had a basin on the landing for three years.

Some people kept their houses up together better than others of course. Alan Nelson for one. He was good with his hands, but even the Nelsons' house looked a bit jaded today as she walked past. His hedge needed clipping and there was a tile loose on the chequered path. Maybe he was spending more time on his boat on the river since the weather had been so good.

Pausing at the top of the road to cross on to the common, Joyce glanced over her shoulder at the last house in the street. Set back from the road in its own gravelled driveway, surrounded by shrubbery, with a side bed of roses, the white, flat-fronted Georgian house with its big spaced windows gleamed almost silver in the bright sunshine.

Nobody could say the Rutherfords didn't look after their house. Everyone knew that Mr Rutherford had the three-storey facade washed from top to bottom every other year by some specialist builders from Croydon. Joyce had seen them at it only last month in the baking hot sunshine, stripped to the waist with hoses and scaffolding and Mrs Rutherford hurrying in and out from the car under the chauffeur's umbrella.

Breathing in the heavy scent of Mrs Rutherford's roses, Joyce crossed over on to the parched grass of the common and felt a small welcome breeze stir her skirt.

Joyce liked the common. She liked the flat, empty plainness of it within its fringe of trees, the way the sky seemed bigger there than it did in the street. Even the sports pitches were empty today, the line markings bleached by the hot sun.

Since the danger of war had loomed, though, the common wasn't as empty as it used to be. They were still digging the underground air-raid shelters and in front of the two great mansion blocks which flanked Cedars Road and dwarfed all the other houses on Northside, even the Rutherfords', they'd built a temporary military camp with Nissen huts and iron fencing. That's where the anti-aircraft guns would be if the worst came to the worst.

If Hitler did decide to bomb London, the residents of those huge chateau style blocks would have a great view. From the top windows at the back, they said you could see north right across the capital to the hills of Hampstead, and east to the high buildings of the City, the dome of St Paul's, and beyond to the docks where the Thames snaked off towards the sea.

Joyce shivered as she passed into the deep shade of the avenue of chestnuts and crunched through the dry scattering of early autumn leaves. She didn't want to think about war, about bombing. But it all seemed so quiet today, there wasn't even much traffic on the Avenue, as though everyone was at home waiting. Waiting for Hitler to make his move.

Hurrying down leafy Wakehurst Road, she was glad to reach Northcote Road and the market. At least things were normal here. The usual bustle, the traders' cries, the sweet pungent smell of fruit and veg, the old crates on the pavement and dogs sniffing around the butchers' shops.

Wiping the sweat off her forehead, Joyce stood under the awning of Lorenz's Pawnbrokers and rang the bell. Since he'd been duffed over one night last winter on his way home, and had the windows of his house broken, Lorenz had had a special lock fitted on his shop door that opened only when he pressed a button inside.

She wondered if he had one on his house too. He lived in Lavender Road too. Next door to the pub. All on his own. Not that that was surprising, Joyce thought. After all, who in their right mind would want to live with a tight-fisted, antisocial old bugger like Lorenz?

Tight as a tart's corset, Stanley called him. Never bought a round in his life. Even when he'd won on the horses. Which he often did. That was his only bit of pleasure as far as anyone knew. Betting. And winning. That's why Stanley hated him so much. Because he won. And because he was Jewish of course. Stanley hated the Jews.

Come to think on it, Stanley hated most people. Nobs, Blackies, Germans, Irish. Irish worst of all. But then everyone hated the Irish just now. What with their bloody bombs all over the place. That young girl killed only two days ago in Coventry High Street and only two weeks before her wedding. And a young schoolboy of fifteen. Pete's age. Terrible.

Joyce felt a wash of despair. It was a feeling she often had recently. Things were bad enough already without bombs and war and all. She'd had enough of all that in her teens. She'd been eleven when the Great War had started and by the end of it virtually all the men she'd ever known were dead. Dead or maimed or nutty with shell shock.

Stanley had been quite a catch in those days. Quite a handsome lad. She snorted. Not any more, lazy fat bugger that he was. The only people who tried to catch him these days were the coppers.

Joyce jumped as Lorenz's buzzer released the lock.

As always, the shop seemed cold inside, even on a scorcher like today, and dark, with its stained wooden cabinets, its inadequate lighting. And as always Lorenz was dressed in black, standing stiff and solemn, hands at his sides. But as her eyes adjusted to the gloom, Joyce realised that behind the neat black beard and wire-rimmed glasses the pawnbroker looked unusually pale.

She peered at him anxiously across the counter and wondered if he'd got the flu. She didn't want him keeling over before she'd completed her transaction. 'Are you feeling all right, Mr Lorenz? You look a bit peaky.'

He seemed to rouse himself, coughed and nodded to the wireless on the counter. 'I've just heard the news, Mrs Carter. Hitler has invaded Poland.'

His voice was oddly hoarse. His faint accent more pronounced. Joyce stared at him. His dark eyes seemed darker than ever, sunk in his thin face. He looked devastated.

'They've been expecting him to invade Poland for weeks,' Joyce said a touch impatiently. Anyone would think it was the first Lorenz had heard of the crisis. 'It's been all over the papers. That's why our forces have been mobilised. That's why the children have been evacuated. The government knew Poland was for the chop. It was expected.'

'That it was expected doesn't make it any easier to bear,' Lorenz said quietly. 'I have many friends living in Poland, Mrs Carter. I fear I will never see them again.'

As she dropped her eyes, embarrassed, from the dark intensity of his gaze, a number of thoughts jumbled in Joyce's mind. But overriding her astonishment at the unexpected force of his emotion and her irritation with him for putting her on the spot, was the extraordinary idea of Lorenz having friends.

She'd never seen anyone visit him at his house. Never once seen him go out of an evening. She'd always thought he was a cold fish. Now she suddenly wasn't so sure. She looked at him, disconcerted, as he battled with his feelings.

She didn't know what to say. She didn't like Lorenz, nobody did, and his emotion embarrassed her. He was the local pawnbroker. A necessary evil. She didn't want to know he had feelings. She didn't want to take on his worries. She had enough of her own. It was easier to say nothing. So she said nothing.

Instead she brought out the bracelet and laid it on the counter.

After a moment, Lorenz picked it up and held it to the lamp.

'My Mam left it me,' Joyce said stiffly. 'I'll buy it back in a week or two. I just need something to tide me over.'

Why did she go through with the pretence? They both knew it had never belonged to her mother and they both knew it would never be redeemed. If Stanley went down, she'd need the bail money to live on. And if he didn't, he'd drink it away in celebration before she ever got her hands on it.

'My Mam left it me'. That was a bad joke and all. The only things Mam had left were a moth-eaten canary, now dead, a box of empties and a dog-eared exercise book full of scribbled recipes. She'd been a good cook, Mam, even though there'd been no money for ingredients. She'd been in service as a teenager and had picked up tips from the cook there.

'It's a nice piece,' Lorenz said, weighing the bracelet on a small chain scale.

'Is it gold?' Joyce held her breath and dug her nails into her palms.

Perhaps aware of her tension, he paused fractionally before nodding. 'Yes, it's gold, Mrs Carter.' He met her eager gaze coolly. 'I'll give you ten pounds for it. I'll keep it for six months. Interest ten shillings a month. If it's not redeemed before that time …'

Joyce hardly listened. She knew the conditions. Ten pound. Her relief was so great she almost didn't notice the ring that lay in the small oak showcase on the counter.

She almost choked. 'That ring …?' She could hardly believe her eyes.

It was the ring. The same diamond ring. She could even seen some flour still encrusted, round the delicate setting.

'That ring, Mr Lorenz,' she pointed. 'I … who brought it in?'

Lorenz glanced at the ring and raised his eyes slowly. He laid her money on the counter and shook his head. 'I'm afraid I can't tell you that, Mrs Carter.'

Joyce stared into his dark eyes. Can't, or won't more likely. She felt something slip inside her, felt her frustration surge. Wished she'd been more sympathetic about his blasted friends in Poland.

'But that ring was mine, I need it. It's all I've got.' Her voice cracked and she swallowed sharply. 'It was my husband, wasn't it?'

Lorenz's eyes flickered to the bruise on her cheek and Joyce instantly regretted her outburst. Lorenz's pity was the last thing she wanted. Or expected.

But he merely straightened his shoulders stiffly. 'I'm sure you appreciate how important it is that I protect the identity of my customers, Mrs Carter.' He held Joyce's eyes. 'The police often ask me for names and I always tell them I don't deal in names. I deal in valuables.'

He dropped his gaze to write out her receipt and Joyce found herself noticing for the first time how extraordinarily long his lashes were behind the steel frames, and thick, so thick, they cast shadows over his thin cheeks. He blotted the paper carefully and folded it neatly. After a short pause, he looked up. 'I generally find a somewhat vague recollection of age and sex satisfies my conscience, Mrs Carter. And the constabulary.'

It was a second, before Joyce realised what he was getting at. She blinked. 'And do you remember the age and sex of the person who brought in that ring?' she asked. But she knew already. It was Stanley. It had to be. Even though he hated Lorenz's guts.

'A young woman brought it in.'

'A young woman?' Joyce stared at him blankly. 'What young woman?'

But there was only one young woman who could possibly have got her thieving hands on that ring. 'My daughter? But Jen's only seventeen.' Joyce felt her temper rise. She wanted to lean over the counter and ring Lorenz's bloody neck. Jen was far too young to use a pawn shop. 'She only left school last month.'

Lorenz laid his smooth, almost delicate hands on the worn wooden surface of the counter. 'The young woman in question assured me she was twenty one years old. I had no reason to disbelieve her. I prefer not to turn business away, Mrs Carter.'

Joyce stared at him. Was he lying? Would he lie? Somehow she knew he wouldn't and was surprised by the thought. He was a shark, but he wasn't dishonest. Not in that way. No, it was Jen all right. Her own daughter. Her own lying, thieving little slut of a daughter, Joyce closed her eyes for a moment, fighting back the mixture of fury and utter despair that threatened to overcome her. Then she squared her shoulders and nodded to the pawnbroker.

'Thank you, Mr Lorenz,' she said tightly, taking the money and the receipt and pushing it into her pocket with a shaking hand. 'You've been most helpful.'

His eyes were expressionless. 'It's always a pleasure doing business with you, Mrs Carter.' He pressed the buzzer to release the door. 'Good day.'

She hesitated in the door and turned. She had to say something. She had to. 'I'm sorry about Poland, Mr Lorenz.'

He inclined his head. 'I know you are, Mrs Carter.'

On her way from Lorenz's to the police station, right by the fish stall, Joyce bumped into Mrs Rutherford. Or rather, Mrs Rutherford bumped into her. Because if Joyce had had her way, she would have brushed past without speaking. She wasn't in the mood to pass the time of day with anyone. Let alone Mrs Rutherford with her condescending, 'my husband owns the brewery' good humour. The last time they'd had words was over Joyce's children climbing over the back wall into the Rutherfords' garden to steal her plums.'

But the other woman stopped and smiled and Joyce had no choice but to stop too, even though the fish stall was ponging a bit in the hot sun.

'It's Mrs Carter, isn't it?' she asked, raising her voice over the noise of the market. 'Doing a bit of shopping?'

Joyce didn't smile back. Stanley had recently stood in line for a job at Rutherford & Berry's and had been turned down. On account of his criminal record.

Joyce shrugged. 'Thought I'd better stock up a bit while I can.' She could hardly say she was on her way to bail out her husband with money raised on a stolen bracelet.

Mrs Rutherford nodded sympathetically. 'Yes, I'm afraid if war is declared we may be in for hard times.'

Joyce took in the other woman's immaculate turn-out, the stylish little hat and matching handbag, the tailored summer jacket, the small diamond brooch pinned discreetly on her lapel and felt a stab of resentment. What did she know about hard times? Nothing.

With her big house and car, rich husband and servants she'd be well buffered from the war. Everyone knew the Rutherfords had had their cellars reinforced and fitted up with beds. They wouldn't be running to a half built shelter on the common when the bombing started, or shivering under that bit of government-issue corrugated iron Stanley and Pete had bodged up in the garden.

What was she doing down here anyway? She didn't shop locally. Oh no, Northcote Road market wasn't good enough for the Rutherfords, They had their food delivered from Fortnum & Mason's in Piccadilly. The van came down for them twice a week. Apart from meat. Give her her due, she did buy that locally in Dove the butcher's. Joyce had stood in the queue behind her once as she had inspected a joint of beef the size of a bowler hat.

'Do you think that would do us for six, Mr Dove?' Celia Rutherford had asked in her nasal BBC voice. 'The boys will be home this weekend.'

It had been on the tip of Joyce's tongue to say that it would have done her for sixteen. And sandwiches for the rest of the week. But she'd saved her breath, waiting till the other woman had left the shop before asking old Dove for half a pound of brawn.

But Mrs Rutherford was looking at her closely now and for an awful moment Joyce wondered if she thought the fish smell was coming from her. Then she realised she was looking at the bruise.

She had dabbed a bit of Jen's powder on before coming out, but in the cruel bright light of day no amount of powder would hide the fact that the black eye Stanley had landed on her the other night was turning green.

All ready with her excuse of falling over the dustbin while practising the blackout, Joyce was put out when Mrs Rutherford asked if she was intending to evacuate the children.

'They've already gone,' she replied stiffly. 'Yesterday, with the school.' What business was it of the Rutherfords what she did with her children? Although there'd been an almighty fuss and a half about it. With Angie screaming her head off and the boys saying they'd go truant.

She'd half expected them to turn up again in the evening. But they hadn't, and God knew where they were now. Devon or Cornwall. 'We'll let you know in due course,' the billeting officer had said.

Mrs Rutherford's delicate brows rose. 'All of them?'

'Just the youngest three.'

'Of course,' Mrs Rutherford laughed lightly. 'Silly me. The others are too old, aren't they? Still, three safe and sound. That will be a weight off your mind, I'm sure. And less work.' She stopped and smiled uneasily before starting again. 'My boys will be at school in the country, of course.' She picked a speck off her sleeve. 'I'd have liked Louise to go somewhere safe now she's left Lucie Clayton's, but she insists on staying in London.' She shrugged resignedly. 'You know what girls that age are like, Mrs Carter. They will have their own way.'

Joyce almost laughed. She knew what her Jen was like all right. Headstrong as a bitch on heat, and a thief too, it seemed. But she would hardly have thought that description applied to the polished and pampered little Miss Louise Rutherford, fresh from her finishing school in Knightsbridge.'

Mrs Rutherford seemed to be working up to another question and Joyce glanced impatiently at the clock above the bank. The smell of fish was making her feel sick now and she wanted to get to the police station before lunch.

And she was anxious to get home so she could get her hands on that thieving little slut of a daughter and wring her bloody neck.

Mrs Rutherford apparently got the message. 'Well, I must get on,' she said backing away hastily and nearly sitting on a tray of sweating smoked mackerel. 'Busy, busy, busy.'

Chapter Two

At lunchtime in the Flag and Garter, the talk was all of Hitler's invasion of Poland.

Tucked halfway up quiet residential Lavender Road, well away from the noise and traffic of Lavender Hill, the Flag, with its well-polished bar and lino floors, had a reputation for being a talker's pub, a smoker's pub, a real local, not full of pushy door-to-door salesmen and wide-boys hawking cheap jewellery for the missus like in the pubs down by Clapham Junction.

Today, even non-regulars popped in for a pint of local, to catch up on the mood of the day, to mull over the implications. Was Hitler using poison gas in Poland? How long would the government leave it before declaring war? Mr Chamberlain couldn't sit on the fence for ever. And what about the French? Were they going to wait until Hitler marched into Paris before reacting?

In the smoke-filled public bar, there was talk of enlisting, talk of the call-up being extended to men over twenty one, talk of decent pay in the forces. And there were jokes too, jokes about Hitler, jokes about West Ham losing all its players to the call-up. Jokes about the landlord's missing leg. 'No Jerry-bashing for you this time, eh Malcolm?' And before Malcolm Parsons, preoccupied with pulling another pint, could respond, a laugh from the other side of the bar, by the dartboard, 'I don't know, an army of hopalongs would save the War Office a packet on boots.'

As the rich Rutherford & Berry bitter went down, the noise level rose and with it the excitement. Of one thing they were certain, war against Germany was inevitable. And on one thing they were agreed; whatever the cost, that jumped-up, strutting, two-faced bastard Adolf Hitler had to be taught a lesson, and quickly, before he started dropping his poison bombs on Britain.

What they didn't realise was that their voices, mingling with the smoke of their cigarettes, rose clearly to the flat upstairs, where seventeen year old Katy Parsons sat swathed in an eiderdown by the window.

She tried to concentrate on the street outside, tried to keep her eyes on Mrs Carter marching up from Lavender Hill, her face red and sweating in the blazing midday sun. She tried to listen to her mother preparing lunch in the kitchen, but all she could hear was the talk of war, of bombs, of gas.

Gas. Katy took a laboured breath, her thin chest heaving with the effort of dragging air into her thickened lungs. She wished she could open the window, but her mother was terrified of her getting a chill. Each time she'd got a cold as a child she'd nearly died, or so she was told. All she remembered was that horrible feeling of congestion in her bony chest, of wracking coughs, of a craving for fresh air.

She coughed now, harshly, trying unsuccessfully to clear space in her lungs, and at once her mother's voice called through from the kitchen.

'Are you all right, Katy?'

Katy closed her eyes and tried to relax the tense muscles in her thin face, forcing herself to breathe slowly, calmly. 'I'm fine,' she said.

'Are you warm enough?'

She moved her legs beneath the heavy eiderdown and a puff of feathers wafted from a tear in the corner. She waved them away before they could catch in her clothes or the soft hazel curls of her hair. 'I'm a bit too hot really.'

Mary Parsons appeared at once in the kitchen door. 'Is the eiderdown too heavy? Perhaps a blanket would be better?'

'I'm warm enough with nothing,' Katy said mildly. But she knew a blanket would appear. Every day this week, even though the sun outside blazed from dawn to dusk, she had started with the eiderdown, scaled down to a blanket at lunchtime and managed to rid herself of any encumbrance by the evening. Her mother was certain that keeping warm was the answer to her breathing problems and although Katy was less convinced, she was reluctant to hurt her feelings by throwing off the covering too soon.

As she tucked the blanket fussily round Katy's legs, Mary Parsons cocked an ear to the stairs and frowned. 'It sounds busy down there. I wonder if your father needs help.'

'I'm sure he'll call up if he does,' Katy said. It was an exchange they had every day. She wished her mother wouldn't fret so much. Sometimes she thought her anxiety was infectious. Her mother worried about little things. Like should she pop down the road for another pint of milk or would one do for the weekend. Like would Malcolm enjoy the new cut of ham she'd bought. Like was Katy straining her eyes by reading so much.

Whereas Katy spent most of her time worrying about big things. Like the war, and what would happen to her if her parents died, and poison gas.

But today Katy knew her mother was concerned about a big thing too. And her father. There had been a Discussion last night. A Discussion she hadn't been meant to hear, but she had. Their voices had carried clearly from their bedroom.

Her parents were in a dilemma. They wanted her to go to the country, to safety. Away from the threat of German bombs. But they wouldn't let her go alone.

She took another laboured breath. She couldn't possibly go alone. And her mother was needed here. Her father couldn't cope alone, not with his half leg. And Katy and Mary wouldn't be able to manage without him anyway. How on earth would they survive alone in the country?

If only they could close up the pub and all go to the country together, Katy thought, to some safe haven where Hitler wouldn't think of bombing or invading. Wouldn't think of using gas.

But her father would never get another job. Not with unemployment what it was, two million they said. Not in the country. Not with only one leg. As it was, Katy was sure that Mr Rutherford only let him stay on at the Flag and Garter because he'd served in Mr Rutherford's father's regiment during the Great War.

'At least Katy can use her gas mask now,' her mother had said.

Katy coughed again and her watering eyes fell on the three fawn, oblong boxes that stood neatly regimented on the sideboard. Their gas masks.

Despite the blanket, Katy shivered and jerked her eyes away. Her mother had worried so much about her not being able to use her gas mask that Katy had eventually had to pretend that it was all right, that she could breathe in it after all, as indeed she could if she twisted her jaw to one side to make a little gap in the seal between the horrible heavy black rubber and her skin. With a little gap, she could breathe. She felt the ominous tightening of her chest now, the sudden hammering of her heart and tried to think of other things.

She hated being such a coward. She also hated being such a trial to her parents, but she was used to that. She was used to being a nuisance, to being 'poor little Katy'. During her childhood she'd grown used to sitting out on games because they made her wheeze. Over the years she stopped apologising to her teachers when she had to go home early. And now she'd finally left school, over the summer she'd grown used to being treated as an invalid.

What she wasn't used to was this awful tense fear.

And the worst thing about it was that nobody else, with the possible exception of her mother, seemed to suffer from it.

Certainly her friend Jen Carter from across the street wasn't worried about the prospect of war. On the contrary, Katy knew that Jen was hoping it might help her in her ambition to become an actress. Jen was hoping that the drama schools might have more places available if everyone left London. That there might be more chance for small parts if actors were called up and actresses volunteered for the women's services.

Lucky Jen. So pretty and healthy and clever at imitating people.

Katy sighed and turned her eyes back out of the window. From her vantage point at the corner window, she could see right up the road to Clapham Common at the end. In a month or two when the chestnuts lost their leaves she would be able to make out the bandstand in the middle of the common, where all the paths met, but at this time of year the big leafy trees blocked her view at the end of Lavender Road.

Katy didn't mind. She was fond of Lavender Road. It might be narrow and shabby, and the houses poky and inferior, as Jen always said, with their outside lavatories and lack of hot water, but they seemed much cosier to Katy than the tall houses overlooking the common. She was amused by the quirky period detail of them, the hideous beige and green ornamental tiles on the insides of the shallow open porches, the stained-glass door panels that some of them still retained. In the winter she liked to see the chimneys smoking. It made the place feel lived in, she felt safe there, away from the high buildings and anonymous bustle of central London.

Over the summer, while her lungs played up, she'd invented things to amuse herself about the neighbours, things she would never dream of saying out loud. And she'd noticed things too. Like this morning, when the Irishman had left late from the Nelsons' house and walked down the street with his shoulders back and a smirk on his handsome face.

She knew things too. She knew it was the young Carter boy, Jen's brother, Mick, and his friends, who had broken poor Mr Lorenz's windows a couple of weeks back. But although she felt sorry for Mr Lorenz, being Jewish and all, she felt sorrier for Mrs Carter, lumbered with those awful rough boys and that beastly husband who drank himself sick in the public bar downstairs then staggered back across the road to duff her up.

Terrible bruises she'd had on her recently. And for no reason as far as Katy could make out from Jen. Joyce Carter might be a bit on the sour side, and looked like something, the cat had brought in, as Jen had once remarked, but she didn't have a fancy man around her, she didn't drink or gamble and, again according to Jen, she wasn't a bad cook when she put her mind to it.

Perhaps things would be easier for the Carter family now the younger children had been evacuated. Katy had seen them go yesterday, arguing as usual, and Joyce Carter watching them silently from her door.

Katy had seen the brave faces of other mothers too, as they'd delivered their children to the school for the last time. She'd seen the buses come. Two red double-deckers, taken off their routes especially for the evacuation, as they were all over London.

As they loaded up class by class, Katy had seen the cherubic little Whitehead boy, George, break away and run back up the street with Miss Hudson in hot pursuit, her huge bust and her gas mask case all bumping about on her, hindering her progress. Even as Katy laughed to herself, she'd seen the little boy kick the teacher viciously on the shins, as he banged frantically on the door, screaming for his mother to come and rescue him. Seen Sheila Whitehead open the door with little Ray, the younger child, in her arms and tears streaming down her pretty face.

Katy hadn't heard the discussion that ensued, but the result was obvious. Sheila took both the children back indoors, leaving Miss Hudson to waddle back down the street alone in high dudgeon.

Katy wondered why Sheila didn't go with the children to the country like some of the mothers of very young children, and decided it was because Sheila couldn't bear to leave her handsome young husband Jo.

Sheila and Jo were In Love. Tears sometimes came to Katy's eyes when she saw Jo Whitehead come home of an evening from the brewery, breaking into a run as he neared the house. Hugging Sheila to death on the doorstep.

Katy knew true love like that would never happen to her: for one thing she'd never be fit enough to go out and meet anyone. If she couldn't dance without coughing and she couldn't laugh without coughing, she certainly wouldn't be able to kiss without coughing. It was a sad fact. A tragic fact. She knew kissing would suffocate her, just like her gas mask. And without kissing you couldn't get a man. Everyone knew that. She was doomed.

Sometimes she tried to imagine whom she would kiss if she could. Certainly none of the fat boozers in the public bar downstairs. No, it would, have to be someone romantic, handsome. Earlier in the year she'd gone to the pictures with Jen and had managed to sit through *Wuthering Heights* without coughing once. Laurence Olivier had been kissable in that. Even Jen thought so, and Jen was hard to please where men were concerned. Jen had actually seen Laurence Olivier once out of costume. Jen thought gorgeous Jo Whitehead was wet.

Katy screwed up her nose. Who else was there? Certainly not Alan Nelson, whose only interest in life seemed to be his dull little boat down on the river at Putney. Katy suddenly thought again of Sean Byrne swaggering out of the Nelson house this morning and felt an odd tingle in her spine. Sean Byrne didn't look one tiny bit wet. On the contrary, Katy had a funny feeling that she wouldn't at all mind being suffocated by him. She giggled nervously at the thought and her mother, coming in with floury hands, frowned.

'Are you all right, Katy? You look quite flushed.'

Katy was saved a reply by the arrival of the Rutherford & Berry dray bringing fresh barrels of beer from the brewery to the pub. As a child she had always rushed down to stroke the horses. She loved the smell of them, their velvet noses and their huge shaggy feet the size of plates. They were shires, a pair, black and white, and it had taken Katy years to admit that the slightest contact with them made her skin itch, her eyes stream and her lungs constrict so badly that for hours after their visit she could hardly breathe.

Nowadays she contented herself with watching them from above. Watching old Cyril, their driver, in his ritual abuse of the lad, Tom, whose job it was to heave the barrels off the dray and roll them down through the trap door in the pavement and down the ramp into the cellar. Jen did a marvellous imitation of Cyril. Somehow she made her eyes go as squinty as his, made her face redden and the spit fly out of her mouth just like his as he yelled at the poor, maligned hardworking Tom. Why the boy stood it nobody knew, although the general feeling was that he wasn't quite all there. One sandwich short of a picnic, as Jen always said.

Katy frowned. Jen knew how to kiss. Jen had spent weeks last summer at school practising kissing the hole in her clenched fist. You had to poke your tongue in and wiggle it around and suck all at the same time, Jen had said. And then one day she had come into school laughing and said it wasn't a bit like that after all. She had been kissed by a friend of her brother's after a bit of a do in the West End and he'd done all the tongue wiggling and all she'd had to do was try not to choke.

'Was it nice?' Katy had asked shyly. And Jen had tossed her head.

'Not nice exactly,' she had said airily. 'A bit like having a huge slug shoved into your mouth on the end of a drain plunger. But good experience.'

Katy had grimaced. But then you couldn't believe everything Jen said. She didn't lie exactly. She just exaggerated a bit. Either that or she short changed you on the truth. Not that Katy minded. She was flattered that Jen even passed the time of day with her.

Sometimes they had walked back from school together and Katy had felt proud to be seen with Jen. Even though her mother thought the Carters were a bad lot. But then, her mother hadn't seen Jen acting in the school play. She hadn't heard Jen singing a solo of *Once in Royal David's City* at the carol service at Christmas. Because her mother hated crowds, she got all hot and bothered in a crowd. So she'd missed Jen's moments of glory.

Katy shook her head. She would never seek the limelight like Jen did. But it must have felt wonderful for Jen to be congratulated, to have a mention in the local paper.

Even though her family was so awful, Jen had so much. Everything was so easy for Jen. Katy envied her. She had good looks, she had personality, she had confidence and drive. And courage and ambition. Loads of ambition. All the things Katy lacked. She sighed and turned her eyes back to the window once more as the Miss Taylors trundled past, loaded with shopping, dragging with them the ancient, elongated animal which they used to refer to proudly as a dachshund, but which had recently in a burst of absurd patriotism reverted to being a mere sausage dog. And a bit of an overcooked one at that.

Katy frowned. She had had enough of the street for now. Enough thoughts of war and impending doom. She wanted to escape her thick lungs, her frail body and mousy hair, she wanted to dream. She reached over to pick up her book, just as her mother came in with a tray of lunch.

Jennifer Carter came home at six o'clock.

And the row started at five past.

As soon as she cautiously pushed open the front door she knew something was wrong. There was an atmosphere hovering around the kitchen door and, wafting down the passage like a bad smell. Jen groaned inwardly as she ran quickly up the narrow staircase to her room, the room she had to herself now that Angie had been evacuated. Swiftly she shoved the bags she carried under Angle's bed and pulled the blanket over to hide them. Then hearing her mother's nagging voice calling her from downstairs, she shrugged off her thin jacket and scarf and threw them on the floor. It was always the same in this bloody house. Always something wrong, always something for her mother to complain about. She'd had a bad enough day as it was, without getting it in the neck from her mother as well.

'What?' She shouted down irritably, checking her face in her hand mirror. She carefully wiped off some smeared eyeliner with her thumb. 'What do you want?'

'I want you down here. Now!'

Her mother sounded more than angry. Jen grimaced to herself in the mirror. She pulled crossly at her hair with her spare hand. The curls were far too tight. She looked like a poodle. 'Why?'

'Because you're a thieving little slut, that's why.'

Jen's hand dropped abruptly. For a second she closed her eyes. Then she opened them again and made a face in the mirror. 'I don't know what you're on about.'

She heard her mother's heavy tread on the stairs and tensed, checking quickly that the bags under Angie's bed were out of sight.

'You know bloody well what I'm on about,' Joyce muttered furiously, as she rounded the top of the stairs and stood red faced in the doorway of Jen's room. 'I'm on about …' She stopped abruptly, her mouth falling open.

When Jen had left the house that morning, her long thick, reddish hair had been tied in its usual plait. But now … For a second Joyce even forgot about the ring. 'What have you done to your hair?'

Jen shrugged defiantly. 'I've had it permed.'

Joyce felt herself groping for words and only managed one. 'Why?'

She watched her daughter lift the mirror to admire her pretty, if angular, side profile. Watched her newly plucked and pencilled eyebrows rise and her red lip curl as she spoke with studied scorn. 'Have you ever seen an actress with straight hair?'

Joyce felt her face contort. Felt her rage surge. Actress indeed. She hadn't been to the hairdresser's in years. 'I suppose my diamond ring paid for that,' she said tightly, clenching her fists. What Jen needed was a good slapping.

But Jen was going to play it to the last. Taking a quick precautionary step back, she put on her most innocent expression and checked it in the mirror. 'What do you mean?'

'You know what I bloody mean.' Joyce's voice rose. 'And put that bloody mirror down.' Sometimes her daughter's playacting drove her nuts. 'That ring was mine. Do you hear me? Mine!'

Jen stared at her coldly. 'It wasn't anybody's. It was stolen.' She shrugged. 'It was there, so I took it.' She smiled at herself in the mirror and licked a speck of lipstick off her teeth. 'I needed it.'

'You needed it?' Joyce yelled at her. '*You* needed it? And what about me? And what would have happened if I hadn't had enough to pay your father's bail?'

'You'd have had to leave him inside,' Jen said indifferently. 'Serve him right.'

'Oh yes, and you try telling him that to his face.'

'I'd say it to his face, all right. If he spent more time at work and less time at the pub, he wouldn't need to steal.'

As much as Joyce wanted to wring her neck, deep down she knew Jen was right. Stanley was a lazy bugger. But he was the man of the house, nevertheless. And deserved some respect from his children. In any case, she wasn't going to take lip like that from Jen. 'You can talk!' she snapped. 'And if you got a job at the factory like all the other girls, you could bring in some money and all.'

But Jen interrupted, 'What other girls? Katy Parsons doesn't work. Sheila Whitehead doesn't work. Pam Nelson doesn't work, not that she counts as a girl exactly. Who else? Oh, Louise Rutherford. She doesn't work.'

Joyce felt a familiar despair welling up as Jen ticked off the names on her fingers. Fingers, she noticed suddenly, that had bright red nails. Jen always had the answers. She was like her father in that. Never in the wrong. Nothing was ever her fault. And she could argue the hind leg off a three-legged donkey.

'Shut up and listen to me for once,' Joyce snapped. 'Katy Parsons doesn't work because she's sick. Sheila Whitehead and Pam Nelson are married. And the Rutherfords are rich.' She waved her hands in helpless rage. 'Rich. Don't you understand that? They're not like us. They own things, a business, a house. Can't you get it into your thick head, Jen? We haven't got any money. If your father goes inside this time, we've had it. If we can't meet the rent, we'll lose the house.'

Jen shrugged sulkily. 'Well, I'll be working soon. I've told you, I'm going to be an actress.'

Joyce stared at her. 'An actress.' She spat out the word, she was so sick of hearing it. 'Whoever heard of an actress coming from a street like this?'

'Gracie Fields came from a back street in Rochdale,' Jen retorted. 'And even you've heard of her.'

Joyce snorted. But Jen was angry now. Her cool unconcern had left her as it always did when talk of acting came up. 'And you'll hear of me,' she shouted. 'I'll make it, you'll see.'

Joyce watched the colour flood Jen's delicate face, watching her fight for control. Saw the defiant squaring of her thin shoulders, the stubborn slant of her mouth. 'Anyway, you can't stop me.'

Joyce had had enough of this acting talk. It was absurd. Jen lived in the clouds. Well, it was all right to dream a bit, but not at the expense of your family. 'I can stop feeding you,' she said coldly.

Jen's tawny eyes flickered, but her fighting spirit was undaunted. She lifted her chin. 'Then I'll go and live somewhere else.'

Joyce stared at her. 'Where?' She asked scornfully. 'Just tell me where?'

'Somewhere where everyone isn't so negative,' Jen said bitterly.

For a second Joyce felt a stab of pity for her. After all, she too had hoped for more at Jen's age. It was a tough life they had, a tough, grey, hand-to-mouth life. And now the war was coming and all.

She tried to gentle her voice. Tried to remember that Jen was only seventeen. 'We all hope for more from time to time,' she said. 'I'm sure everyone does. But we have to live with what we've got. And do things we don't want to do. Look at me. I'd like to have my hair done once in a while too. And go down the social club. But I don't. I have to live on nothing to keep food on the table for you all.'

For a second Jen did look at her, her eyes hard and angry like a tiger. 'I don't want to be like you,' she hissed. 'I want to get out, to escape.' Her lip curled scornfully. 'Who cares about the social club? She lifted the mirror and smiled bitterly at herself in it. 'I want to live in the real world where people have real ambitions and real glamour and aren't just content to look like beaten-up old drudges and live off sardines.'

At that moment Joyce almost hated her daughter. She stepped forward and snatched the mirror out of Jen's hand and flung it against the wall where it smashed, showering them both with glass.

Then she pointed at the door. 'If you want to start living in the real world, Jen Carter, then just bloody get out there and try it.'

For a moment they stood there, shocked, mother and daughter, in a glittering mess of broken glass.

Then Jen bent down and picked up her jacket. She shook the glass off it. 'OK, then I will,' she said and walked out of the room, out of the house.

*

It was still warm outside, a dull, grey, clammy heat that hung in the air like the grime in her brothers' Friday-night bathwater. And, as far as Jen was concerned, that just about summed up Lavender Road too. And her stupid family. Dull, grey and grimy. If she hadn't been the spitting image of Bob, only female, she'd have thought she was adopted. Not that her mother would have adopted. She hated kids. She was always shouting at the boys to get out from under her feet. Jen couldn't understand why she had so many if she hated them so much. Except for Angie of course. Pretty little delicate Angie couldn't put a foot wrong as far as her mum was concerned.

As for her dad, he was a dead loss. The only thing he'd ever done for her in his life was take her along to the New Theatre where he had worked as a scene changer for John Gielgud's *Romeo and Juliet* for a while. And that was only because she'd pleaded with him till she was blue in the face. And then just when she was beginning to get to know one or two of the dressers and had glimpsed Laurence Olivier once and Peggy Ashcroft twice, he got drunk, missed a couple of nights and got sacked. Since then he'd only done odd jobs locally, and most of those on the wrong side of the law.

Jen sighed. She didn't particularly mind her father and Bob going on the make. But why on earth did they have to let themselves get caught all the time?

Because they bragged in the pub, that's why. And got grassed on. They had no self control. No brains.

And then there was young Pete, fifteen and spotty and thick as two short planks, earning a pittance as an apprentice bricky, having ducked out of school with not one exam pass to his name.

No, Jen thought, as she unknowingly followed the same route her mother had taken earlier, marching up Lavender Road to the common, ignoring the passers-by, ignoring the catcall from two lads on their way to the pub, she was definitely different. She would show them. She would make them sit up. She was the one that everyone had clapped in the school play. Not that any of them had bothered to come. She was the one who could sing and dance. She was the one the newspaper had raved about: 'Jennifer Carter has undoubted talent and a maturity beyond her years. Her dying Juliet moved everyone in the hall; an unusual achievement for a young actress in a low cost school production.'

Jen shook her head. She wasn't going to give in and become a factory worker with a white mobcap and a shapeless overall.

But as she reached the top of the road by the Rutherfords' house and looked through the trees over the flat, grassy expanse of Clapham Common, she began to acknowledge that she had nowhere to go. She still had three pounds left from the five that tight, grassing bastard Lorenz had given her for the ring. She supposed she could go to a hotel. But Jen had never been inside a hotel in her life. She had no idea how much it would cost. Anyway, she had no luggage and she'd heard they wouldn't let you in without luggage. And she might need that money for drama school.

Jen sighed. She knew she couldn't afford Central or LAMDA, let alone RADA at seventeen guineas a term, but surely there were other places. Places that would make her speak right. She'd made herself look the part now, with the hair-do and the new clothes. But there was no doubt she talked wrong for the theatre. Earlier in the week she'd self-consciously bought herself a two-bob matinee ticket for *The Importance of Being Earnest* at the Globe, and all the actresses spoke like newsreaders, like the Rutherfords.

Crossing the road on to the common, she turned round and glared at the windows of the Rutherfords' house. It was all right for that fancy Louise Rutherford. Presumably she could do anything she wanted with her classy voice and her father's money. She wouldn't have to stand all afternoon in a long auditioning queue, only to have the theatre doors closed on her before she'd even got inside.

'They've seen enough,' the doorman had explained.

'But they haven't seen me,' Jen had complained indignantly. And he had glanced at her with faint sympathy.

'Better luck next time, luv.'

Next time. Next time, Jen vowed to be front of the queue. She'd had no idea there were so many stupid stage-struck girls in London all hoping for a chance. But she wasn't stage struck. She just knew she wanted to be an actress. An actress with the power to hold an audience in her hand like she'd done in the school play. The feeling of that power was amazing. She couldn't describe it. It was like a shot of whisky in the blood. Better than that. More like a double, swallowed straight down.

As she stood there dreaming, a car swung round the corner, catching her briefly in its headlights and stopped sharply outside Mrs d'Arcy Billière's, the other big house at the top of Lavender Road, the opposite side from the Rutherfords'. Jen watched two men get out, both well dressed, dapper almost, both smoking. She caught a snatch of a foreign language, spoken in deep husky tones, and a low chuckle as they stamped out their cigarettes and rang the doorbell.

The foreign woman, Mrs d'Arcy Billière, opened the door herself with a cry of joy. Intrigued, Jen wished she was standing closer. Wished the dusk wasn't settling in. But even through the falling darkness she could see the gallant heel-clicking way the two strangers kissed their hostess's hand on the doorstep. And then the door closed behind them and Jen wished she knew what was going on inside.

She was an odd woman, that Mrs Arsey Billière, or whatever she called herself. Odd, but glamorous in a dark, foreign kind of way. She wore her black hair pulled back in a tight bun like a ballet dancer. And in the winter she wore a wide brimmed fur hat like a Russian Cossack. Most people disapproved of her because she lived alone and entertained men. She had a lot of parties. Nobody knew who went to them. Foreigners mostly. Russians, somebody had said. Maybe one of those had brought her the hat.

Katy Parsons reckoned she was a foreign spy, a kind of Mata Hari, tempting secrets out of the government. But then Katy was always imagining things, making things up because she was bored to death sitting in that poky flat above the pub all day long.

Jen stood under a tree and smoked two cigarettes, half hoping there might be more glamorous arrivals she could watch. Then when it began to get really dark she toyed with calling on Katy.

Katy would be sympathetic. Katy was always sympathetic. And she'd admire Jen's new hair-do too. But her weedy mother would be there fussing around disapprovingly, and they wouldn't be able to talk, and Katy would probably wheeze and cough all over her. She felt sorry for Katy, but she was a bit wet. She should tell her mother not to carry on so much. Jen smiled sourly. Katy Parsons wouldn't last five minutes in the Carter household.

She stubbed out her last cigarette on the bark of the tree. She'd have to go back of course. If nothing else, she'd left her new clothes there, under Angie's bed. But she wouldn't eat her mother's food tonight. Not after that comment about not feeding her. Not after she'd smashed her mirror and all. No, she'd get fish and chips and then go home and eat them in her room.

Chapter Three

In St Aldate's on Sunday morning, there was an air of nervous anticipation, which hung about above the waiting congregation like the dust on the shafts of multicoloured sunlight streaming through the high stained-glass windows.

Unlike the more famous Holy Trinity up on the east side of the common, with its fanciful Doric columns and history of Evangelism and missionary zeal, St Aldate's had a sturdy Victorian porch and tower, and its services were firmly embedded in the Book of Common Prayer. St Aldate's was a good, solid, middle of the road church. No irritating new versions and no incense, that was what Greville Rutherford liked about it, and his family therefore patronised it without fail every Sunday morning. This Sunday, 3 September 1939, was no exception.

In the front pew, the one reserved for their use, Louise Rutherford sat between her mother and her brother Bertie and watched her father helping the verger, Mr Trewgarth, set up the wireless on the edge of the pulpit.

'The Prime Minister, Mr Chamberlain, will be addressing the nation at eleven fifteen,' the vicar had announced portentously after he had processed into church behind a much depleted choir. Most of the local children had already, been evacuated to the country, and as some of the men had already been called up, only a selection of rather busty women were left, vying for airspace with half a dozen or so rather half-hearted tenors and basses. 'We will interrupt the service to listen to his words.'

But then Mr Trewgarth had kicked over the wireless as he stood for the first hymn and instead of the expected organ introduction to *Love Divine, All Loves Excelling*, the congregation had been treated to a rousing blast of the popular hit, *Run, Rabbit, Run*.

Bertie and Douglas had got the giggles and had been severely frowned down by their father before he had stepped out of the pew and gone forward to assist.

Undaunted, Douglas swivelled round to see who else in church was amused, then swivelling back again, leaned round Bertie to whisper to Louise, 'Who's that man sitting with the Miss Taylors?'

'How should I know?' she hissed, frowning as her mother glanced at her sharply. 'Shh.' But something in Douglas's expression made her want to look, and a minute later as they all stood again for a second attempt at the hymn, she glanced casually over her shoulder and nearly dropped her hymn book.

The Miss Taylors were in a pew about five rows back, and standing between them in a dark, well cut suit was the most startlingly good-looking man Louise had ever seen. Dark haired, with a healthy-looking summer tan, he stood head and shoulders above the two old women, head slightly bowed, studying his hymn book diligently, as though unfamiliar with the words.

Sure enough as he looked up at the end of the first line to draw breath, Louise caught a glimpse of a wry, faintly deprecating expression in his eyes and a humorous grimace on his lips.

What on earth was a glorious-looking man like that doing in St Aldate's, and with the dotty old Miss Taylors of all unlikely people? For the first time in ages Louise felt her spirits rise.

After a wonderful lazy summer holiday in Cornwall with a school friend, she had been bored to death for the last three weeks with all this talk of war and her father banging on about air raid precautions and her mother endlessly measuring blackout material and moaning about the maid leaving. And yet she had fiercely resisted the idea of going to stay with dreadful Aunt Delia in Shropshire. That would be a fate worse than death. There weren't likely to be any nice, eligible men up there, for goodness' sake.

No, Louise wanted to be where the action was, where the men were. Knightsbridge would have been preferable but her father wouldn't hear of her sharing a flat there like some of the Lucie Clayton girls were going to do. And what fun they would have. Right in prime position for all the balls and dances and nobody to check what time they came in.

A sharp nudge in the ribs from her mother brought her back to more godly thoughts. The hymn was over and everybody was getting down on their knees for the general confession. Closing her eyes, Louise at once embarked on a devout prayer of thanks to the Almighty that she had had the foresight to dab on some lipstick and powder her nose before coming to church. She wished she had done something about her hair too, the pink, ribbon at the back was a bit childish, she thought, but at least she was wearing one of her more fetching hats, a navy velvet beret which showed off her pretty profile to full effect.

As they stood up for the psalm, Louise caught another glimpse of the handsome stranger, and this time, having left her hymn book on the pew behind her as a pretext to turn round again, she found herself gazing straight into a pair of steady grey eyes.

Even as she stared, spellbound, one dark eyebrow lifted slightly in quizzical amusement, and for that instant Louise's thoughts were entirely ungodly. And then everyone was suddenly sitting down and a hushed expectancy filled the church as the wireless was switched on.

Suddenly, right on cue, Mr Chamberlain's clipped vowels filled the church. 'I am speaking to you today from the Cabinet rooms at number ten

Downing Street ...'

As he went on, to report that the Germans had failed to respond to his ultimatum to withdraw from Poland, and that consequently, 'This country is now at war with Germany,' Louise felt her heart begin to pound.

'We are ready,' Chamberlain said, but she wasn't ready, she had brushed off all the talk of war as boring, getting in the way of her summer. But now suddenly here it was. War. And she didn't know what to think, how to react.

She glanced along the pew and caught sight of her father patting her mother's gloved hand. Louise was astonished. Her father never touched her mother in public. He was far too correct and strait-laced for anything like that. Then, even as Louise's eyes widened, he withdrew his hand and stiffened his back, while her mother fumbled in her handbag for a hanky and blew her nose.

On her other side Bertie was looking rather pale, but Douglas was grinning with gleeful satisfaction and behind her the whole church seemed to be muttering and shuffling excitedly.

Louise longed to turn round to see how the handsome stranger had taken the news, but just as she began to ease her bottom round a fraction on the hard, narrow pew, the vicar turned off the wireless and stepped forward with folded hands and a grave expression. 'Let us pray.'

It was only as the congregation took their seats again for the lesson that Louise had the chance to glance round once again. Only to discover, to her horror, that the object of her interest was no longer there. The coy, carefully arranged smile fell from her lips as her eyes frantically raked the church. The two Miss Taylors sat alone in their pew. The handsome stranger had gone.

The rest of the service dragged interminably and then finally after the rather more relevant than usual prayers for peace, for the King and the Royal Family, the vicar finally got to the blessing. And they had barely mouthed the final amen when a sudden eerie wailing started up outside.

Louise clutched Bertie's arm. 'What on earth is that?'

He looked at her in surprise. 'It's an air raid siren, stupid.'

Louise blinked. 'What do we do?' She asked nervously. 'Where do we go?'

But before he could answer, her father was marshalling them out of the pew and down the aisle, even as the vicar clapped his hands and called for calm and invited the congregation to stay in the church. 'Our Lord will guard his flock,' he promised.

'Why doesn't he tell them to go to the shelters on the common?' Louise asked as her father bundled them into the car. She couldn't quite bring herself to believe that the Lord would consider the congregation of St Aldate's worthy of his personal attention.

'They're not finished yet,' Bertie said.

'I thought Mr Chamberlain said we were ready,' Louise said crossly. It seemed extremely stupid to declare war on Hitler if the bomb shelters weren't even finished. Thank God her father had reinforced the cellar at home.

'Be quiet, Louise,' Their father shot a quelling glance over his shoulder. 'What are all these people doing on the road?' he muttered irritably. 'Didn't they hear the siren?'

'They're probably rushing back home to their private air-raid shelters,' Bertie commented dryly. 'I hope it doesn't last too long,' he added. 'I'm starving.'

Douglas was peering out of the window at the clear blue sky over the common. 'I can't see any planes.'

Mrs Rutherford looked anxiously at her husband as they turned off the common into the Cedars House driveway. 'Shall I ask Cook and Jane to serve lunch in the cellar, Greville?'

'Aren't Cook and Jane allowed to take shelter?' Bertie asked.

'Of course they are, Bertie,' Mrs Rutherford flushed faintly. 'Your father's talked to Cook about it already.'

'I told her that if things got bad, I'd put up an Anderson shelter in the garden for them,' Greville Rutherford said, pulling up in front of the house. 'Until then they can use the cellar. I expect we'll find they're in there now.'

They were, with their feet up, listening to the wireless. But the ethical dilemma of letting them stay down there, versus having lunch, was resolved a few minutes later by the all-clear sounding, and at one o'clock the family sat down to Sunday lunch in the dining-room as usual.

And, as usual, Louise munched her way through the meal wishing that her parents would talk about something marginally more interesting than the quality of the beef, the flaccid texture of Cook's Yorkshire pudding, and the problem of ensuring that all the Rutherford & Berry pubs were properly blacked out now war had finally been declared.

'It's going to be murder being back at school,' Douglas said suddenly, stabbing a roast potato with his fork. 'I wish I was old enough to join up.'

Louise rolled her eyes, but her mother looked deeply shocked. 'Don't be absurd, Douglas. You've got three more years at school to do and then university before you need even think of joining up.'

'You don't have to do university first,' Douglas pointed out. 'As long as you're eighteen. Bertie could join up next year if he wanted to.' Apparently unaware of the sudden tension at the table, he appealed to his father. 'Couldn't he?'

Greville Rutherford laid down his knife and fork. 'In theory, yes, he could. But there would be little point as the war will be long over by then.' He smiled complacently at his younger son. 'I'm afraid Mr Hitler has bitten off rather more than he will be able to chew, Douglas. He seems to forget that we gave Germany a sound thrashing only twenty years ago and mark my words, we're quite ready to do it again.'

'It took us five years then,' Bertie commented mildly, chewing a carrot. 'And a lot of loss of life.'

An ominous silence greeted his words.

As her father flung down his napkin and abruptly stood up, Louise glanced nervously at her brother. It was a new departure for Bertie to needle her father. She had thought she was the only one in the family to find his autocratic, old-fashioned views stuffy and restrictive.

Now his mouth tightened into an ominous line as he fixed Bertie with an icy glare 'I will not hear defeatist talk like that in this family, Bertram.' He leaned forward stiffly, hands on the table, to make his point. 'Is that clear?'

There was a moment's tense pause, then to everyone's profound relief Bertie nodded and apologised. 'I'm sorry, I didn't mean to sound defeatist,' he said, swallowing the carrot. 'I just think the crisis might have been better solved politically than militarily, that's all.'

'I see.' Greville Rutherford nodded seriously. 'You're entitled to your opinion, of course, Bertram, but in this house I want to practise positive thinking.' He smiled briefly at his wife and daughter. 'We need to keep up the morale of our ladies.' With that he sat down again and then as though to clear the air he rang the bell for Jane to clear the dishes.

He waited in silence as Jane stacked the plates and brought in the steamed suet pudding. Then, with a deliberate change of subject, he turned to his wife and asked if she had had any luck finding a replacement for Jane who was leaving at the end of the week.

Celia Rutherford paused in serving out the pudding. 'I asked Mrs Nelson as you suggested, but she refused most adamantly.'

Greville Rutherford frowned. 'That's very poor form. Very odd. She should have been pleased. I'd better have a word with her husband about it.'

'Oh no, Greville. I don't think there's really any point,' Celia Rutherford said hastily. 'She said she'd rather look for some secretarial work.' She finished serving and lifted her spoon and fork to allow the others to start. 'She did suggest I ask that Mrs Carter,' she added doubtfully. 'But she's such a dreadful woman.

'Rather attractive daughter,' Bertie put in.

'Bertie, really!' His mother looked appalled.

Louise giggled. 'I know the girl you mean. Jennifer, she's called. But she's frightfully common, Bertie. I don't think she would be your type.'

'Louise! For goodness' sake,' Celia Rutherford glanced anxiously at her husband. But luckily he was involved with a scalding mouthful of suet pudding.

Bertie grinned slyly at Louise. 'How would you know my type?' He turned to his mother. 'Talking of which, who was that man with the Miss Taylors in church?'

Louise pricked up her ears but to her disappointment her mother answered distractedly, 'I didn't notice.'

Douglas made a leering face at his sister. 'Louise did.'

'Oh, do shut up, Douglas,' Louise said witheringly. 'Why don't you go and play with your toy soldiers?'

But his words hit their mark. And all afternoon, as she reluctantly helped her mother hem up the blasted blackout curtains, she was half dreaming of a handsome, dark-haired man with quizzical grey eyes and a wry smile who didn't know the words to *Love Divine, All Loves Excelling*.

Jen Carter woke the following morning with butterflies in her stomach. Today was the day she had been waiting for. Her first real chance to get into an acting school. Croydon Repertory Theatre School.

OK, so it was only Croydon, not London, but the London schools she'd visited, RADA and Central, had been snooty, expensive and not at all encouraging. The lady at Croydon had been very friendly and helpful, even down to suggesting pieces that she might want to use for her audition. One Shakespeare and one contemporary.

Jen had decided on Juliet's dying speech from *Romeo and Juliet* and one of Eliza Doolittle's in *Pygmalion*. You couldn't get more contemporary than that. She had practised them endlessly. And now she was ready. She hoped.

At least she had her new sophisticated hair-do and her new 'audition' outfit, a stylish black and white plaid cotton suit with a neat short jacket with large, slightly racy black buttons and a fashionable skirt that swung just enough to show the lacy petticoat underneath. It had cost her an arm and a leg. She had never owned anything anywhere near as glamorous in all her life. But even though it had depleted the ring money badly, it was worth it. It was important to get the right image. That was obvious. They weren't going to look at someone who didn't look the part, were they? She smiled suddenly, pushed back the covers and swung her feet out on to the cold lino floor. She was going to look the part all right, with her manicured nails and her red lipstick.

But she had barely reached for her new uplift bra and figure hugging knickers when the wailing of the air-raid siren started up at the end of the street. She swore violently. She was damned if she was going to miss her audition just because of a stupid siren. Anyway, it was probably another false alarm, like yesterday. She padded over to the window and peeled back the corner of the thick brown paper her mother had stuck over the glass. She couldn't see the street from the window because it was at the back of the house, but she could see most of the neighbouring back gardens, or yards they were really, some of them already with Monday washing hanging from the line, and most of them with the ungainly, government issue air-raid shelter with the corrugated-iron roof.

There didn't seem to be much activity out there. No sign of anyone rushing to safety. Jen snorted. Everyone had learned their lesson yesterday.

Jen had been with Katy Parsons, in the flat over the pub when the air-raid warning went off yesterday. She'd called over to tell Katy she'd bought them both tickets for next Saturday's matinee performance of Noel Coward's *Design for Living*.

'It's my treat,' she had said when Katy looked dubious. 'I came by a bit of money last week. And it's only at Streatham Hill. We can take the bus and be back before dark. I thought you wanted to go. You loved Anton Walbrook in *Victoria the Great*, and that dishy Rex Harrison is in this one too.'

And Katy had been muttering that she'd have to ask her mother, what with war having just been declared and all, when the sirens had sounded.

For a moment the two girls had stared at each other, then they heard rapid footsteps on the stairs up from the pub and Jen had giggled irreverently. 'Oh my God,' she said. 'Here comes Adolf Hitler already.'

But in fact it was only Mrs Parsons, in a terrible state, rushing in from the front where she'd been helping her husband tape the pub's precious stained-glass windows against bomb damage. 'What are you two girls just sitting there for? Can't you hear the siren?'

Jen had toyed with shaking her head or cupping her ear expectantly towards the window through which the siren was wailing at a near deafening pitch, but she could see that Katy's mother was too far gone for comedy, so she merely winked at Katy and was surprised to see that Katy was as white as a sheet and looked as though she was about to vomit.

'Thank goodness we went to the early service today,' Mrs Parsons muttered as she grabbed the gas masks off the sideboard and hurried over to help Katy to her feet. 'Whatever would you have done if we'd been at church?'

'It's probably only a test, Mrs Parsons,' Jen had commented mildly as Katy's mother rushed into the kitchen, and reappeared with a great box of food. 'And even if it's not, I can't believe that Hitler said to himself this morning, 'Jawohl, now zat war has finally been declared I can go and bomb Lavender Road'.'

She had grinned, pleased with her German accent, but Mrs Parsons didn't seem amused. She paused momentarily in her panic. 'You'd better go back over the road, Jennifer,' she had said stiffly. 'Your mother will be worried about you.'

Jen had snorted. 'Worried? She won't worry. She'd be delighted if Hitler dropped one on me.' Anyway, there was no way she was going to go and sit in that cramped bit of metal in the garden. Not with her parents. Not after the row over the ring money.

She frowned now and turned away from the window. She reached for her clothes. She wouldn't go yesterday and she wouldn't go today.

It had been quite nasty when her father came home on Friday evening. Her mother had bubbled her about the ring and he had taken a vicious swing at her. But luckily Jen had been quick on her feet and he had been too drunk to make contact. And she'd screamed that they'd all be glad if he was put away and that they'd get on a lot better without him.

Actually that wasn't true because her mother was just as bad. What with smashing that mirror and all. She'd take her time forgiving her for that. No, after a weekend like that it wasn't surprising that she'd rather spend a couple of hours in the dusty old cellar of the Flag and Garter yesterday than venture home.

And the pub cellar had been dusty, dusty and cold and, as far as Jen had been able to see by the dim light, full of meowling cats. She had almost sat on one of the damn things and jumped out of her skin when it scrambled away with an angry hiss from right under her bottom.

Jen giggled now as she eased herself into the new suit. Thank God it had only been for half an hour. The Parsons had wittered on endlessly about gas masks and why wasn't she carrying hers, and Katy had sat in glassy silence like a corpse. Jen had tried to calm her down with a bit of gossip about the street. The news that Jo Whitehead's TA regiment was being called up. That there had been two rather glamorous foreigners calling on Mrs d'Arcy Billière on Friday night. And more recently, that she'd only that morning spotted the Miss Taylors going off to church with some nice-looking man in a racy little Austin.

But all she'd got out of Katy was a nervous giggle and a lot of coughing and she was thankful when the all-clear sounded and she was able to escape.

Jen smoothed the suit and slipped on her new neatly heeled shoes. A moment later there was a knock on her door.

She swung round warily. 'Who is it?' She didn't want her mother to see her new clothes. No point in starting the rows all off again.

'It's Pete.' Her fifteen year old brother's voice came through the door. He knew better than to open it before being invited to. 'Mum says you're to come down to the shelter.'

Jen rolled her eyes. 'No fear. Tell her I'm going out.'

'You can't go out when there's an air-raid warning.'

'Can't I?' Jen swung open the door dramatically and glared at him. 'Who says?'

'I dunno. You just can't.' Pete's eyes widened as he took in the vision before him. 'Where did them clothes come from?'

'Never you mind.' Jen preened slightly, pleased with his astonishment.

Then she smiled at him sweetly. 'Go and bring me up a jam sandwich, Pete.'

Pete looked at her suspiciously. 'Why can't you get your own?'

'I haven't got time.'

Pete turned away, then stopped at the top of the stairs. 'What shall I say to her about the shelter?'

Jen tossed her head. 'Tell her I'm not going to waste my life sitting around waiting for Hitler to drop bombs on me. I've got better things to do.' Her eyes narrowed and she lowered her voice. 'Where's Dad? I bet he's not in the shelter. Not after the rage he was in about the false alarm yesterday.'

Pete nodded nervously along the passage. 'Still asleep. Mum said it was best to leave him.'

Jen smiled: 'Good.' With any luck she could be ready and out of the house before he woke. She certainly wasn't going to hang around waiting for the all-clear. War or not. She had a life to lead. A career to launch. War or no war, it didn't make any difference. And that stupid little man, Adolf Hitler would have to land one right on her before she was going to take any notice.

She laughed to herself as she went back into her room. And minutes later the all-clear sounded. Another false alarm.

But later, as the bus trundled down through Streatham towards Croydon, Jen had to admit that suddenly the war was making a difference. Almost overnight the whole look of the place had changed. For a start, the windows of the bus had been painted black with only a small diamond shape left in the middle to see out of, the kerbs on the main road had all been painted white so drivers could see the road without lights at night. Many of the glass-fronted shops on Streatham High Road were hidden behind sand bags and the windows of the flats above were blanked out with drab brown paper.

Jen frowned as she peered through the restricted window. There was a great flabby silver-grey barrage balloon over Streatham Common and there were an enormous number of green army vehicles about. Particularly as they neared Croydon Airport, where from her vantage place on the top deck, she could see military planes moving about on the runways, and another coming in to land, a Hurricane, she thought, but she wasn't sure.

In sunny Croydon the newspaper men were screaming the headlines of the late morning issues. That Winston Churchill was back in the Cabinet as First Lord of the Admiralty. That Canada and Australia and New Zealand had thrown in their lot with England and France. That Luftwaffe bombs were devastating Poland. That thousands upon thousands of Poles had already been killed or captured. That the magnificent Polish mounted cavalry was being pulverised by the German tanks.

Two large women in flowery mob-caps were leafing through the paper they had just bought. 'Them poor horses,' one of them muttered. 'They didn't ask for no war.'

'Nobody did,' her friend replied sourly. Then, after a moment, added, 'At least it don't seem as he's using his poison gas on them poor Polish buggers.'

'Not yet,' the first woman responded dryly. 'Probably saving that for us.'

Jen glanced down at the oblong box that contained her gas mask and felt a shiver trickle down her spine. Away from the familiar houses of Lavender Road, it all suddenly seemed more real.

And more frightening.

Then she saw the time on the church steeple and quickened her step. She was damned if she was going to be late. The war would have to wait. This was her chance to make her break, and she was going to make the most of it.

But by the time she reached the door of the theatre school, she was so keyed up and nervous that she deliberately walked straight past. She couldn't go in with her heart thudding audibly in her chest, with shaking knees and clammy palms. What if she had to shake hands with someone?

At the corner she leaned against the wall and tried to calm herself down. Silently she mouthed through her audition pieces to convince herself she knew them off pat. For a second she faltered in the Juliet soliloquy and sweat broke out again. Then the words came back to her and she breathed again.

An open army car cruised incongruously down the street and one of the soldiers in the back whistled at her. They all grinned as she looked up, surprised. 'Don't look so sad, lovey,' one of them called, 'It may never happen.'

Their smiles were openly admiring and Jen straightened herself and smiled graciously back as though they were adoring fans.

It was the confidence boost she needed.

I can do it, she said to herself. I've got what it takes. And squaring her shoulders and lifting her chin, she swung on her heel and walked back to the theatre school.

Chapter Four

Pam Nelson took one look at Sheila Whitehead's tear-stained face and said she'd put the kettle on.

'Daddy's going to war,' little George Whitehead said as he followed his mother into Pam's kitchen, apparently completely recovered from his frantic flight from the evacuation bus. 'He's going to fight Mr Hitler. I'm staying with Mummy and Ray.'

Pam's heart twisted as she smiled into the eager cherubic face of the little boy and wondered how many other sweet, innocent families like the Whiteheads were going to be torn apart over the next few months.

'He's being sent to a training camp,' Sheila said as she sat down at Pam's kitchen table, pulled out a chair for George and set the two and a half year old Ray down on the floor to play about around the table legs. 'He doesn't know where. It's all so secret.' Her voice rose slightly. 'I don't know how I'll know where he is.'

'He'll write to you,' Pam said soothingly as she laid out the cups. 'And he'll get leave, won't he? Soldiers always get leave. Furlough they call it, don't they?' She turned away to warm the pot and prayed that Jo Whitehead would be close enough to come home often. She wasn't at all sure how Sheila would cope for long periods without him. They were such a perfect couple, Sheila and her Jo. Almost like one person divided into two. They even looked alike with their gentle blue eyes, sandy hair and scatter of freckles. It was no wonder they'd produced two of the prettiest blond, blue-eyed children Pam had ever seen.

'Will he write to me too?' George asked eagerly.

'He'll write to all of you,' Pain said quickly as Sheila's eyes reddened alarmingly. She nodded at the smiling child swinging on the table leg. 'Even Ray.'

George wrinkled his freckled nose. 'Ray can't read.'

'I can,' Ray said.

George grimaced at Pam. 'He can't really.'

Pam smiled. 'Mummy can read Ray's letters to him.'

'What's Alan going to do?' Sheila asked suddenly. 'Jo said he was looking for war work. ARP or something, is it?'

Pam nodded. 'He wants to do something to help.' She poured the water into the pot and stirred it carefully. 'He wants to feel useful.'

Poor Alan. He felt so useless just now. Pam felt a tightening of her throat and took a quick steadying breath. They both did. Useless and hopeless. And it was increasingly hard to hide it. Luckily Sean Byrne had been out yesterday when the siren had gone and Alan had been down at the river tinkering with his boat. So nobody knew that Pam had sat in her kitchen, drinking tea, half hoping that Hitler would bomb number twenty four Lavender Road and put her out of her misery.

But Hitler hadn't obliged. And this morning when the siren had gone again, Sean Byrne had been still in the house and Pam had felt a sudden and dreadful panic at the thought of them cloistered up together in the poky air-raid shelter that Alan had dug into the back yard. But as his landlady, she'd felt obliged to offer him the option of taking cover.

He'd smiled slowly, leaning against the banister where she'd caught him just coming downstairs. 'To be sure, Mrs Nelson,' he'd murmured. 'It's a tempting offer but I'd better decline.'

To her horror, Pam had felt a stab of disappointment and hoped to God he wasn't aware of it.

But he just laughed softly, 'I'm a good Catholic,' he said and his lips curved slightly as he looked down at her. 'I would hate to shock the priest at confession Mrs Nelson.'

Pam stared up at him blankly from the foot of the stairs.

His blue eyes held hers. 'It's a very small shelter, Mrs Nelson.'

A rush of colour had flooded into Pam's, shocked face. She fought for composure and nearly succeeded. 'There wouldn't be anything to confess,' she said stiffly.

He had smiled as he came lightly down the stairs and opened the front door. 'There'd be my thoughts, Mrs Nelson. That's quite enough for any priest.'

Even now as she poured the tea for Sheila, Pam could feel the warmth on her cheeks, the sudden thudding of her heart, and she hated herself for it. And she hated Sean Byrne. The blatant cheek of him. Those damned blue eyes and that lazy, knowing smile.

'You're spilling!' George commented delightedly. 'Look, it's all going in the saucer.'

'Oh my goodness!' Pam jerked back to the present, shocked.

Sheila looked at her in concern. 'Are you all right, Pam?' she asked, watching her empty the saucer into the sink. 'Your hand is trembling and you look ever so flushed. I hope you're not sickening for the flu.'

Pam tried to laugh it off. 'To tell the truth, I'm nervous,' she said. 'I'm thinking of applying for a job.'

Sheila stared at her as though she had said she was applying for the French Foreign Legion. 'What job?'

Pam sipped her tea. 'It was in the paper this morning. They need people who can type in the new Ministry of Information,' she said diffidently. 'I thought it sounded quite interesting.' She didn't say that all the other jobs sounded either too high powered or too boring. Nor that she had already sent off for an application form.

'But you're married.'

Pam smiled wryly. 'I don't think that's going to matter too much now.'

'A job.' Sheila shook her head in awe. She put down her cup. 'What does Alan think about it?'

Pam grimaced guiltily. 'I haven't told him.' And she didn't intend to. Not until she had found something. There was no point in upsetting him and it might never happen. Quite likely she would be turned down flat anyway. After all, she hadn't worked for years. And, as everyone kept pointing out, she was married.

She frowned. It had always seemed so unfair that married women were penalised against. If they had children, fair enough, but if they didn't, then why shouldn't they do something a bit interesting? Were they supposed to be chained to the kitchen sink their whole lives, preparing endless meals for their husbands, and making jam for the WI?

She hadn't told Alan about last Friday's visit from Mrs Rutherford either. After all, Mr Rutherford was Alan's boss at the brewery. And Alan hated to put a foot wrong with him. She smiled sadly. Dear Alan, he hated to put a foot wrong with anybody. He really was the nicest person. But she did wish just sometimes he would take a bit of positive action. Like asking Mr Rutherford about a bit of a wage increase, perhaps, or suggesting a day out occasionally at the weekend instead of spending all his time down at the river with that damn boat.

Sheila was looking miserable again. 'If you get a job I'll be stuck here all on my own all day long,' she said glumly. 'Who will I have elevenses with?'

Pam smiled bracingly. 'It may never happen.'

'You got me, Mummy,' George piped up suddenly. 'And Ray, You can have elevenizzez with us.'

Sheila laughed and hugged him to her. 'My babies,' she said, pulling Ray up on to her lap too. 'Yes, I'll always have you.'

As the two little blond heads nestled eagerly into Sheila's chest, Pam had to turn away abruptly, to hide her look of longing, the tears in her eyes, the sudden empty ache in her heart.

Straightening her suit, taking a deep careful breath, Jen frowned and banged on the theatre school door again. Why was it locked? Last time she had come here, she had walked straight into a hall teeming with people. It had been lunchtime and there had been a lot of shouting about sandwiches and coffee and where was so-and-so, and Jen, somewhat awed by the dark oil portraits adorning the arched hall and the wide stone staircase, had been impressed by the students' apparent confidence and easy camaraderie.

But this time, the place seemed deserted. Presumably term hadn't started, but nevertheless it seemed odd that there was nobody to open the door. She glanced up and down the street wondering if perhaps the receptionist had popped out for a paper or some cigarettes, but there was no sign of anyone who looked as though they belonged to the theatre school. No one rushing back apologetically to let her in.

She banged again forcefully, almost bruising the sides of her hands, and then stood back in relief as she finally heard footsteps on the other side of the door.

An old man opened the door and regarded her through rheumy eyes. 'Can I help you?'

Jen breathed slowly to steady her pulse which had accelerated the moment she'd heard the footsteps. She smiled winningly. He was old but he might be important for all she knew. 'My name is Jennifer Carter,' she said. 'I've come for an audition with Mrs Frost.'

The old man blinked at her. 'I thought they'd finished all that,' he said.

'She said eleven o'clock in her letter,' Jen offered helpfully, wishing she was dealing with the nice admissions lady she had met last time.

The door keeper frowned and sucked his teeth, then finally came to a decision and stood back. 'You'd better come in,' he said gruffly. 'Mrs Frost is upstairs. She didn't say as she was expecting anyone.'

'Well, she is,' Jen said firmly with a bright smile, following him inside. 'She's expecting me.'

But when Mrs Frost appeared at the top of the stairs a few minutes later it was clear she wasn't expecting her at all.

She was a large, imposing woman with a prominent nose and iron grey hair pulled back into a severe bun.

She stared down at Jen with ill-concealed irritation. 'What is it you say you've come for?' she barked, striding down the stairs.

'An audition,' Jen said stiffly. 'I was …'

'An audition!' Mrs Frost interrupted harshly. 'Good Lord. Don't be absurd. We've closed.'

Jen felt the blood drain from her face. 'Closed?' she whispered.

Mrs Frost seemed either unaware or uncaring of Jen's private agony. 'The school has closed for the war,' she said briskly. 'We notified all the students and applicants last week that we'd close in the event of war being declared.'

Jen felt an icy hand crushing her heart. 'I didn't receive anything.'

'Well, you should have,' the woman snapped as though it was Jen's fault. 'The letters were certainly sent out.' She moved towards the door and added grudgingly, 'I hope you haven't come far.'

'Only from London,' Jen said bleakly. She couldn't believe it. Could not believe that her one big chance had been snatched from under her nose by this horrible, hawk-nosed woman.

'Not too bad then.' Mrs Frost smiled thinly.

Not too bad? Jen felt like hitting her. Felt like punching her hard in the stomach. Felt like scratching that supercilious uncaring smile off her painted mouth. How dare she dismiss her so heartlessly? Jen's eyes flashed dangerously as she followed her to the door.

'What difference does the stupid war make?' she asked suddenly. 'It's not going to make any damned difference to Adolf Hitler if Croydon Repertory Theatre School keeps going or not, is it? I thought we were supposed to keep a fighting spirit in the face of war, not close up shop and run away the minute things get a bit rough.'

Despite her disappointment Jen was secretly pleased with her tirade. That would show her, the vicious old dragon. But Mrs Frost did not look at all taken aback. On the contrary, her expression was entirely unimpressed.

'You need to learn to control your feelings, young lady,' she said, chillingly dismissive. 'Particularly if you want to become an actress. She nodded abruptly to the old man who was standing by imperviously. 'Show Miss Carter out, Mr Bates. Before she says something she regrets.'

Her icy disdain was like a red rag to a bull. Angry colour flared in Jen's cheeks. 'I won't regret it,' she hissed. 'I wouldn't have wanted to come here anyway if it's got beastly horrible people like you here. I'll go to RADA or somewhere where they give people a chance instead of shutting the moment any one wants to join.'

But of course she did regret it. By the time she had walked back to the bus stop, she wished she had maintained an icy cool. That would have shown that cold-faced bitch.

Reaching the bus stop, she leaned on a park railing crossly. She shouldn't have lost her temper. That old dragon was right. To be a successful actress she needed to control her feelings. She glared at the trees until her eyes watered. Then she kicked the railing angrily and hurt her toe. How on earth was she going to become a successful actress if she was thwarted at every turn?

'I pity the man that upset you,' a soft voice said beside her and she swung round angrily. All ready to tell an intrusive stranger to leave her alone, in no uncertain terms, she found herself blinking into a vaguely familiar face. Wasn't it the man who lodged with the Nelsons in Lavender Road? The Irishman?

She glared at him, annoyed at being intruded upon. Annoyed by the faint smile that played on his lips and in his eyes. Annoyed by the gentle mockery in his lilting Irish voice. She didn't like the Irish. Particularly not Irish men who made unasked-for, insinuating remarks like that.

'It wasn't a man, it was a woman,' she said, shortly, turning back to her contemplation of the trees.

'Is that right?' he said, leaning his back against the fence beside her and lighting a cigarette. 'And that does surprise me. That an attractive young girl like yourself should be more interested in women than men.'

Jen gaped at him. 'I'm not interested in women.' She was deeply shocked. 'Not in that way.' She blushed.

He smiled slowly and the blue eyes glinted. 'I'm awful glad to hear it. Those beautiful lips and fiery eyes would surely be wasted on a mere woman.'

For a strange second Jen felt a flicker of excitement somewhere in the region of her stomach. She had never had that reaction to a man before and, for a moment, it unnerved her badly. Then she reminded herself he was Irish and took a step away. 'Look,' she said carefully. 'I'm not in the mood for flirting.'

'Flirting?' Sean Byrne looked outraged. He opened his hands innocently. 'Who said anything about flirting?' He shook his head mournfully and took a drag on his cigarette. 'Sure and it's a sad state when a man can't pass comment on a woman's beauty without being branded a flirt?'

Feeling the unwelcome heat in her cheeks again, Jen looked impatiently up the street for the bus. But there was no sign of it and anyway, she suddenly realised, presumably Sean Byrne would be getting on it too. Why else would he be waiting at the bus stop? She grimaced to herself and slanted him a quick glance as he blew out a lazy stream of smoke. He was nice looking, it was true, very nice. She wondered suddenly if he would sit next to her on the bus and felt a flicker of excitement which she quickly quashed. She wasn't going to get silly about a stupid Irishman.

'Will you not tell me what the woman did to rouse you?' he asked suddenly. 'If only to stop my fevered imagination running away with me.'

Jen tried to resist his wry smile and couldn't. 'She closed her stupid drama school because of the blasted war being declared.'

'Is it an actress you are, then?' He sounded impressed and Jen warmed to him slightly. Most people scorned her ambition.

'I'm going to be,' she said stiffly. 'It's just a bit difficult to get started.'

'It's a competitive world, to be sure,' he agreed. 'But with your looks, you should have no problems.' He exhaled slowly and his eyes narrowed against the smoke. 'You have a look of Vivien Leigh about you, don't you? Do you have her talent too?'

Jen stared at him. Vivien Leigh! Her heroine. Laurence Olivier's beautiful lover. She couldn't think of anyone she would rather be compared to. As for having her talent ... For a moment she remembered Vivien Leigh's stunning performance in *Fire over England* and wondered. Then she came to her senses and lifted her chin. 'Of course I do. Everyone says so.' She frowned. 'I got a review in the paper for a part I had when I was at school which said I had great potential.'

He nodded absently. 'There's a lot of actresses without talent in my opinion.'

Jen bristled. 'You won't be saying that about me in years to come.'

He smiled suddenly. 'Well, look at that, an English girl with ambition.'

Jen frowned. 'Do Irish women have more of it, then?'

He laughed. 'Some do, but being Irish they're mostly spending their lives having babies.'

'God forbid.' Jen thought of her mother, fat and bloated, pregnant with the younger children, thought of her shouting at them all, thought of her uncaringly drab appearance, the bruises on her, her apparent willingness to live her life in drudgery, and shuddered dramatically. 'Well, I'm not getting married until I'm successful,' she said abruptly. 'I'm not going to let anything spoil my chances of a good career.'

'Are you not?' He smiled slowly, his blue eyes glinting as they flicked down over her slender body and back to her face. 'Then there'll surely be a string of broken hearts behind you by the time you're famous. Just like Vivien Leigh.'

Jen laughed delightedly, for a moment forgetting her earlier disappointment. It was nice to be flattered, admired. Even by an Irishman, It was nice to have someone take her ambitions seriously. 'I wish I was going to play Scarlett O'Hara in *Gone with the Wind*,' she said wistfully. 'I can't wait for it to open over here.'

Sean Byrne smiled. 'Perhaps she'll go sick and they'll call you up as a replacement.'

'If only!' Jen laughed. It made a nice change to meet someone who understood her dreams. 'You live in Lavender Road, don't you?' she said suddenly. 'With the Nelsons? That's where I live too. My name is Jennifer Carter.'

'Is that right?' He feigned surprise. 'Well, think of that.'

'You knew, didn't you?' she accused him.

'I've seen you about, all right.' He shrugged off her surprise. 'To be sure, I could hardly miss noticing such a pretty girl living only just a few doors away.'

She waited for him to say something else. To suggest they meet again. To ask her for a drink maybe, but he merely nodded up the road. 'Here comes your bus.'

Jen felt an unexpected jolt of disappointment. 'Aren't you catching it?'

He stubbed out his cigarette and glanced at his watch. 'No, I have to get back to my work.' He stood back as the bus drew up. 'Goodbye Jennifer Carter Leigh. Good luck with your career.'

Jen hesitated with one foot on the platform. Wasn't he intending to see her again? Why didn't he say something? Something positive.

The conductor clicked his fingers impatiently. 'Come on, love, make up your mind.'

Jen glared at him then turned to Sean who was watching her with a faint, complacent amusement.

'I've got tickets for Noel Coward's *Design for Living* in Streatham on Saturday afternoon,' she said suddenly. 'The matinée.' Katy wouldn't mind. She'd been half hearted about it anyway. 'You're obviously interested in the theatre. Would you like to come with me?'

Sean Byrne shook his head slowly, 'Not Saturday. I'm busy in the afternoon.'

The bus conductor put his hand on the bell.

'The evening performance then,' Jen said urgently. 'I'm sure I can change the tickets.'

He met her eyes and smiled slowly. 'OK, Jennifer Carter, the evening performance it is.'

As the bus pulled away, the conductor shook his head. 'Theatres are all closed, love. Haven't you seen the papers?'

Jen stared at him. 'They can't be.'

He shrugged impassively as he took her money and rolled out her ticket: 'Suit yourself.'

And sure enough as they drove past Streatham Hill Theatre half an hour later Jen saw the sign draped across the hoarding. 'Closed by government order until further notice.'

Her heart sank. Sean Byrne would think she was a complete idiot. She wished she'd never mentioned the stupid play.

She saw the conductor watching her and turned her fury on him. 'Why didn't you say so before? In Croydon. When I asked him?'

The conductor shrugged. 'None of my business,' he said. He rolled out a ticket for a woman in a black hat. 'Don't like the Irish myself,' he added laconically as he went upstairs. 'Don't trust them.'

When notification came that her three youngest children had arrived safely in Taunton and had been taken in by a Mrs Baxter of Redlake Farm near Barnstaple, Joyce Carter experienced a profound sense of relief.

It had worried her not knowing where they were. Now she knew they were settled, she could put her mind at rest and tuck away that little niggle of guilt that it was a relief having them gone. The boys, that was. Particularly Mick. At fourteen he'd thought he was too old to be evacuated. But he'd been such a bloody nuisance recently that Joyce had been glad to see the back of him. And his bloody conkers. Always under her feet they were at this time of year, before he fixed them to their little strings ready to smash the knuckles of an unsuspecting challenger.

She would miss Angie, though. Angie wasn't a bad child. Jen always said she spoilt Angie, but it wasn't that. It was just that in general Angie did as she was told, which Jen had never done. Even as a small child Jen had thrown her weight around. Perhaps it was having so many brothers, or more likely it was having a dad who drank.

Joyce grimaced as she swept the kitchen floor. Even now Stanley was lying in bed, sleeping off last night's excesses. His trial date had come in yesterday and he was making the most of his freedom. Joyce paused in her sweeping and wondered for a second if she would be relieved if Stanley was put away.

Financially it would be a disaster, not that he brought in much these days, but occasionally he found a bit of work, or more likely brought home something they could pawn or even sometimes sell, and there was his unemployment of course, although that was barely worth sneezing at. Sometimes she wondered if Stanley was right going on about those Communists giving everyone a decent wage, everyone equal and all that. It sounded like a good idea but it was hard to imagine everyone being equal in this road; there'd still have to be bosses, wouldn't there, like the Rutherfords?

Stanley said when the revolution came, people like the Rutherfords would be shot, and had got angry when Joyce said that seemed a bit hard on the Rutherfords, for all their fancy ways. And he'd got even more angry when Jen chipped in and asked if he wanted to end up equal with all the blackies and Jews and all, people like Mr Lorenz.

Joyce swept the dirt out into the back yard. Jen's problem was that she was too smart. Too clever by half. With her brain she could train for something worthwhile, secretarial or Civil Service or something. And bring in a bit of cash. And perhaps find a nice husband to marry to get her off their hands.

But no, she was set on this acting lark, stupid little madam, and there didn't seem to be a damn thing they could do about it.

Joyce banged her brush on the back step. She was still angry about Jen stealing that ring. She hadn't forgiven her for that, nor for her nasty remarks the other night. Nor would she. She half wished she'd bolted the door so she couldn't get back in. That would have served her right.

Joyce propped the broom against the wall and glanced in the mirror. Maybe Jen was right. What with hair like old string, the creases across her forehead and the bags under her eyes, it wasn't a pretty sight. Once in the long distant past she had looked all right, quite attractive some had said, despite the heavy chin. You'd never know it now. Not that she cared, she told herself, not really. After all, who did she have to be pretty for?

Stanley? The days had long gone when Stanley cared what she looked like. He'd hardly notice if she went to bed dressed up like Adolf Hitler. Not unless he was in the mood. Which thankfully, he wasn't often these days. And then he'd most likely be tanked up and have a bit of a job getting the swastikas off.

She glanced in the mirror again and was surprised to see that she was smiling. It seemed a long time since she'd smiled, and it made a difference to her face. Made her look younger, just a bit. She snorted and turned away. What had she got to smile about? A husband about to be locked up in jail? One son already in jail and another earning a pittance as an apprentice bricky? A daughter who refused to work? The prospect of being thrown out on the street if she couldn't meet the rent next month?

Hearing movement upstairs she quickly put the kettle on and then jumped as someone knocked on the front door.

The Rutherfords' chauffeur was standing on the step. 'Mrs Rutherford asked me to deliver this,' he said, with faint disdain, offering her an envelope with *Mrs Carter* written on it in an elegant italic hand. 'What is it?' Joyce asked suspiciously.

He shrugged. 'Mrs Rutherford did not inform me as to the contents,' he said pompously and turned away. 'I was not required to await a reply.'

Joyce watched him get back into the car, with a sour expression. Jumped-up little git, she thought, everyone knew he only came from Peckham, so why he thought he could put on airs was anybody's guess.

Then she went back indoors, shut the door and quickly tore open the envelope.

Mrs Carter,

I have been given your name as someone who might be interested in helping out in the house a couple of days a week. My housemaid is going back to the country and will leave us shorthanded. I believe three shillings a day is the standard rate for this kind of work. I look forward to hearing from you.

Yours sincerely, Mrs Rutherford.

Joyce blinked at the letter, wanting to be certain she had understood it. The last thing in the world she wanted to do was work for the Rutherfords, but three shillings a day, and with the children away ... She felt a flicker of hope stir in her chest, which was quickly quashed as Stanley's voice came roughly from upstairs. 'Who was that?'

'Nobody.'

'What do you mean, nobody? I heard you talking.' Joyce tucked the letter into the pocket of her apron. Stanley would never countenance her going to work for the Rutherfords.

'It was someone lost asking the way,' she said quickly. 'Now they've taken down the signs on the common, people are always asking.'

She'd wait for a good moment to ask him. She had to choose it carefully. Because Stanley just had to agree. Because this was the answer to all her prayers.

Chapter Five

The elegant, white, three storey facade of Cedars House at the Clapham Common end of Lavender Road gave an impression of genteel tranquillity. But behind those regular Georgian windows, Louise Rutherford spent most of the first week of the war arguing with her parents about a party she had been invited to at the Leander Club in Henley by one of the girls she had met on her Lucie Clayton finishing course.

The fact that Lucinda Veale's father was a Sir weighed slightly in her favour, but absolutely everything else seemed to be against her. The outbreak of war. What if the bombing started? How was she going to get there?

People were already being asked to conserve petrol. Some people, it was said, had already put their cars up on blocks, rationing was expected. And then, how late would it be? Where would she stay? And how was she going to get back? Who else was going? Was it going to be properly chaperoned?

Letters flew back and forth between Celia Rutherford and Lady Veale.

Eventually it was agreed that if the bombing hadn't begun by Saturday, Louise could go. She would be conveyed down on Saturday, and back on Sunday by Mrs Rhoda Hesketh, a personal friend of Lady Veale who was also attending the party. They would spend the night at the Veales' country house which was situated on the river just outside Henley.

This was not the outcome that Louise had desired. The prospect of a long journey in the company of some respectable middle-aged woman did not appeal anywhere near as highly as travelling down by train or by car with a number of Lucinda's racy young London friends, but at least it allowed her to go to the party, which was the main thing. In any event, as Bertie pointed out to her at a crucial stage of the negotiations while they were playing cards on the veranda, it was that or nothing. There was no way their ultra conservative parents were going to allow her to racket about all over the country with a lot of unidentified young men at all hours of the night.

'I'm eighteen, for goodness' sake,' Louise had grumbled, discarding a two of hearts. 'You'd think I was old enough, to go to a party without all this fuss.'

Bertie had shrugged. 'Perhaps they've noticed that hungry look that comes into your face whenever any vaguely handsome man between seventeen and thirty crosses your path.'

'Don't be absurd, Bertie,' Louise pouted crossly. Then she saw he was laughing at her and she made a face and giggled. 'Anyway, you're miles out. Thirty is far too old. And I wouldn't dream of marrying a seventeen year old.'

'Oh, it's marriage we're talking about, is it?' He rolled his eyes as he trumped her hand with a jack of spades. 'Sorry, I thought it was something quite different.'

'Bertie, really!' Of course she was thinking of marriage. Her whole life had been geared towards making a good marriage. That's why she had gone to Lucie Clayton's finishing school, that well known training ground for fashionable young ladies. OK, so her family wasn't quite as classy as some of the girls there. But she'd been to a good school, she was well spoken and well dressed, and quite a bit more pretty than some of the real top-drawer girls. All she needed now was a handsome, rich, cosmopolitan man to fall in love with her.

And if she occasionally kept an eye open for any likely contenders, like that lovely-looking mystery man who had been in church with the Miss Taylors, there was nothing wrong with that, was there? Nevertheless, Under Bertie's wry gaze, she was put out to feel herself blush.

He smiled knowingly but his eyes were serious. 'Well, just be careful, big sister,' he said condescendingly. 'I'm not sure that marriage is always the first thing that men think about when they see a pretty girl. Not nowadays.'

'Bertie!' Louise was shocked. She lifted her chin. 'I do know the facts of life, Bertie,' she said witheringly. They had talked about very little else at Lucie Clayton's. Although, to be fair some of the finer details were still a little bit hazy. But she didn't intend admitting that to her brother. He was far too big for his boots as it was. 'I'm not stupid.' She knew perfectly well that you withheld your favours until someone offered to marry you. Certainly her parents would not tolerate anything else. They still thought they were living in the last century. Bertie had only last week commented, in private, that the ownership of the Rutherford & Berry pubs and the brewery, a key local employer, made their father see himself as some kind of feudal overlord.

That might have been a touch unfair because there was no doubt that Greville Rutherford was an important local figure. Chairman of both the Parish Church Council and the local Conservative Society, a long-standing Mason, and now since Monday some kind of local ARP official as well, he was by any standard a highly respected pillar of the community. Certainly he had spent much of their childhood reminding them of their Position.

In those days, their Position meant that they had to brush their hair and dress tidily if they were going to set one foot out of doors. They had to nod appreciatively if ever their father's employees addressed them, avoid conversing with the local children, and save any sweets from the local shops until they got home, on no account could they be seen chewing in the street.

Things had changed a bit recently, Louise realised. New rules had been added. Or perhaps they had always been there but untested. Nowadays, they had to provide precise details of where they were going, for how long and with whom. Only clothes approved of by their father could be worn and nobody, not even their mother, was apparently allowed to contradict him on his views, political or otherwise.

Bertie had come up against this last rather more frequently than Louise or Douglas, but Louise had had major problems over the clothes. For one thing her father abhorred slacks. 'I will not have you wearing trousers. It's unladylike and that's all there is to be said about it.'

The fact that even Vogue was now featuring women in slacks, party pyjamas and trouser suits seemed to pass him by. Louise wasn't allowed them and that was that.

Nor was she allowed to have her ears pierced. That was apparently 'common', even though last year's debs had all had pierced ears. As did the Royals.

Nor would he allow her to learn to drive. 'Ladies do not drive, Louise. We have a perfectly good driver in Mr Wallace. Your mother has never needed to drive. Can you imagine her cranking the Riley? No, you cannot. It would be quite unsuitable. Cars are dirty, complicated pieces of machinery, much best left to men.'

That the glamorous Mrs d'Arcy Billière in the house opposite had recently dismissed her chauffeur and acquired one of the new seventy miles an hour Flying Standards with white mudguards and running boards which she drove herself seemed only to confirm his view that it was unsuitable.

'I gather Mrs d'Arcy Billière is taking in some refugees,' Celia Rutherford had commented mildly as the conversation threatened once again to become heated. 'Austrians, I think she said.'

'Jews probably,' her husband said briskly, 'Wouldn't surprise me if she hadn't got some Jewish blood in her, herself.'

'Greville, really!' Celia had admonished mildly, but he merely shrugged and lifted his newspaper, effectively dismissing the subject of women drivers, and Mrs d'Arcy Billière with them,

'I'd agree to go to Henley with Lady Veale's close personal friend, if I was you,' Bertie said now, flicking through the records by the gramophone. 'Let's face it, she's your only chance.'

So Louise had given in grudgingly and had turned her thoughts instead to what she might wear.

She found just the thing at Debenham & Freebody: a sleeveless evening dress in pressed pleats of bright emerald with a modern cropped jacket to top it off. She also bought herself two jaunty gas-mask holders from a street trader in the Strand and while the boys had end of holiday haircuts at Trumpers, her mother bought her a pair of leather gloves with special white palms for extra visibility, because of the increase in traffic accidents due to the black out.

By the end of the week Louise was more than ready for the party. The boys had been sent off on the school train from Paddington on Thursday, since when her mother had hardly stopped complaining about the mess they had left behind. She was also fretting about why Mrs Carter had not come back to her about the cleaning job.

'Honestly, you'd think these women would be grateful to make a bit of pocket money, wouldn't you?' she grumbled over lunch on Friday.

'I suppose so,' Louise replied, entirely uninterested. What concerned her more was whether the velvet ribbon headband she had chosen for the party was quite the thing or not.

Celia sighed. 'It really is most thoughtless of the Carter woman not to respond. It puts me in quite an embarrassing position.'

'Perhaps she's forgotten,' Louise suggested.

'Of course she hasn't forgotten,' Celia said irritably. 'I sent a note. If she doesn't want the work, she only has to put pen to paper. Then I can make alternative arrangements.'

Louise shrugged. 'Perhaps she can't write.'

Greville Rutherford snorted and looked up from his boiled ham. 'Can't be bothered, more likely. Too lazy, I expect. They're a bad lot, those Carters.'

Celia frowned anxiously. 'Oh dear, Greville, do you think I shouldn't have asked her?'

'It's your decision, of course,' he said magnanimously. 'But if it is laziness that's delayed her, it doesn't bode particularly well for her standard of work, does it?'

Louise rolled her eyes inwardly. That was typical of her father. To pretend to leave the management of the house to her mother and then niggle about her decisions. Mind you, he was probably right. That Mrs Carter was an awful-looking woman, and she couldn't see anything in favour of the daughter Jennifer, despite what Bertie had said. She'd seen her yesterday, hanging about in the street with red lipstick and a ridiculous tight perm in her gingery hair. Louise was going to have her own long dark tresses washed and set in gentle waves tomorrow morning before leaving. Much more sophisticated.

'Is it all right if I telephone Lucinda this afternoon?' she asked casually. Anything to change the subject. 'I want to find out who else is going.'

'Darling, do you really think that's necessary?' Celia said quickly, as her husband reddened alarmingly. 'You know Daddy doesn't like your using the telephone. Trunk calls are frightfully expensive and you'll find out quite soon enough tomorrow.'

*

53

Jen had had a frustrating week. The letter announcing the closure of the Croydon Theatre School had finally arrived, having been misdirected to Lavender Hill.

'I expect the post is up the creek at the moment because so many postmen have been called up,' Katy said sympathetically when she heard.

Katy was also sympathetic about the theatres closing. It really did seem to be terribly unfair, they agreed, that just as Jen was about to launch herself on the acting scene, the blasted theatres closed. There was absolutely nothing Jen could do now except wait. Either for the Government to come to its senses and reopen the theatres, or for the bombs to fall and finish them all off.

Katy had gone quiet at that point and Jen had been forced to regale her with details of her meeting with Sean Byrne and enlist her help in the problem of what to do about Saturday night in order to take her mind off her imminent demise.

In fact the prospect of another encounter with the blue-eyed Irishman had been about the only thing that had kept Jen's own spirits up. Her father was edgy as hell about his impending court case and her mother had hardly addressed a word to her all week. It was all about that stupid, diamond ring of course. As though five pounds made any difference to anyone.

Except to her, of course. It could help her get started on her career. But they didn't seem to understand that. And her mother kept on whining about the children and how it would cost twelve-and-six train fare plus a thirty-bob taxi fare to go and see them in Devon or wherever they were, and how they couldn't possibly afford it.

Not that she'd have gone anyway, Jen thought sourly. Her mother had never gone further than Croydon in her life, as far as Jen knew, and she could hardly see her trundling all the way to Devon just because Angie had written a pathetic letter saying she had wet her bed because she was homesick and that Mick and Paul were playing up.

Jen had avoided the house as much as possible. But there was a limit to the places she could go, particularly in the evening, and she was glad she would be able to escape tonight with Sean. Katy had ingeniously suggested she should explain to him about the closed theatre by means of a note dropped surreptitiously through the Nelsons' door, and in it propose an alternative plan, of meeting at the Lyons Corner House at Clapham Junction at seven o'clock. It seemed forward, but Jen felt she had to suggest something because she and Katy both agreed it would be a complete raving disaster if he called at the house.

Her father would go berserk if he found she was going out for five minutes with an Irishman, let alone a whole Saturday evening.

But Jen's plan of creeping into the house, quickly getting changed and creeping straight out again was foiled by a sudden craving hunger. By six o'clock, her whole stomach was churning in nervous anticipation of her assignation with Sean and she knew she would have to eat if she wasn't going to be embarrassed the entire evening by a rumbling stomach.

As she slid into the kitchen in search of a piece of bread and jam, her mother looked up from the sink.

'Oh, there you are,' she said shortly and nodded to an envelope on the sideboard behind her father's chair. 'That came for you earlier.'

'Thanks for giving it to me when I came in,' Jen muttered sarcastically as her heart accelerated in a painful lurch. She knew it was from Sean. It had to be. Nobody else she knew called her Miss Jennifer Carter. She opened it and read it quickly. He wrote in an attractive slanted hand. The gist of it was that he knew a pub up in Kilburn where there'd be a bit of a sing-song later and thought they might as well go there. He'd wait for her at South Clapham Underground station at seven o'clock. It was signed simply, *Sean*.

Jen felt a surge of excitement. It was a real date after all. Her eyes were sparkling as she looked up.

'What is it?' her father asked suspiciously, glancing up from his meal. 'Who's writing you notes, then?'

Jen folded the note carefully and shrugged. 'Just a friend.'

'Who?'

Jen shook her head impatiently. 'Look, it's just a friend, all right? Nobody you know.' She turned to her mother. 'Can I have a sandwich?'

'If you would only eat proper meals like everyone else you wouldn't be always asking for a sandwich,' Joyce grumbled crossly, reaching for the loaf of bread.

But her father was not to be distracted. He banged his fist on the table. 'Who is the note from?'

Jen rolled her eyes. 'Oh, for God's sake. It's just someone I'm meeting up with tonight. A girlfriend, if you must know.'

Stanley Carter pushed back his chair with a menacing scrape on the concrete floor. 'Don't you talk to me like that, madam. I'm your father and I have every right to know who you are gallivanting around with.' And before Jen could take evading action he had reached forward violently and snatched the note out of her hand.

'That's private,' Jen screamed, trying to grab it back and knocking over the chair he'd been sitting on. She appealed to her mother in desperation. 'Stop him. That's my letter.'

Her mother ignored her and her father fended her off with a powerful swipe while he read the note. He wasn't a great reader at the best of times.

He looked up with beady eyes. 'Who is Sean?' He pronounced it 'Seen'.

If Jen hadn't been so angry, she would have laughed in his face. She tossed her head, her eyes bright. 'I said, she's a friend.'

'It's Sean,' her mother said suddenly, treacherously. 'It's that Irishman from Pam Nelson's, isn't it?'

'That Irish bugger?' Stanley roared incredulously. 'I've seen him. All mouth and trousers.' His eyes bulged dangerously. 'You're not going out with him.'

Jen took a step back. She knew that angry frog look. 'I am.'

'You're bloody not.'

'I bloody am.' She'd end up with a job in pantomime if they kept this up much longer.

'You'll do as your father says,' Joyce said mildly and Jen glared at her furiously. Trust her stupid mother to take his side when the chips were down.

'I'll do what I like,' Jen spat at her. 'And I'll go out with who I like.'

Joyce folded her arms across her chest. 'You will not.'

Jen lifted her chin. 'Why not? Just tell me why not?'

'He's bloody Irish, that's why not,' her father shouted, advancing across the kitchen.

She was going to get thumped in a minute and she was damned if he was going to bruise her. She thought fast. 'I don't see what's wrong with an Irishman,' she said, holding her ground. 'At least I'm not demeaning myself by working for the bloody Rutherfords.'

Her father blinked and paused, taken aback by the change of subject. 'What's that?' he blustered. 'What about the Rutherfords?'

Joyce shook her head. 'Nothing,' she said, nervously. 'It's nothing.'

He leaned across the table. 'Tell me,' he bellowed, making the bowls shake. 'I'll not have secrets in this house.'

The sudden silence was startling. Then Joyce folded the tea cloth, she was holding. 'Mrs Rutherford has offered me a couple of mornings' work in her house. Cleaning. I was going to ask you …'

'Cleaning? Cleaning! I'll not have you getting down on your knees for those bloody Rutherfords.'

'She's not praying to them, she's cleaning for them,' Jen chipped in.

It was a mistake. He swung back to her. 'Shut your mouth. And get that stuff of your lips. God, you bloody women!' He raised his fist and thumped it down on the table. 'You'll do as you're told, do you hear me. You'll bloody do as you're told.' He fixed Jen with a dreadful stare and pointed upstairs. 'Get in your room.'

Then when she didn't move he grabbed her arm, shook her violently and dragged her screaming and kicking out of the kitchen and up the stairs. He flung her into her room, slammed the door and with surprising dexterity wedged a chair under the handle, effectively locking her in.

Back in the kitchen he glared at Joyce who was watching him warily from behind the table. 'And if you let her out you'll pay for it. Do you hear me?'

'I won't let her out,' Joyce said quickly.

He laughed hoarsely, cruelly knowing. 'Damn right you won't.' He picked up his cap. 'I'm going over the road. And if I hear another word about you skivvying for those Rutherford swine, you'll pay for that too.'

'I won't say another word about it.'

But he can't stop me thinking about it, she added silently to herself as he slammed the front door. And what I'm thinking is if he goes down for a couple of years next week we're for the high jump anyway.

Joyce sat down heavily at the table and was annoyed to find she was trembling. She needed that money. She wanted that job more than she had wanted anything for ages. She chewed her lip. He needn't know. Not after he was locked up. With Bob inside, Pete out at work all day and the younger children safely in Devon, nobody need know. She'd force that little bitch upstairs to silence. Jen never went to visit him when he was inside anyway.

The sash window of Jen's bedroom was stiff, the cord had gone on one side. Normally she only opened it an inch or two. But she knew it could open wide because her brother Bob had come through it once, last June. After some job, one of the ones that had gone wrong. He'd come through, the window and ripped off his clothes as he ran through her room and was in bed pretending to be asleep by the time the coppers were banging on the front door.

He'd got off that time. Jen grimaced as she struggled with the heavy frame. But not the next time. And now he was over at Brixton, wasting two precious years of his life. When if only he'd had the sense to keep his mouth shut he could be here now, helping her to open this damned window.

She swore as the window moved an inch and then jammed. Why the hell didn't someone keep the house up together a bit? Bob had occasionally thrown a bit of paint at a wall, but since he'd been put inside, nobody had done anything. Pete ought to do it. He was meant to be a blasted builder and decorator, wasn't he? But he never lifted a finger. The place was falling to bits, nothing worked, the roof leaked, the toilet outside was a disgrace.

Jen frowned. It really was no place for a budding actress to live. I bet the Nelsons' place is better, she thought, pausing to lean on the window sill, imagining Sean, at this very moment getting ready to meet her. I bet Mr Nelson keeps their place up together. He's meant to be good with his hands, what with rebuilding that boat of his and all.

Jen had seen Mr Nelson's boat once, down at the river in Putney. It had been on a Saturday school expedition. Something to do with biology. And there had been Alan Nelson, cruising past like Admiral bloody Nelson himself, standing up at the back of his boat with his shirt open at the collar and a proud smile on his face.

She'd waved but he hadn't seen her. And she'd remembered thinking it looked quite fun. Odd really that a dull little man like Alan Nelson should do something that looked like fun.

Jen resumed her efforts on the window and snorted in satisfaction as it at last slid open. She peered out dubiously. If Bob had got in, presumably she could get out. It was only a matter of sliding down to the toilet roof, jumping down into the back yard and letting herself out through the alley which ran along the back of the houses where the dustbins were kept.

Chapter Six

The River Thames at Henley is not the wide, muddy expanse it is in London, but it is still an impressive stretch of water, and the Leander Club, occupying prime position by the bridge on the opposite bank, facing the pretty town across the river, is one of the most exclusive rowing clubs in the world.

Membership is restricted to members of winning crews at the famous Henley Royal Regatta held every year in early July, when eights, fours and sculls from all over the world compete for the glittering trophies and the honour of being invited to join the elite circle of Leander members, with their elegant clubhouse and distinctive pink tie.

From time to time distinguished members of the club were able to hire its facilities for their own private functions, and Sir Edwin Veale, whose name adorned several of the oars which hung on the walls of the club had availed himself of this privilege for the purpose of his son Freddy's twenty-first birthday.

Louise had been expecting a sumptuous event, but the thing that most shocked her about it when she walked self-consciously up the stairs into the pink-trimmed candlelit Leander clubroom, in her emerald-green dress and matching jacket, was just how many of the extraordinarily large number of young men present were already in uniform.

She had seen the papers, of course, and listened to the news on the wireless, like everyone else. But despite the scare stories of Hitler's intentions, all the blackout precautions in London, the buckets of sand and gas masks had seemed to her like a bit of over-reaction, particularly as there had been no sign of the Luftwaffe bombers and the news was only of Nazi conquests miles and miles away in Poland.

No, it was the sight of all these handsome young men, swaggering round proudly in their fancy, brand new dress uniforms, that suddenly brought it home to her that there really was a war on. And the thought that they were all apparently prepared to go and fight and die for England, brought an unexpected lump to her throat.

'Louise! You made it.' Lucinda Veale danced up and kissed her on the cheek. 'How was awful old Rhoda?' she whispered, nodding at Louise's travelling companion who stood, dressed entirely in black, speaking to Sir Edwin and Lady Veale a few yards away by one of the heavily shrouded windows. 'Isn't she a fright?' she giggled. 'You should have come down with all the other London crowd. They got here this afternoon and Daddy organised rowing boats for everyone and we've all been out on the river. And Felicity Rowe got swept downstream with Harry Davenport and nearly capsized. Ralph had to rescue them. He wasn't terribly amused.'

Louise giggled obligingly at the thought of Lucinda's rather serious older brother, Ralph, having to act as lifeboat man, but inwardly she groaned. If anyone was going to get swept anywhere with a good-looking young man like Harry Davenport, it was Felicity Rowe. That girl attracted men like jam attracted flies. And as far as Louise was concerned, Felicity Rowe was rather like a pot of strawberry jam: pink and gooey and sweet and extremely sick-making if you had too much of her.

But despite Felicity's activities, Louise still wished her parents had allowed her to come down with the others. An afternoon out on the river would have been enormous fun. Certainly it could not have been worse than the stilted journey she had passed with that dreadful old dragon, Mrs Hesketh, whose conversation in the back of her chauffeur-driven car had consisted of a turgid diatribe about some Member of Parliament Louise had never heard of, followed by a long and rambling description of 'Piggy', who at first Louise had assumed to be Mrs Hesketh's former husband, but who had subsequently, and somewhat embarrassingly for Louise, turned out to be her recently deceased bull terrier.

Louise recounted this misunderstanding later to a group of Lucinda's friends as they ate supper from the splendid buffet, and was gratified by their hysterical laughter. She was particularly pleased that Harry Davenport, handsome as anything in the high-necked Rifle Brigade officer's dress uniform, seemed to find her story especially funny and made her promise to dance with him after supper.

'Watch out for his sword,' Lady Helen de Burrel smiled over the rim of her glass. 'Willy Wilkinson nearly cut Felicity Rowe's leg off at the Grosvenor last weekend.'

'Where is Felicity?' Lucinda asked. 'I haven't seen her for ages.'

'She's over there,' Harry said at once, pointing to the far end of the room.' Talking to that Canadian friend of your brother's.' Cross that Harry obviously had Felicity so firmly in his sights even as he asked her to dance, Louise reluctantly allowed her eyes to follow his glance, and froze in utter astonishment.

Felicity Rowe was as usual dressed in the sexiest dress in the room. How she managed to get away with an almost entirely bare back and a garment that hugged her curvaceous figure to quite that extent when her father was a bishop nobody knew. But she did.

However, on this occasion it wasn't Felicity's appearance that caused Louise nearly to drop her glass and choke on her mouthful of Highland smoked salmon. It was who she was with.

The man that Felicity was looking at oh so coyly from under her long blonde lashes was none other than the grey eyed mystery man who had accompanied the Miss Taylors to church.

But today, instead of the well-cut suit, he was in the full evening dress of the Royal Air Force with the rank of Flight Lieutenant. For a moment Louise could not believe her eyes. And she clearly was not the only one.

'Who is that man?' Lady Helen's voice asked softly in awe.

And Lucinda giggled. 'He's rather gorgeous, isn't he? He's called Ward Frazer. He's Canadian. A rowing friend of Ralph's. He's a member of Leander but I think they actually met at the Berlin Olympics.'

'He was meant to be in the Canadian eight,' Harry Davenport offered obligingly. 'But he did something to his knee just before his event so he didn't take part.'

The girls sighed in unison.

'I bet he's married,' Helen said. 'The really handsome ones always are.'

'No, he's not,' Lucinda replied. 'On the contrary, I gather he has something of a reputation.'

'What sort of a reputation?' Louise asked, for a moment tearing her eyes away from the handsome Canadian.

Lucinda giggled. 'The best sort, of course. Women.' She leaned closer and lowered her voice. 'Ralph wouldn't really say, but I gather there was some kind of scandal a couple of years ago and his parents have cut him off without a bean. So he's come over here to join the RAF.'

'How exciting!' Lady Helen de Burrel's eyes were shining. 'A black sheep. I've always wanted to meet one of those. Particularly one that looks like that.' She handed her plate to a passing waiter and nudged Louise. 'Let's go and cut in on dear Felicity.'

Louise thought quickly. It seemed crass to march brazenly over there as just one of a gaggle of adoring girls. Meeting the Canadian suddenly seemed very important. But she wanted to get their first encounter exactly right. Even just looking at him across the room made her insides tremble.

She turned suddenly to Harry and smiled her best smile. 'If this lot are going to start singing the Canadian national anthem, maybe we could have that dance now?'

Harry nodded courteously. 'It would be my pleasure.'

But before they could move, Helen had clutched Louise's arm. 'They're coming over.' She hissed. 'Felicity's bringing him over.'

Louise disengaged herself firmly from Helen's clutching fingers. The last thing she wanted was this Ward Frazer to think she was nervous. Yet she suddenly had an overpowering urge to escape. To lift up her skirts and run for it. Determinedly avoiding glancing at the rapidly approaching couple, she glanced up at Harry and rolled her eyes resignedly.

'I suppose we'll have to stay to say hello now.' Her voice came out rather louder than she had expected and she had a nasty feeling that the Canadian might have heard as he greeted Lucinda and kissed her on the cheek.

'Lucinda, good evening. You look very lovely tonight.'

Lucinda blushed scarlet, preened, and glanced proudly round her friends before suddenly remembering her manners, or half of them. 'I think you've met Harry Davenport,' she said in a rush and then stopped and giggled. 'And these are two other friends of mind, Lady Helen de Burrel and Louise Rutherford.'

The Canadian nodded to Harry then glanced at Helen and held out his hand. 'Lady Helen de Burrel,' he said. 'Or is it Hélène?' He raised his dark eyebrows humorously at the pretty heiress.

Helen smiled. 'Helen will do. I am only a quarter French.'

And then suddenly it was Louise's turn.

'Miss Rutherford.'

As they shook hands, he frowned. 'Haven't we met somewhere before?'

Louise swallowed hard. She could feel everyone staring at her.

She longed to nod eagerly. To gabble off about church and the Miss Taylors. She was pretty sure from the sudden curve of his lips that he remembered. But she couldn't be sure. It wasn't worth the risk. He could so easily make her look a fool. A fool for remembering the briefest, most meaningless glance.

Instead she forced herself to shake her head, wishing his pronunciation of her name wasn't so spine tingling, wishing the mere touch of his hand hadn't brought her out in goose bumps, wishing just something about him was normal, ordinary, or dull, so she could stand in his presence without her heart leaping about wildly in her chest.

'No, I don't think so.'

'I'm sure you would have remembered, Louise,' Felicity simpered slyly and Louise shrugged dismissively.

'I don't have a very good memory for faces,' she said lightly. A complete lie. This man's face had somehow become branded on her very soul. She had even dreamed about him. She glanced in some desperation at Harry, who obligingly rose to the occasion.

'I was on the verge of taking the lovely Louise away to dance,' he murmured.

Ward Frazer inclined his head gravely as though permission lay with him. 'By all means.'

Louise nodded at him coolly. 'Thank you, Mr Frazer,' she said with faint sarcasm. And was quite pleased with her self control.

Everyone knew it wasn't a good idea to throw yourself at men. Not ones that looked like Ward Frazer. They were far too used to it. It was much more interesting to be a bit reserved, to play it cool, wasn't it?

She glanced at him swiftly from under her lashes as she moved away. It seemed to have worked. His grey eyes were on her. He looked interested, as though her snub had piqued him. At least she tried to convince herself that he did. But actually, deep down, she had an annoying feeling he thought it was rather funny.

Later she saw Ward Frazer dancing with Lucinda, twice with Felicity, and later again with Helen, and wondered with a jolt if he might ask her.

But he didn't. And even as she laughed and chattered brightly with Harry and danced eagerly with his friends, she was aware of a dreadful sense of disappointment: Her plan had misfired. Ward Frazer was surrounded by the prettiest women all evening. Virtually clothed in them. It seemed unlikely that he had spared her even one moment's thought.

And then suddenly the party was over and everyone was leaving. There was much hilarity in the Henley blackout about whose car was whose, and who would inadvertently end up spending the night with whom or, worse, in the river.

And as Louise hung around despondently, having to wait for the very last goodbyes to be said before she could be conveyed to the Veales' nearby mansion for the night, she wished she was older, prettier, funnier. Anything that might have made Ward Frazer take more notice of her. Even when she had daringly removed the jacket of her dress he had barely spared her pretty shoulders a passing glance.

She hugged her evening shawl around her now against the cool night air and watched the dimmed torches bobbing around among the cars like dying fireflies.

'Is that you, Louise?' Lucinda was groping her way towards her in the gloom. She indicated the dark figure behind her and giggled. 'Lieutenant Frazer wanted to say goodbye.'

Louise felt her heart jolt painfully in her chest. She was incapable of speech as she felt the pressure of his hand on hers and wished she had had time to rip off her glove.

'Goodbye, Louise Rutherford.' She felt rather than heard his soft laugh 'See you in church, perhaps?'

Lucinda peered at Louise as he melted away into the night. 'What on earth did he mean by that?' She wrinkled her nose. 'I didn't know you were religious.'

'I'm not,' Louise said carelessly, glad that the darkness concealed her suddenly heightened colour. 'He must be drunk.'

But she knew he wasn't drunk and her heart was already singing.

It sang all night, all through a very formal Veale family breakfast and all the way back to London with Mrs Hesketh and her morbid memories.

And oddly enough the song it sang was the very one Ward Frazer didn't know: *Love Divine, All Loves Excelling, Joy of Heaven to Earth Come Down.*

Jen woke late on Sunday morning, feeling as though she had been run over by a train. Every limb ached, but none of them as badly as her head. Her throat and eyelids felt as though someone had used a cheese grater on them, her stomach was painfully cramped and queasy and her mouth tasted of unprocessed sewage.

As she gradually came to she remembered she had been sick on the way home. Twice, in fact. In the car of Sean's friend.

Her whole body clenched in sudden renewed embarrassment, and then the rest of the previous evening's events impaled themselves on her awakening consciousness and for a terrible moment she thought she was going to be sick again.

It had started off well. She had been keyed up with the ease of her escape through her bedroom window and had found Sean lounging against a wall at the station reading a newspaper.

'Good evening to you,' he had said with a slow smile in his blue eyes and Jen had immediately felt a trickle of excitement course down her spine. He was even more good looking than she had remembered.

'I'm sorry about the theatre,' she said nervously.

He shrugged. 'Not to worry. Maybe we'll go when they open up again.'

Jen glanced at him eagerly. 'Do you think the government will open them again, then?'

'Sure they will.' He smiled and folded the paper. 'They won't want people to start thinking dear old England isn't much of a place to live. Not at a time like this.'

Jen frowned uncertainly. 'That sounds cynical.'

He shook his head. 'Not cynical, realistic.' He chuckled and straightened up. 'Anyway, Miss Jennifer Carter Leigh, they'll have to open up again. How else will you make a career for yourself?'

Yes, the evening had started off well. It was so nice to have her aspirations taken seriously. To have someone on her side.

There was a delay on the Tube so they took the bus to Kilburn, or rather two buses, the first down through shabby Vauxhall and across the river to the clean wide streets of Victoria, and then a number two up past the high walls of Buckingham Palace gardens, round Hyde Park Corner, up elegant Park Lane to Marble Arch and then on north up the shop-lined Edgware Road and into the seedy, busy Kilburn High Road. And all the way Sean sat with his arm resting along the back of the seat, nearly but not quite touching Jen's collar as he listened to her life story and smoked an endless round of cigarettes.

And his friends in the rowdy pub in Kilburn had all been flatteringly interested in her too. They had the gift of the gab, those Irish boys, that was for sure, even though they could hardly hear themselves speak over the music pouring from the fiddlers on the makeshift stage in the corner. It was pure Irish blarney. The way they teased Sean about his luck in living in the same road as her. They laughed at her jokes, clapped her impressions. They made her feel like a famous actress already.

And after half a pint of Guinness and two Irish whiskies, she liked their roguishness too, their irreverence about everything, the government, Hitler, the British army. It made a change from the wireless and the newspapers banging on about King and Country.

'What happens when you get called up?' she asked, sipping her whiskey and giggling uncontrollably at a rather rude joke about a British sergeant-major that she didn't quite understand but which was clearly tremendously funny.

'We're not going to get called up, sweetheart,' one of the men laughed.

'We're neutral,' Sean explained. 'Ireland is neutral.'

'Anyway, we have our own war,' somebody else said, rather shortly, ignoring Sean's frown. 'We don't want to get ourselves tangled up in yours.'

It was quite a few drinks later when Sean slid an arm round her shoulders, and leaned closer to her. 'There's a show going to start,' he shouted in her ear over the din. 'Do you want to stay? Or will we go now?'

'A show?' Jen murmured, liking the feel of his arm, the scent of his body, the way his blue eyes dilated when he looked at her. 'What kind of show?'

He grinned. 'Something to amuse the boys.'

Jen looked lip at him eagerly, 'A comedy?'

He laughed tolerantly. 'Something like that. Have you not seen a pub show before?'

Jen didn't like him laughing at her. Not when she wasn't trying to be funny. 'Of course I have,' she said with a toss of the head that made her feel slightly sick.

If only they had left then, Jen thought now, reluctantly levering her legs from under the bedcovers on to the cold lino floor. But they hadn't.

Sean had been doubtful, but by the time she had realised the show might not be entirely proper, it was too late.

'We can't go anyway,' Sean had said suddenly. 'They've locked the doors now.'

Jen had stared at him blankly. 'Why would they lock the doors?'

'Against the police.'

'The police?'

'I thought you said you'd been to pub shows before.'

Jen had giggled. It all seemed so illicit, so exciting. But she wasn't giggling by the end. Not even by halfway through. Never in her entire life had Jen been so embarrassed.

It had started with a faint unease when the three first girl singers had suddenly hitched up their tawdry skirts and done a lively can-can with apparently very little on underneath. To Jen's astonished eyes, it seemed they only wore scarlet thigh garters and only the very briefest of black panties. Everyone had started to clap in rhythm as the music got faster, and each time the legs went up more and more of their skimpy underwear was revealed.

A fat bejewelled belly dancer came on next to moderate applause. And then a pair of tap dancers whose cheap, badly fitting outfits were cut so low that it seemed to Jen that at any moment one or more of their bosoms would pop out due to the rigour of the dance, until the end, when to yells and whistles of appreciation they did. Jen squirmed in her seat as the two protruding girls quickly gathered the coins that had been hurled up on to the makeshift stage.

Other acts followed in quick succession, teasing the predominantly male crowd with increasing amounts of exposed female flesh to part with their money, until the grand finale, a buxom black woman, who, to Jen's utter and complete horror and the howls of delight of the rest of the audience, slowly and deliberately took off all her clothes until for a brief second she was entirely naked except for a gaudy Union Jack painted rather badly across her gleaming naked torso.

The lights went out immediately but not before Jen had glimpsed the heavy large-nippled breasts and the curly black hair on the secret folds between her legs and despised herself utterly for looking.

She could hardly bear to think about it this morning. Nor about Sean's evident amusement at her reaction.

'What's the matter, sweetheart? You look quite pale.'

'How could they?' She could hardly speak. 'How could they do it?'

He laughed. 'There's nothing wrong with it. The female body is a thing of beauty. Why shouldn't it be admired?'

But it wasn't admiration Jen had seen on the faces of some of the men in the pub. It was another expression. An expression that scared her. A greedy salacious gleam in their eyes, beads of sweat on their skin as they groped in their pockets for cash to throw at the girls.

She tried to smile back at Sean and failed. She felt a fool. Torn between her desire to impress him and her revulsion. Inside she was squirming. She was scared he'd think she was too young. Too naive. But much as she tried to hide it, she was shocked. Not so much by the girls, surprisingly, but by the men. The look on their faces.

She was revolted, shocked to the core of her being. Oh, she might pretend to be a woman of the world. But if the truth be known, she had had quite a sheltered upbringing.

In a family of brothers it was perhaps strange that she had such a prudish streak. Or perhaps it was just for that reason. Her mother had always been insistent that Jen and Angie should have their own room. And her older brother Bob had always seen off any interest in her from unwelcome sources. Without really being aware of it, she had always been heavily chaperoned.

But now Bob was in jail and she was on her own. And she had seen a slice of life that appalled her. 'But those girls must feel so degraded.'

Sean shrugged. 'They don't have to do it. They have a choice.'

'I suppose so.' She shivered. Perhaps she should blame the girls after all, but it seemed so shameless. The thought that a man might look at her that way made her feel physically sick. But she couldn't mention that to Sean. He was already looking at her with an odd expression in his blue eyes.

'And they make quite a bit of cash out of it if they're good.'

Jen stared at him in horror. 'It's not worth it. Money could never be that important.'

He laughed dismissively. 'And there I was thinking you were a liberated woman.'

And then to crown it all, she had had to get his friend to stop the car to be sick on the way home. Right in the middle of Chelsea Bridge. And not just once. Twice. And everyone had laughed at her. And cheered as she retched up her guts into the river. Even Sean. And as they drove off, a policeman guarding the entrance to Battersea Power Station had shouted to them that the van lights were showing, and they'd laughed even more at that.

The only miracle was that she'd managed to climb back into the house without waking her father. The chair was still wedged under her door. So presumably nobody had realised that she'd gone out. At least she wouldn't have to have another row about it this morning.

For a long time Jen sat on the edge of her bed with her head in her hands and wondered how she was going to face the day. Let alone how she was ever going to face Sean again.

In the cold light of day her reaction to the strip show seemed absurd. How could she have been so stupid about it? Sean would think she was pathetic. Young. Naive. The last things she wanted anyone to think about her. Let alone the handsome young Irishman. She'd have to blame it on the drink, she decided at last. That revolting Guinness. Or say she'd eaten something that disagreed with her and made her tetchy.

Even if she blamed the drink, it wasn't as bad as seeming a prude. Everyone had too much to drink once in a while, didn't they? Her father did most nights. She groaned as she stood up, and felt the nausea again.

*

Joyce pushed the sleeves of her best cardigan up under her overall and carefully levered open the tin of floor polish. Last week she had caught her cuff in the tin and it had been the devil of a job to get the grease off. By rights she knew she shouldn't be wearing her good clothes for a menial cleaning job, but she wanted to make a good impression.

Mrs Rutherford had seemed a bit off when Joyce had called round after Stanley's court hearing to accept the job. She had looked disconcerted by Joyce's threadbare coat and down at heel shoes, and had hesitated so long that for a dreadful moment Joyce had thought she might be going to change her mind.

But then Mrs Rutherford had nodded abruptly and suggested a month's trial of three days a week and Joyce's nervously held breath had all been expelled at once in an embarrassing wheeze of relief.

So she had put on her best clothes, what there was of them, which wasn't much to be honest, and now, having seen at close quarters the immaculate outfits that Mrs Rutherford wore even to do her gardening, she was nervous to let the standard slip. She didn't mind humbling herself to work in their house but she didn't want their scorn. Even the cook seemed to look down her toffee-nose at the shabby coat and string bag Joyce left each morning in the pantry.

It was bad enough that she hadn't known how to operate their machines. Labour-saving household machines they were called, and that was a joke and a half. On the first day she had been introduced to an enormous new Hoover which had a mind of its own and roared about the house like a maddened bull, making the noise of one and all, drowning any form of conversation.

Not that Mrs Rutherford seemed inclined to chat of course. Nor did the stuck-up little madam of a daughter. Except on the telephone.

On that very first day Miss Louise had gesticulated frantically to Joyce as she thundered through the hall clinging for dear life to the Hoover's handles, to indicate that she should turn the infernal machine off while she was on the phone. But Joyce didn't know how to.

In the end, Mrs Rutherford had to be fetched from the laundry room before the raging bull could be silenced. By the end of that first day Joyce felt as though she'd done ten rounds with Joe Louis, her arms ached so much.

Now, a week later, as she chased the newfangled electric polisher over Mrs Rutherford's beautiful parquet wooden floor in the dining-room, hoping she'd fixed the brushes on securely so they didn't fly off and catch her employer on the shin, as one of them had done last time, Joyce tried to work out how many days she would have to work before she could afford a new dress and a hair-do. With Stanley safely inside and without the three younger children to feed, clothe or worry about, some of the pressure had already lifted off her shoulders.

Not that she was in the clear yet. Not by any means. Still, she was earning now and that would help. And the pittance young Pete brought in paid for his food, even though he ate like a carthorse with tapeworm.

But some of the prices had shot up, even in Northcote Road market, and that was a worry. Everyone said price controls would come in soon, and rationing. Some of the shops were already cleaned out of sugar and flour as people tried to stock up.

And Jen was still off her food anyway. Last weekend, when she had screamed to be let out of her room and vomited on and off all morning, Joyce had had a sudden terrible thought that the little slut might have got herself pregnant.

She spent two hours summoning up the courage and the words to ask her. Because a baby in the house was all they needed. And if it was the result of that young Irish bugger's attentions, Stanley would throw her out. No question about that. Truth be told, he'd most likely throw her out anyway. He still had his morals, Stanley, even if he didn't have anything else.

Not that Joyce had mentioned her fears to Stanley, of course. She had more sense than that. He'd have gone bananas, skin and all. Especially after a Saturday night on the bottle. His last, as it had turned out, for a year. Not much booze available in Reading Jail, she wouldn't imagine. Though why he'd been sent to Reading was anybody's guess when Wandsworth and Brixton were right on the doorstep. Maybe they didn't want the prisoners getting bombed.

Anyway, finally she accosted Jen in her bedroom. Stood over her while she groaned self indulgently on the bed, white faced, clutching her stomach. Asked her straight out if she was up the duff.

Jen stared at her in naked astonishment. And then sudden colour flooded into her face. 'Of course I'm not,' she snapped.

Joyce shrugged, slightly surprised at Jen's vehemence. 'You can't blame me for wondering. What with strange men writing you notes and all. And you tarted up to the nines. And out gallivanting all hours of the day and night.'

She knew Jen had climbed out of the window last night, and that she'd come back in the small hours, but she wasn't going to mention that specifically. Not yet. That was a precious piece of information and she intended to use it to her advantage.

'Sean is not strange,' Jen's eyes flashed defiantly. 'You don't know anything about it.'

Joyce sniffed. 'I know what men are like.'

'You don't know anything.' Jen sneered. 'All you know is Dad.' She spat out the word. 'Sean's not like Dad. Not one bit.'

Joyce smiled at her bitterly, wanting to shock her, wanting to hurt her.

'They're all the same underneath. If you don't know that now, you'll learn it soon enough. Just don't let them into your knickers, that's all I say, or you'll get into trouble and there'll be nobody to help you then.'

'Don't be so disgusting!' Jen shouted with tears in her eyes.

With immense relief Joyce went back downstairs. The girl had seemed genuine in her denial. She was a good actress. But for once she believed her.

Later that same afternoon, taking advantage of Jen's weakened state, she took her up some tinned tomato soup and a slice of bread and made a deal. She wouldn't mention to Stanley that Jen had been with Sean Byrne last night, if Jen kept her mouth shut about Joyce taking the Rutherfords' cleaning job.

Jen looked shifty. 'How did you know I'd gone?' she asked, then snorted sarcastically. 'Don't tell me you were going to let me out.'

'No, I wasn't,' Joyce said sharply. 'I don't approve any more than your father does. The Irish are bloody murderers if you ask me. But you left your light on and the window open, and that damned ARP man came round shouting his head off about a ten pound fine for showing lights in the house. Lucky for you your father was still at the pub.'

'Ten pounds!' Jen looked horrified. 'You didn't pay it, did you?'

Joyce laughed sourly. 'Of course I bloody didn't. You're the only one with spare money in this house,' she said. 'And I'll tell you, I was sorely tempted to tell him to bugger off and leave you to pay up. But out of the kindness of my heart I went into your room instead and turned off the light. You're lucky I didn't shut the window and all while I was about it.'

She saw Jen's frown and knew her sharp little brain was thinking through her offer, assessing, deciding. Jen pretended not to be scared of her father but nobody in their right minds would willingly lay themselves open to his anger. Even if he was in prison. He had enough friends and relations round and about who could give her a hard time.

'OK,' Jen said stiffly at last. 'I won't say anything. But I still think it's demeaning to clean for those Rutherfords.'

'And I think it's demeaning to walk out with an Irishman,' Joyce responded smartly. 'So we're quits. Is it a deal?' To her surprise Jen grudgingly offered her hand and Joyce shook it, the first time they'd voluntarily touched each other in years. Joyce couldn't help noticing how slender her daughter's hand was, and smooth, compared to her heavy, calloused one, but she put that thought to one side.

'And when you next see your precious Sean Byrne, tell him you're to be home by ten thirty or the deal's off. I'll not stand for you staying out all hours of the night, however different he is.' She nodded briskly at the soup. 'Bring the bowl down when you've finished.'

But if Joyce had thought their conspiracy might ease relations between them, she was wrong. Jen had been like a bear with a sore head ever since.

On the other hand, Mrs Rutherford had become increasingly civil. When she paid Joyce at the end of the second week, she even smiled.

'Thank you, Mrs Carter, you've been a great help. And I think you've got the measure of the Hoover at last, haven't you?'

To her astonishment Joyce felt herself smiling back. 'I reckon it's got the measure of me, Mrs Rutherford. But at least it knows I'll stand up to it if it comes to a fight. Anyway, if the worst comes to the worst I can always turn it off.'

Mrs Rutherford smiled. 'I wish the same could be said of Mr Hitler,' she said dryly. Then she looked at Joyce anxiously. 'And you're not finding three days too much?'

'Oh no,' Joyce said hastily, suddenly terrified of being cut down to two, or even, God forbid, to one day. 'It's fine. What with the children away and all.'

Mrs Rutherford nodded. 'And your husband, he's happy about it, is he?'

Joyce hesitated for a second then decided not to lie. The Rutherfords would find out sooner or later. And knowing her luck it was bound to be sooner. 'My husband's inside,' she said. 'He doesn't know.'

'Inside?' Mrs Rutherford frowned and then her eyes widened. 'Oh, you mean ...?' She looked appalled and Joyce's heart sank.

'He's in jail,' she said stiffly and dropped her eyes, shrinking from Mrs Rutherford's obvious horror. Then a moment later she raised them again. She had to know. 'Does that make any difference?' she asked and wished she'd managed to keep the pleading note out of her voice. She saw the other woman's eyes flicker, and regretted the question. She didn't want to grovel. She straightened her shoulders, ready for the dismissal, but before she could speak, Mrs Rutherford shook her head slowly.

'No. It doesn't make any difference,' she said. 'I'm pleased with your work. It wouldn't be fair to punish you twice.'

She saw the relief on Joyce's face and touched her on the arm. 'I appreciate your honesty, Mrs Carter. It would have been easier to lie.'

And Joyce blinked. It was nice to be appreciated for once.

As she walked home, she saw Mr Lorenz on the other side of the road going into his house. To her surprise, he turned and raised his hat to her and she felt her spirits lift another notch. Then she laughed at herself. She must be in a bad state if she got a lift out of a civil gesture from a surly Jewish pawnbroker.

Nevertheless, she was humming as she put on the kettle. And it was the first time in a long while that she had hummed.

Sean Byrne was right about the theatres reopening. On the twelfth of September the government announced the formation of the forces'

71

entertainment organisation, ENSA. The Drury Lane Theatre was allocated as its headquarters. And by the end of the month most of the other theatres and cinemas were back in business.

'You need an agent,' Katy said to Jen. 'I read about it in your Stage magazine. Hardly any producers take people straight off the street these days. You need to get photos done too to send with a letter of introduction.'

Jen sighed. For once her heart wasn't in it. She had stood in three separate audition queues this week already with no luck. Each time she had run through her pieces. Each time she had thought she'd done them well and each time she'd been turned down. Once because she had no professional experience, once because she wasn't drama school trained. And the third time they had given no reason at all.

'The agents only take people who are trained or who already have experience,' she said now. 'I read that article too.'

'Well, that's not fair,' Katy said hotly, fiercely loyal to her friend. She paused and bit her lip, then she lowered her voice conspiratorially even though they were alone in the flat. 'Couldn't you pretend you had got some experience?' she asked. 'How would they ever find out?'

Jen blinked in surprise. 'I don't know,' she said doubtfully. 'They might have cast lists or something.'

'Couldn't you say you'd been a stand-in in something with a big cast?' Katy asked eagerly. 'Just in a chorus or something. They probably wouldn't know then.'

Jen looked at Katy with new respect. She wouldn't have thought she would have a shifty thought in her body.

'It's not really dishonest,' Katy said, reading her mind. 'After all, you have had experience. It's just that it happened to be at school.'

'They don't take any notice of that,' Jen said crossly. 'They just laugh when I say I've been in a school play.'

She stood up moodily and looked out of Katy's window up the street. And at once her body stiffened as she saw Sean Byrne strolling up the road towards the Nelsons'.

She had only seen Sean once since that awful evening in Kilburn.

For a couple of days she had felt too sick to see anyone.

And then she had got a spot on her chin and had avoided seeing anyone at all until it had gone. Honestly, whoever heard of an actress with a spot?

Anyway, the last thing in the world she wanted was for Sean Byrne to see her with a spot. Not that Sean Byrne had shown much sign of wanting to see her again, spot or no spot.

For a week she had waited for him to get in touch. Waited for a note, a knock at the door. Waited for him to do something. Anything.

And the simple truth was that he hadn't. He hadn't lifted a single finger to see her. As far as he was concerned she might have died of vomiting. Or fallen off her window ledge and broken her neck. Or been carried off by a white slave trader to Arabia.

And then suddenly she had bumped into him on the Underground one Saturday lunch time waiting for a train and he'd been as charming and flattering as ever, apart from teasing her about the strip show, which she hadn't liked.

She had tried to laugh off her reaction, saying that if girls were going to take their clothes off she thought at least they should be young and pretty and that some of the women in the pub show had been well past their prime. And anyway, why was it just women? Weren't there any male strippers around? It was an excuse she had spent a week thinking up and she was quite pleased with it. But she should have known she couldn't pull the wool over Sean Byrne's blue eyes.

'Oh, was that it?' he said with a mocking smile. 'I'm sorry the show wasn't good enough for you. In my innocence I forgot you were a wicked woman of the world.'

It was her innocence he was mocking, she knew that. Not his. And it rattled her.

She felt the sweat break out on her palms. She tried to smile coyly. 'No, but seriously, Sean, that last black woman in the Union Jack was far too fat.' She sniffed. 'You didn't even clap her at the end.'

Sean's eyes narrowed. 'It was the flag I objected to, not her figure.'

Jen looked at him uncertainly. 'Do you prefer big girls, then?'

He smiled slowly then and leaned gracefully back against the wall to light his cigarette. 'No, Jennifer Carter, to be perfectly honest with you, it's girls like you that I prefer, slender and sexy and with a bit of go about them.'

Jen gaped at him, shocked out of her careful poise. 'I'm not sexy,' she stammered.

'Are you not?' He drew on his cigarette and laughed out the smoke just as the train came in. He took her arm and stepped on board. 'And what in the world makes you so sure about that?' he asked as they sat down.

Jen blushed. 'I just don't think ...' She stopped, entirely disconcerted, as the other people in the silent carriage began to stare at them.

'Oh, come now, Jennifer Carter Leigh.' Sean's blue eyes gleamed wickedly. 'You're surely not asking me to prove it to you, are you?'

Even now Jen could feel the way her skin had tingled at his words. The sickening clench of her guts. It was no wonder she had been off her food.

She had shaken her head. 'No, of course not,' she had said crossly. But he had laughed unconcernedly at her anger, and told her she was about to miss her station.

That was a week ago and she hadn't seen him since.

And now there he was, cool as a cucumber, strolling up the street as though he owned it.

She frowned crossly, heart thumping like a drum. How was it that when she hung about trying to bump into him accidentally he never came past?

Behind her Katy coughed. 'Who is it? Who have you seen?'

'Nobody,' Jen said shortly and turned away from the window. She felt stupid that she'd got so excited about Sean Byrne and then nothing had happened.

It was even worse with her mother. Having made the stupid pact with her over Sean, she felt a fool that she hadn't been out with him since. Not that her mother cared one way or the other, Jen thought crossly. She was far too wound up with the namby-pamby Rutherfords and their stupid cleaning machines.

Jen frowned. Her mother's accusation about being pregnant had rattled her more than she cared to admit. Why on earth would her mother assume she had had sex with Sean? With anybody, come to that? Did seventeen year old girls normally have sex with their boyfriends? Was she the odd one out? Had her mother had sex when she was seventeen? It seemed inconceivable. But then Bob was twenty one and her mother wasn't forty yet.

Jen shivered. It was disgusting. The thought of her mother and father in bed. She swallowed hard and realised that Katy was watching her in concern.

Abruptly she picked up her coat. She didn't want Katy's questions. She didn't want her sympathy. What she wanted was Sean Byrne. And if she hurried she could catch him before he went indoors.

Chapter Seven

Left alone in the flat Katy frowned. Under her careless, carefree exterior, Jen was like a coiled spring these days, edgy and secretive and tense. And yet normally she was so self-confident, so under control, so clear about what she wanted.

Katy knew it was partly her frustration with not getting going with her acting, but she also guessed it had a large amount to do with Sean Byrne. She had a feeling that Jen was far more keen on the handsome young Irishman than she let on. Jen was funny like that. She was completely open about some things, shockingly so sometimes, Katy thought, and generous to a fault. But other times she was like a dog with a bone and however good a friend you were, she wouldn't let you have a sniff of it.

And she was like that about Sean Byrne. Oh, she said he was nice, charming and all that. She'd even imitated his Irish brogue to make Katy laugh. And she'd told her all about the dreadful strip show they'd seen, which had shocked Katy to her core.

Not that Jen had minded it, it seemed. No, on the contrary, Jen had been quite blasé about it, saying that the girls all earned good money for it and after all it was their choice.

Jen was so grown up like that, Katy thought, so sophisticated. Katy knew she herself would have died of embarrassment if she'd had to watch even one woman taking her clothes off in public, that's if she hadn't died of a coughing fit first. She couldn't sit for five minutes in a smoky pub before starting to wheeze.

But for all her show of being amused by Sean's attentions, Katy knew that deep down something was unsettling Jen and she wished she had more experience of life so she could do something to help.

Hearing the door bang downstairs and Jen's heels clicking away rapidly up the street, she stood up and went to the window and was just in time to see Sean Byrne pause at the Nelsons' door and turn slowly with his hands in his pockets to greet Jen on the pavement.

Katy couldn't hear what they were saying of course, not right along there outside the Nelsons' house, but even at that distance, she could see that Sean Byrne was smiling. She saw Jen toss her head coyly at something he said and then they both laughed and Katy felt a stab of envy.

It was absurd of her to think of Jen needing help. Jen had everything, good looks, good humour, good health, a lovely figure, talent, ambition, all the things Katy so badly lacked, and now it seemed she even had a boyfriend.

Katy Parsons wasn't the only person who saw Sean talking to Jen. Pam Nelson, laying up his tea in the front room, had seen him open the gate and tried to ignore her sudden shortening of breath. She was a married woman, for goodness' sake, far beyond getting into a tizz over a pushy young Irishman. It was just that she wanted to talk to him, that was all.

But when she saw him stop and turn back to greet Jen Carter with easy familiarity and that lazy intimate smile she knew so well, she couldn't ignore the sudden stab of jealousy she felt. And was shocked by her reaction.

'Oh my God,' she said to herself, leaning on the table, as a sudden irrational hatred of Jen Carter swept over her. 'Please don't let this be happening to me.'

But it was happening. Over the past few weeks Pam knew she had been slowly and surely falling under Sean's spell.

Not that he made any improper advances towards her, he was too clever for that, he knew if he overstepped the mark she would throw him out. Or she hoped he knew that. No, it was just that he was interested in her and her life. She had found herself confiding in him, not about Alan of course, nothing like that, but about some of her hopes and aspirations.

Like the job she had now been offered. She hadn't even mentioned to Alan that she'd applied, let alone that she had had an interview, let alone that she had practised her shorthand with their lodger for two hours last weekend while Alan had been down on the river painting his boat. Sean had even offered to borrow a typewriter from his work so she could brush up her speeds. But Pam hadn't dared agree to that. Alan might be blind to her sense of dissatisfaction with her humdrum little life, but even he would notice a damn great office typewriter sitting on the table in the front room.

She would have to tell him of course, but it wasn't going to be easy. Poor Alan, desperate to earn a little bit extra and keen to do his bit, had offered his services not only to the military but to virtually every one of the new Civil Defence organisations too. But despite the huge posters everywhere asking for help with the war effort, Alan had never been quite the person they needed. He was always too old, too short, or too flat footed.

Even the voluntary services had turned him down. They were all oversubscribed already. He would have to stand by, they had told him, until his services were required. Pam thought it was cruelly unfair. He must be the only man in London who hadn't managed to get himself some kind of armband or uniform. And he wasn't that old, that short or that flat footed.

The door opened just then and Sean Byrne came strolling in with an irritating little smirk on his lips.

'Good evening, Mrs Nelson,' he said easily as he shrugged off his coat.
'I saw you talking to Jen Carter.'

It sounded even to her ears like an accusation and she kicked herself. Why couldn't she keep her stupid mouth shut?

Sure enough his eyebrows rose. 'Oh, isn't that allowed?' he asked innocently. 'I thought it was just yourself, Mrs Nelson, that I wasn't allowed to talk to, not other women as well.'

'You are allowed to talk to me,' she said crossly.

He smiled to himself as he hung his coat in the cupboard under the stairs, then closed the door and turned the smile on her. 'Oh yes, I can talk all right,' he said. 'But sometimes talking isn't quite enough, is it, Mrs Nelson?'

Pam felt herself blush and looked away. Not enough for whom, did he mean? For her or for him? She stared after him as he ran lightly up the stairs and couldn't help thinking that nobody in their right mind could accuse Sean Byrne of being too old, too short or too flat footed.

'I got the job,' she called after him suddenly and he stopped at once and leaned over the banister rail.

'I knew you would,' he said. And for once his blue eyes held a genuine smile of pleasure. 'They'd have been crazy not to take you on. Wasn't I telling you that all along?'

Pam smiled back up at him. 'I know you were, but I didn't believe you.'

He laughed softly. 'You don't believe in yourself, Mrs Nelson, that's your problem.'

She had laughed off his comment then, saying coyly that she didn't have any problems thank you very much Mr Byrne.

But later as she lay in bed beside Alan, having confessed about the job and seen the hurt and sense of inadequacy plain on his face, Pam wondered if once again Sean Byrne had hit the nail on the head.

She didn't believe in herself any longer. That was the truth of it. She had done once. In the old days. When she worked at the LCC she had taken pride in doing a good job and had accepted the praise of her bosses as her due.

But just now she had nothing to be proud of. She was being a poor wife to Alan. She was not giving him the love and affection he deserved and craved. She had let him down by not getting pregnant. She had applied for a job behind his back. And worst of all she was carrying on a mild flirtation with another man.

For that was what it had come to, she knew, however much she wished to deny it. She was attracted to Sean Byrne.

'Alan,' she said suddenly. 'Will you make love to me?'

For a second when he didn't reply, she thought he might already be asleep, then she heard him move, turn his head in surprise. 'It's not the right week,' he said.

Pam felt a spurt of anger against him. Sean Byrne wouldn't wait for the right week.

'I don't care,' she said fiercely. 'I don't care about the right week.'

'But the doctor said ...'

'I know what the damn doctor said. Surely we don't have to live our lives by what a bloody doctor says.' Pam was horrified to realise she was almost in tears.

Alan roused himself and sat up. 'What's the matter, darling?' He took her hand and patted it gently. 'I've never seen you so strung up. I'm sorry I wasn't more enthusiastic about the job.' He sighed. 'I just don't like the thought of you going out to work, that's all. I know it seems old fashioned but that's just how I am. I'm the one that ought to provide for us. But it seems I'm not providing enough.'

Pam felt a rush of affection for him. 'Oh Alan.' She lifted his hand to her cheek. 'Why is everything different, why has everything gone wrong? Is it the war?'

Alan shook his head and. leaned over to kiss her neck. 'Nothing is different. Nothing has gone wrong. I still love you, Pam, you know that.'

She did know it. But she also knew something had gone wrong. And even as his hands crept under her cotton nightgown, even as he obligingly stroked her smooth thighs, the soft curves of her breasts, even as he kissed her and eased himself gently on to her, even as she moved obediently to his rhythm, she knew what it was.

The fun had gone out of it. The days when they had played naughty teasing games with each other's bodies and giggled over their stupidity had passed. The simple truth of it was that Alan no longer made her feel sexy.

Pam sighed, even as her husband gasped and groaned his release. Sean Byrne was the only person who made her feel sexy these days.

And he was also the only person who made her laugh.

Celia Rutherford was becoming concerned about the effect the war was having on her daughter. Since the Veales' party, Louise seemed to have become increasingly devout.

Not that Celia had anything personally against the Church, she knew religious faith could bring a lot of comfort, but to go to both the morning service and evensong each Sunday seemed just a little excessive. And instead of the jolly popular songs, *Run, Rabbit, Run*, or *South of the Border*, which seemed to blare out of the wireless whenever it was turned on, Louise mooched dolefully around the house humming hymns.

And with Louise's newfound faith seemed to have come a strange new concern for the welfare of the old.

'Do you think it would be a good idea if I visited some of the old people locally?' Louise asked one day last week as she helped arrange some flowers in the hall.

Celia eyed her with carefully concealed astonishment. 'That's a lovely idea, Louise,' she said as visions of scabrous, lice-ridden East End poor flashed before her eyes. 'What sort of old people exactly did you have in mind?'

Louise shrugged. 'I don't know. Ones like the Miss Taylors perhaps. I thought they looked a bit lonely in church on Sunday.'

Celia breathed a sigh of relief as the Stepney slums receded.

'Well, I'm sure the Miss Taylors would appreciate a visit,' she said doubtfully, carefully positioning an awkward rose. Actually she thought the Miss Taylors were a couple of terrible old women and well left alone. They were on her husband's Parochial Church Council committee and caused him and the vicar all kinds of problems with their ridiculous High Church ideas. There had been a terrible row over incense at the last meeting, she recalled. Greville had come home ranting about bead-swingers and why didn't the Miss Taylors join the Catholic Church if they wanted all that kind of nonsense.

'I thought I might offer to walk their dog.'

Celia nearly knocked over the vase. 'What? That awful smelly old dachshund?'

Louise looked put out. 'It's not smelly, it's sweet.'

Celia put down her flowers. 'I think perhaps you should ask Daddy first,' she said diplomatically. 'He's not frightfully keen on the Miss Taylors.'

Louise must be seriously deranged, she thought. She would have to speak to Greville about it herself. And if necessary, the vicar.

Jen's first kiss with Sean was nothing at all like what she had expected. It bore as much resemblance to the disgusting mouth-to-mouth assault she had suffered from the friend of her brother last summer as a butterfly did to a frog.

Sean's kisses were tantalisingly short, more like caresses of the lips than the deep French kisses she'd carefully practised on her hand. And each one left her increasingly dissatisfied. She could feel her whole body starting to tingle. Her skin suddenly seemed to be on fire and strange unnerving things were happening in her stomach, and below.

Suddenly these light playful kisses under a moonlit tree on the common weren't enough. Half of her wanted more but the other half was scared. When his hand brushed her breast she nearly jumped out of her skin. But he just laughed when she tried to kiss him again and ran his finger over her open mouth in a spine-chilling caress.

'Take it easy, Jennifer Carter,' he said, 'It's a shame to rush these things. And haven't we got all the time in the world?'

'We've only got till ten thirty,' Jen muttered. 'My mum will kill me if I'm much later than that.'

Sean laughed and leaned back against the tree to light a cigarette, his teeth flashing white in the light of the sudden match. 'We'll be frozen to death by ten thirty,' he said. 'What would you say to popping into the Flag and Garter for a quick pint before closing?'

Jen was appalled. 'We can't go there she said. Not in Lavender Road. What would everybody think?'

'They'd think you'd found yourself a feller,' he said.

Jen knew exactly what they would think, and what they would say. And it wouldn't be flattering. And if her father got to hear of it, even in jail, she'd be sunk.

'I'd rather go somewhere where nobody knows me,' she pleaded.

'Is it ashamed of me you are, then?' Sean asked softly.

To Jen's sensitive ears it sounded like a threat. Suddenly terrified of losing him, she shook her head and took hold of his arm. 'No, Sean, it's not that,' she said urgently. 'But I'm only seventeen and my father is funny about the Irish and if he got to hear ...'

'I see,' Sean said coldly, releasing himself from her grip. 'So it's not your age that's the problem, it's my nationality. I suppose you think I'm a member of the IRA and all?'

Jen blinked at him. 'Of course I don't,' she said truthfully. Such a thought had never crossed her mind. Beautiful, sensitive Sean Byrne as a murdering bomber? It was ridiculous.

Sean laughed shortly. 'Of course you don't. Why should you?' He smiled and seemed to relent. 'OK, we'll go over to the Windmill instead. You're a lovely girl, Jen, but just a few kisses can't beat a pint of Guinness.'

He took her hand and started to walk across the moon-shadowed common towards the popular pub over on the other side, indistinguishable at this distance in its blacked-out state from the other buildings around it. His thumb caressed her bare palm as she stumbled along beside him on reluctant jelly legs. She didn't want to go to the Windmill any more than she did the Flag and Garter. She would have preferred the anonymity of the Falcon down by Clapham Junction or even the seedy Windsor Castle pub on St John's Hill. But she didn't dare say so to Sean. In case he sent her home and went in on his own.

As they skirted the iron mesh fence which protected the newly dug gun emplacements and accompanying Nissen huts from prying eyes, she wished she could think of some way of changing his mind.

As though he guessed her thoughts, he touched her cheek gently with cold fingers. 'Of course, if there was a little bit more on offer, the Guinness might not appeal quite so much.'

Jen felt her heart jolt. 'What sort of more do you mean?' she asked in a small voice.

He stopped and smiled at her. 'I think you know what sort of more, Jennifer Carter.' He squinted briefly up at the barrage balloon floating high above them, an ominous dark shape on its long curving silver wire, and then back at her. 'You've got a lovely body, it would be a crying shame not to make use of it.'

As the moonlight glinted in those beautiful blue eyes Jen felt something snap inside her. She knew what he meant. Her body knew.

And even as her mind whispered caution, all her insides seemed to churn and melt with one accord. He desired her, and that knowledge was like a powerful drug.

At that second, as a sudden cold breeze ruffled the leaves of the dark trees behind them, he could have done with her anything he wanted. Anything. 'Go on then,' she whispered, bracing herself. For a moment he stood in silence looking at her, then he laughed softly and took her hand again. 'Maybe next time, sweetheart,' he said. 'Just now the pull of that Guinness is a touch too strong.'

Bumping into Felicity Rowe in Harrods at the beginning of October was, for Louise, rather a mixed blessing. On the one hand she was pleased to meet someone who might furnish her with some news about Ward Frazer, about whom she had been thinking constantly day and night, on the other she certainly didn't want to hear that Felicity had been seeing him frequently since the Veales' party.

Louise had had no success at all in her ploy to meet Ward Frazer in church. Nor had her suggestion that she call on the Miss Taylors been met with any enthusiasm from her father. On the contrary, he had expressly forbidden it, apparently concerned that she would get herself indoctrinated in their High Church dogma.

If she wanted to visit anyone, he had said, she would be better served visiting young Katy Parsons at the Flag and Garter, who apparently was very handicapped by her bad chest and unable to get to church. 'She's more or less your age,' he had added. 'Quite a nice little thing, apparently. So the vicar says. But scared to death at the prospect of bombing.'

Louise had groaned inwardly. The last thing on earth she wanted to do was sit around comforting some pathetic invalid, however old she was. That wasn't likely to get her any nearer to meeting Ward Frazer again. Or anyone else, come to that.

Felicity Rowe was a much better bet on the man front, even though Louise couldn't stand the sight of her. And she was particularly annoying today because as well as being hatless, scarfless and gloveless, she also seemed to be wearing a padded bra under her tight ribbed black jersey and, even more racy, a pair of rather clinging, bottle-green Corduroys that Louise would have died for, even though she knew her parents would rather die themselves than see her wearing slacks. Not that Felicity's trousers could really be called slacks. There was certainly nothing 'slack' about the way they clung to her shapely bottom.

But apparently blissfully unaware of Louise's antagonism, Felicity screamed with delight as though they were best of friends and led her to a huge green sofa in the black and white hall.

'Goodness, you're still carrying a gas mask,' she exclaimed, as Louise disentangled herself from hers to sit down. 'We've all given up dragging ours around. Such a nuisance. Although I suppose you are a little bit further from home.'

Louise gritted her teeth. She hated being reminded that she lived in a socially inferior part of London. And it was most irritating that having found such a chic little case for her gas mask it now seemed it was unfashionable among the smart set to carry it at all.

As Felicity started gabbling on about Hitler's ludicrous, recently broadcast peace proposals, and the British Expeditionary Force and how Hitler must be mad if he was thinking he could breach the Maginot Line, Louise was wondering how she could get her off the subject of war and on to the subject of men.

'So which of the boys have gone over to France with the BEF?' she asked. 'Anyone I know?'

'Well, it's all hush-hush of course.' Felicity glanced about furtively as though Adolf Hitler himself might be doing a spot of early Christmas shopping in Harrods' ladies' department. 'But I think nearly all the army chaps we know are going or have already gone. Certainly Harry Davenport has and Freddy Veale. Not that they could say, of course. But when they stop telephoning and turning up at parties, then you know.'

Louise frowned. She didn't like hearing about parties she hadn't been invited to. Nor did she like the few young men she knew disappearing off to France. 'What about the RAF chaps?' she probed casually. 'Have you seen any of them?'

Felicity nodded eagerly. 'Oh yes. I saw Willy Wilkinson only last week, he's still in training somewhere in Oxfordshire. He was in cracking form.'

Louise groaned inwardly. It seemed they were going to run through every man they knew before blasted Felicity got to the one she wanted. It would be just her luck to be swept away by her mother before Felicity had even mentioned his name. 'Wasn't there another RAF chap at Lucinda's party?' she asked in some desperation. 'A Canadian?'

Felicity's expression changed. 'Oh, you mean Ward Frazer,' she said stiffly. 'Ralph Veale's friend. I have seen him once or twice.'

Louise leaned forward expectantly but Felicity's former willingness to supply information seemed to have waned somewhat. She took an elegant gold powder compact from her handbag and carefully powdered her nose.

'So he's still around, then?' Louise prompted.

Felicity sniffed. 'Oh, he's around all right.' Having finished her powdering, she pulled out a daringly red lipstick and applied it carefully to her pouting lips. 'But if you take my advice, Louise, you'll steer well clear of him.'

Louise's eyes widened. 'Why? What's the matter with him?'

'There's nothing the matter with him.' Felicity said. 'That's the problem. He's handsome, intelligent, amusing, charming, sexy.' She stopped abruptly and grimaced. 'Basically, you name it, he is it.'

Louise almost moaned out loud. Trust Felicity to include sexy. But clearly their liaison, if there had been one, hadn't been a bed of roses. She looked at Felicity curiously. She had never seen her cross like this. Not about a man, normally she had them eating out of her hand. 'So what's the problem with him? He sounds gorgeous.'

Felicity snorted, 'The problem is that he isn't interested in women. At least, he is interested,' she added dryly, 'extremely interested, but not in a relationship. You can't tie him down. He'll be as charming as anything one evening.' She blushed slightly and Louise wondered just how far Ward Frazer's charm went. Felicity snapped the compact shut. 'And then the next time you see him, he's with another girl.'

'Oh.' Louise was shocked. But less by Ward Frazer's habits than by Felicity's reaction. She looked at her more closely and realised that behind the powder and lipstick, Felicity looked pale and drawn. Louise blinked. Surely Ward Frazer couldn't have broken Felicity's heart? Not man-eating Felicity's heart of stone? Not in such a short time? For goodness' sake, they'd only met for the first time at the Veales' party.

'So watch out, Louise,' Felicity said with a light laugh that didn't quite reach her newly reddened lips. She stood up. 'And if you see him give him a wide berth.'

'Thanks for the advice,' Louise said with absolutely no intention whatsoever of taking it. If she saw Ward Frazer again she'd make every effort to berth as close to him as possible. She got to her feet. 'I don't suppose I'll ever see him again anyway,' she added wistfully.

Felicity sniffed. 'I expect you will. He said he was related to some people who live in your street.'

'Related?' It seemed inconceivable that someone as gorgeous as Ward Frazer could actually be related to two awful old crones like the Miss Taylors. 'Are you sure?'

'So he claimed,' Felicity said, rather offhand. 'He seemed to have taken a bit of a fancy to you.'

Louise gaped as her heart did a double somersault and landed flat on its back. 'Did he?' she stammered. 'How do you know?'

Felicity shrugged. 'He asked about you.'

'He asked about me?' Louise repeated, trying to stop her voice rising in excitement. 'What do you mean? When? What did he ask?'

'It was at the Veales' dance.' Felicity looked bored. She picked up her handbag off the sofa and clipped it shut. 'Don't get excited. He only asked if Harry Davenport was your boyfriend.'

Excited wasn't the word. Louise felt as though she was about to take off. 'What did you say?'

'I can't remember,' Felicity said. 'Presumably that Harry Davenport was actually in love with me.' She glanced at the Harrods clock. 'I must go. I promised to call in on Helen de Burrel at her ambulance post.'

Louse gaped at her. 'Helen de Burrel is driving an ambulance?'

'Didn't you know? She's in some dreadful underground ARP place near the Adelphi.'

Before Louise could elicit any more details about Lady Helen de Burrel's extraordinary new role in life or about Ward Frazer, she saw her mother approaching.

Introductions were effected and after a brief exchange of rather stilted pleasantries, Felicity strolled off.

'Who on earth was that, darling?' Celia asked.

'Felicity Rowe,' Louise answered shortly. 'She's a girl I met at Lucie Clayton's.'

Celia frowned. 'Is she quite suitable?'

'Oh, honestly, Mummy.' Louise rolled her eyes impatiently. 'She was a deb last year. You surely can't get more suitable than that.'

'A deb?' Celia's eyes lingered in amazement on Felicity's receding, tightly clad bottom. 'What is the world coming to?'

But Louise didn't answer. She was already dreaming of her next encounter with the now infamous Ward Frazer.

'When we get home we must sort out some old clothes and blankets for the Red Cross,' Celia said as Mr Wallace drove them home. 'They've put out an appeal. And we must see what we've got in the garden for the Harvest Home service next Sunday.'

'Oh yes,' Louise said eagerly, emerging with a beatific smile from her daydream. 'We must find something really nice for that.' Surely the Miss Taylors would invite their Canadian relation to come to Harvest Home.

And, as she imagined herself walking up the aisle under Ward Frazer's interested gaze and tenderly laying a large marrow on the altar steps, she was unaware of her mother's uneasy glance.

Chapter Eight

Despite the complete dissimilarity of their backgrounds, the enormous disparity of their respective financial states and the mutual mistrust of their families, by the end of the first month of Joyce's employment, Joyce Carter and Celia Rutherford, to their surprise, had begun to discover that they had a number of things in common, not least of which was the fact that they both had difficult teenage daughters.

One October morning, Joyce heard Louise shouting across the landing, 'I can't go to Granny's on Sunday! I just can't. What about church? You and Daddy are so mean. You don't want me to have any fun.'

And Celia, coming out of her room, saw Joyce caught on the stairs in the crossfire and sharply told Louise to keep her voice down. Later she apologised to Joyce.

'It's a difficult age. She's not really old enough to go off on her own and yet she's bored at home.'

Joyce nodded sympathetically, somewhat surprised that Celia felt the need to explain. After all, family rows were an everyday event in her house. In any case, wanting to go to church was normally considered to be a good thing. But Celia looked quite upset by it, or perhaps just embarrassed that Joyce had overheard the discord. Normally the Rutherford household seemed to run so perfectly. The perfect happy family. An example to the neighbourhood.

'I'm sure your daughter does what she's told,' Celia said.

And Joyce stared at her in amazement. 'Jen, you mean? She does exactly the bloody opposite more like,' she said and wished she hadn't said bloody as Celia looked shocked. 'I never know where she is or who she is with,' Joyce added quickly.

Although she had a pretty good idea these days. She was with that shifty Irish bugger, Sean Byrne, and God only knew what they got up to. But any time Joyce tried to find out, she got her head bitten off and told to mind her own business.

'And don't you mind that?' Celia asked curiously. 'Doesn't it worry you?'

Joyce put down her duster. 'Oh, it worries me all right,' she said. 'I do mind. But there's not much I can do short of locking her in her room. And then she only climbs out of the window. Mostly nowadays I leave her to get on with it. If she gets into trouble, that's her problem. Good luck to her.' She shrugged as Celia looked appalled. 'It's different for the likes of us, of course,

Mrs Rutherford. I suppose we haven't got so much to lose.'

She picked up her duster again. She had a job now and she was damned if she was going to lose that. She wondered about telling Mrs Rutherford what a difference the job had made to her but decided against it. With her beautiful house, her newfangled machines, her gardening and all, Mrs Rutherford wouldn't know what she was talking about if Joyce said the cleaning job had given her a kind of purpose in life. Something to look forward to. Something she did well.

And the money, meagre though it was, helped. And with the little bit of extra money and the freedom she had since the children had gone, and without Stanley, she had taken on a new lease of life. Yesterday she had even popped into the cinema to catch the cartoons and the Pathé news.

That was another thing she and Mrs Rutherford agreed on. That Hitler was a terrible man. And a fidget too. They had both noticed it. He just couldn't stand still. And they'd even had a chuckle over the news that he'd sacked his favourite astrologist after she had made the rather obvious mistake of predicting his untimely end.

'Well, I hope she's right and his end comes soon,' Celia said. 'I don't like the blackout and it'll get worse as winter comes on. Greville said Mr Wallace nearly ran someone over yesterday evening on Nightingale Lane. It was one of those Jewish refugees from that home they have for them over there. They will wear such dark clothes.'

Joyce knew the place she meant. The Home for Aged Jews. It always reminded her of Mr Lorenz. Not that the pawnbroker was all that aged of course, but he had the same look about him, that dark foreign look. And he always wore black.

'There was two or three of them up here yesterday,' Joyce said as she started to polish the table. 'Refugees. I saw them standing about on the common just over the road from here. In a terrible state they were, all skin and bone. The clothes hanging off them. I think they were children but they look old, if you know what I mean.'

Celia nodded. 'Those are probably the ones Mrs d'Arcy Billière has taken in from Austria.' She frowned. 'It really is rather good of her to have them. I did wonder if we should offer. I feel awful I'm not doing anything for the war effort. But I don't think Greville would like to have strangers in the house.'

'He's probably like my old man,' Joyce said. 'Doesn't like change. Leastways, not at home. Stanley's quite happy to use a new bookie or try a new fence, but if I try to slip a mushroom into his steak and kidney pudding he'll throw the whole lot straight in the rubbish.'

She shrugged and stood back to admire the gleam on the table. 'Not that he dislikes mushrooms, mind. He's quite partial to them really. It's just he doesn't like change. As for having Jews in the house, he'd throw a fit and a half.' She glanced at Celia. 'Mr Rutherford is most likely the same. Stuck in his ways.'

Celia looked rather taken aback by the comparison, then surprisingly she chuckled. 'Yes, Greville is rather like that, actually. I hadn't thought about it before.'

The following day Celia asked Joyce to help her pack up some old clothes she had put out for the Red Cross appeal.

Joyce was astonished by the quality of the things the Rutherfords were happy to give away. There were cardigans that seemed barely worn, several of Miss Louise's summer dresses, some boys' sweaters, lots of shoes, two or three good quality if a bit faded tweed skirts, and one of Mr Rutherford's old suits that would fetch a fortune in the nearly new shop on Lavender Hill.

There was one cardigan in particular that Joyce could not help but notice. It was in a lovely soft, sky-blue wool with small dots of pink and seemed brand new. As she folded it carefully and added it to the jersey pile, she wondered what lucky refugee woman would receive that and hoped they would appreciate it. She had never in her life owned anything as gay as that.

Celia Rutherford looked up from the pile of shoes she was sorting. 'Do say if there's anything there you'd like for yourself, Mrs Carter.'

'Oh no.' Joyce stepped back from the pile, shocked and offended. 'I wouldn't dream of it.' She felt herself flush. 'I have all the clothes I need, thank you.'

It was one thing to buy second hand clothes in the nearly new shop but to be offered them as charity from her employer was quite another thing altogether. Did Mrs Rutherford think she looked as though she needed her cast-offs, then? Clothes fit only for refugees. After all the effort she had gone to to come in looking her best. For a second Joyce thought of walking out. She felt a fool and she had her pride. But then she saw that Celia Rutherford looked genuinely embarrassed and realised she hadn't meant to offend her.

'I'm sorry, Mrs Carter,' Celia said, breaking the sudden awkward silence. 'Of course I didn't mean you to take our cast-offs. It's just that I saw you looking at the blue cardigan and thought it would be wasted on refugees. It's brand new. Greville's mother gave it to me. I've never worn it.' She hesitated. 'Are you sure you wouldn't like it, just as a thank-you for all your hard work?'

She smiled appealingly and it seemed rude now to refuse. 'It is very nice,' Joyce said grudgingly.

'It would suit you,' Celia said. 'It was too young for me. I felt like mutton dressed as lamb.'

Joyce blinked. She thought of pointing out that they must be much the same age, but the truth was that she wanted that cardigan. She wanted to look like a lamb for once. She'd been mutton for too long. And she'd never in a million years be able to afford anything like it for herself.

'Thank you,' she said stiffly. 'If it's all right with you, I'll take it and try it on at home.'

'Of course you may,' Celia said. Then she glanced at the rest of the clothes, now mostly in neat piles waiting to be packed up, and nodded. 'Now if you wouldn't mind finishing off here, Mrs Carter,' she said briskly, 'I'll pop down to the scullery to find some paper and string. And then we can parcel it all up. You can go off a bit early today if you like, there's no point in starting on something else just for half an hour.'

She was all right, that Mrs Rutherford, Joyce thought as she hurried home early to try on the cardigan. It was just that toffs had a different way of going about things. They didn't think the same. They lived in a different world, her and Mrs Rutherford. Like chalk and cheese.

It was the same with their houses. Up there on the common, the Rutherfords' house looked out over a proper main road with buses, cars and recently even the odd military convoy passing by, whereas the most excitement they ever saw in Lavender Road was if something frightened the massive Rutherford & Berry dray horses or if someone fell drunk off their bicycle after closing time.

Today's excitement was the sight of the Miss Taylors trying to protect their dachshund from the amorous advances of a large black mongrel.

'Yours must be on heat,' the mongrel's owner shouted angrily at the old ladies as he finally, red faced, managed to grab his dog and drag it out of reach.

'He's a boy,' the older Miss Taylor shouted back pluckily, picking up the geriatric animal and brandishing his undercarriage in the man's face. 'See for your bloody self.'

Grinning to herself, Joyce brushed past the small crowd that had gathered to enjoy the confrontation and walked on down the road.

There was no sign of Mr Lorenz in the street today, but as she let herself into the house she knew at once that Jen was home. Her coat was thrown carelessly over the banister and there was noise from her room upstairs. Joyce's heart sank. She had hoped she would have the house to herself. She had wanted to have a private look at herself in Mrs Rutherford's cardigan in the long mirror that Jen had bought herself last week. Crossly she banged the door shut behind her and frowned as the noise above ceased abruptly. Then she distinctly heard the scrape of a window opening.

The cardigan forgotten, in dawning suspicion Joyce took the stairs two at a time. On the landing outside Jen's room she paused, took a steadying breath, gritted her teeth and pushed the door open.

Jen was standing by the half open window, fully dressed, but flushed and dishevelled. Next to the bed stood Sean Byrne.

Joyce's first thought was how extraordinarily attractive the young Irishman was. She hadn't seen him close to before and certainly not without his shirt. Straight shouldered and slender-waisted there wasn't an ounce of extra fat on him, not like Stanley who had several stones extra on him. And what's more he had the grace to look embarrassed.

Not that Joyce cared whether he was embarrassed or not. She certainly wasn't going to let him get round her with his seductive eyes and coy smile.

As he opened his mouth to speak she held up her hand. 'I don't want to hear any excuses,' she said icily, meeting his blue gaze squarely. She took a quick breath. 'Or any of your Irish blarney.' She dragged her eyes away and pointed at the door. 'Just get dressed and get out.'

By the window, Jen jerked into life. 'Don't speak to Sean like that. He's my boyfriend.'

'I don't care if he's Rip van bloody Winkle.' Joyce turned to her, trying not to notice the reflection of muscles rippling in Sean Byrne's chest in the new mirror as he slowly shrugged on his shirt. 'I'll speak to him any way I like,' she said. 'I will not have naked Irishmen in my daughter's bedroom. Nor anywhere else in the house. What do you think your father would say?'

'He's not here to say anything,' Jen said sulkily.

Joyce nodded grimly. 'Luckily for you.' She turned back to Sean, thankful that he was now decently clad. 'If my husband found out about this, you'd be dog meat. Do you understand me?'

He inclined his head and smiled faintly. 'I understand you perfectly, Mrs Carter.' His voice was like honey but his eyes were not smiling. He smoothed his hands through his hair and nodded coolly at Jen. 'See you around, sweetheart.'

Mother and daughter stood in rigid silence while Sean ran down the stairs and let himself out into the street. Then as the door banged Jen turned furiously on Joyce.

'You said I could see him.'

'I didn't say you could see him here. Not half bloody naked,' Joyce retorted heatedly, then she sighed wearily. 'You've got the whole of blinking London. Why do you have to bring him here?'

Jen flushed. 'There's nowhere else to go. Not where you can be private.'

Joyce gaped at her cheek. 'Well, you needn't think you're going to 'be private' here. For God's sake, girl, you're only seventeen. What the hell do you think your father would do if he found out? And don't say he wouldn't find out. Anybody could have seen the two of you coming in here. Anyone.'

Joyce felt faint at the thought. If Stanley got some of his heavies to come over to see what was going on, it would be the end of her newfound freedom, the end of her job, that's for sure.

She shuddered and eyed her daughter with loathing. 'I'm already working my fingers to the bone so that you can play at your acting. I'm damned if I'm going to do it so you can sit around here playing with your so-called boyfriend.

'He is my boyfriend.'

'Oh yes?' Joyce sneered. 'And he's probably the boyfriend of every other girl in London who's prepared to drop her knickers for him too.'

'He's not,' Jen cried, close to tears. 'You don't know anything. He's not like that. I wasn't going to go the whole way.'

Joyce shrugged and turned away. 'Good God, Jen, I sometimes wonder if you're all there.'

She was just about to leave Jen's room when someone knocked at the front door.

Joyce blinked in surprise, it was rare for them to have callers. With a last sour look at Jen, she went downstairs and opened the door.

A pretty young post girl stood there with a telegram.

For a second Joyce stared at the flimsy paper blankly. Telegrams were never good news. Everyone knew that. Although the land war had not yet begun in earnest, nor the expected bombing, the vicious German U-boats had been active since the day war had been declared. It had recently been given out that twenty Allied ships had been sunk in the first month of war. Everyone locally knew that Mrs Phelps in Northcote Road had lost her son when the aircraft carrier HMS Courageous was torpedoed three weeks ago.

So, even though she had no relations serving, Joyce was filled with dread by the sight of the telegram. And even as her heart began to pound, she opened it.

It came from Mrs Baxter, Barnstaple, Devon. It was a moment before Joyce grasped what it said.

Her fourteen year old son, Mick Carter, had run away from the farm the previous day.

Pam Nelson was delighted with her new job at the Ministry of Information. She liked her office on the sixth floor of the big white building with a window that gave her an excellent view across Whitehall into Horse Guards Parade with the green leafy expanse of St James's park beyond.

Pam felt at the hub of things here. Below, in a haze of exhaust fumes and pigeons, the traffic roared up and down Whitehall, and military officers from all over the Commonwealth hurried along the wide pavements with important-looking documents under their arms, saluting each other as they disappeared into one or other of the great high buildings of government.

It was a far cry from the narrow back streets of Clapham. Here there was a sense of action, of progress, of serious international decisions being made, and Pam liked being part of it.

Pam also liked her boss. Mr Shaw, an eccentric but kindly man with whom she struck an immediate rapport, was unstinting with his praise and had already begun to trust her to carry out certain tasks without his supervision.

From the first he treated her more as his equal than as his assistant. He thought nothing of asking her opinion on the phraseology of a document he was working on. Twice he took her to lunch at the nearby heavily sandbagged Lyons Corner House in the Strand to discuss some work issue in more congenial surroundings, and surprised her only last week by offering her his copy of Adolf Hitler's *Mein Kampf* to read. 'You've got a bright future here at the Ministry of Information, Mrs Nelson,' he said. 'But to understand our role fully, you need to know what we're up against.'

Pam glowed with pride. And even though Hitler's exposition of his world view was far and away the heaviest thing she had ever read, she ploughed her way doggedly through it on the way to and from work, determined not to let Mr Shaw down.

In fact the only problem with Pam's new job at the Ministry of Information was that her friends and neighbours expected her to know what was going on.

Sometimes she did know things in advance before they were given out. Like that rationing, planned for December, was going to be delayed until January, Like that the leaflets dropped on Germany by the RAF instead of bombs seemed to have had little effect on the German people despite widespread rumours of mass revolt in Berlin. Like that the government were very anxious about Nazi infiltrators, rumour mongering and propaganda.

But more often than not, unless they directly concerned the department in which she worked, she was as much taken by surprise by the endless new regulations and announcements as everyone else.

Nevertheless, working for a government department did give her some credibility with people who asked her opinion. And if her responses put their minds at rest, then as far as Pam was concerned it was worthwhile.

When one evening she found Sheila Whitehead sobbing on her doorstep that her Jo had finally been sent to France with the BEF and that he was sure to be killed the moment he set foot on French soil, Pam was able to tell her reassuringly that the Secretary of State for War, Mr Hore-Belisha, had recently announced to the House of Commons that the army he had sent to France was equipped in the finest possible manner which could not be excelled. 'Our army,' he had said, 'is as well, if not better equipped than any similar army.'

Pam didn't add that Alan had told her privately that several of the brewery lorries had been commandeered in early October to transport the troops and equipment to France.

It seemed somehow unpatriotic to worry that the decrepit Rutherford & Berry beer lorries were neither the most effective nor morale-boosting mode of transport for a fighting army. After all, who was she to doubt the Secretary of State for War? For all she knew the Wehrmacht trundled about in brewery lorries too, although it seemed unlikely.

And Sheila had enough to worry about as it was. Little George was missing his father dreadfully, and the toddler, Ray, had recently discovered how to open the front door and had twice been found by passers-by halfway down the street looking for his dad.

As her best friend, Pam helped Sheila as much as she could, but with the full time job, her time was short. Already she was aware that virtually the only times she saw Alan alone were in bed and then she was too tired to do anything except sleep, even in the 'right week'.

'I'm sorry,' she muttered into the darkness as she turned away from him. 'What with the new job and the war and everything, I'm not sure that now is the right time for a baby.'

He was silent for a while, then she felt him groping for her hand. 'I don't want to lose you, Pam,' he said when he found it, and a terrible guilt washed through her. He was having a bad enough time without this. He had been for a pint at the Flag and Garter earlier, perhaps to build up some courage to approach her, and two recently enlisted lads from Cedars Road had teased him about his lack of uniform.

Someone had even asked him if he was a conscientious objector and they hadn't believed him when he had said he'd tried to get war work. He was quite upset about it when he got back.

'You won't lose me,' she said. But even to her, her voice sounded more doubtful than reassuring. Her hand felt like a dead fish in his.

'I've finished repainting the boat,' he said suddenly. 'Perhaps you'd like to come down and see it on Saturday.'

Pam bit her lip. She had said she'd go to the pictures with Sean Byrne on Saturday afternoon. It had never occurred to her that Alan would ask her to go down to the boat. She didn't want to spend a cold October afternoon on the river. Nevertheless Alan was her husband. It was her duty to comply with his wishes.

'That would be nice,' she said, wondering who Sean Byrne would take to the pictures in her place. She detached her hand from Alan's. 'Now I think I should try to get to sleep. I've got a busy day tomorrow.'

Sean Byrne took Jen to the cinema on Saturday afternoon. It was the first time she had seen him properly since he had been caught in her bedroom by her mother and Jen was uneasy about the amount she had minded his neglect.

She found that she missed his lazy flattery, she missed his kisses, she missed the way his blue eyes sparkled when she amused him. She knew he was cross with her. Not just for letting them get caught, but for her reluctance to acknowledge her interest in him publicly and also for not wanting to go further in their lovemaking.

Her mother didn't know it, but Sean had in fact been getting dressed when she came in that day, not undressed. He had wanted Jen to take her top off, and her bra, so he could feel her breasts against his chest as they embraced. He had taken off his shirt to encourage her, had sat next to her on the bed, gently caressing her back, her neck, but when his fingers had slid under her shirt and eased under her bra, Jen had suddenly got cold feet.

The feel of his fingers on her skin had sent shocking shivers coursing through her body. She had felt suddenly she was slipping out of control and had leaped to her feet in alarm. And even the look of irritation in his handsome face as he reached for his shirt had not changed her mind. To be perfectly honest it had been a bit of a relief that her mother had come home when she did.

But even though Jen's mind told her it was for the best not to see him, for a while, her body still craved his attentions and she had had great difficulty in preventing herself from knocking on the Nelsons' door and offering herself to him lock stock and barrel.

Instead she had been careful to fill her time. She had made some headway in finding the names and addresses of theatrical agents to whom she could apply for acting work. She had taken Katy's advice, had some lovely photos taken in a studio in Oxford Street and rewritten her introductory letter to include a mythical stand-in stint in the chorus of the Lambeth Walk musical *Me and My Girl*. But even so, she had so far failed to get any of the names on her list to see her.

What's more, her mother was beside herself because there was still no news of Mick. Jen had tried to reassure her. After all, he was a tough little bugger, Micky. At school he was constantly being caned for fighting. One term he and his pals had terrorised the playground so badly, the parents of weaker kids had complained to the headmaster.

The headmaster had complained to her parents, not that they'd been able to do anything about it. Her dad had just clipped Mick round the ear and told him if he had to beat people up to pick on more deserving victims. It was shortly after that that Micky and his pals had broken Mr Lorenz's windows.

Jen shrugged. No, young Micky was well able to look after himself. He was like a bad penny and would turn up soon enough. It was absurd of her mother to talk about going down to Devon, what on earth good could she do there? It would just be a stupid waste of money.

Jen was far more worried about Sean. She couldn't bear the thought of not seeing him again. She was worried that he would think she was too young for him. She was worried he would make her suffer longer than she could bear. She was worried that he would only have her back on his terms. But worst was the terrible worry that he would have found another girl.

So when she bumped into him in the street and he casually asked if she'd like to go to the pictures with him on Saturday afternoon, she nearly died of relief.

And then on Friday as though to compound the good news, one of the agents to whose receptionist she had just presented her letter, walked into the outer office just as she was leaving, asked who she was and what she wanted, and said he'd see her there and then.

Nev Cooper was a brisk, impatient man, with a bristly moustache. Taking Jen's letter and photograph out of his receptionist's hand, he marched straight back into his office and sat on a piano stool facing a small cleared area of floor space. Evidently his audition stage.

'Right,' he said, glaring at Jen, who was hovering in terror by the door. 'What are you going to do for me?' His voice was like gravel.

It hadn't occurred to Jen that she might be asked to perform straight away. To be honest it hadn't occurred to her that she might be required to perform at all. She had received so little interest for so long she could hardly believe anyone would ever want to see her act again.

'I can do one of Juliet's speeches from *Romeo and Juliet*,' she mumbled.

'Speak up,' Nev Cooper shouted at her. 'And take your coat off. Juliet didn't go about swathed like an Egyptian mummy.'

Jen gritted her teeth as she unbuttoned her coat. The agent watched her impassively.

'Pretty face, nice figure. Are you any good?'

'Yes. I am,' Jen said, but he didn't appear to hear her and she began to wonder if he might be deaf.

As she moved self-consciously to the bare patch of carpet he waved his hand impatiently. 'Come on, girl. I haven't got all day.'

He heard her high volume Shakespeare in silence.

As soon as she finished, he asked if she could sing and even before she replied he had swung round to the piano behind him and started thumping out a tune that Jen dimly recognised as coming from *Me and My Girl*. Her heart sank. She certainly didn't know the words, let alone how they fitted to the music. Suddenly she wished she hadn't followed up Katy's suggestion.

'OK, OK,' she shouted, as he looked over his shoulder at her quizzically. 'I admit it, I wasn't in the show. You've caught me out.'

She glared at him as he stopped playing and turned to face her. 'But I can sing. And I can act. I just need to be given a chance.'

For a long moment he sat and stared at her then he crossed his arms and closed his eyes. 'Sing, then.'

Nonplussed, Jen racked her numbed brain for a song she knew all the way through without music, and the only thing she could come up with was *Once in Royal David's City*. For a second she hesitated. A nativity hymn certainly wasn't going to be what he expected. Then, damn him, she thought, at least it shows off my voice, and she squared her shoulders and launched into it.

Nev Cooper's eyes flew open. By the end of the first line he had taken hold of his surprise but he didn't close his eyes again and by the end of the first verse he was smiling.

As Jen took a deep breath and doggedly prepared to start the second verse, he held up a hand, laughing. 'Enough.' He sobered and stared at her grittily. 'You've got a voice, I'll give you that, and you can hold a tune. But you can't sing hymns for the likes of Manny Jay or Vivian Van Damm. It's not godliness that they are looking for.' His eyes narrowed thoughtfully. 'You're a pretty girl. How easy are you with your favours?'

Jen stared at him aghast. 'Not at all easy,' she stammered, flushing. What was he saying? That she might be expected to sleep her way on to the stage? She'd heard rumours of course, who hadn't? But she had hardly believed it could be true.

He shrugged. 'Pity. That cuts down the options.' He shook his head dismissively and Jen's heart sank. Dully she picked up her coat.

As she moved towards the door he seemed to take pity on her. 'Can you dance? Tap?'

Reluctantly she shook her head. 'But I could learn,' she said loudly and clearly.

'Then learn,' he said briskly and stood up, He wrote a name on a piece of paper and handed it to her. 'And find a piano and learn some decent songs too. Come back in a month,' He smiled dryly. 'It's not going to be the Old Vic. But we might get you into one of the Christmas shows if you're lucky.' He shook her hand courteously. 'Oh and, Miss Carter, I'm not deaf.' He paused to note her confusion, 'But I've no time for mumblers.'

Jen smiled. 'I'll never mumble again,' she said, and to her immense gratification he laughed.

Out in the street Jen blinked. The whole thing had only taken ten minutes. She realised her knees were shaking. And her hands. And her heart. She shook her head helplessly as she leaned weakly against the wall for support. Whatever happened with Sean Byrne would be child's play after what she had just, been through.

For a moment she stood there trembling. Then she glanced at the scrap of paper in her hand. Max Rivers Dancing School, Great Newport Street, it said. And suddenly she felt her spirits lift. She had finally found someone who was prepared to help her. Surely that was a start. What had he said? A Christmas show?

Her mouth curved in excitement and a new light came into her eyes. She clenched her fists and looked up at the mottled autumn sky. She would give up everything she possessed to be in a Christmas show.

Chapter Nine

'I've missed you, Jennifer Carter.'

Sean's breath caressed her face in the cinema darkness. She could still feel the tingle of his kisses on her lips. She still had the smoky taste of him in her mouth. Her heart was pounding like there was no tomorrow. She had no idea what was happening on the screen. Admittedly it was only the B film. *Secret Service of the Air*, it was called, about a pilot who got involved in smashing a drugs ring. But the dashing young American actor Ronald Reagan could be flying to the moon for all she had seen of him. She and Sean had been kissing and cuddling ever since they had sat down.

'I've missed you too,' she murmured, leaning towards him again, craving his touch, craving his admiration. He liked her to kiss him. To touch him.

'Making love is a two way process,' he had told her earlier as they walked to the cinema. 'Give and take.' He had stopped to light a cigarette and had eyed her steadily through the smoke. 'I've got a lot to give you, Jennifer Carter, but I'll be wanting something back. And I'm not at all sure you're prepared to give it to me.'

Jen had felt her heart leap at the word love. Nobody had ever talked about making love to her before. She was surprised how much she liked the sound of it. She stared into his beautiful blue eyes. 'Oh, I am,' she had said eagerly. 'I'm just not sure how to.'

He didn't smile. 'If you do what your body tells you, you won't go far wrong.'

Now he responded to her tentative kiss by pulling her head hard against him and deepening the kiss until Jen's head was spinning and her whole body was juddering with a force outside her control. This time when Sean's hand slid under her jersey she made no attempt to stop him and he stifled her scream of excitement with his mouth.

'Take it easy, Jennifer,' he muttered against her lips. 'We're in a public place.'

'Oh Sean,' she whimpered helplessly as something seemed to explode in her groin. 'Please stop.'

Abruptly he stood up and dragged her to her feet. 'Pick up your things,' he hissed at her and blindly she gathered up her coat and scarf while everyone around them started hushing and tutting about the noise. Ronald Reagan and his feminine lead, the beautiful Ila Rhodes, were looking at each other lovingly and nobody wanted them disturbed.

Outside in the unexpected brightness of the warm October afternoon, Jen stared at Sean miserably as he stopped to light a cigarette outside Arding & Hobbs. What had she done wrong now? She hadn't really meant for him to stop. It was just that it was all so frightening, so unexpected somehow, the reaction of her body to his touch.

'I'm, sorry,' she mumbled as he stared across the street, smoking moodily. 'I'm sorry I'm so hopeless at all this.'

He turned to her then. 'Oh, you're not hopeless Jennifer Carter. Not at all. But do you have no idea what you do to a man with all this stopping and starting?'

'What do you mean?' It hadn't occurred to her that Sean might be physically affected too. He seemed so experienced, so in control all the time. She stared at him. Did she have some power over him the same way he had power over her?

'What do you think I mean?' He looked away from her and dragged on his cigarette. 'You're driving me crazy with desire for you. I can't sleep at night for it. And if I do sleep I dream of you. Kissing you. Making love to you.'

'I dream of that too,' Jen admitted shyly.

He shook his head impatiently. 'The difference between us is that you only want to dream. You're not prepared to follow through.' He glanced back at her. 'I thought you loved me.'

'Sean, I do. I'm a bit scared, that's all,' Jen said pleadingly'. 'And I ... I don't want to get pregnant.'

'Oh, you won't get pregnant,' Sean said dismissively. 'I've told you, that's easy to avoid.' His eyes narrowed. 'You can't use that excuse, Jennifer. If you don't love me enough to trust me then it's no good.' He saw her stricken expression and shrugged. 'If that's the case then there's nothing for it but we'll just have to stop seeing each other. Never mind. I'll have to find myself another girl, an older girl, to put me out of my misery.' He leaned forward and kissed her cheek resignedly. 'Goodbye, Jennifer Carter Leigh, good luck with your acting career.'

Jennifer stared at him, her heart thudding. Another girl? What other girl? She grabbed his arm as he went to turn away. She hated him thinking she was too young. 'Sean, please wait. Stop seeing each other completely? But why?'

'You really don't understand, do you?' He dropped his cigarette and ground it impatiently under his foot. 'If you love someone, you want to please them, don't you?' Jen nodded. 'Well, if you're a man it's a physical thing. It's a physical reaction. And after a while it becomes too painful to stop. It's a terrible dangerous thing for a man then.' He thrust his hands into his pockets. 'There are names for girls who do that to a man.'

'I don't mean to do that,' Jen whispered. 'I didn't know.' She had no idea she was putting him in pain, in danger. She would hate to be called names. She had sometimes heard her brother Bob call girls names.

Sean shrugged, 'Well, you know now,' he said shortly. Then seeing her look of despair he relented and touched her cheek with a gentle smile. 'It's your choice, Jennifer Carter. You know what I want. I want to make love to you. To make you mine.'

When he smiled at her like that Jen was putty in his hands. She took a deep breath. He wanted her. Wanted her to be his girl. Her inhibitions fell away. So long as she didn't get pregnant what did it matter what she did? Who would know, anyway? And the thought of not seeing him again or, worse, of perhaps seeing him with another girl, was too painful to bear.

Sean was the only person who took her seriously. He was the only person who respected her ambition. The only person she could admit her anxieties to. She remembered his questions about her missing brother. His interest earlier when she had told him about the agent. His enthusiasm. His high expectations of her.

Nobody else cared one way or the other. Well, Katy Parsons did a bit, but it wasn't the same as Sean Byrne. Katy didn't have the power to turn her knees to jelly, her blood to fire. Jen didn't want to lose him and if letting him make love to her was the way to keep him then it was definitely worth it. So long as nobody knew, of course.

She took a quick breath. 'I think I want it too.'

To her dismay, Sean shook his head. 'Think isn't good enough,' he said coolly, watching some girls on the other side of the street. 'If you pull back this time I can't say what would happen.'

'I won't pull back.' Jen felt her heart lurch as she passed the point of no return. After all, if the bombing started she might be dead tomorrow. And then she would have missed her chance. She glanced up at Sean's handsome profile. The firm chin, the sensual mouth. And then suddenly she wanted to do it. To get it over with. 'But where can we go?'

Sean looked at her. 'The Nelsons are out for the afternoon,' he said, smiling. 'We can go there.'

They walked hand in hand back up busy Lavender Hill, with its constant stream of traffic, and for once Jen didn't dare suggest they separated at the end of Lavender Road. Sean was in an odd mood today. And she didn't dare annoy him again.

Already she felt she was on trial. Her last chance to please him before he went searching for another girl. And she knew that for Sean Byrne it wouldn't be a long search. She had seen already the way other girls looked at him. She knew he noticed too, although he didn't say anything. It made her anxious about losing him. Anxious to please him, flattered that he had chosen her over them. But once they had made love she would be his girl and she wouldn't have to worry any more.

As they turned up Lavender Road her train of thought stopped abruptly.

Ahead of them outside her own house was a figure she recognised. A figure she hadn't seen for a while. Surely a bit taller than she remembered. She stared in disbelief. Micky.

'Sean.' She stopped and grabbed his arm excitedly. 'Look. There, just going to my house. That's my brother. The missing one. He's come home.'

She was all set to fly off up the street. But then she looked up at Sean's face and saw the danger and dropped her clutching hand from his arm.

'Go if you want to,' he said coolly. 'It's your choice, remember.'

For a fatal torn second she hesitated as her loyalties rearranged themselves.

Then she shook her head. 'Micky can wait. He's kept us waiting a week.'

'You've kept me waiting six weeks,' Sean said leading her across the road to Pam Nelson's house and pulling out his key. As he pushed it slowly into the lock he smiled into her eyes. 'Tell me you love me.'

'I love you,' Jen whispered. She must do, mustn't she, if she would rather be with him than with her errant brother? She shivered. And now she was going to have to prove that love.

Joyce couldn't believe her eyes. One moment she had been alone in the kitchen having a recuperative cup of tea after hurrying back from Clapham Junction, and the next she was staring blankly at her missing son, who was lounging in the kitchen doorway.

She stood up. 'Micky,' she said flatly.

He grinned. 'So you remember me, then.'

Joyce blinked. How could she forget that thickly freckled face, the sticking-out ears, red hair and foxy eyes? She stared at him, wondering how you were supposed to react when confronted with someone who had given you a week of intense anxiety. Who had cost her pounds in weight and in anxious telegrams. Even now she had a rail ticket in her pocket that had cost seventeen and six. Money loaned from Mrs Rutherford, who had been surprisingly sympathetic and tolerant of her distraction all week.

'Where the hell have you been?' she said roughly at last. 'We've all been worried to death about you.'

She watched his face fall. He'd grown in the time he'd been in Devon. Her initial stab of relief that he was alive and apparently well, turned into a nagging unease about how she was going to feed him. How she was going to persuade him to go back to Devon. And worse, in the meantime, how she was going to keep him quiet about her job.

She had lied outright last week on her first monthly visit to Stanley in

Reading Jail. He had asked what she had said to the Rutherfords and she had said she'd refused. Amazingly even Pete hadn't noticed that she was working three days a week. He left for his building job before she did and wasn't back until well after she was home.

But Mick was much sharper than Pete. And with the schools closed because of the evacuation he would be hanging around all day if he stayed here. Not that Mick had ever spent much time in school. He was one of the worst truants there was. And if he stayed, Jen would suffer too. Mick had picked up his father's attitude towards the Irish. He wouldn't keep his mouth shut about his sister's unsuitable liaison. And all hell would be let loose then.

'You should have known I was coming home,' Mick said sulkily.

'You took your time about it,' Joyce said sharply. For the first time she took in that he was more dishevelled than usual. The journey obviously hadn't been plain sailing. Serve the little devil right.

'I had to hitchhike,' he said. 'And there wasn't much traffic apart from military. So it took ages. I didn't have enough money for the train. I had to sleep rough.' He shrugged. 'I thought you'd be pleased to see me.'

'I'm pleased you're not dead,' Joyce said grudgingly. 'Although you've nearly been the death of me. You'll have to go back, you know,' she added after a moment. 'You can't stay here. All the schools are closed. And they're still expecting bombing every day.'

He stared at her, his jaw hardening ominously. 'I'm not going back. I don't care about school. Or bombing. I don't have to go to school any more anyway. Not now I'm fourteen. I'm going to get a job.'

Joyce groaned inwardly. She knew that stubborn look. She also knew the chances of a fourteen year old boy finding a job were minimal. 'You'd better have a cup of tea,' she said. 'And you're probably hungry after your journey. I'll make you a sandwich.'

For the first time Mick grinned. 'I'm bloody starving.' He sat down at the table as Joyce began to cut the bread. 'Oh, I nearly forgot. I brought you a present,' he said.

Suddenly Joyce felt a terrible sense of guilt. He'd thought to bring her a present and all she wished was that he hadn't come back. But she didn't want him here rocking the boat. Everything had seemed to be going so well for the last week or two.

Mick fished in his pocket and pulled out a necklace of what looked like pearls. Joyce stared at it aghast as he proudly handed it over.

Mick looked disappointed. Don't you like it?'

'Where did this come from?' Joyce asked suspiciously.

'I'm not saying.' Mick looked sulky. 'You never asked that when Dad and Bob brought things back.'

'Is it Mrs Baxter's?'

He shook his head crossly. 'I'm not stupid. I don't know whose it is. Look, if you must know, I picked it up on the train down to Devon. I've been saving it for you. I thought if you didn't want to wear it, at least it would be a bit of keep for me, what with Dad being inside and all. Until I find a job. But if you don't want it I'll have it back.' He reached out his hand truculently and for a second he looked just like his father. And just like with his father Joyce felt she had let him down.

'Oh, Micky.' She sat down abruptly and put her head in her hands. She felt bad for being so ungrateful. In the past she would not have given another thought to a bit of petty theft, the odd bit of jewellery could always be turned into a bit of useful cash after all, he was right about that. But now suddenly she didn't want it.

She didn't want to worry about the police knocking on the door at dead of night. She didn't want the house searched from top to bottom. As far as she was concerned, she had reached the bottom already with two of the family men inside. The only way now was up.

She had a job now, something of her own, and she didn't want it jeopardised by her family. Nor did she want any more rows. She'd had enough recently with Jen.

She heard his voice, puzzled and a bit aggrieved. 'What's the matter? I thought you'd be pleased with it.'

She looked up. 'I am pleased with it,' she said weakly. 'And I am pleased to see you, Micky. Although you shouldn't have run off without saying anything. Everyone has been worried. Angie has cried every night apparently.'

He shrugged indifferently and reached greedily for the slice of bread she had cut, apparently uncaring that it hadn't been buttered. 'If I'd said where I was going they would have stopped me or sent the police after me. I'm not stupid, you know.' His jaw stiffened again as he chewed. He spoke through his mouthful. 'But you can't do nothing now I'm back. I'm not going back to that bloody farm whatever you say. I hated all them fields and cows and sheep and what have you. And them yard animals and all, horses and dogs and that, growling and snapping at you as soon as you turn your back.'

He swallowed and wiped his mouth with the back of his hand as he looked up at Joyce, 'This is my home and I'm staying put this time. Hitler, or no Hitler. I'm not scared of a few bombs.'

In Sean's bedroom Jen was standing awkwardly in her bra and knickers, trembling all over.

Sean was still fully dressed. She watched him pour a generous measure of Irish whiskey into a glass he'd been to fetch from downstairs and tensed as he turned round.

'What is it?' he asked, raising the glass to his lips. 'I thought you'd be in the bed by now.'

Jen didn't move. She felt suddenly sick.

Fortified by the drink, Sean frowned and stepped towards her. 'It's not shy you are, is it, Jennifer Carter?'

Miserably, Jen nodded as he touched her cheek with cold fingers. 'A bit. And a bit scared too,' she admitted, wishing her knees weren't knocking quite so obviously. She'd always thought she'd got quite a nice body but then she'd never stripped off in front of anyone before, not even for gym at school, not right to the buff, and now she found herself terribly conscious of her white bony shoulders and small pointed bosoms under her new uplift bra. And worse even than that, she was suddenly very aware of the wiry reddish hair under her knickers. She just couldn't believe that Sean would be expecting that. She could feel herself flushing all over at what he might say about it.

'Here, have a sip of this,' he said, thrusting the glass into her hand. 'And get in the bed. You can't do it standing up, not the first time.'

Jen blinked. She didn't know you could do it standing up any time. Sean was obviously far more experienced in these things than her. She took a gulp of the whiskey and was momentarily distracted as it burned a path down her dry throat.

She put the glass down on the bedside table and glanced at the narrow bed and then at Sean. 'What about ... Should I ...?' She flapped her hand nervously over her bra and knickers.

'Take them off,' Sean said briskly as he shrugged off his jacket and unclipped his braces.

As he turned his back to unbutton his trousers, Jen struggled rapidly out of her underclothes and scrambled into the bed pulling the sheet up to her chin.

It seemed odd being in bed in the middle of the afternoon. The sheets were pleasantly cool on her bare skin. She wondered how often Pam Nelson changed them. Every week most likely, they seemed clean and crisp enough. She must iron them too.

She heard a clink and a rustle and Sean's trousers dropped to the floor, and turning her head at once all thoughts of Pam Nelson's linen arrangements shot from her mind as her eyes rested on Sean's bare torso.

Only the back view admittedly, but the smooth back and buttocks were quite enough to send the goose bumps over her skin again. She had never seen a naked man. Not a fully grown one. Once they were out of short trousers, her brothers had all been very coy about their equipment, as Katy Parsons had once blushingly referred to it.

As Sean turned round Jen quickly averted her gaze. She didn't want to see anything else. Not yet. Already a hot flush of embarrassment was prickling over her skin. As he walked over to the bed and climbed quickly in beside her in a muddle of hairy limbs and cold skin, more than anything Jen wished she was still sitting in her cosy velvet seat at the cinema.

She wished they could talk, relax a bit, but at once he was kissing her, and his hands were pulling her close to him so she could feel the strange cold, rough and smooth texture of him all the way down her body.

Jen didn't know what to do. She felt stiff and anxious and the more Sean muttered for her to relax as his hands roamed her body, the stiffer she felt. Any minute now he'd find that wiry patch between her legs, she knew, and she found herself clinging close to him just to stop his hand creeping down there.

But he found her bosoms instead. 'That's more like it,' he smiled suddenly and Jen felt a stab of pleasure. It was pretty much the first time he'd smiled since they'd left the cinema. She realised suddenly she'd do virtually anything to make him smile.

'What do I have to do?' she whispered nervously as his hands started roaming again. Perhaps in a minute she would feel something, that stirring sensation she'd felt in the cinema. But his hands weren't as gentle now as they'd been then and even his kisses seemed rougher, as though he was in a hurry.

Leaning over for the glass on the bedside table, he drained the whiskey in one swallow. Then he looked down at her with glittering eyes. 'You have to relax,' he said gruffly. 'And you have to stroke me.' Taking her hand he guided it down between their bodies.

Jen was so startled to find that he'd got a tangle of hair down there too that she hardly realised what he was asking her to do.

From then on it all became too embarrassing to think about.

'Are you ready?' he had whispered suddenly.

'I don't know,' she said nervously and he laughed softly.

'You're a good girl, Jennifer Carter,' he said.

Jen had had no idea how much it would hurt. There just didn't seem to be room inside her for Sean's equipment. But after a lot of pushing and squeezing, to her astonishment it did eventually go in. But then it all got even worse. If Sean hadn't so obviously been enjoying it, she would have shouted at him to stop, As it was she suffered the burning, grating thrusts in silent agony until, to her enormous relief, he suddenly yanked it out, shouted and collapsed on top of her in a sticky, sweaty mess.

It was over. And suddenly Jen was crying.

It was all so horrible and she hadn't felt anything. Nothing except pain and embarrassment. And now she was all rumpled and messy and Sean seemed to have gone to sleep.

But her sobs roused him and he gently kissed away the tears.

'It's never much fun for a girl the first time,' he said, easing himself off her and stroking her hair gently. 'That's why it's better to get it over quickly.' He smiled his old beautiful blue-eyed smile. 'You'll be all right next time. I'll get some French letters, then we won't have to be so careful.'

Next time? Jen's heart sank despite the smile. It hadn't occurred to her that she'd have to go through it all again.

But thankfully Sean was getting up and reaching for a handkerchief. 'I'd better get you cleaned up and out of here before Mrs Nelson comes home,' he said. Then he stopped and looked at her, curled red eyed and foetus-like on the crumpled white sheet. 'It's a beautiful body you've got Jennifer Carter.' He shook his head. 'I think I forgot to tell you that in the heat of the moment.'

The following weekend, after weeks of putting it off, Louise finally gave in to parental pressure and went to visit Katy Parsons at the pub. She was shocked by the claustrophobic stuffiness of the small first floor room where Katy apparently sat all day, and was hard pressed not to show her distaste for the sour-sweet smell of beer that drifted up from below as Mrs Parsons washed the floor of the public bar.

Looking around her surreptitiously while Katy made a pot of tea in the poky kitchen, Louise marvelled at the extraordinary idea of taste that some people had. For there was no doubt that the hideous lilac cushions had been carefully chosen to tone with the purple and beige chair covers, and that the grotesque family of white china dogs on the mantelpiece had been bought to complement the gold-framed print of three beribboned poodles that hung above them.

Surprisingly Katy Parsons herself didn't look too bad. She certainly wasn't the pathetic wasted invalid Louise had expected. Her mousy bob wasn't very flattering, admittedly, and she could do with using some blusher and lipstick, but she had a sweet, rather shy smile and thoughtful grey eyes under some thick, enviably curly lashes. She was a bit on the thin side and her high-necked white blouse and navy pleated skirt weren't by any means the height of fashion, but they were neat and tidy, and the blouse had unusual pearl-coloured buttons and some rather pretty lace at the cuffs.

Mindful of her father's comment that Katy was scared to death of the war, Louise initially tried to avoid mentioning it. A difficult task considering nobody seemed to talk of anything else these days and Louise was conscious that her descriptions of Dodie Smith's *Dear Octopus* that she'd seen the previous evening and the Myra Hess lunchtime concert she'd been to with her mother at the National Gallery, were rapidly running out of steam. Desperately she racked her brains for another safe topic and was relieved, if somewhat surprised, when Katy asked if she had heard about people in

Edinburgh earlier in the week actually being able to watch a dogfight between the RAF and the Luftwaffe over the Firth of Forth.

'Can you imagine? They could see all the markings on the planes. One of the reports said, they could even see the German pilots' faces, they were so close. But the RAF saw them off of course.'

'I think the RAF pilots are the bravest men on earth,' Louise said.

'Or in the air,' Katy added and they both giggled.

'They are certainly the most handsome,' Louise said knowledgeably and was gratified by the sudden interest in Katy's eyes.

'Do you know some Royal Air Force pilots, then?' Katy asked in awe.

Sensing that Katy was a fellow romantic, Louise nodded and without knowing quite how it had happened, suddenly found herself talking about Ward Frazer.

And not just talking, but pouring out all the details of the party in Henley, his irritating interest in Felicity Rowe and her report of his cavalier behaviour, his tantalising remarks about Louise and, finally, his mysterious connection with the Miss Taylors and her fury about his apparently empty promise of seeing her again in church.

'Honestly,' she finished dramatically, quite flushed with the frustration, of her story, 'I've been to the blasted church so often that my parents think I've turned into a religious freak and the vicar is about to enrol me in a nunnery. I know all the hymns off by heart.' She groaned as Katy giggled. 'I know it sounds funny. But it's not. Why did he say it, if he didn't mean it?'

Katy shook her head. 'I don't know,' she said sympathetically. 'All I do know is that it all sounds terrible romantic.'

Louise sighed. 'Do you think so?'

'Oh yes,' Katy said, leaning forward in her chair eagerly. 'All that being the black sheep of his family and everything. And your friend Felicity falling in love with him and being rejected. It's like a story out of a film or something. Or a novel, like *Gone with the Wind*. Yes, that's what it's like. Your Ward Frazer sounds a bit like Rhett Butler.' She wrinkled her nose, puzzled. 'The only thing is, I can't imagine what the Miss Taylors have got to do with a man like that. It sounds most unlikely. I'll have to ask my mother.'

Louise gaped at her. 'Your mother?'

Katy nodded. 'Mummy is quite friendly with the Miss Taylors. They sometimes do the church flowers together.'

Louise groaned. 'The church flowers? Why didn't I think of that? I've been searching desperately for an excuse to talk to the Miss Taylors. We did blasted flower-arranging endlessly at Lucie Clayton's.'

Katy shook her head. 'They'd never let you on to the rota,' she said knowledgeably. 'They guard their positions fiercely. No, I'll get my mother to find out when he's next coming to see them.' Her eyes gleamed. 'And then

I'll let you know.'

'Would you really?' Louise looked at her uncertainly. Most of the girls she knew would make every effort to get hold of a man like Ward Frazer for themselves. Not pass details of his whereabouts to somebody else. But then, let's face it, a man like Ward Frazer was hardly likely to be interested in a sickly, mousy little thing like Katy Parsons, was he?

Katy seemed surprised to be doubted. 'Of course I will. I'll let you know straight away,' she said. She smiled wistfully. 'It might turn out to be a real love story.' Like Jen and Sean Byrne, she thought. It seemed to happen to everyone at the moment. Perhaps it was something to do with the war.

Louise smiled as her hope was renewed by Katy's optimism. 'I think I've fallen in love with him already,' she said dreamily. Normally that was the last thing she would admit to anybody, but somehow it seemed safe with Katy Parsons.

After she had gone, Katy watched her walking briskly away up the street in her fashionable little black felt hat and chequered scarf. It really was no wonder that this mythical, glamorous Canadian was interested in her. Louise Rutherford was the sort of girl any man would be interested in. Like Jen. They were alike in many ways, those two, Katy thought, despite their different backgrounds. They were both pretty and lively and funny. And they both dreamed of bigger and better things than their regular humdrum lives. Not that Louise Rutherford's life was particularly humdrum, of course. With all the parties and concerts she seemed to go to. And all the society friends she had.

She heard the click of Louise's heels change direction and glanced again out of the window in time to see her cross the road to avoid passing too close to Mrs d'Arcy Billière's Jewish refugees who seemed to stand at the corner of the road for hours on end.

They were better dressed today, Katy noticed, but they still had that awful ravaged look about them. She shivered, unable to imagine a quarter of what they had been through and wishing idly she could do something to help them. To help anyone, come to that. She felt wasted sitting here all day long. Even Jen's mother had managed to get herself a job.

Jen had ranted on for hours about her mother cleaning for the Rutherfords. She thought it was demeaning and Katy hadn't liked to say that she thought it was nice for Mrs Carter to have a job. She herself would give anything to have a reason to get out of the flat for a few hours each day. She had tentatively suggested doing a training course with the Red Cross. But her mother wouldn't hear of it, citing the terrible diseases she would certainly catch from contact with ill and injured people.

Hearing voices outside, Katy again glanced out of the window. Louise had disappeared round the corner, but to her horror Katy saw Jen's recently returned brother, Mick, and two or three other boys advancing noisily on the silent Jews. She couldn't hear what they were saying but it didn't take a genius to know it wouldn't be kindly.

She banged on the window but they didn't hear her or didn't care. She tried to open it but the sash cords were stiff. She saw the Jewish boys glance at each other anxiously.

There was only one thing for it. Katy grabbed her mother's coat and ran down the stairs.

Her mother looked up from her mop in amazement as Katy slithered across the wet floor. 'What on earth are you doing?'

'There are some boys teasing the Jews,' Katy gasped and shot out into the street before her mother could find the words to stop her. Wheezing and holding her chest, she half ran, half walked down the road towards the tense little group.

Mick and his pals were standing very close, pushing at the Jews, but the Jews were holding their ground. All six turned to look at her in astonishment as she panted up to them, doubled over and started to cough.

As she got her breath back, she straightened up. She was daunted to find that Jen's brother was inches taller than her. 'Leave them alone,' she said. Her heart was pounding. Her knees shaking.

Mick Carter looked surprised. 'They're Jews,' he explained.

'They're human beings,' Katy said.

There was an astonished moment's pause.

'Oh, is that what they are?' One of the boys said sarcastically and the others giggled inanely. 'They don't seem to be able to speak. Not English, at any rate.' He turned back to the Jews and prodded the smallest one in the chest. 'Do you? Eh? What's the matter? Cat got your tongues?'

Katy saw the dark fear in the young Jewish boy's eyes. And realised they only understood the danger not the words. She looked at the others and saw the emptiness in their faces. The terrible resignation. She felt her blood boil. 'Stop it,' she shouted. 'Just stop it. These people have suffered enough.'

Her hands clenched involuntarily into fists. She glared at the local boys one by one and was glad when they dropped their eyes from hers.

'You should be ashamed of yourselves,' she said weakly.

'They're the ones that should be ashamed,' one of the boys ventured with some remnant of bravado, nodding at the Jews. 'They should have stayed to fight. Not run away.'

Katy stared at him. She thought of the reports of the terrible purge of Jews in Germany this time last year. Kristallnacht they had called it because so much glass had been broken. Jewish homes, businesses and synagogues had been attacked, their windows smashed and many destroyed, 'Oh yes,' she said grimly. 'And how effective do you think the bare hands of homeless children would be against Nazi tanks and guns?'

The boy who had spoken shifted uneasily and glanced at the others. 'I don't know,' he said when neither of the others showed any inclination to speak. 'At least it would have shown guts. We've got more guts than that.'

'Have you?' Katy asked witheringly. 'Guts like trying to beat up some defenceless half-starved refugees? I don't call that guts. I call that pathetic.' She wished her knees weren't shaking so obviously. It was absurd to be scared of fourteen year olds. 'Now clear off and leave these poor people alone.'

For a second they stood there and her heart quailed. Then just as she was wondering what to do or say next, to her immense relief they turned and sloped off, kicking a pile of leaves along the gutter, laughing defiantly as soon as they got a safe distance away.

The Jews watched them go. Then to her astonishment the oldest one turned back to her, clicked his heels slightly and bowed. 'Thank you,' he said in heavily accented English, his eyes dark and surprisingly bold in his thin, pale face.

Katy nodded awkwardly, embarrassed, and smiled faintly and then she turned back the way she had come and stopped in surprise.

Behind her, a few yards back, stood her mother and, incongruously, Mr Lorenz the Jewish pawnbroker.

'Katy, what were you thinking of?' Her mother scolded, rushing forward to steer her back down the street. 'Coming out with no hat or scarf. You'll catch your death. Really, you are a silly thing. I'm sure those boys didn't mean any harm. Boys will be boys, I always say.'

Mr Lorenz stood to one side as they passed. He didn't speak but Katy saw the pain in his eyes and she smiled at him. 'I'm sorry,' she murmured, and flushed, not quite sure what she was apologising for. For the boys perhaps, for the inadequacy of her intervention, for the suffering of his race. Perhaps all three.

He seemed to understand. To her surprise he raised his hat, to her courteously. 'What you did took courage, Miss Parsons, I am grateful for that. It is only courage like yours that will defeat the tyrant in Germany.'

Chapter Ten

'Oi, you! Redhead! Will you bloody concentrate!'

Jerked abruptly out of her reverie, it was a moment before Jen realised the booming command was directed at her. She stared in alarm at the black man at the front of the room.

'Me?'

'Yes, you!' Danny Grey bellowed, waving impatiently at the gramophone girl to stop the music. The other ten dance pupils relaxed their poses.

'Are you with us or not? I'm damned if I'm going to waste my teaching time if you're going to spend the whole lesson dreaming about your boyfriend.'

Someone sniggered. Jen felt herself flushing. She had indeed been thinking about Sean. Reliving the illicit hour they had snatched yesterday lunchtime in Pam Nelson's sitting-room. Remembering the grazing of the Nelsons' rough carpet under her back, the touch of Sean's fingers on her cold skin, on her breasts and on the other secret places that made her hot even now to think about. Recalling, in retrospective horror, the risk of it; anybody could have come to the door and seen them through the window. Her cries of uncontrollable astonished delight would have been enough to make anyone peer in.

'I'm sorry,' she stammered. 'I just lost the rhythm for a moment.'

'That's not all you've lost by the look of you,' the black man commented dryly and Jen gaped at him in horror. Was it that obvious? Could anybody see? She certainly felt different so perhaps she looked different too. After yesterday.

Yesterday was the fourth time Sean had made love to her. After that first time it was for reasons more to do with being scared of losing him than a desire to repeat the process, that she steeled herself to let him do it again a few days later when Pam and Alan had gone up to North London to Pam's mother's birthday.

To Jen's relief, it was a vast improvement. Sean had been in a much better mood and took immense trouble to relax her first. The third occasion, on a pile of autumn leaves behind some bushes out on the common one warmish evening last week, she had even begun to see how it could be thought to be enjoyable.

And then yesterday, for the first time, on Pam Nelson's carpet she nearly exploded with the sudden, overwhelming, bursting sensations that caused her whole body to thrash and writhe for release, and even though she was embarrassed by her wild, involuntary screams as the throbbing release finally came, she was also highly gratified by the smug look on Sean's face afterwards.

'You're a sexy lady, Jennifer Carter,' he said as he buttoned his fly and lit a cigarette. 'To be sure, didn't I know it the first time I clapped my eyes on you? And I wasn't wrong.'

After that, it took her hours to get to sleep when she got home. And then falling into a heavy slumber in the early hours of the morning, she nearly overslept, and only the terror of getting on the wrong side of her dance teacher's acid tongue had dragged her out of bed and into her clothes.

And now her sluggish limbs and distracted manner had drawn her to his attention anyway and she waited to be dismissed from the class. Danny Grey had said right from the start that he expected them to work, and work hard. And anyone that didn't would be out. And as she had used the last of her money to pay for the five-session course, the last thing Jen wanted was to be thrown out.

It had been hard work. By the end of the first session Jen had decided that she had little aptitude for tap dancing. Her feet just didn't seem to hear the music and compared to her teacher's incredible flexibility and light, rattling feet she felt like a retarded baby elephant.

He was advancing towards her now, a glittering look in those strange, dark eyes with the white surrounds. Jen wondered idly what her father would say if he knew she was paying a black man to teach her to dance.

'What's your problem, dahling?' Danny Grey asked smoothly. 'You using up too much of your energies elsewhere?'

Jen shook her head. 'I don't know what you mean,' she said.

He smiled, displaying a set of perfect, very white teeth. One of his hands snaked up to touch the side of her neck and the sniggers in the room grew even louder. 'I mean this, dahling. You got a love bite on you the size of a rose, and as red. And you got black bags under your eyes and we all know what that means.' He chuckled. 'You got to sleep at night if you want to dance by day, dahling.'

Jen wished the floor would open and swallow her whole. A love bite. No wonder they were all laughing at her. If only she hadn't been in such a rush this morning she would have noticed it in the mirror. She could kill Sean. It was obviously his revenge for her teasing him yesterday that one of the boys in the class wanted her to go with him for a coffee.

'I hope you told him you were taken,' Sean said as he slowly undid her buttons. 'Or will I have to come and punch him in the face?'

'Oh, that would be a shame.' Jen remembered giggling nervously. 'You might break his nose and he's quite handsome.'

'Then I'll have to think of some other way of showing him,' Sean had murmured, peeling off her blouse and lowering his head to her neck.

And he clearly had. A highly effective way. Out of the corner of her eye now she could see that the boy who had fancied her wasn't laughing with the rest.

Jen raised her head and looked at the teacher. 'I was concentrating,' she said. 'I was just going through the steps my head, that's all.'

Danny Grey smiled. 'Then perhaps you could now go through them on your feet,' he suggested, waving to the girl who operated the gramophone. 'The rest of us will watch.'

As she self-consciously waited for the music to start, Jen knew he wanted her to flunk it and suddenly she felt her spirit rise. She wasn't going to be intimidated by a studio of laughing students. She wasn't going to be intimidated by a black man. She wasn't going to give him a chance to throw her out. She lifted her chin and smiled straight at him. Sean Byrne thought she was sexy. That was enough to buoy her up. She had overcome her fears about sex. She wasn't a child any more. She was Sean Byrne's girlfriend. Surely to God, she could tap dance as well.

With a big effort she kept up perfectly for the first few bars but then it began to slip away. She could feel it go, feel the giggles starting up again. But she was damned if she was going to stop. For the first time in ages she had an audience, and she was going to perform for them whether they liked it or not. She couldn't do it right so she deliberately began to do it wrong. As she ran on the spot to catch up and yet again failed to get the beat, it became a comedy show.

She began to imitate Danny Grey. Imitation was always her fallback. She knew she was good at it, so she schooled her face to wear his expression, widening her eyes to show the whites and made her legs and arms bend elastically like his and although her feet were well out of step with the music, nothing like the time step he had so laboriously taught them, she was dancing. Albeit more like Charlie Chaplin than Ivor Novello.

And suddenly, as the students realised what she was at, they were laughing with her not at her. She could feel the change and it made her exaggerate even more. She would be thrown out after this for sure, so she might as well go out with a bang.

When the music finally stopped she was panting. To her delight, the students burst into spontaneous applause, the clapping sounding odd in the small studio. Jen hardly dared to glance at Danny Grey. He wasn't clapping. Slowly the applause died away.

And then she saw he was smiling slightly. 'You can't dance to save your life, Miss Carter,' he drawled, 'but you're a natural performer, I'll give you that.'

Jen stared at him, astonished. A natural performer. He thought she was a natural performer. Her pounding heart jumped with excitement. It was a compliment. Who cared about dancing? She wanted to perform. To hold an audience.

She grinned at him. 'Will you write that down?' she asked, and she saw his mouth curve again.

And then, even as he started to laugh, a terrible, shattering explosion sounded outside and the whole building shuddered alarmingly.

For a moment they stood frozen in disbelief. And then they all started talking at once.

'What the …?'

'I didn't hear any planes.'

'Why aren't the sirens going off?'

'Do you think we ought to go to the shelter?'

Jen ran to the window with everyone else. 'You're meant to stand back from windows during bombing,' someone said but no one took any notice.

Jen could see people running down the street towards Piccadilly Circus. Some police were miraculously already there.

She could see them pushing people back. Shouting over loudspeakers. 'Go away. Stand back. There may be more explosions. You're in danger. Clear the area. Stand back please.'

Jen looked up to the sky. It was a cold clear blue November day. There was no sign of any planes. Suddenly they could hear screaming. A terrible heart-chilling sound of pain and fear.

'I bet it's not Hitler,' someone said behind her. 'I bet it's the sodding IRA.'

Joyce hadn't heard the news; she had been hoovering at the Rutherfords' all day. But when Micky announced over tea that three IRA bombs had gone off at Piccadilly earlier, she couldn't help but glance anxiously across at Jen who was sipping her tea somewhat distractedly.

Mick caught the look and frowned. Then his eyes widened and he swung round on Jen, pointing his sandwich at her aggressively. 'You're seeing that Irish bastard at Mrs Nelson's, aren't you? I punched Bill Wiggs on the nose when he suggested it. But he's right, isn't he? You are.'

Jen looked up and her eyes narrowed. She wasn't scared of her younger brother. Joyce thought it was a miracle she had kept it quiet from him for so long. After all, he had been roaming the streets ever since he got back. Him and his little gang of ne'er-do-well friends.

Joyce had been mortified to hear that Katy Parsons had had to stop them baiting Mrs d'Arcy Billière's Jewish refugees. And she suspected they'd been baiting Alan Nelson recently too. He had always been a butt for their jokes, what with his boat and all. The Admiral, they called him, and now he had failed to find war work, they thought the nickname was even funnier.

Certainly Alan had been looking very down last time she'd seen him. What with Pam working so hard and all. It was a shame because he was a nice man, kinder than most and so much in love with his wife. You could see that a mile off.

Just as you could see that Jen was about to fly at Mick's throat. Jen's eyes were glittering dangerously. 'And so what if I am? What's it got to do with you?'

Mick stared at her incredulously, his sandwich hanging in mid-air halfway to his mouth. 'What's it got to do with me? How do you think I'm going to be able to show my face round here if my sister is seeing a Paddy? I'll be a laughing stock.'

'You're a laughing stock in the street already for picking on those Jewish kids,' Jen said scornfully.

'At least I'm patriotic,' Mick said through a mouthful of bread and jam. 'At least I'm not dating an enemy.'

'Ireland is not an enemy. It is neutral,' Jen hissed. 'And as for you, Micky, you are nothing.' Her voice was withering. 'Nothing.' She nodded at Pete who was sitting quietly watching the scene with anxious eyes. 'At least Pete brings in a bit of cash.'

Joyce glanced fondly at Pete. The one thing you could say about Pete was that he wasn't any trouble. He was a bit slow on the uptake, but at least he didn't argue the toss.

Jen stood up and prodded Pete on the shoulder. 'Don't you, Pete?' She turned back to Mick with burning eyes. 'What do you bring in, Mick? Nothing. You're just a bloody nuisance. You always have been. All you do is eat.'

Despite Mick's sullen face, Joyce almost laughed. Jen could hardly have expressed it better. Despite all his big talk, Mick had failed to find an employer prepared to take him on. As she smiled, she realised it was the first time in a long while that she had agreed with her daughter. Although she was tempted to ask Jen exactly what she herself brought in.

'I brought that necklace home,' Mick said defensively, and Jen laughed shortly.

'Oh, brilliant. A string of fake pearls. Dear old Mr Lorenz was frightfully impressed with that, wasn't he, Mum?'

Joyce groaned. She hadn't admitted to Mick that his stolen gift was a fake. That Mr Lorenz had cut clean through one of the pearls with a sharp little knife to prove it to her. She saw the flush of hurt pride on Mick's face and sighed. Why were families so difficult? 'Mick wasn't to know they were fake,' she said placatingly.

Jen turned in the doorway: 'No, Mick wasn't to know,' she mimicked. Then her expression hardened. 'That's not surprising because Mick doesn't know anything. It would be much better for all of us if you sent him back to the country. That's where he belongs. With a bunch of farm animals. Why didn't you like it, Micky? Because they wouldn't let you live in the pig sty?'

She swung on her heel and walked out then and it was as much as Joyce could do to stop Mick from going after her. But surprisingly it was Pete who convinced him.

'Leave her, Micky,' he said. 'It's not worth it. She's like a bear with a sore head today. It's never worth arguing with her when she's in that mood.'

Joyce frowned. It was true. Jen had been more vicious than usual. And she suspected it was all to do with those bombs. She had seemed upset when she first came in this evening. Edgy and preoccupied. And her reaction to Mick's attack had been like that of a cornered tiger. Joyce hoped to God that handsome bugger Sean Byrne wasn't mixed up with the IRA.

'It's never worth arguing with Jen at all,' Mick said crossly. He hacked himself off another slice of bread and waved the knife angrily at the door. 'But I'll show her. Just you wait and see.'

Joyce sighed. She would much rather not wait and see. She would much rather Mick went back to the country. But she couldn't say so. She had made a pact with him that he could stay so long as he didn't let on to anyone about her job at the Rutherfords'. He hadn't like it but she had been tough. Tougher than usual, actually. She'd waved the train ticket in his face and told him she'd get the police to send him back. And eventually he had reluctantly agreed. He'd had to.

And thank God he had. Joyce stood up and began to stack the plates and smiled to herself. Mrs Rutherford had only yesterday asked her tentatively whether she might consider standing in for their cook while she went to visit her family for two nights after Christmas.

Joyce had been unbelievably flattered. Mrs Rutherford trusted her. Trusted her to manage the kitchen. To cook for the whole family. Trusted her not to pinch from their copious supplies of food. She could hardly believe it. She would cook them such a lovely meal that they would wish that that sour old cook of theirs would never come back.

Pam Nelson stood in her kitchen and waited for Sean Byrne to come home.

Nervously she straightened the tea towel, on, its hook and repositioned some cups on the drainer. For the third time she glanced at the clock on the wall. He was late. Sheila would be over with George and Ray before long. She often popped over when Pam got home from work. Pam was happy to see her. She loved the two cherubic little boys, but tonight she wanted to see Sean Byrne first. She looked at her hands and was annoyed to see they were shaking. She was just about to walk up to the hall to check her face in the mirror when she heard his step and the front door opened.

'Mr Byrne. Would you mind coming in here a moment?' Pam called, hoping he couldn't hear the shake in her voice.

He walked slowly down the narrow passage in silence and stood in the doorway. He was smiling slightly but his eyes were wary and Pam's heart twisted.

'Mrs Nelson,' he drawled. 'What can I do for you? You know your word is my command.'

Pam swallowed. Wishing he meant it. But knowing he didn't. He had been acting strangely with her recently. Since she had refused to go to the cinema a month or so ago, in fact. He had been cool with her after that, less inclined to chat.

And to her dismay she had found she missed his company. She would have liked to tell him about her job, some of the funny things that happened in the office. Things she couldn't tell Alan because he never seemed to laugh any more. But she knew Sean would be amused. And she liked to make him laugh. Liked the appreciation in his eyes.

She missed his subtle flattery, and, truth be told, suspected that Jen Carter was the recipient of it now. And more than just flattery too by all accounts.

Pam wished she didn't mind. Wished she could convince herself that it was for the best, but she couldn't. It was burning her up. And the thought that Sean might have made love to Jen Carter here, in her house, made her blood boil. Not that she had any proof. It was only suspicion.

'Mrs Nelson?' Sean's soft innocent voice interrupted her uneasy thoughts. 'What was it you wanted to ask?'

Pam took a quick breath. 'Mr Byrne. Three IRA bombs went off today at Piccadilly Circus.'

Pam wondered if she imagined that his eyes flickered as he inclined his head. Or was she merely becoming paranoid about this as well as everything else?

'I know,' he said calmly. 'I saw the evening paper.'

'Nobody was killed.'

'I saw that too,' he said impassively.

Pam felt sick. It was clear he wasn't going to make this easy for her. 'Did you ...? I mean,' she flushed as his brows rose slightly and looked away. 'You don't have anything to do with that sort of thing, do you?'

There was a long pause. Cautiously Pam raised her eyes. His eyes were hard. Her heart sank.

'Are you asking me if I'm a member of the Irish Republican Army, Mrs Nelson? Is that it?'

Pam shook her head. 'Oh no, I didn't mean that.' She stopped and gritted her teeth. Yes she did. She had got this far, it was stupid to back down now. She had to know. 'It's just that when I was cleaning your room I couldn't help noticing an article you'd cut out of the paper about the four IRA men who were convicted last month.'

'I see.' Sean Byrne took out his cigarettes. As he lit one, he seemed to relax slightly. He blew out a cloud of smoke and frowned. 'I grew up with one of those boys, Mrs Nelson. A childhood friend.' He shrugged his shoulders. 'It will be twenty years now before I see him again. And that's if he doesn't hang for his so-called crime.'

Pam blinked. 'Oh,' she said inadequately. What was it about Sean Byrne that made her feel disloyal? Made her want to throw herself into his arms and ask forgiveness?

'You could always go and visit him in prison, I suppose,' she said tentatively. After all, she knew Joyce Carter went each month to see her son in Brixton and her husband in Reading. Not that she wanted to think of the Carters just now. Or at all, come to that.

Sean laughed shortly. 'If I went to visit him, I'd be branded a terrorist. And even if they didn't trump up some make believe charge for me, I'd certainly be expelled.' He looked up and held her eyes. 'The English are very quick to be suspicious, to jump to conclusions. Don't you think so, Mrs Nelson?' He shrugged as she dropped her eyes in confusion. His voice hardened. 'I'm Irish, so I'm a murderer. Isn't that right? Isn't that what people think?' He drew on his cigarette. 'I thought you were different, Mrs Nelson, more enlightened than most.'

Pam felt stupid. Why had she ever brought the subject up? He was hardly likely to say, 'Yes, Mrs Nelson, you're right, I am a member of the murdering IRA,' was he? Whether he was or not. The truth was that she wanted him to deny it. Wanted him to convince her. So she could carry on liking him. Because she did like him. She liked him a lot.

She looked up and found his eyes on her, blue as ever and piercing right to her soul. 'I thought you trusted me,' he said softly.

She nodded, mesmerised. 'I do.'

He moved across to stub his cigarette out in the sink and stopped beside her. 'Haven't I kept my hands off you, Mrs Nelson? Even though your smile is enough to tempt the very devil himself.'

Pam felt her heart accelerate. Perhaps she was wrong about Jen Carter. Perhaps she had been over suspicious. Perhaps the rug in the front room had moved three feet across the floor of its own accord. 'You have,' she whispered.

The silence in the room seemed suddenly heavy with meaning.

'And is that what you really want, Mrs Nelson?' Sean's voice caressed her skin. 'Or am I right in thinking the devil is prodding at you as well?'

Pam shivered. 'What about Jen Carter?'

Sean's brows rose. 'What about her?'

'You're seeing her, aren't you?'

He smiled slowly. 'A man must take his pleasure where he can, do you not think?' He laughed softly. 'Jennifer Carter is just a girl, Mrs Nelson. Quite a pretty one to be sure. But you're a woman. An experienced married woman, and that is a very different thing altogether. You're off limits to the likes of me, Mrs Nelson, are you not?'

His eyes caught hers and snared them, asking a question.

'I don't know,' she stammered as her body and her mind fought a fierce battle of lust over loyalty. She didn't feel experienced just now. She felt all at sea. Just as she had the first time with Alan all those years ago.

Poor Alan. How could she think of betraying him? He would be devastated if he ever found out. Everything was going wrong for him just now. He had admitted only the other day that Mr Rutherford had given him a hard time over her refusal to take their cleaning job. The job that Mrs Carter now seemed to be enjoying. Mrs Carter, mother of Jen, who was quite clearly enjoying Sean Byrne's favours.

'Tell me what it is you want,' Sean murmured, touching his cool fingertips to her hot cheek.

Pam closed her eyes and then opened them again alarmed as he withdrew his touch.

He shook his head. 'Oh no, Mrs Nelson. That's too easy. I'm not prepared to seduce you. If you want something you must ask me for it.'

Pam stared at him. Saw the curve of his sensual lips, the predatory light in his blue eyes. Her whole body felt as though it was on fire. She could feel her breasts pressing against her thin jersey. She could feel the throb in her groin.

'I want you to kiss me,' she said faintly and swayed towards him as though drunk. 'Just once. Quickly, before Sheila comes over with the children.'

Sean's hands cupped her chin. 'Is that right?' He smiled complacently. 'It's a kiss you want, is it? Well, Mrs Nelson, don't forget it was you who asked me.'

But, as his lips closed on hers, for Pam it was more than a kiss. It was the explosion of a frustration that had been building in her ever since Sean Byrne had first set foot in the house two and a half months ago.

She tried to stop herself from clinging to him, tried to keep it cool, as impersonal as possible, but inside she was lost on a wave of pleasure so intense that she didn't even hear the front door opening, didn't hear the scamper of small feet in the passage. It was only Sean's abrupt withdrawal and low chuckle that brought her back to her sense.

In horror and shame, she raised a hand to her mouth and in doing so caught a small movement by the door.

Heart pounding, she swung round and met the saucer-eyed gaze of little Ray Whitehead.

For a second he stood there in silence, then George spoke behind him.

'Daddy's coming home for Christmas,' he said gruffly, pushing past his younger brother into the kitchen. 'Mummy sent us over to tell you.'

'Oh, good,' Pam said weakly, clutching the kitchen table for support, trying to smile, trying to forget what had just happened, trying to make herself believe that little Ray had not seen what was going on, had not witnessed her disgrace. Trying to convince herself that he was too young to understand. Trying to forget that Sean Byrne was still standing there only inches away from her, apparently amused. Trying not to cry in mortified shame. She gulped. 'That's wonderful news.'

Jen had never anticipated how painful and difficult it would be to be in love. She had stood up for Sean against her mother, against her brother, and yet Sean, when she had challenged him about the IRA bombs at Piccadilly, had refused to stand up for himself.

'You either trust me or you don't,' he had said. And she had tried to.

But then, only days after he'd offhandedly told her she'd be safer to travel by bus for a week or two, a second set of bombs went off at Victoria and King's Cross stations. One man died in that blast and many more were seriously injured.

'You knew, didn't you?' Jen accused him.

'It was obvious,' he said easily sitting on the edge of the bed to do up his shoelaces. 'The IRA aren't going to be satisfied with a couple of pathetic bombs at Piccadilly Circus.' He looked up. 'It's a campaign, don't you see that? They have a cause.'

'What cause?' Jen asked scornfully. 'To murder as many English as possible?'

He shrugged. 'It's as good a way as any to make the English government listen. The Republicans want the English army out of the Six Counties. They want a united and independent Ireland. It's a war, Jennifer Carter, the same as your war against Germany.'

He saw her sceptical expression and leaned forward. 'Ireland is occupied by unwelcome forces. Your forces. Your brave British soldiers. It's no different to Poland. Except the brave soldiers there are German.'

He stopped abruptly and reached for his cigarettes. As he lit up, he rested his eyes thoughtfully on Jen, standing uneasily by the door, and then he shook his head.

'Oh, forget it, sweetheart.' He sat back on the bed and leaned his shoulders against the wall. 'It's not a history lesson you're wanting, is it?' He smiled. 'I have much better things to teach you than that. Come here and kiss me instead.'

Jen frowned. She didn't care about Ireland. Or Poland particularly. But she cared deeply for Sean Byrne. And it infuriated her that he was sometimes so dismissive of her. She didn't even know for sure that he loved her. Once in a café, when she had dared to ask him, he had eyed up some pretty girls at a neighbouring table and wondered in an embarrassingly loud voice whether they would be better pupils than she in his school of love.

Now, as usual, he read her mind. 'I can't love you until I'm sure you trust me,' he said softy.

Jen took a step forward. 'I do trust you,' she said 'But you did tell me not to use the stations, Sean. You even mentioned Victoria specifically.'

He stood up angrily. 'So you don't trust me. For God's sake, girl, I was only trying to make sure you were safe. Would you rather I sent you to your death?' His blue eyes bit into hers. 'I suppose you're just waiting to run to the police. 'My boyfriend knew a bomb was going to go off, Inspector,' he mimicked cruelly. 'I think you should lock him up for twenty years. Or better still, hang him.'

Sudden unexpected tears sprang to Jen's eyes. 'Sean, don't! That's a beastly thing to say. I would never do that.'

He laughed then and lay back on the bed. He waved his cigarette at her, 'Prove it, then. Prove it by taking off your clothes and making me the happiest man in the world.'

Jen gulped back her tears and tried to smile. 'Sean, we can't. Not again. Mrs Nelson will be back any minute. If she caught us she might throw you out.'

Sean shrugged lazily, blew out a cloud of smoke, 'She won't throw me out. She's half in love with me herself.'

Jen took an involuntary step forward. She gaped at him. 'Mrs Nelson is? How do you know?'

He chuckled and leaned forward to unbutton her shirt. 'Sweetheart, I know you're young, but do try not to be naive.'

Jen felt as though someone had stabbed her in the heart. She stilled his hand on her chest with hers. 'Sean,' her voice faltered. 'You wouldn't, would you?'

He glanced at her clutching hand with slightly raised brows and Jen quickly released her grip. He didn't like her denying him access to her body.

To her relief, he looked up at her with a lazy smile. 'Not while you're keeping me happy, Jennifer Carter.'

Sean and Mrs Nelson. Jen thought about nothing else for days. Surely it was impossible. And yet Mrs Nelson was quite a nice-looking woman. But what about Mr Nelson? Stupid man. Why didn't he spend more time at home and less at his stupid boat? On the other hand if you put Alan Nelson up against Sean Byrne it was no contest. Jen bit her lip. No wonder Alan Nelson looked so hangdog these days.

Two days later she was still worrying about it as she despondently climbed Nev Cooper's stairs.

She had called at Nev Cooper's theatrical agency three weeks running and had been told each time he had nothing for her, the same as at a dozen other agencies who now had her letter of introduction.

So she was taken aback when the receptionist said Mr Cooper wanted to see her.

Nervously, she stood in front of his desk, waiting for him to look up.

Finally he did. 'Jennifer Carter, isn't it?'

She nodded.

'I might have something for you.'

'You do?' Her breath caught in her throat.

'So,' Nev Cooper smiled faintly. 'I gather you've taken my advice and learned to dance? You can at least do the time step?'

She nodded eagerly. 'I'm brilliant at it.'

His brows rose. 'That's not what I hear. But Danny says you deserve a break.'

'Danny Grey said that?' Jen was astonished. After that one incident when she had taken the floor in the dance studio, Danny Grey had given her no more attention. To be honest, she was surprised he even knew her name.

Nev Cooper nodded. 'He did.' He looked down at the paper in front of him. 'It's a chorus part. Pantomime. *Cinderella*. Wage two pounds a week. Carlisle. Find your own lodgings.' He looked up. 'You're lucky. They're short because so many girls up there have taken war work. Particularly as that area seems to be seeing most of the action at the moment.'

But Jen was hardly listening. She had waited so long for this moment she wanted to savour every second of it.

She was being offered a job. A job. A real paid job. She thought she was going to explode. And then she stopped. What had he said? Carlisle?

Carlisle? She blinked. Her mind spun. Carlisle was miles away. Right up near Scotland.

It had never occurred to Jen that she would be offered a job outside London. For a second her heart buzzed with excitement. Scotland. She had never been further north than Watford.

And then her face fell. What about Sean? If she went so far away she would lose Sean.

She shook her head, shocked how much she minded about that.

On the other hand she wanted the job badly. Very badly. It was only pantomime but it was a start. A good start.

She felt the pain of indecision. She was torn. Swung, backwards and forwards between love and career.

Nev Cooper was watching her impassively. 'Well?'

Jen looked at him miserably. 'I don't know. I don't think …' She stopped and swallowed. 'Could I have a couple of days to think about it? To ask my er … family.'

He looked at her for a long moment through narrowed eyes then he closed the file. 'I must know by tomorrow morning, Miss Carter,' he said crisply. 'But I must warn you that chances like this do not grow on trees.'

'I understand,' she said.

She understood only too well. And the worst thing was that she was sure if she asked Sean what he thought about it, he would tell her to go.

She was wrong.

'A pantomime job? In the chorus?' Sean stubbed out his cigarette and leaned over the chequered café tablecloth. 'Surely to God, you deserve more than a back row chorus part?'

'It's a start,' Jen said doubtfully. Perhaps he was right. Perhaps she did merit something a bit more than that. 'It's *Cinderella*, though,' she added eagerly. 'That's a popular pantomime.'

Sean took her hand and smiled. 'With your lovely looks you should be Cinderella herself, sweetheart. You don't want to throw yourself away on a nothing part. I think you should wait for something big. Something you'd be proud of.'

'Something you'd be proud of, you mean,' Jen said gruffly. She was torn. With Sean massaging the back of her hand with his thumb like that, the last place in the world she wanted to be was Carlisle. On the other hand she wanted a job. Christmas was coming up and her finances were at rock bottom. Sean was generous about buying coffees and drinks and. cinema tickets but she couldn't rely on him for everything. She could hardly expect him to pay for his own Christmas present.

'I'd be proud of you whatever you did,' he said now. 'You know that. But I just don't think it's worth rushing off all over the bloody country to slog your guts out for a pittance in the back row of a chorus.'

Something in his voice, a slight catch, a faint hesitation, made Jen look up at him sharply. What she saw in his blue eyes made her heart leap in her chest. Suddenly she understood. He didn't want her to go. Not because it was a chorus job, not because it was badly paid, but purely and simply because he didn't want to lose her.

She smiled and reluctantly he smiled back. 'Sean?'

He lit a cigarette. 'What?'

'If I turn it down, will you promise to smile at me every day?'

He laughed and she saw the tension drop from his shoulders. 'When you look at me like that, Jennifer Carter Leigh, I'd be happy to smile at you all day and all night to eternity.'

Katy was beside herself with excitement. She could hardly wait for her mother to go into the other room for her bath, so she could grab her coat and sneak out. Her mother would never let her go out. Not on a dark, drizzly December night like this.

When the moment came, she grabbed the torch with its blue paper shading and crept down the stairs.

Outside it was pitch dark. Her heart was thumping in her chest as she stumbled along the pavement, coughing as the chill damp air got to her lungs.

There was no chink of light anywhere in the street, Mr Rutherford and his team of ARP officials had seen to that over the last couple of months of this odd nonexistent war. Sheila Whitehead had been fined five pounds last week for showing light. And it hadn't been her, it had been the children looking out for their dad. Everyone agreed it was cruelly unfair. Poor Sheila was suffering enough without that. But she'd had to pay up nevertheless. The law was the law, especially in wartime.

Katy could hear the Whitehead children now, shouting with excitement in their shrouded house, probably putting up the Christmas decorations they'd been making all week. Jo Whitehead was expected back any day now. For Christmas. Everyone knew. The children had told everyone they saw. There was a whisper that he had applied for compassionate leave as Sheila was coping so badly in his absence.

Katy swallowed nervously as she crept past, following the eerie blue beam of her torch. It was going to be a strange Christmas this year. And everyone was saying that Hitler was saving his bombs for when everyone was relaxed at home for the festivities.

She passed the Miss Taylors' house, or at least she thought it was. It was difficult to see where you were in the blackout. And she felt a tremor of anticipation. Louise was going to be so pleased when she heard the news.

And then she was at the corner and the great, black common loomed empty ahead of her. You couldn't see the anti-aircraft guns from here, not at night. And there were no barrage balloons up tonight, perhaps due to the low cloud.

Katy shivered and swung the eerie blue beam of her torch. Two cars were parked outside Mrs d'Arcy Billière's house and it sounded as though festivities were going on in there too. She could hear music, the faint strains of *South of the Border, Down Mexico Way*, and laughing and the chink of glasses.

The Rutherfords' house was silent. Katy stared up at the imposing dark facade and wondered how on earth much blackout material they had needed to cover all those windows. As she rang the electric bell on the front door, she heard a rustle in the bushes behind her and jumped in alarm. Swinging round, she thought she saw a shadow flit round the corner of the large house. But before she could catch it with her torch, the front door opened and one of Louise's brothers peered out into the darkness.

'It's Katy Parsons,' Katy said nervously. 'Is Louise in?'

'I'll just get her for you.'

A moment later Louise was at the door. Katy hardly waited for her greeting. 'Louise!' she whispered. 'Listen, Ward Frazer is coming to see the Miss Taylors tonight. They told my mother this morning. But I haven't been able to get away until now.'

Even as she spoke they heard a distant car, Louise clutched her arm. 'That might be him now. Wait, I'll get a coat.'

A few seconds later, they stood on the corner giggling. They saw the dim lights of a car approaching up Lavender Road. Sure enough it pulled up outside the Miss Taylors'.

Creeping closer, they heard the slam of the door. They saw the shadowed outline of a tall broad-shouldered man. Heard the mild muttered oath as the gate impeded his entry. Then a firm knock on the Taylors' door. Then the older Miss Taylor's distinctive call of enquiry from within.

And then his voice, loud in the silent street, that deep, warm, slightly accented, very male voice Louise remembered so well.

'It's Ward, Aunt Esme. I hope you're expecting me ...?'

The girls clutched each other and then nearly jumped out of their skins as, without warning, another car started up noisily behind them. One of Mrs d'Arcy Billière's guests was leaving. The car swung into Lavender Road, passing them quite fast, its engine drowning out the rest of Ward Frazer's words.

And then suddenly everything went wrong.

The door of the Whitehead house flew open, spilling sudden yellow light into the street. And the two children darted out with a shout of, 'Daddy!'

Louise and Katy saw Ward Frazer swing round sharply. Saw the look of surprise on his handsome face turn to horror. Saw him turn back and struggle frantically with the gate. Saw him vault the wall and lunge forward. Saw the brief silhouette of a child in the road, caught in the dimmed headlight of the oncoming car.

And then they heard the frightful screech of brakes, the dull thump, the child's cry lost in the shadows. And as one they began to run down the street.

Chapter Eleven

As the girls ran up, the engine died and with it the headlights. The sudden dark silence was startling.

Katy played her torch around frantically. Ward Frazer was there, alive, leaning against the Nelsons' wall on the other side of the road. The older child, George, was in his arms, struggling for release. For a split second Katy's blue beam caught a glimpse of the Canadian's handsome face as he reluctantly lowered the child to the ground, heard his hiss of exhaled breath and her heart jolted involuntarily. Then she spun the beam on. Where was the other child? She was certain both had run out.

And then suddenly she saw it.

There, some way ahead, half in the gutter, was something she had at first thought to be some street rubbish, some old clothes, a discarded rag doll. Trying to keep the torch steady in her shaking hand, Katy took a few hesitant steps towards it and heard Louise's shocked scream behind her.

'Oh my God,' Katy whispered to herself, running forward and crouching down. The child must have taken the full impact of the car's big bumper to be flung so far. And yet the little cherubic face was undamaged, the eyes closed. With trembling fingers, wishing her mother had let her do the Red Cross course, Katy felt the tiny limp wrist for a pulse.

She leaned over to see if she could feel breath from his mouth and as she did so she noticed a stain on the road beside her and stared at it for a second before realising what it was. Blood. Purple in the blue light of the torch. Carefully, instinctively gentle, kneeling now, she edged forward to cradle the child's head in her lap.

Behind her she could hear voices, people stumbling out into the dark street, some muffled questions. The current hit song, *Run, Rabbit, Run*, blasted out of someone's open front door. Angry voices. A child crying. Louise's distant panic-stricken voice.

'We need an ambulance,' Katy shouted urgently. 'Can somebody get an ambulance?'

'Someone's gone to telephone.' The voice approaching her was steady and faintly accented. Katy looked up but could only see the outline of Ward Frazer's body.

He crouched beside her in the blue darkness. 'How is he?'

Katy groped for the torch and shone it on the child's face. It cast a ghostly light on the small angelic features and she quickly turned it off. She wished someone would turn off the music too.

'I don't know,' she stammered into the sudden darkness. 'There's a pulse but it's very faint.' Already she could feel the dampness on her legs and knew the child was bleeding profusely.

Silently, in horror, wishing she was anywhere but here, she slid her hand under Ray's little head, feeling for the wound, tried to hold the pumping blood back, trying to save his life. 'I think he might have fractured his skull,' she said shakily. 'Or broken his neck. I daren't move him, but it's so cold for him here.'

'Are you a nurse?' Ward asked crisply.

Katy shook her head and then realised he couldn't see her. 'No,' she said. 'I'm not. I wish I was. I wish I knew what to do. I'm trying to hold the wound closed, b-but he's bleeding so badly.'

Just for a second she felt Ward Frazer's hand on her shoulder. 'You're doing just fine,' he said. Then he shrugged off his jacket and laid it carefully over the inert little body, apparently uncaring of the dirt and blood. 'The ambulance will be here in a moment. Somebody's gone in to tell the mother. Poor woman was taking a bath.'

'What about the driver of the car?' Katy asked quickly, scared he would leave her. Scared he would leave her alone with the dying child and the jarring refrain of *Run, Rabbit, Run, Rabbit, Run, Run, Run*. The other voices seemed a long way away and nowhere near as calm as his. 'Is he all right?'

'It was him I sent to phone for the ambulance,' Ward said. 'It's better he stays out of the way. People can get quite nasty in situations like this. Particularly as he's foreign. Polish, I think.' Katy heard him shift his weight slightly. Heard him draw a sharp breath. 'It wasn't his fault, poor guy. Those children must have run out right in front of him.'

'I know,' Katy said. 'I saw them.'

He was silent for a moment then he swore softly. 'I should have seen there were two of them,' he said bitterly. 'I thought there was only one.'

Katy blinked, wishing she could see his face. 'Don't be ridiculous,' she said angrily. 'It's not your fault. You saved the other child.'

She hated the thought that he blamed himself. She saw again his split-second reaction, the image of him throwing himself in front of the car. Heard again the sickening thump. 'It was nobody's fault,' she said firmly.

'Oh yes it was,' he said quietly as he got to his feet. 'It was Adolf Hitler's fault.' He was speaking almost to himself and Katy blinked in surprise at the ice-cold tone of his words. Nobody liked Adolf Hitler. But the Canadian's voice had held more than the usual scornful hatred of the enemy. It was more like a bitter, private anger. As though Hitler had caused him some personal tragedy.

She shivered. But when he spoke again, his voice was steady with that faint but appealing accent and Katy wondered if she had imagined that dangerous, bitter edge to his previous comment.

'How is he now?' he asked. 'Is there still a pulse?'

She reached for the tiny wrist. Her eyes were more accustomed to the darkness now. 'Just. But it's awfully faint.' She shivered again, convulsively, coughed, clamped her teeth to stop them rattling and prayed she wouldn't cry.

He leaned down to touch her cheek briefly with the backs of his fingers. 'You're freezing,' he said abruptly. 'You should have said. I'll get you a blanket. Can I borrow your torch?'

Silently she handed it to him. She didn't want him to leave her. His voice reassured her, took away some of the horror, and his brief touch had strangely warmed her. Without him she thought she might break down. But he took the torch and strode away, ripping off the blue tissue impatiently, leaving her in darkness.

Almost at once she heard Mr Rutherford's furious bellow from the far end of the street. 'What's going on? Put that light out. Don't you know there's a war on?'

And Ward's steady, undaunted reply. 'I'm afraid it's an emergency, sir. There's been an accident. A child's been hurt. We need all the light we can get.'

And then a scream. Sheila Whitehead's scream. And running feet and urgent voices. And Katy swallowed hard and tried to ignore the sticky dampness oozing between her fingers.

From then on everything seemed to move as in a hazy dream. A nightmare. There were people suddenly crowding round. Hushed voices. Loud voices. A police car. Torches.

A voice telling everyone to stand back, which only belatedly she realised was hers. Sheila Whitehead's terrible, choking sobs as she fell on her broken child. Pam Nelson's stricken face, white as a ghost, as she crouched with Sheila. Ward Frazer wrapping a blanket round her shoulders. Ward Frazer saying the ambulance was on its way. Ward Frazer quietly telling the policeman that it wasn't the driver's fault. Ward Frazer crouching by little forgotten George, trying to calm his agonised sobbing.

And then the ambulance came.

Two brisk, overalled men slid Ray's little body on to an enormous stretcher. Pam and Sheila went in the ambulance van too with George, who Sheila at the last minute refused to leave behind even though he was on the point of hysterical collapse.

And then suddenly it was all over.

Katy stood up stiffly and blinked. Somewhere along the line, the mocking melody of, *Run, Rabbit, Run*, had given way to the poignant *Love Never Grows Old*.

And even as unwanted tears sprang to her eyes, someone was trying to pull her away. Her father.

'Katy, whatever are you doing? I thought you were in the flat. You'll catch your death ...'

And her mother's scream. 'You're all covered in blood. Are you hurt?'

And Katy pushing her away. 'It's not my blood,' she muttered, as people turned to stare. People were still milling about, perhaps reluctant to leave the scene of such excitement. Katy could hear the Rutherford boys' plummy voices. Mrs Rutherford was saying something about the Wilhelmina Hospital to Alan Nelson. The Miss Taylors were there, twittering anxiously. The policeman and Mr Rutherford appeared to be measuring the road.

Someone's torch beam fell on Ward Frazer as he bent to pick up his bloodstained coat from the pavement. As he straightened up again, Katy saw at once that there was something wrong. His breathing was shallow. He looked in pain.

She stumbled forward to touch his arm. 'Are you all right?'

He glanced in her direction distractedly, but his face was in shadow again. Her torch was still in his hand. She didn't like to ask for it back.

'I'm fine,' he said. But for the first time his voice was shaky. The torch beam wavered on the ground as though he was in too much pain to control it.

Katy felt sick. 'The car hit you too, didn't it?'

He shrugged and winced. 'It only touched me. Nothing serious.'

'You should have gone to hospital.'

He shook his head. 'It's nothing, maybe a couple of bruised ribs, that's all.' He glanced about vaguely, frowning. And then suddenly a door closed and the haunting strains of *Love Never Grows Old*, were silenced abruptly, leaving another sound behind them. The sound of tears. Someone was sobbing quietly nearby.

Ward took a step towards the noise, raised the torch and caught Louise Rutherford in the beam.

'Louise?'

She was sitting on the Nelsons' wall with her face in her hands.

Katy watched in silence as Ward strode forward and pulled the other girl into his arms, saw the beam of the torch jump, saw the fleeting pain on his handsome face as Louise clung to his bruised chest, the involuntary clench of his jaw as he tried to hold the bloody jacket away from her clothes.

'It's all over,' he said gently, smoothing Louise's sleek dark hair. 'It's over now. Let me take you home.'

For a second Katy stood numbly, watching him lead her away, his arm round her slender shoulders. What about me? She wanted to shout. I'm upset too.

But even as her heart twisted painfully in her chest, and her lungs constricted, she held her tongue. It was Louise he was interested in. Pretty, sophisticated Louise Rutherford. It was quite understandable.

Slowly Katy turned away, the blood congealing on her hands. And then her mother grasped her arm and dragged her away.

Cedars House seemed deserted as Ward Frazer escorted Louise up the drive and she glanced about, surprised to find the front door was wide open and the hall light was on spilling out on to the drive. Her parents and brothers must have heard the crash and rushed straight out with no thought to the blackout.

'They must all be still out on the street,' Louise said, walking across the spacious panelled hall and pushing open the drawing-room door.

Now she was away from the scene of the accident and alone finally with Ward Frazer, she felt decidedly better. Until that moment, a few minutes ago, when he had held her in his arms, she had felt left out, useless and sick. He had seemed far more interested in Katy Parsons than her. OK, so Katy had been holding the injured child and everything, but Louise felt that Ward could at least have acknowledged her presence. He could have comforted her a bit earlier. Instead of talking to Katy all the time. After all, it had been very upsetting.

She pulled off her gloves and smiled as he helped her off with her coat. He was very well mannered. She liked that. She liked him. She liked him a lot and just looking at him made her heart beat fasten She smiled again and nearly melted when he smiled back. She had forgotten the devastating effect of his smile. In all the dreams she had had about this man, in all the mental re-runs of their brief encounters, she had failed to recall the way her knees went weak when he smiled.

She took a nervous jerky step back and would have fallen if he hadn't stepped forward quickly to support her.

'You'd better sit down,' he said, leading her into the drawing-room and seating her in an armchair. Striding to the fireplace, he kicked some life into the dull fire in the grate, threw on a couple of logs, then glanced around and located her father's drinks cabinet. Before Louise could speak, he had opened it up with an easy familiarity, selected a couple of glasses and poured out two generous brandies.

He handed her one and smiled at her wide-eyed look. 'Medicinal,' he said and, raising his glass in a wry toast, took a good slug.

Louise watched him swallow, watched the movement in the strong column of his throat as he tipped back his head, watched the satisfied curve of his lips as he drank again and lowered his glass.

Flushing as his eyes fell on her with a faintly quizzical expression, she quickly gulped from her own glass and nearly choked as the fiery liquid scorched down her gullet.

He raised his dark eyebrows. 'That's put some colour back in your cheeks.'

Louise suddenly felt very gauche and unsophisticated. She hated the amusement in his eyes, hated him to see her at anything other than her best. She wished dearly she could check her appearance in the mirror. She was certain her face was unattractively tear stained, and she hadn't powdered her nose or done her hair in hours.

But it was Ward Frazer who moved towards the large ornate mirror over the mantelpiece. He threw her a wry glance over his shoulder. 'Would you mind averting your eyes for a moment?'

Louise blinked in surprise. 'Of course, but ...'

Before she had a chance to look away he had untucked his shirt from his trousers and was pulling it up over his chest, half unbuttoning it as he went.

Louise stared in numb amazement feeling suddenly hot and cold. What on earth was he doing? Surely he wasn't going to strip off there and then and jump on her, was he? She had heard about his reputation, and admittedly she was pretty keen on him, but this was ridiculous. In any case, her parents would be back at any moment.

Abruptly she stood up and then stopped in horror. He wore no vest. She could already see his smooth, tanned, muscular lower back, but now she was on her feet she could see reflected in the mirror the unnerving image of his bare chest and side.

And across the base of his ribs on the right hand side was a wide congealing graze. And behind it a dull, dangerous-looking, red and black bruise. As Ward prodded it tentatively with his other hand, Louise gasped and sat abruptly back in her chair, feeling sick.

He grinned round at her. 'I told you not to look.'

'I ... I couldn't help it,' she admitted and then kicked herself as his brows rose in amusement. Recovering quickly, determined not to appear unsophisticated, she smiled coyly and crossed her legs. 'I'm not used to thoroughly handsome men suddenly stripping off in my parents' drawing-room,' she said.

'No?' He chuckled appreciatively as he tucked in his shirt. And there was something unconsciously alluring about the way he smoothed it down carefully under his belt. He was still smiling when he looked up. 'Does that imply that you are used to thoroughly handsome men stripping off in other locations?'

Louise gulped. 'No, ... I mean ... yes.' She stopped abruptly and swallowed.

What did he want to hear? Would he prefer her innocent or experienced?

She glanced up at his strong handsome face and caught the thoughtful expression in his steady grey eyes. It was impossible to tell. All she knew was that she would admit to anything if it would make him like her. More than anything, she wanted him to like her. She took a sharp breath and a sip of her brandy, choked again, and was still coughing when her parents walked into the room.

Had she not been so flustered, Louise would have been amused by her father's three shocked, disapproving glances: one to the brandy, one to the handsome stranger and one to the now blazing fire.

Even though he owned a brewery, her father was not a great drinker, nor a particularly generous host. His measures were notoriously small and slow in coming. Her brothers always joked that nobody ever got drunk in Cedars House.

Nor was he much of a one for stoking the fire, believing that two pieces of coal smouldering in the grate were quite enough. He was always going on about people getting soft and consequently the house was always freezing. And as for a tall, somewhat dishevelled, stranger standing over his flushed daughter, intimately patting her on the back, it was a wonder he didn't have a heart attack on the spot.

It was Ward who stepped smoothly into the astonished silence, apologising that there had been no time for introductions out on the street earlier, introducing himself as some kind of distant nephew of the Miss Taylors and explaining that he had met Louise once before.

'I'm sorry about the brandy, sir,' he said easily, once the appropriate handshakes had taken place. 'But Louise was very shaken and I thought it might be the best remedy.'

Everyone looked at Louise and she smiled weakly. She was shaken, but not for the reasons her parents assumed. She was shaken by her reaction to Ward Frazer. By her strange longing to feel the texture of his bare skin, by her crazy desire to rip off her clothes and throw herself into his strong muscular arms.

'Yes of course, quite the best thing,' her father was saying, rallying to the unexpected raid on his drinks cabinet. Clearly the presence of the hero of the hour in his drawing-room had a mellowing effect,

'Terrible thing. Terrible accident. Not at all the thing for ladies.' He glanced at Celia who was standing beside him. 'A sip of brandy might steady you too,' he suggested gallantly.

Celia blinked at him in surprise. 'No, no. I'm quite all right, thank you,' she said and glanced at the grandfather clock in the corner. 'Actually we really ought to get ready, Greville. We're due at the Perrys' at eight.'

Louise suddenly remembered that her parents were going out to dinner

131

and her mind raced. 'Could Mr Frazer stay to supper here?' she asked eagerly.

'Well, I don't know,' Celia started with an uneasy glance at her husband. But she was saved a reply by Ward's polite interruption.

'I'm afraid my aunts will have prepared something for me,' he said. 'I can't let them down.'

Louise bit her lip. 'What about tomorrow? Tomorrow would be all right, wouldn't it, Mummy?' Her parents would be there tomorrow but it was better than nothing and she had this awful feeling that Ward Frazer was about to walk out of her life with no further meeting arranged and then she would spend another few weeks of agony wondering if he would contact her again.

'Don't be pushy, Louise,' Celia said gently. 'I'm sure Mr Frazer has other plans for tomorrow.'

They both glanced at Ward who inclined his head. 'I'm afraid I have,' he said with polite regret.

Louise felt the situation slipping away from her. 'He was injured,' she said suddenly. 'In the accident.'

'Oh dear.' Her mother eyed him with some concern as if wondering exactly which portion of his anatomy was damaged, and not quite liking to ask. 'Is there anything we can do for you, Mr Frazer?'

Ward shook his head. 'No, it's nothing,' he said, patting his side and wincing involuntarily. 'Just a scratch.'

Louise frowned. The painful bruised gash she had seen could hardly be described as a scratch. It made her sick to think of it. She caught his eyes on her and smiled weakly.

He smiled back thoughtfully then turned back to her parents. 'Next weekend I have been invited to a charity Christmas carol concert. I wondered if I might ask Louise to accompany me?'

Louise stared at him. And then at her parents. She could see they were dismayed. She wasn't as a rule allowed to go out with anyone they didn't know and approve of. And certainly not alone with a strange man. But you could hardly find anything more innocuous than a carol concert. A charity carol concert. And Ward Frazer was a relation of the respectable, if somewhat infuriating, Miss Taylors. And he was the hero of the hour. And he was injured.

'Well … providing it isn't too late and that you see her home.' Her father nodded reluctantly.

'Oh, it won't be late. Certainly not later than midnight,' Ward said easily and Louise nearly burst out laughing. Midnight! She was never allowed to stay out until midnight. Not unless it was a ball or something formal.

She waited for her parents to object but before they could Ward spread his hands courteously. 'Please, don't let me delay you. Louise can see me out.' He shook hands again with Greville Rutherford. 'Thank you for your hospitality, sir.' He raised his glass slightly. 'I'll just finish the brandy and then I'll be on my way.'

'Yes, yes, of course,' Greville blustered as the wind was firmly taken out of his sails. 'A pleasure.' He glanced back uneasily from the door as Ward bade farewell to his wife. 'Well, we'll just be upstairs if you need us, Louise. And the boys will be back in a moment.'

As her parents departed, Louise glanced round at Ward with sparkling eyes. 'I think they're worried about leaving me alone with you,' she said breathlessly. He had asked her out. OK, only to a carol concert, but it was a start. It must mean he liked her. A bit. She prayed her parents' stupid over-protectiveness wouldn't have put him off. 'They must have heard of your reputation,' she added.

He looked surprised. 'What reputation is that?'

'Well,' Louise giggled and lowered her eyes coyly, 'Everyone says you are a bit of a heart-breaker.'

'Do they?' he said and she looked up. He sounded amused. But behind the smile his expression seemed to harden fractionally. Then he shrugged easily and Louise wondered if she had imagined it.

'Maybe they're right,' he said. He finished his brandy and smiled again. 'I don't mean to be. It's just that English girls seem to fall in love so easily. I guess they're disappointed when I don't fall in love with them.'

So that was it. He wasn't in love with Felicity Rowe. No wonder the pretty blonde had been so full of sour grapes about him when they'd met in Harrods.

'What, never?' she asked flirtatiously. 'Never ever?'

This time he didn't smile. 'Never,' he said.

It sounded horribly like a warning. Louise ignored it. You will with me, she said to herself. Just you wait and see.

He shook his head and set down his glass on a side table, 'I must go.'

In the hall, he took her hand and raised it to his lips. 'So, Louise Rutherford. Will you come with me to the carols?' He grinned over her hand and lowered his voice. 'There'll be a bit of a party afterwards.'

Louise's eyes widened. So he had fooled her father. Deliberately. She could hardly speak for excitement. 'Yes, of course I will,' she said.

'I'll come and fetch you around six thirty.'

She smiled at him as he picked up his bloodied jacket. 'I can't wait.'

He laughed. 'I'm afraid you'll have to.' Then he stopped as he caught sight of the torch lying on the chair and frowned. 'This torch belongs to that other girl.' He looked at Louise. 'Who was that? Katy somebody, was it?' He shook his head. 'She did a good job out there. If that poor child lives, it's only due to her.'

Louise frowned. All Katy had done was sit by the child until the ambulance came. Surely that wasn't much to write home about.

'It was Katy Parsons,' she said. 'She's a funny little thing. Asthmatic and really shy. Her father runs the pub. The Flag and Garter down the road. It's one of my father's pubs.' She dropped her eyes deprecatingly. 'Daddy owns the local brewery.'

He nodded, not quite as impressed as she had hoped, his mind apparently still on Katy. 'The Flag and Garter, was it? I'll drop the torch off there, then.'

'Oh, don't worry about that,' Louise said quickly. 'I'll give it back to her tomorrow.' She turned off the main hall light and opened the front door. Blackout precautions had become second nature after four months of her father's nagging. She peered out of the door and shivered. 'Unless you need it now.'

He shook his head. 'No, I don't need it. I have good night vision.'

'That must be useful in your job,' Louise said and he looked surprised. 'For night flying,' she said. Perhaps he didn't know that she knew he was a pilot.

'Oh yes,' he agreed and smiled a slightly strange smile. 'It's useful for that.'

And then he touched her lightly, fleetingly, on the hand and was gone into the darkness.

She was about to shut the door when she saw the dim, bobbing torches of her brothers at the gate. She saw them illuminate Ward Frazer with the eerie blue glow, heard his casual Canadian greeting, 'Hi,' heard the surprise in their voices as they replied.

And then behind her, her mother's voice.

'Louise, darling, have you seen my diamond brooch?'

Louise turned back into the house and blinked. She shook her head dreamily. 'No. You were wearing it the other day. You said the catch was faulty.'

'I know. Mrs Carter noticed it was undone. Oh dear. I do hope it hasn't fallen off somewhere.'

'You can borrow mine if you want,' Louise said. Her grandmother had left her a pretty diamond brooch when she died, together with some money she would get when she was twenty-five. It seemed a long time to wait. But at least she had the brooch. 'I'll get it for you.'

She ran upstairs, glad to have a moment to recover before facing the boys' questioning. She could hear them coming into the hall now, knew they had recognised the visitor from that time in church and knew she was in for an evening of teasing and schoolboy humour.

She went to her dressing table and stared at herself in the mirror. Her eyes were sparkling like the diamonds she had come to find. I'm in love, she said to herself. In love. With the most handsome, most wonderful man in the world.

She heard her mother's voice on the landing and glanced quickly about for the brooch. She usually left it just by the mirror. It wasn't there. She opened her jewellery case and frowned. It wasn't there either. Nor was the pretty gold bracelet she had been given by her parents for her seventeenth birthday. And yet her pearl necklace was there, lying alone on the red velvet.

'Mr Frazer seemed very nice,' Celia said behind her. 'When was it you met him before? At the Veales', was it? You didn't mention it.' She folded one of Louise's jerseys and put it in the cupboard. 'Did you know he knew the Miss Taylors then?'

'I saw him in church with them once,' Louise said distractedly, pushing things about on her dressing table. She looked round worriedly. 'Mummy, I can't find my brooch. Or my gold bracelet.'

Celia stopped and stared at her. She looked unusually stern. 'When did you last see them?'

Louise bit her lip. 'Yesterday. I wore them at supper.' She shivered. 'Please don't tell Daddy I've lost them.'

Her father was a tyrant where losing things was concerned. Being utterly meticulous and ordered in his own life he was fiercely intolerant of other people's mistakes. And if it happened to be something precious that was lost or broken, his anger was even more virulent. Louise had been once confined to the house for a week for breaking a vase in the drawing-room while trying to swat a fly. She dreaded to think what the punishment would be for losing a diamond brooch. If he stopped her going out with Ward Frazer she would die. Tears sprang to her eyes.

Celia put a reassuring hand on her shoulder. 'I don't think you've lost them, darling.' Her voice was oddly stiff, reluctant. 'I think they've been stolen.'

Louise gaped at her. 'Stolen.' She stood up abruptly and looked around as though a posse of jewel thieves were even at that moment lurking under the bed. 'But when? Who?'

Celia looked uneasy. 'I don't know. But your father has just been shouting about some money missing from his desk drawer. What with your brooch and mine, it's too much of a coincidence.'

'But when?' Louise said. 'How could anyone get in? There are no broken windows or anything, are there?' She stopped and breathed quickly. 'Unless it was someone who was inside already. Who's been in the house recently? Cook? It wouldn't be her, she's been with us for years. The plumber? But you were with him all the time. And Mrs Carter was here anyway.'

She stopped and stared at her mother. 'Mrs Carter,' she repeated slowly and watched her mother go pale. 'You think it's Mrs Carter, don't you, Mummy?'

Celia shook her head. 'I don't think anything, Louise. I don't know. I hope not.' She sighed. 'I really hope not.'

When Jen discovered that Sean was going back to Ireland for Christmas, she was furious.

'I wish I'd gone to Carlisle now,' she snapped, hoping she wasn't going to cry. She had looked forward so much to sharing the festivities with him. And now she was going to have to struggle through it on her own, jobless and broke.

Not that Christmas was going to be particularly festive this year, of course. Not with the war and all. There were no illuminations in the West End, no lights anywhere come to that.

Christmas was never anything much in the Carter household at the best of times. But it would be worse than ever this year. Her mother hadn't even bothered to get a tree in with the younger kids still being away and she'd said only yesterday that a turkey was out of the question.

Jen glared at him through tear-filled eyes. 'I only turned down that job because of you, and now you're buggering off without me.'

'It's only a couple of weeks,' Sean said, reaching forward to take her hands. 'And I'll be thinking of you every day.' He smiled as he pulled her slowly towards him. 'And every night.'

They made up of course, Sean had only had to kiss her these days to bring her round. Anyway he was clearly going to Ireland whether she liked it or not and she didn't want to put him off her in case he never came back, or worse, came back with a nice little Irish girl in tow. Terrified of losing him, she tried to be especially nice. She even gave him one of her precious photographs to take with him.

He was nice back. His last evening, the evening of the crash, he took her to a jitterbug contest at the Grand, Clapham Junction. They weren't placed, Sean wasn't much of a dancer and Jen kept getting the giggles, but they enjoyed the opportunity to touch each other in public.

The following morning, when he called to say goodbye, Sean presented her with two parcels: one large one, a box tied with string, which was something he wanted her to keep for him while he was away, and one small one, Christmas wrapped, which was her present.

'What is it?' she asked, eagerly fingering the smaller package.

He smiled. 'Now do you really think I'd be telling you that?'

Jen wrinkled her nose. 'Well, what's in there, then?' she said looking at the larger one.

'Just a few clothes,' he replied.

'Why can't you leave them at the Nelsons'?' she asked and he frowned.

'If you don't want to keep it for me, just say and I'll find someone else who will.'

Jen shook her head quickly. She hated it when he suddenly froze on her like that. 'Of course I don't mind. I was just wondering, that's all.'

Sean's blue eyes narrowed. 'You're just wondering if it's full of gelignite and alarm clocks, aren't you?'

'No, I was not wondering that,' Jen said crossly. 'I was just wondering why you make everything a secret and wishing you would come straight out with the truth for once.'

He smiled. He liked it when she was cross. He ran his hand round the back of her neck and pulled her towards him. 'I'm not sure if you're ready for the truth, Jennifer Carter,' he murmured against her lips. 'Because you still don't trust me. If the police came to the door now looking for IRA sympathisers, you'd hand me over without a backward glance.'

'I would not,' she said hotly, flushing as shivers of desire coursed down her spine. 'Honestly, Sean, I wouldn't.' Not if he carried on kissing her like that.

'Good. Then stop wasting time asking questions,' he said, easing her shirt over her shoulders and nipping her neck with his teeth. 'And tell me instead what it is you've bought me for Christmas.'

Jen pulled away. She didn't want another love bite. In any case her mother was in the kitchen, 'I'm not telling you if you won't tell me!' she said sulkily. And then cried in alarm as he caught her arm and tumbled her on to the bed. She stared up defiantly into his blue eyes and giggled. 'You'll just have to wait and see, won't you?' As she wriggled away she caught sight of the clock and her eyes widened. 'Sean, you'd better rush or you'll miss your train.'

The truth was she had agonised for hours over what to get Sean. Katy had suggested socks or some fancy shaving soap, apparently that was what her mother usually gave her father. But Jen wanted something more personal than that and had finally plumped for some silver cufflinks she had seen in Lorenz's 'unredeemed' window which, although they weren't new, were very elegant and. had the added advantage of already being engraved with a swirly S.

Mr Lorenz had seemed surprised to see her in the shop. And even more surprised by the item she had chosen to buy. But then she realised that he assumed they were for her father and laughed inwardly. No wonder he was surprised. Cufflinks wouldn't be much use to a man in prison, would they?

'They're for my boyfriend,' she said as she handed over the money.

'I see.' Mr Lorenz nodded his head gravely as he counted it carefully. 'A generous gift.'

It was indeed a generous present, she'd had to borrow the money off Katy Parsons, but she wanted to get Sean something he would like, something he would remember her by when he was in Ireland with all those pretty Irish girls. And she would pay Katy back as soon as she got work.

She watched Mr Lorenz wrap the cufflinks in cotton wool and slide them in a small brown envelope. 'I haven't seen your mother recently,' he remarked abruptly as he handed the package over the counter. 'Not to talk to.'

Jen blinked. Lorenz didn't usually enter into conversation with his customers, as far as she knew. And she could hardly imagine him passing the time of day with her mother. What on earth would they talk about? The price of diamonds?

'Well, she hasn't had call to come in, I suppose,' she said awkwardly. 'What with my dad being inside and all.'

'Of course.' Lorenz nodded and brushed a speck of cotton wool off his counter. Then he stroked his neat beard and looked up at Jen through his wire-rimmed glasses. 'It must be hard for her without him. Is she managing all right?'

Jen was surprised by the question. What would old Lorenz care if they managed or not? She felt like telling him to mind his own business but something in his eyes made her hesitate.

'She's got a job now,' she said gruffly. 'A couple of days a week. I think she's OK.'

To be perfectly honest it hadn't occurred to Jen that her mother might not be OK. That she might miss Stanley. Or be finding things hard without him. If Jen was in her shoes she would be thanking her lucky stars that he'd got nicked. Stupid bugger. Jen had no time for her father. And it annoyed her that her mother took so much stick from him when he was there.

She glanced at Lorenz now and shrugged indifferently. 'I don't know if she misses Dad or not. Personally, I reckon we're all better off without him.'

Mr Lorenz hadn't commented one way or the other. He had merely inclined his head. 'Perhaps you would be kind enough to convey my best wishes to her,' he said courteously. 'Compliments of the season.'

Compliments of the season indeed, Jen thought sourly, shivering as she stepped out of the warm shop into the damp foggy street. What with it getting dark at three o'clock, the blackout, the fog and the cold, as far as she was concerned, there was nothing to compliment the season about. Sometimes, quite often actually, she wished she lived in Australia or America, somewhere where the sun shone all the time and there was no stupid war lurking in the background making everyone edgy and preoccupied as they waited for something to happen. And then she remembered that she wouldn't have met Sean if she lived in Australia, and changed her mind.

When the police knocked at her front door later that day, Joyce thought they had come about the accident. She knew that they had been taking statements from other people in the street. She knew that some long-lost Canadian nephew of the Miss Taylors had been the hero of the hour. That sickly little

Katy Parsons had held the injured Whitehead child on her lap until the ambulance came and was now ill herself with a serious chill.

She had also heard on the grapevine that the driver of the car was some rich foreign gentleman who had been visiting Mrs d'Arcy Billière. Bloody foreigner. A Polish count, somebody said, but Joyce didn't believe that. Although give the poor man his due, he'd already offered Sheila Whitehead money for the best hospital treatment for little Ray, even though everyone said the accident wasn't his fault.

Either way when she opened the door to find two policemen standing on her step, for once she was not unduly concerned.

'Mrs Carter?' It was the shorter of the two who spoke.

She nodded.

'May we come in? We'd like to ask you a few questions.'

She shook her head. It wasn't a good idea to let policemen into your house. Even if for once you were in the clear. 'I wasn't there,' she said. 'I didn't see it.'

There was a moment's pause and Joyce suddenly realised the policeman was looking blank. 'The accident,' she prompted him. 'I was busy cooking. I did hear a squeal of brakes but I didn't go out.' She didn't add that she had been trying out a recipe she was going to use for the Rutherfords when she cooked for them after Christmas. That she had rashly blown two and six at Dove the butcher's on some lamb chops to practise on.

It was nothing fancy, just a nice rich stew. But she wanted to make a good impression. It was a long time since she had done any proper cooking and she was terribly nervous of getting it wrong.

As it happened it had come out perfectly and the boys had eaten up every scrap when they'd come in after the crash, dumplings and all. Jen had enjoyed it too. Joyce sighed. She'd cook for them more often if she could afford the cost of the ingredients.

'It's not the accident we have come about, Mrs Carter,' the short policeman said now. 'It's the burglary.'

Burglary? Joyce stared at him blankly. This was horribly like old times. But Stanley and Bob were safe inside now. She was safe. Wasn't she? She swallowed hard as her throat tightened. You never knew with the police. She eyed them warily. 'What burglary? Where?'

'Cedars House,' the policeman said. 'The house at the end of this road. Home of the Rutherfords.'

Joyce was astonished. 'The Rutherfords have been burgled? When? I was only there yesterday.'

The policeman nodded. 'Exactly, Mrs Carter. You were there yesterday. That is why we want to ask you some questions.'

Joyce didn't like the tone of his voice. It sounded sarcastic to her. She was all set to give him a piece of her mind when she stopped and caught her breath. It wouldn't be wise to lose her temper. In any case, he was carefully unfolding a document, the contents of which looked painfully familiar. He flourished it in front of her nose and her vision swam.

A search warrant.

She could not believe it. She just could not believe it. Why her? Surely the Rutherfords didn't suspect her?

But the answer was obvious. They did suspect her. It was there in black and white.

She felt a sudden sick pain of disappointment in her stomach. She took a step back. 'You'd better come in,' she said.

And, taking off their helmets, they followed her indoors.

Chapter Twelve

Jen was upstairs in her bedroom, moping, when the police arrived. She heard their stiff exchange with her mother and without at first even really realising why, her heart began to pound.

For a second she stood rigid in her doorway. It was an instinctive thing to fear the police. To fear the consequences of a search warrant, the mess and disruption, the humiliation of them going through her drawers, touching her things, let alone the possibility of them finding something. But then she shook her head. They wouldn't find anything this time. She was certain her mother wouldn't rip off the Rutherfords, wouldn't rip off anyone come to that. Deep down she knew her mother was honest; it was only the necessities of day to day life that made her tolerate the petty crime that kept the family's heads above water, above the poverty line.

Jen stepped back silently into her room, and glanced around thankfully, at least she had nothing to hide.

And then her eyes stopped on the box Sean had asked her to look after while he was away and her heart kicked.

She didn't know what was in that box.

Clothes, he had said. But could she trust him?

Suddenly, even as she heard the police moving about in the kitchen downstairs, the truth of her relationship with Sean hit her like a bullet. She loved him, she desired him, she revelled in his attention and enjoyed his company. She was crazy about him, but she just didn't trust him. She didn't know whether he was IRA or not. He could be. Certainly he loved his country and resented the British presence there. But he had always got touchy if she pressed him further. And so she hadn't pressed. Basically, she hadn't wanted to know.

Sean Byrne was an experienced charmer and she hadn't wanted to lose him. The truth hurt. It had hurt for weeks. But it hadn't stopped her getting involved. And she kicked herself for letting herself get into such an intolerable situation. What's more, she had given up the chance of a paid job to be with him and all he had done in return was bugger off to Ireland for two weeks.

And now her position was even worse. She was stuck in the house with two policemen and a box that for all she knew really did contain gelignite and alarm clocks as Sean had mockingly suggested.

There was no time to open it now. It was all tied up with brown paper and string and knotted. Jen glanced round frantically. Nor could she hide it. Not a damn great suspicious-looking box like that. Not from a team of police searchers.

She could see them outside in the back yard now, looking in the Anderson shelter of all places. Well, good luck to them, she thought, keeping well back from the window, the stupid shelter had flooded up to the ankles with all the recent rain. She hoped they spoiled their uniform shoes. Then she shook herself and bit her lip. They'd be coming upstairs in a minute and she and Sean's box would be caught red handed.

She glanced at the window: There was nothing else for it. She would have to climb out of the window and take the blasted box with her.

Impatiently, she waited for the policemen to go back indoors, then, holding her breath, she eased open the window, wincing as it creaked and stuck.

Mouthing vicious curses both at it and at the absent Sean she forced it up and peered out gingerly. It was one thing to climb out of the window on a hot summer's night, but quite another when everything was soaking wet and slimy with winter grime.

As she perched precariously on the cold, slippery sill, she wondered for a moment if she was doing this to protect Sean or to protect herself. She would have liked to think she was doing it for him, but deep down she knew that wasn't entirely the case.

She had gone out on a limb already for Sean, gone against her family and friends just by having him as a boyfriend. She would look a fool now if she was proved wrong. If he was exposed as an IRA bomber.

Hearing footsteps on the stairs, swearing under her breath as she nearly lost her footing, Jen grabbed the box and clambered quickly down on to the toilet roof, reaching back only to pull the window down as far as she could, before closing her eyes and half slithering, half jumping painfully to the ground.

Aware of them already in the room above her she pressed herself silently to the damp wall of the house, then when the coast seemed to be clear, sped across the yard and out of the back gate into the dustbin alley with a sense of profound relief.

Shivering on the corner of the street, wondering where to go for sanctuary, she caught sight of her errant younger brother swaggering up the street. His escape from Devon and his reinstatement in London seemed to have gone to his head. In the absence of any form of schooling or work, he and his little gang of equally cocky youths had taken to hanging around street corners, smoking, making smart remarks at passers-by and generally being extremely tiresome.

'I wouldn't go home just now if I was you,' Jen said as he approached. 'The police are there.'

'The police?' Micky stopped abruptly.

Jen grimaced, pleased to see the wind taken out of his sails. 'Someone's gone and burgled the Rutherfords' and now of course they are suspecting Mum.'

She glanced away down the street and bit her lip. Would this be the end of her mother's job? For the first time it came home to her how precarious their financial situation actually was. Without the money Joyce brought in, they would be stony broke. And to think if it hadn't been for Sean Byrne she could have been working now. In Carlisle. Starting her career. Earning money. Meeting real professional actors and actresses, instead of skulking around the back streets of Clapham like some shifty criminal, freezing to death and with her heart still going like the clappers.

'Stupid buggers,' Micky said scornfully. 'Mum wouldn't burgle nobody.' He shifted from one foot to the other and blew on his hands. His ears were bright red with cold. 'So the Old Bill are there now, are they? I'd better keep clear for a bit, then.'

Jerked out of her thoughts, Jen eyed him balefully. She was sick of his big talk. 'Why? What have you gone and done now? Beaten up a few more school kids?'

He shrugged off her sarcasm with an irritating smirk. 'That's for me to know and you to find out. But put it this way, Dad would be proud of me.'

Jen stared at him, her eyes hardening in suspicion as the meaning of his words sank in. 'They are searching our house, Micky,' she said with deliberate emphasis. 'If they find any stolen stuff in there you'll be for the bloody high jump, I can tell you. We all will. They'll accuse Mum and that'll be the end of us.'

Mick stepped back a pace from her glittering eyes. 'They won't find anything,' he said, but some of the bravado had gone from his voice.

Jen felt a hint of anxiety. 'I'm serious, Mick. If they find anything. Anything hot and we're done for.' She stopped abruptly as he dropped his eyes.

'There is something, isn't there?' She knew that stubborn, sulky expression. Knew he was hiding something. Wished she could thump it out of him. But he was far too big for that these days.

'Oh my God. It's not the Rutherford stuff, is it?' she asked. 'Surely to God, Micky, even you aren't stupid enough to burgle your own mother's employers.' She saw a muscle move in his jaw and felt a flicker of horrified doubt. 'Or are you? Are you really that stupid after all?'

As she stared at him with rising fury, his expression changed.

'Why do you always think the worst of me, Jen?' he shouted at her

143

suddenly. 'Why do you never give me the benefit of the doubt? You treat me like a child. Everyone does. Nobody takes me seriously. Well, let me tell you, I'm not as stupid as you think. I'm not a child. And I don't leave stolen things around for the police to find.'

Jen stared at him, surprised by his outburst. For an extraordinary moment she had thought he might burst into tears.

'Well, good,' she said sarcastically. 'Thank God for that.'

He flushed and turned away. Then a few steps away he turned back again. 'You think I'm stupid. Well, I think you're stupid, prancing around with that Irish bastard. You're bringing shame on the family, that's what you're doing. He'll never marry you. He's just using you.'

For a long second Jen just stood there, her fierce pride bruised by his scornful words. Then suddenly her eyes narrowed.

'Oh yes?' she shouted after him. 'Well, if you're suddenly so grown up, I'm surprised it hasn't occurred to you that I might not want to marry him. That I might be using him?'

But it wasn't true. Or it hadn't been up till now. Jen was painfully aware that Sean had always had her exactly where he wanted her. Under his thumb. Ready and willing to please him whenever and wherever he wanted and utterly terrified of losing him. Ever since he'd left she had been worrying about what he might be up to in Ireland. Worrying that he might go off her. Worrying that he might meet someone else more suitable.

She swore silently as it began to rain. Well, after today, things were going to change. She was damned if she was going to be anybody's doormat. Sean Byrne was only a man, albeit a thoroughly sexy one, but he should be treated as such. As a man. A mortal. Not as some all-powerful god to be endlessly worshipped and feared and placated.

She glanced down at the box at her feet and frowned. It was beneath her to open it. Beneath her to care what was inside. She would open her Christmas present from him privately on Christmas day and that was all. It was his body she wanted, nothing else. And if she couldn't have that, never mind. She would get on with her career instead.

Feeling the cold rain seeping through her thin clothes, she lifted her chin and smiled to herself. Sean Byrne was in for a shock when he got back. But it was his own fault. He'd had it all his own way for long enough. Now the tables had turned. She was in charge once more. She glanced at the box again and chuckled evilly. Whatever was in there was getting nice and wet.

It took a lot of courage for Joyce to present herself at Cedars House the following morning. But she knew if she didn't go it would be like admitting guilt.

So she went promptly at eight thirty as usual with her chin held high.

But instead of Mrs Rutherford opening the door with her bright, welcoming smile, Joyce found herself confronting a very unwelcoming Greville Rutherford.

Joyce didn't like Greville Rutherford at the best of times. But as she stood on the step, listening in silence to his thin, cold voice telling her they would no longer be needing her services, not for cleaning, nor for the period when their cook was away after Christmas, she decided she had never hated anyone so much in her entire life.

'My wife and I have talked it through at great length and we both agree in the circumstances it would not be in our best interests to continue your employment.'

So Mrs Rutherford was in it too.

Joyce had had no idea how much that would hurt. That her employer didn't trust her. And, worse, that she didn't have the guts or the gall to tell her to her face. So she'd got her husband to do her dirty work for her.

Fighting off a stab of self-pity, Joyce realised that Greville Rutherford had finished speaking and was looking at her disdainfully. 'Have you anything to say, Mrs Carter?'

Joyce met his eyes. She had a lot to say but she didn't trust herself to speak. She would rather die than cry. She waited for an apology, for a hint of remorse, even regret. But none was forthcoming.

After a moment's stony silence she shook her head. 'If you've quite finished, Mr Rutherford, I'd like to go home. It's rather chilly standing out here.'

Pleased to see he looked slightly taken aback, she turned and walked stiffly away. If he calls Happy Christmas after me, I'll go back and shove a Christmas tree up his arse, she promised herself bitterly. Baubles and all.

But the thought didn't help, in any case he didn't offer any apology or seasonal greeting, and by the time she reached the gate there were tears running down her cheeks.

Louise wore a brand new Norman Hartnell dress to the carol concert with Ward Frazer. She had bought it specially. It was called Maginot and was fashioned in the new shade of khaki and caught up on one side with sequins. Over it she wore a long fox fur coat, borrowed from her mother. It was a beastly cold, foggy night and there was talk now of possible snow at Christmas.

Luckily Ward Frazer came for her in a taxi, so there no need to wear boots and carry her shoes, nor was there any time for stilted conversation with her parents or brothers before departure. Not that there was anything the slightest bit stilted about Ward Frazer.

On the contrary, he seemed unnervingly relaxed, certainly in comparison to Louise who felt as nervous as though this was her first ever date, which in a way it was. The first date that really mattered, at least. With a man who was older and significantly more sophisticated than her. One who had a bad reputation with women. Goodness knew what might happen. Her brothers had teased so much about the likely dire consequences of the evening, that she had become scared her parents would withdraw their permission.

But Ward Frazer was courteous and well mannered. In the taxi he sat well away from her, lounging comfortably in the corner, his long legs stretched out in front of him as he chatted amiably about the terrible weather. It was difficult to believe he was a black sheep. Louise wondered again if the rumour of a rift with his family was true and if so what had caused it.

As they crossed Albert Bridge with its ornate metalwork barely visible through the wispy fog, he asked her about the Whitehead child and was delighted to hear that little Ray Whitehead was not only still alive, but, according to her mother who had called on Sheila Whitehead only yesterday, improving daily now that he had been moved to St Thomas's Hospital, the teaching hospital down by Westminster Bridge, for specialist treatment.

'And what about the poor mother?' he asked. 'Is she coping all right?'

'I think so,' Louise said. 'Although her husband hasn't got back from France yet as far as I know.' As a rule she didn't take much interest in the other occupants of Lavender Road. And as Katy Parsons had been ill ever since the accident Louise was a bit out of date with local gossip. She'd only called once, very briefly, just to drop off Katy's torch. After all, the last thing Louise wanted was the flu.

There was one thing she had heard, though. 'You know the man who was driving the car that night?' she said to Ward now. 'Apparently he is some kind of exiled Polish count.'

Ward smiled faintly at her awed tone. 'I know,' he said dryly. 'The police told me. They seemed impressed too.' And Louise bit her lip in the semi darkness in the back of the taxi, wishing she could have said something rather more intelligent. Ward obviously wasn't impressed by their close brush with nobility, which was a shame because she would have liked to have asked him what this Count looked like. But instead she changed the subject.

'It's ironic you're taking me to a carol concert when one of the first things I noticed about you was that you didn't seem to know the hymns in church.'

He smiled, amused by her comment, the admission of her interest, or perhaps just by her powers of observation.

'You're right,' he said, leaning back and resting an arm negligently along the back of the seat. 'I didn't know the hymns. Although the tunes seemed familiar, perhaps from schooldays.'

Louise was astonished. 'Haven't you been to church since you were at school, then?'

He shrugged. 'I confess I'm not a great believer. I have always had difficulty in accepting the existence of an omnipotent benign deity. Particularly one that tolerates the kind of thing that is currently going on in Germany.'

'But surely that's Hitler's fault,' Louise said, shocked. 'Not God's.'

Ward smiled easily. 'If God made us all, I don't see why he should only take the credit for the good bits.'

Louise stared at him. She had waited around in church for him for weeks on end and now she discovered he didn't even believe in God. Everyone believed in God.

She realised he was looking at her. 'I've shocked you,' he said, suddenly contrite. 'I'm sorry. I'm afraid I have a bit of a thing about religion. Or religions, perhaps I should say. The branding of a group of people into a religious group, and then using their beliefs as a reason for domination or persecution.'

'The Jews, you mean?' Louise asked. She realised she wasn't entirely sure what Jews did believe in. She glanced at him, wondering whether to expose her ignorance, and caught an unexpected flash of anger in his profile as he looked out of the window. It came to her with a terrible blow that Ward might be Jewish. He didn't look it, but then apparently you often couldn't tell. Perhaps that was why he didn't believe in God.

'Are you Jewish?' she asked.

He glanced round at her surprised. 'No, I'm not. Why do you ask?'

'I thought you looked cross for a moment.'

'Did I?' He seemed taken aback. 'I didn't mean to. But I guess I always feel kind of cross about any kind of persecution.'

He changed the subject then and Louise was relieved. She wasn't strong on theology; her own belief was based on little more than the fact she had been to church every Sunday all her life without question. It had never occurred to her that it might all be a myth. That the God that all the millions of churches had been built for might not exist. All those prayers she had recited as a child kneeling at her bedside. It seemed awful to think that she might have been saying them to nobody.

However, God or no God, the carol service was lovely. They sat in a pew with some other people Ward obviously knew quite well, a rather glamorous, rich-looking American couple who Ward told her were somehow connected with the American Embassy. They didn't seem a bit surprised to see Ward with a girl they had never met. On the contrary they made a joke of it, saying that he seemed to have a monopoly on the prettiest girls in London.

To her horror Louise felt herself blushing. But Ward was entirely unfazed. 'I'm working on it,' he drawled. 'I've always fancied the idea of a harem.'

The Americans laughed as they were clearly intended to do, but Louise had the uneasy feeling that Ward might not be entirely joking. Behind his charm and his lazy, knee-trembling smile was a certain detachment, almost a sense of world weariness that disconcerted her. It made her feel young. Young and a bit naive. And she found that very unnerving.

At the party afterwards there was talk of the American ambassador Joseph Kennedy and his outspokenly pacifist views which people feared would prevent America giving the Allies the military support they wanted.

The party was held in a private house in Pimlico, the secluded, fashionable area between Victoria and the river. In a stylish square, one of several built in the early nineteenth century to imitate Belgravia, it was exactly the sort of discreetly elegant place Louise would have loved to live in. A tall, pale-brick town house, rising behind a smart black railing fence. With wide steps and strong pillars supporting the balcony over the front door, it overlooked the square's high pavemented road and central communal garden. Apparently well tended, with gravel paths bordered by ornamental shrubs and well-pruned trees, the communal garden too was fenced in by high, matching railings and ornate lockable gates. A much better system than stupid Clapham Common, Louise thought, which was open to all and sundry from all directions.

She smiled to herself as she followed Ward up the steps. It was odd to think that the shabby, narrow Victorian terraces of Clapham were less than a mile away on the other side of the river.

Indoors she was impressed by the unusually pale decor and minimalist furnishings. Most of the rooms had bare polished floorboards and instead of pictures there were mirrors on the walls and strange unidentifiable white sculptures on elegant stands. It was a far cry from the flowered chintz, patterned carpets and dark heavy furniture of her parents' drawing-room. But then her parents didn't know people who called each other 'darling' and smoked cigarettes through ivory holders.

There was no doubt it was a chic affair, with drinks and finger snacks in one spacious room and dancing in another.

Louise was glad she had worn the Norman Hartnell dress. She wished she could have worn her diamond brooch to go with it, but of course that had been stolen and the police were apparently no nearer to finding it. Louise had been sure it would be in Mrs Carter's house and was disappointed that the police search had been fruitless. But her mother was clearly relieved. From the start, she had seemed reluctant to join the rest of the family in outright conviction that Joyce Carter was the culprit.

'Honestly, Mummy,' Louise had argued. 'We know her husband is already in jail for burglary. It's obvious they're short of money.'

'That's just why I feel sure she wouldn't jeopardise her job,' her mother had insisted. 'Exactly for that reason. Because she needs the money so badly.'

But Greville Rutherford had been adamant that Mrs Carter should be sacked. And had angrily said that if Celia wouldn't do it, he'd do it himself. And he had.

Louise knew her mother was upset about that, and even more so when, later that day, she found some cardigan she had given Mrs Carter on the step with a curt little note from Mrs Carter saying she would no longer be needing it.

Honestly, Louise had thought, what a cheek. How ungrateful could people get?

'What do you Brits think about America's attitude?' someone asked suddenly. 'Do you think they should come in?'

Realising they were addressing her, Louise blinked. Politics was never her strong point. She smiled at Ward who was watching her through slightly quizzical eyes and to her horror she felt herself blushing again. 'Well, if they are as nice as the Canadians I'm all for it,' she said lightly and everyone laughed.

'On that note perhaps I could claim a dance?' Ward said, offering his arm, and Louise took it eagerly.

'Oh, yes please,' she said.

He didn't say anything as he led her through to the dancing room and Louise wondered if he thought she was too flippant about the war. After all, one of the few things she knew about him was that he had come to England to join the RAF.

'I don't really see the point of America coming into the war,' she said now, 'because nothing seems to be happening.' Seeing he looked surprised, she went on quickly, 'I mean I know some ships have been sunk, which is sad, and Russia is trying to invade Finland and everything. But do you think anything is really going to happen? To us?'

'Oh, it's going to happen all right,' he said dryly as he took her into his arms. 'And I'm afraid it may start happening rather more quickly than people realise.'

It was certainly happening to her heart, Louise realised, as her concentration suddenly faded. The proximity of his hard lean body, the touch of his hand on hers, was almost more than she could bear. She had spent the whole evening secretly staring at his handsome face, trying desperately to glean from his expression, from the compelling cadences of his voice, some flicker of genuine interest in her. But all she had found were those faintly detached, courteous good manners and a hint of wry amusement.

And now, just when she should be matching his detachment, playing hard to get, she was going all weak at the knees and gooey eyed. She thought of the reflection of his bare chest and flat stomach in the mirror after the crash and an involuntary shiver coursed through her.

'How's your injury?' she asked abruptly.

He smiled. 'Fine as long as I don't breathe too deeply.'

Suddenly Louise was hardly able to breathe at all.

'I'm sorry,' Ward added after a moment, 'About what I said before. I didn't mean to scare you. But I still don't think people appreciate that Hitler really does mean business. Even if he's taking his time about it.'

'I'm not scared of Hitler,' Louise said, stoutly. She looked up at him earnestly. 'Daddy says it won't last long anyway, even if fighting does start in France. He says our troops will thrash Hitler's.'

Ward's brows rose. 'Does he?' He looked directly into her eyes for a moment, making her heart buck helplessly in her chest. 'Then we don't need to worry, do we? We can just concentrate on enjoying ourselves.'

Somewhere in there was a hint of sarcasm, but Louise didn't care, her pulses were throbbing too hard for that. She smiled nervously up at her handsome escort, suddenly feeling very young again. 'Don't forget I've got to be home by midnight.'

Ward's expression softened slightly as he looked down at her. 'I won't forget, Cinderella,' he said. 'I certainly don't want to get left with a damn great pumpkin on my hands.'

In fact, to Louise's dismay he got her home by eleven thirty. When she remarked regretfully of the earliness of the hour as the taxi drew up at the gate of Cedars House, Ward merely smiled. 'Best to make a good impression on the first date.'

Louise hoped he was being serious but it niggled her that he had bored of her company.

'Will you go back to the party?' she asked bravely as he walked her to the door. It had still been in full swing when they left. And several women had greeted him with unnerving familiarity. One in particular had looked quite put out by Louise's leech-like presence at his side.

He shook his head. 'No. I must get some sleep. I'm on duty tomorrow.'

'Flying?' Louise asked, peering at him in the thin moonlight.

For a second he hesitated, then he nodded. 'Probably.'

'I suppose all your missions are highly confidential,' she said reluctant to let him go, but unsure how to provoke a goodnight kiss. She licked her lips.

He smiled. 'Highly,' he agreed gravely.

'Well, thank you for a lovely evening,' she said lamely.

He inclined his head. 'Thank you too. I enjoyed your company.'

'Did you?' Louise asked eagerly, then bit her lip when he laughed softly.

'Yes, I did,' he murmured, reaching forward and putting her out of her misery with a brief kiss on the lips.

He touched her cheek with cold fingers. 'Goodnight, Cinderella. And Happy Christmas.'

Louise's heart sank. 'Won't I see you before Christmas?'

He shook his head. 'No,' he said. 'But I should be back in January. In the meantime, will you give my best wishes to the lady with the injured child? I hope he picks up OK. And to your parents, of course. Oh, and also to that nice girl from the pub.' He frowned. 'Kate, wasn't it? Say hi to her too.'

And then before Louise could respond, before she could speak, before she could move, he was gone, crunching away briskly across the gravel, back to the taxi. Back to war.

And her first date was over.

Chapter Thirteen

After fighting for his life in a semi-coma for five days, Ray Whitehead died on the twenty third of December, aged three and a half, twenty minutes before his father arrived back from France.

What made the tragedy of his death even worse was that since he had been moved down to the smart St Thomas's Hospital, in its prestigious position on the river by Westminster Bridge bang opposite the Houses of Parliament, Sheila had told everyone he was getting better. It was as though she just couldn't accept that he wouldn't. And everyone had gratefully believed her. So it came as a double shock both to her and her friends and neighbours when he gave up the struggle and died.

For his father, Jo, arriving back for Christmas, tired after a difficult journey and a long rough sea crossing, unaware even that there had been an accident, it was like a homecoming to hell.

Even the knowledge that Ray had had the best possible treatment didn't make the loss any easier to bear.

Pam Nelson's grief was so painful she had to take time off work. And even more difficult to bear than the grief was the guilt, a dreadful debilitating guilt that after her initial shock and pain on hearing the news, for a few terrible moments she had felt a profound relief that at least now no one would find out about her illicit embrace with Sean Byrne.

It ate her up. She could not believe she had it in her to be so callous. So self-centred. So heartlessly selfish. And because she couldn't tell anybody the shocking truth, it festered inside her, undermining the newfound self-esteem she'd gained from her job, leaving her listless, unable to sleep, to work, to eat, unable to do anything but cry.

Alan tried to help her, offered to get the doctor, sat with her for hours on end trying to cheer her up, trying to make her eat. But she was unable to respond. Certainly not to Alan, who, in her trauma, she felt she had betrayed. Even in her despair she knew he blamed himself, blamed himself for not providing her with a child of her own. For he believed that her misery was because she had become over-attached to the Whitehead children, giving them all the love she should have reserved for her own child. And perhaps for him too.

It was a reasonable guess, perhaps partly true, but the knowledge of it only made Pam feel worse, for she knew that it was Sean Byrne who had taken the love Alan deserved, not Ray Whitehead, and the knowledge of that only intensified her guilt.

But finally it was the thought of Sean Byrne's return after Christmas, even though she dreaded it more than even the threat of a German invasion, that dragged her out of her lethargy. The thought of him finding her languishing in bed, and the conclusions he might jump to, forced her to get a grip on herself.

And by the time he did reappear at the frozen beginning of January, handsome and blue eyed and provocatively charming as ever, she was over the worst, or so she seemed on the surface. She was back at work at least and, to Alan's profound relief, she no longer cried at night. She was even able to sit with Sheila and Jo and little George, to try to help them come to terms with their loss.

Only her thin unresponsive smile and pale skin gave the game away, the only visible remnants of a painful self-inflicted wound that had cut her to the very core of her being.

The news of little Ray's death hit Katy Parsons badly too. Still in bed with aching joints, sore throat and a grinding cough, she had plenty of time to think over the events of that night of the crash, to wonder if there was anything else she could have done, to imagine Sheila Whitehead's suffering.

Gazing out of the window a few days later, up the grey, wind-blown street, seeing the pathetic little funeral cortege, the drab, chilled mourners gathering for the walk across the common to the church, Katy wondered what was there really to get better for.

With half the street in mourning, no lights and little cheer, it had been a sad, half-hearted Christmas. The weather was consistently terrible. There were no leaves on the trees. Everything seemed bleak and grey and cold.

Even Jen wasn't herself. She insisted she wasn't missing Sean, but she had been pleased as punch with the pretty silver earrings he'd bought her for Christmas. When she saw them, Katy couldn't help wishing she had a boyfriend to buy her jewellery. She didn't want to be ungrateful for the numerous small gifts she had received. But some delicate silver drop earrings would make a change from bed socks and knitting bags.

The only bright spot in an otherwise dreary Christmas day had been hearing, out of the blue, Jen's younger sister Angie on a special evacuee broadcast on the radio from the West Country saying what a lovely Christmas they were having on the farm there, with a great big turkey and a Christmas pudding with silver sixpences in it.

And poor Joyce Carter hadn't even heard it; she'd been up on the common with Pete picking up wood blown down in the storms. It seemed that with no money coming in from the Rutherfords any more, they couldn't afford any coal.

And lucky they did collect the wood, because it snowed all over the New Year. It was so cold the ponds on the common froze solid. Seagulls stood about forlornly on the white playing fields. At night you could hear ducks and geese calling as they flew overhead in search of water.

Katy had been shocked to hear that the Rutherfords had sacked Joyce on suspicion of stealing their jewellery. It seemed cruelly unfair.

She wished there was something she could say to convince her new friend Louise, that Joyce deserved a second chance. But Louise probably wouldn't have listened anyway. When she had called round briefly on Boxing Day she had been far more interested in telling Katy all about her evening with Ward Frazer, what a lovely dancer he was, how witty he was, how charming and attentive.

Katy had been torn between wanting to know and being fiercely jealous of Louise's luck. Not that she could say so, of course. It turned, out that Ward Frazer hadn't even remembered her name. Kate, he'd called her, Louise said, giggling. Kate. Katy had smiled weakly as though she didn't mind, but afterwards she had wondered if Kate wasn't a better name than Katy, which after all was a bit babyish.

And then the fog came and her parents refused to let her go to the Grand at Clapham Junction to see the variety show on account of her chest, so Jen went alone and came back with reports of real lions, a pretty but uninspiring soubrette, and the brilliance of the Battersea-born Sparks brothers, who were the reason they'd wanted to go in the first place.

And then Sean Byrne came back from Ireland and Jen's visits stopped abruptly.

And then to cap it all, on the sixth of January, reports came in that the Germans had gained ground in a fierce onslaught on a hundred and twenty mile front north of Paris. And suddenly, after the Christmas lull, the war seemed real again. Real, and getting closer.

Jen didn't care about the war. All she cared about was Sean Byrne. She was shocked by how much she had missed him. Not that she would admit that to him in a million years. Even though he tried to make her say it, she wouldn't. Not under her new regime of being more in charge. Being more cool, more detached. More grown-up. And anyway she was cross with him. Cross about the box. Cross about the pressure he had put her under and cross that he seemed unrepentant when she told him about her dramatic escape from the window of her room. And not just unrepentant, downright amused.

'You needn't have bothered. I told you it was only clothes.'

Jen eyed him suspiciously. Had she sensed a faint hint of relief in his voice? They were in Lyons at Clapham Junction. He was wearing the cufflinks she had given him. They looked good. Smart. He'd said he really liked them. He was smiling. He seemed relaxed. Too relaxed.

'But it was so heavy,' she said watching his eyes follow his favourite waitress across the café.

'It had shoes in there.'

'Why?' Jen leaned over the table crossly. 'Why did you give me a box of clothes and shoes to look after?'

He didn't respond for a moment. Then he took out his cigarettes and lit up.

Jen raised her eyebrows. 'Don't I get offered one?'

Sean looked surprised. 'You know I don't like girls to smoke.'

'I don't care what you like,' Jen said coolly. 'I got the taste for it over Christmas and it's only polite to offer me one.'

He looked at her thoughtfully through his exhaled smoke. 'You've changed.'

'I haven't.'

'Oh, and I think you have,' he said. 'You didn't used to argue with me so much.' His eyes were very blue, very steady. 'I liked it better when you agreed with every word I said.'

Jen gritted her teeth, ignoring the flicker of alarm that coursed through her. She didn't want to lose him but she didn't want to be his doormat either. 'I'll agree with you when you're right but not when you're wrong,' she said stoutly, holding his eyes. 'And now I want a cigarette and then I want to know about the box.'

It was Sean who looked away first. In silence he pulled the cigarette packet out of his pocket and offered it to her. 'Your cigarette, madam,' he said with faint sarcasm. 'And is there anything else you want while you're about it?'

'Yes,' Jen said, taking the matches off the table and calmly lighting up. 'I want to go to bed with you.'

But even as she saw his eyes flicker with surprise and with something else, shock perhaps, or even a faint grudging respect, her heart sank. Where could they go? Not to her home, not with Mick around. It was far too bitterly cold now to stay outside as they had done occasionally before Christmas. Sean worked weekdays. And Pam Nelson always seemed to be on guard at her place in the evenings and weekends. Preventing any sneaked hours of passion.

'Well, on that we're agreed at least.' Sean was stirring his tea with a faint complacent smile. 'I missed your beautiful body, Jennifer Carter. I looked at other girls but couldn't find anyone to give me quite what you give me.'

Jen breathed carefully. 'I don't care about other girls, Sean,' she lied. And was pleased to see him look up sharply. She held up her cigarette and glanced meaningfully at the ashtray by his elbow. He didn't move. She smiled grittily.

'I want to know about that box. I guarded it with my life and I want an explanation.'

He shrugged and pushed the ashtray towards her and she knew she had won a small battle. She smiled inwardly and watched him draw deeply on his cigarette.

'You know yourself it's not easy times for an Irish fellow in England just now,' he said blowing out smoke. 'If we're not getting it in the neck for being neutral we're getting it for letting off bombs.' He glanced at her. 'And whether we're involved or not we're under suspicion, even from our own girlfriends.'

His expression hardened fractionally as he reached over and stubbed out his cigarette. 'People have been wrongly accused. Your Brit police want convictions and they don't care too much how they go about getting them. It's the devil's own job to prove your innocence.' He sat back in his chair. 'I don't know about other fellows, but I don't want to find myself wrongly accused and fighting for my freedom.'

He paused and looked up at Jen seriously. 'Nor do I want to find myself hanged.'

Jen stared at him, startled. He moved his shoulders and leaned forward again. 'There are two fellows going to the gallows any day now and one of them is innocent. I swear it.'

Jen swallowed. This was a Sean she didn't know. A serious Sean. But none the less attractive for that.

'But what about the clothes?' she asked doggedly.

'A precaution. Some of those boys would have escaped if they'd not had to go back to their digs after a tip-off.'

'But you weren't here to escape,' she said puzzled. 'Not over Christmas.'

He looked at her for a moment then sighed. 'It's money too. I didn't want Mrs Nelson to find money in my room.' He saw Jen's surprise and shrugged. 'Money and papers. I couldn't take the risk. She's not been herself at all since that child got run down.' He frowned. 'She doesn't know her own mind any more. I don't trust her.'

Jen almost laughed. Money and papers. Trust. It all suddenly seemed like a spy thriller. But then she saw Sean's expression and sobered. 'You didn't trust me enough to tell me what it was.'

He lifted his shoulders. 'I trusted you to keep it safe. And I want to go on trusting you. I want you to keep the box for me.'

Jen took a deep breath. 'It got wet.'

'What?'

'It got wet. It was raining when the police came. I was cross and I let it get wet. I hope the money isn't spoiled.'

He grinned and the atmosphere suddenly lightened miraculously, 'I hope none of it is spoiled. I don't want to make my escape in trousers stinking of mould.'

'It would serve you right.'

'For what?'

'For not telling me, for being Irish, and for leaving me alone for weeks on end.'

'So you did miss me?'

Jen shrugged. 'Not particularly, but now you're back I'm not averse to seeing you occasionally, when I'm not too busy.'

Sean smiled complacently, ignoring the faint challenge in her tone. 'Mrs Nelson is taking that child George from over the road out to the pictures on Saturday,' he murmured, leaning forward to run his fingers across her lips. 'And I may be able to get back one or two lunchtimes next week.'

Jen felt her heart shiver. It was a dangerous game she was playing. She had forgotten Sean's power, the anticipation that knotted in her stomach every time he touched her. She glanced nervously around the restaurant but nobody seemed to be taking any notice of them. Nobody but her seemed to be feeling the sudden electricity in the air. Nobody else seemed to be sitting on a chair that thumped in time with her heart. 'I think I'm free Saturday,' she whispered.

'Good,' he said, sliding his fingers round the back of her neck and pulling her towards him across the table for a kiss. 'Because if I don't get you to bed soon I'll explode.'

Louise was sick of her brothers and sick of their incessant teasing. It seemed that Douglas had for some reason been peering out of his window at exactly the moment that Ward Frazer had kissed her goodnight after the carol service. All the next day, whenever their father was out of earshot, he played an imaginary violin and made stupid smacking noises with his lips. He thought it was hilarious.

Louise thought it was childish in the extreme. But she didn't help herself by floating round the house with a dreamy, distracted smile on her lips. But when Christmas came and went without any word from Ward at all, not even a card, she became somewhat less dreamy and rather more irritable.

Matters were not helped by the lack of a cleaner and then, the weekend after the New Year, the lack of a cook as well.

To her disgust Louise found herself roped in to help her mother in the kitchen. At Lucie Clayton they had learned how to organise cocktail parties, how to choose a tasty menu for a dinner party. They had even learned what problems to expect with weekend house parties. But nobody had mentioned anything about raw hands from scrubbing muddy, gnarled vegetables from the garden, nor that she would be facing a mound of beastly washing-up after every meal.

What was worse was that her mother perversely seemed to be quite enjoying it. 'It's the war,' she said with gritty brightness, struggling with some unidentifiable meat that Mr Dove had delivered that morning. 'We all have to do our bit.'

'Louise thinks her bit is to entertain the troops,' Douglas remarked dryly, carrying in a worm-infested bowl of potatoes from the garden for Louise to clean and slice. 'Particularly the foreign troops. Of course I'm sure they are very homesick and need some er … comforting. Although not, apparently, over the festive period.'

He stopped abruptly and ducked as Louise swung round and flung a bunch of wet but unwashed carrots right at him.

Missing Douglas, the carrots hurtled on across the kitchen and splattered noisily against the opposite wall. Wet earth flew everywhere and in his attempt to avoid the carrots, Douglas spilled the potatoes which rolled in all directions depositing mud and worms all over the kitchen floor.

'What on earth …!' Celia turned round and stopped abruptly, staring in absolute horror at the sudden comprehensive devastation. 'Louise! What are you thinking of?'

Louise bit her lip. 'It's not my fault.'

Celia looked at her incredulously. 'Of course it's your fault. Entirely your fault. You've just thrown two dozen perfectly good carrots at the wall.'

Louise swallowed. 'It's not fair, Mummy. The boys tease me the whole time about Ward.'

'Well, it's your own fault. You should try and grow up a bit. You're behaving like a silly schoolgirl.'

'I'm not.' Louise flushed scarlet at the cruel injustice of it. 'I haven't said a word about him.'

'You haven't needed to, mooning about the house like a wet blanket,' Douglas chipped in helpfully and got a quelling look from his mother for his pains.

'Go back upstairs, Douglas, and for heaven's sake prevent your father coming down here.' She waited till he had gone then turned back to Louise. 'Now what's this all about?'

Sensing a hint of sympathy Louise put on her most pitiful look. 'Ward hasn't telephoned me, Mummy.'

Celia stared at her. 'Why on earth would you expect, him to? He's probably busy. There is a war on, you know.'

Louise groaned. 'I might have known you wouldn't be sympathetic.'

'Sympathetic?' Celia frowned. 'Why should I be sympathetic? After all, he's hardly a boyfriend, is he? To my knowledge you've only met him three times.' She shook her head. 'Anyway, darling, you're far too young for a man like that.'

Louise flinched. 'Mummy, I'm eighteen.' She wanted to go on, to explain, to discuss her hopes and fears, but she saw her mother's impatient, sceptical expression and gave up and turned away in sullen despair. 'You don't understand.'

'I understand very well. You've got a silly crush on the poor man, that's all.'

'It's not a crush,' Louise yelled at her furiously, tears springing into 'her eyes. 'It's more than that and he likes me too. I know he does. That's why I'm upset he hasn't called.' She stared at her mother, her glittering eyes pleading for moral support, for a hint of sympathy. Surely she would understand. She must understand. Even her mother must have been in love once upon a time. In the long distant past.

But Celia was angry now. 'If this is the way you behave I'm not surprised he hasn't. For heaven's sake, Louise, a man like that isn't going to be interested in adolescent tantrums and tears. I'm quite sure he only took you to that carol concert out of kindness.'

She turned away and nodded coldly at the mud-splattered wall and floor. 'Now pull yourself together and clear up this mess before your father sees it.'

Unable to speak, unable to argue, with angry tears streaming down her face, Louise dabbed at the mud with a cloth and only succeeded in smearing it even worse.

'Oh, for goodness' sake,' Celia said crossly. 'Leave it for now. Mrs Carter is coming back tomorrow. I'll get her to see to it.'

Almost choking on her humiliation and hurt, Louise flung the cloth back in the sink and headed for the door. She didn't care about leaving her beastly, hard-hearted mother to prepare the dinner alone. She just did not care. Nor did she care if stupid drab old Mrs Carter had to clear up the mess she had made. She'd be paid for it. And she was lucky to have her job back at all.

Oddly it was Katy Parsons who had indirectly helped Joyce get her job back. Katy had woken one night with the vivid recollection of seeing someone skulking around the Rutherfords' house on the evening of the crash. A man, she thought, certainly not Mrs Carter.

Mary Parsons had mentioned Katy's theory to the Miss Taylors over church flower arranging and they had put it forcefully to Celia Rutherford after the Sunday service. Celia tentatively brought the subject up at the family Sunday lunch the same day. And, thinking back reluctantly to that gruesome evening, Louise had recalled that the front door of the house had been wide open when she and Ward staggered back after the crash. That someone could have been in while everyone was out in the street. Although personally she thought it extremely unlikely.

Now, though, as she fled the kitchen, she was grateful that Mrs Carter was going to be reinstated. And Cook would be back on Monday too.

Louise kicked the door shut and sat on her bed. Why should she help clear up? She was sick to death of housework. It had ruined her Christmas. She never wanted to see a duster or polish again. Or that vicious man-eating Hoover. And as for cooking, luckily she clearly had no aptitude for it at all. She would be more than happy to leave it to the staff.

She stood up and stared at herself in the mirror. She would make sure she married someone who would provide her with staff. Plenty of staff. Someone tall, handsome and well-to-do. Someone who didn't make her cook and clean when they were short handed. Someone who knew sophisticated people. Someone who went to sophisticated parties.

She bit her lip as the tears threatened again and turned back to the bed.

Impatiently, she kicked a pair of shoes out of her way. How could her mother be so beastly? So brazenly, condescendingly unsympathetic? So short sighted and hurtful. Her own mother.

Louise bunched her fists and gritted her teeth and swore silently to herself that she would never tell her mother anything important ever again. Ever.

Joyce scooped out the sardines from the tin and began to mash them with a fork, bones and all. They went further mashed. Sardines. She laughed sourly. Who would ever have thought that she, Joyce Carter, who took a pride in her food, in her cooking, would be serving up sardines and boiled potatoes for her family's tea?

But there wasn't much in the shops suddenly. The German U-boats were beginning to take their toll on British merchant ships. And their cargoes. And what provisions there were on the shop shelves, Joyce couldn't afford. A pound of decent sausages cost nearly a shilling now and she hadn't seen an onion or a banana for weeks.

And the rationing that had finally come in January was a bad joke and all. You were allowed four ounces of bacon and ham and butter per person and a pound of sugar a week. Where on earth did the government expect her to find the money for all that? She'd had to pay one and seven for a quarter of butter alone yesterday and ten pence for a dough cake. It was laughable. Old Dove raised his eyebrows if she ordered more than half a pound of brawn. God knows what he'd do if she waltzed in for a pound of best back bacon at two and six a pound. Faint clean away most likely.

She remembered the four lamb chops she had bought to practise her recipe for the Rutherfords. Old Dove had got ever so excited about that. Thought she must have come into the money. Little did he know those chops were the last decent meal she'd had.

And now the Rutherfords wanted her to go back. Worse than that, they expected her to go back.

I will expect you Thursday morning as usual, the note had said.

Joyce had been speechless with the bare-faced cheek of it. They sacked her without a moment's warning because they wrongly thought she had pinched their jewellery. And then, when they clicked their fingers, they thought she would come running back. Just because they couldn't find anyone else to skivvy for them for peanuts. And the bitter truth of it was they were right. She would come back. She had no choice. She needed the money, peanuts or not. Needed it badly.

I do hope the delay hasn't caused you any inconvenience, Celia had written.

Inconvenience. That was an understatement. It had only completely ruined her Christmas. Ruined all her plans for a weekend trip to Devon to see Angie and Paul. If it hadn't been for a couple of pounds that Micky had casually produced from out of the blue, she wouldn't even have had enough to send them a new jersey each, a couple of pairs of socks and some chocolates for Christmas Day.

Thanks to the suspicious, untrusting Rutherfords, Stanley and Bob, in the nick, had had to make do with just the socks.

And now they wanted her back. Expected her back. Well, she would go back with her head held high. So high she wouldn't be able to open her mouth. If Mrs la-di-da Rutherford thought she was going to be all chummy and grateful this time, she had another think coming. She had cooked her goose. And as for that stuck-up brat of a daughter, as far as Joyce was concerned, Louise Rutherford had cooked hers long ago. She hoped that handsome young Canadian nephew of the Miss Taylors would give her a good run for her money. Word had it that he hadn't been seen since before Christmas. It would serve that little madam right if he never called to see her again.

At the end of the second week of January, Jo Whitehead was sent back to the front in France. It seemed his compassionate leave had run out. After all, what was one child's life in a war where hundreds of grown men were soon to be killed every day?

Pam had secretly suspected that poor Jo almost wanted to go back. That he thought killing Germans might be easier than dealing with his distraught wife. Certainly less emotionally draining. Less painful.

But whether he wanted to or not, he had gone and Sheila was in a terrible state. She craved support and reassurance. Pam had tried to give it. But nagging her behind her brave words about early British victory and minimal danger were the dry, cynical questions of Mr Shaw, her boss in the Ministry of Information. Had Neville Chamberlain always been such an optimist, he wondered. Could he really be expecting poor little Finland singlehandedly to fend off the might of Russia? Did he really think Hitler would take any real notice of countries declaring neutrality? Did he really believe the British troops would fight effectively under French command?

Mr Shaw had never had much time for the French, he told Pam confidentially. Their wine and their food, yes, those were excellent. Magnificent. But he'd never been particularly impressed by their powers of leadership. Even now he imagined their generals in their grand requisitioned houses and comfortable chateaux along the Maginot Line, immaculately dressed with their feet up after a good meal, sipping a full-bodied red and smoking Gitanes. It wasn't somehow the stuff that battlefield victories were made of, he thought.

In the company of Sheila Whitehead, Pam tried to ignore those wickedly unpatriotic thoughts.

'Daddy's gone to kill Mr Hitler,' little George had said with such trusting faith that tears filled Pam's eyes and she had had to grope blindly for the door handle.

George opened it for her. 'And then the war will be over,' he added confidently and Pam had hugged him quickly and rushed out before the tears began to fall.

As she crossed the road a car pulled up and the Miss Taylors' nephew got out, the handsome young Canadian, Ward Frazer. Pam hadn't seen him since the accident before Christmas, but she knew he had called on Sheila yesterday to offer his condolences.

She waved at him now and he waved back and smiled.

He had been so kind, Sheila had said, so nice with George. He had stayed for two hours and hadn't minded her ranting on and on about how she still couldn't believe Ray was dead and how much she was already missing Jo.

Looking back at Ward Frazer as she opened her gate, Pam suddenly wished she had stopped to talk to him. Offered him a cup of tea even.

The thought surprised her. Normally when she felt down the last thing she wanted to do was talk to anyone, but there was something strong about Ward Frazer, something sympathetic yet non-judgmental that appealed to her. She had noticed it instantly the night of the accident. It was those thoughtful, guarded eyes, she thought. They made him look as though nothing would ever shock him. Or, rather, as though something had once shocked him so badly that nothing else would ever matter again.

Pam stopped suddenly and turned. But across the road the Miss Taylors had already let him in. For a second Pam stood there, indecisive, then she straightened her back and shook her head. She couldn't burden a virtual stranger with her problems. It wasn't fair. Her problems were her own affair. Affair. She shuddered at the word and let herself quickly into the house.

Chapter Fourteen

As soon as she stepped inside her front door Pam knew something was wrong, but it took a moment longer for her to work out what it was.

Cigarettes. She could smell the faint lingering smell of cigarettes.

Neither she nor Alan smoked. She never had and smoking made Alan cough. But Sean Byrne smoked. And Jennifer Carter smoked. Pam had seen them up on the common only last weekend, sitting on a bench together, smoking and chatting and laughing, unaware of Pam suddenly changing direction to avoid them, to avoid a difficult encounter, to avoid the bitter taste in her mouth, the stab of jealousy.

Now that jealousy turned to anger. She flung open the door of the front room and saw the bruised-looking rug once again slightly out of position. Her eyes narrowed and she crouched by the grate and stirred the ashes, swearing as they glowed red under her stick. They couldn't possibly still be smouldering from this morning, not on an ice-cold day like today.

In the kitchen two cups and saucers lay on the draining board, and one of them still had a smear of lipstick on the rim.

It was too much. Pam felt a strange overwhelming fury. It wasn't often that she lost her temper, but when she did she certainly knew it. At that moment she could quite easily have killed Jen Carter. How dare she come into her house and make love to her lodger? For Pam had little illusion about what Jen and Sean might or might not have been up to. She knew Sean Byrne too well to suppose that an impetuous, pretty young thing like Jen Carter would have the strength to resist him, if he put his mind to it.

And he obviously had put his mind to it, been putting it to it for some time. Thinking back, Pam could number several occasions when the front room had been indefinably different when she came home. She had never said anything. Scared to rock the boat. But she was damned if she would turn a blind eye this time.

The wireless was playing the *Londonderry Air* when Sean Byrne came in. Pam was waiting for the news. Like everyone else in the country she was heartily sick of the BBC's endless renderings of the *Londonderry Air*. It was either that or some condescending advice to housewives about how to make half a pound of sausages go just that little bit further.

Pam was strung up tight as a noose without the extra irritation of the BBC, so it was almost a relief when she heard Sean Byrne open the door.

She faced him in the passage, determined this time to have her say before he somehow contrived to take the wind out of her sails.

'Did you come back here at lunchtime today, Mr Byrne?' she asked.

'Yes, I did, Mrs Nelson,' he said. 'I forgot something.' He spoke easily but his eyes were watchful as though awaiting her next move. If he had only known it she would have liked to slap him hard across his sexy mouth.

But instead she crossed her arms on her chest. 'And it took you so long finding it that you had to light the fire to keep you warm?' The unaccustomed sarcasm sat uneasily on Pam's tongue, but she was pleased with it nevertheless.

Sean inclined his head. 'I'll pay for the coal.'

'Yes, you will,' Pam agreed. 'And you will also pay for your last week's rent and then pack your bags. It was not part of our agreement that you could entertain your lady friends in my house.'

For a long moment Sean stood there with his hands in the pockets of his overcoat. Then he lifted his blue eyes to hers.

'You wouldn't turn me out on the street, would you, Mrs Nelson? Not after what we have shared.'

Pam swallowed. 'We haven't shared anything,' she said sharply.

He didn't move. Nor did his eyes. 'Oh, come now, Mrs Nelson, we have shared dreams. You surely can't deny that.'

She couldn't. Nor could she help remembering that Alan would be home any minute. She had wanted Sean gone by then. Now she realised she had been hasty. Sean would not go without a fight. And if he fought dirty it could be very awkward indeed for her. Things were not good between her and Alan just now. And she knew Sean knew it too.

'My agreement was with your husband, Mrs Nelson,' he said, pushing home his advantage. 'I think it is up to him to throw me out.'

'I don't want Alan involved in this,' Pam said. 'He has enough on his plate as it is.'

'Is that right?' Sean raised his eyebrows with a hint of sarcasm and Pam bit her lip more sensitive than ever to slights about Alan just now. But she wasn't going to get into an argument about poor Alan.

'I just think it would be easier, for all of us, if you left,' Pam said weakly, hating the faint pleading note in her voice.

Sean took his hands out of his pockets and ran them slowly through his hair. 'I don't think you really want me to go, Mrs Nelson. You just don't like me seeing Jennifer Carter.'

Pam winced. It was so true. 'I don't care who you are seeing,' she said angrily. 'But I must insist you don't see them here.'

'I'm sorry it upsets you,' he said slowly. His eyes were very blue, very direct. 'But a man has to have his pleasure, Mrs Nelson. Surely you know that, a beautiful red-blooded woman like yourself.'

Pam felt her stomach turn over inside her. She hadn't felt very red-blooded recently. Not where Alan was concerned at least. Alan hadn't had much pleasure recently. Neither of them had. Pam sighed suddenly. If only she had got pregnant when they had been trying. None of this would have happened. And now the last thing on earth she wanted was Alan's baby. And knowing that tore her up inside.

Realising Sean Byrne was looking at her, she tried to pull herself together, only to find the anger flare up again. This time against Sean Byrne, against his smile, against herself for the stupid, debilitating attraction she still felt for him.

'Just leave me alone,' she snapped. 'Take your pleasure with Jennifer Carter if you must. But if I find you've been here with her again you'll go, and damn the consequences. And you won't find it easy to get another lodging, you know. Not being Irish and all. Not with all these poor refugees flooding in from Europe.'

Sean dropped his eyes then raised them slowly again. 'I would much prefer to take my pleasure with you, Mrs Nelson,' he said softly. 'You do know that, don't you?'

Pam stared at him, speechless. Then before she could even frame a thought, let alone speak it, they heard a step outside, the front door swung open and Alan came in together with a draught of icy cold air.

If he noticed the odd angry tension that hung in the hallway, he made no sign of it, merely stamping his feet as he shrugged off his coat, and commenting on the arctic conditions outside.

'They are saying the river might freeze tonight,' he said rubbing his hands, glancing quickly from Pam to Sean. 'I see you are still in your coat, Sean. I don't blame you. I've never know it so cold. I'll get the fire going in the front room.'

He missed the look that passed between his wife and his lodger.

'Why don't I do that for you tonight, Mr Nelson?' Sean offered and Pam saw Alan cover his surprise with a grateful smile.

'Why, that's very good of you, Sean. Thank you.'

The sudden silence seemed deafening to Pam.

Sean nodded awkwardly to the stairs. 'I'll just go up and get out of my coat.'

Pam was cringing. It all seemed so fake, so obviously tense. Sean's provocative remark still seemed to hang in the narrow passage between them. Alan's joviality didn't ring true. She felt sick.

'Are you all right, dear?' Alan asked. 'You look a little pale.'

'I'm fine,' she said crossly. 'Mr Byrne and I were just discussing the refugee situation,' she added rather desperately, in an effort to change the subject. 'They're mostly Jews, of course. I heard one of the government ministers today saying he didn't know where we were going to put them all if the situation gets any worse.'

'I know.' Alan rubbed his cheek with the back of his hand. It was a gesture he often used when he was worried or upset about something. 'Poor things. I did wonder if I ought to offer the boat.'

'The boat?' Pam stared at him. 'Don't be absurd. Who on earth would want to live on the stupid boat? It's far too small. Anyway they'd freeze to death.'

Alan looked hurt. 'It sleeps two at a pinch,' he said mildly. 'And I've got that little gas heater in there now.'

Pam almost laughed. That damn boat. Alan couldn't think of anything else these days. For a moment she looked at him in angry despair. Then looking up and seeing Sean standing silently on the stairs, she abruptly turned away and went into the kitchen.

Later that very same night, with guilty glee, Sean and Jen took the bus down to Putney, and with the aid of an illegal torch, located Alan Nelson's little boat, the Merry Robin, moored with two others to a narrow planked platform jutting into the river, and climbed aboard.

While Jen explored the tiny cabin, Sean at once got busy with his matches lighting Alan Nelson's new gas heater. On the fourth attempt he was successful and the thin blue flame threw a flickering light around the curved walls of their floating hideout. Decked out in brass-edged wood, with a bunk seat that folded ingeniously down from the wall, a big compass fixed to the table and maps carefully strapped to a shelf alongside a navy captain's hat, it was all very spick and span. It smelt faintly of beeswax and Brasso and it was clearly Alan Nelson's pride and joy.

It was pretty perfect for Jen and Sean's purpose too.

'Sean, this is fantastic,' Jen whispered, peeling off her gloves as the cabin temperature gradually crept above freezing. 'What a brilliant idea.'

Sean grinned and put Alan Nelson's navy cap on his head. 'I've always fancied myself as a bit of a sailor.' Fumbling around in the cramped space he located a locker from which he withdrew two tartan car rugs and a couple of cushions. He tossed them to Jen. 'Make the bed, darling.'

Bumping his head as he straightened up, he swore and Jen giggled. 'Aye aye, Captain.'

A moment later, Sean was tumbling her on to the bunk.

At first keyed up by their trespass, and still too cold to take off their clothes, they romped and laughed on the tiny bunk. But gradually, lulled by the creak of the wooden joints and the gentle, lapping of water, and for once not having to keep their eyes on the clock, their lovemaking became more tender and romantic than ever before.

Afterwards they inadvertently fell asleep and were woken shortly after midnight by a strange fizzing and cracking sound as the mighty river, for the first time in years, froze around them.

'To be sure, I would have thought the heat of our passion would have kept the ice at bay,' Sean remarked when they finally realised what had happened. And they laughed and laughed over the bottle of Irish whiskey Sean had thoughtfully provided as sustenance.

It was a bright moonlit night and as they tentatively emerged from the cabin and stood shivering on the small tilted deck gazing out across the glistening, strangely still river, Jen experienced an odd sense of excitement. For a moment she felt almost tearful with the emotion of it. Catching, her mood, Sean pulled her into his arms and kissed her gently. But it was so cold their lips were already almost numb and they retired hastily back into the cabin, realising with guilty but humorous satisfaction that they had left it too late to go home.

When Lady Helen de Burrel telephoned and told Louise that everyone was meeting up to go skating on the river on Saturday, Louise's first thought was that she hadn't got any skates and the second was to wonder if Ward Frazer was included in 'everyone'.

She had been furious to learn from the otherwise frosty and tight-lipped Mrs Carter that Ward Frazer had recently visited Sheila Whitehead.

'Perfect gentleman, she said he was,' Joyce had added. 'Most solicitous. Brought in her coal for her and all. Stayed chatting with her for ages.'

Inwardly seething, Louise had listened to this eulogy of her absent heart-throb with a gritty smile pinned on her lips, but just when she reluctantly opened her mouth to ask when exactly this had been, Mrs Carter had abruptly turned on the Hoover, rendering any further discussion on the topic impossible.

So Ward Frazer had been in the area without bothering to call on her. After her mother's slighting comments Louise found that a snub hard to take.

Having once read *Tess of the d'Urbervilles*, she even lifted the hall carpet to see if a note from him had inadvertently slipped underneath. It hadn't.

Now she summoned up the courage to ask Helen de Burrel whether he was to be included in the skating party and Helen laughed. 'Well, of course I've asked Felicity to ask him, but you know what he's like.'

'No, what is he like?' Louise asked irritably, alarmed that Felicity Rowe was obviously in closer touch with the Canadian than she was.

'Oh, you know,' Helen said airily. 'Here today, gone tomorrow. Nobody seems able to pin him down.'

Louise found this a very unsatisfactory reply and determined to be cool with Ward Frazer next time they met.

But when she arrived at Hampton Court a few days later to find Ward among a dozen or so other skaters, carving figures of eight on the frozen river, he looked so unutterably gorgeous in his thick, high-necked sweater and sleek corduroy plus fours that her heart lurched at the sight of him and all her brave intentions immediately dissolved on the thin cold air.

It wasn't just the skaters who were enjoying the crisp air and frozen river. The towpath was teeming with people, their breath puffing out of their mouths in little clouds as they walked or stood about enjoying the unusual spectacle. A horde of children were playing on the ice below them, screaming and shouting as they slithered around, chasing and catching each other. Somebody was even trying to ride a bicycle on the river with little success.

A bit further along the frozen bank, Louise could see Helen kneeling on a rug, pouring something from a Thermos, while her group of friends, in bright scarves and balaclavas, stood about chatting. Louise knew manners decreed that she should really go and say hello to Helen first, but instead she pushed back the hood of her duffel coat, patted her hair, took a deep breath of ice-cold air and crunched over to the edge of the river. Ward Frazer was, after all, the only member of the party she wanted to talk to.

Tentatively she waved. He saw her at once and she waited nervously as he swooped over, sliding to a flashy standstill at the bank, his sharp blades grating on the ice, sending a spray of silver frost high into the air behind him.

He smiled up at her, windswept and handsome and apparently pleased to see her. He wasn't wearing a hat, and flecks of ice sparkled like diamonds in his thick dark hair. 'What a pleasure,' he said. 'I never knew Cinderella could skate.'

Blushing, Louise looked doubtfully at the hard, bumpy ice, at the people wobbling about on jelly-looking legs, periodically crashing down with shrieks of pain. It had all sounded quite easy from the warmth and comfort of her home. 'She can't,' she admitted, reluctant to make a fool of herself. 'I think I might just watch.'

'Oh no,' Ward said at once. 'It would be a shame not to have a go. It's only a matter of balance. I'll teach you,' he added gallantly, a smile warming his grey eyes. 'We'll start right at the beginning by finding you a pair of skates. Helen brought some spare.'

And so passed one of the most pleasant afternoons of Louise's life. Skating involved a lot more than balance, she quickly discovered, but the pleasure of nestling into Ward's body as he steered her around, the pleasure of holding his hands while he skated backwards in front of her, the pleasure of his warm encouraging smile when she managed a few yards on her own, was worth any amount of bruises, any amount of fear and cold.

Helen had provided a magnificent picnic and they all huddled together on rugs on the bank, muffled in hats and gloves, munching through chicken sandwiches and, extraordinarily, some smoked salmon that one of Helen's relatives had sent from Scotland. As Ward reached over for the Thermos of tea, Louise felt his shoulder close to hers.

She looked up at him eagerly and he smiled at her. 'Not too many bruises, I hope?'

Louise shook her head. 'Not too many,' she said, very aware of Felicity Rowe's narrow gaze from across the rug. Whatever had happened between those two clearly wasn't happening any more. Felicity had been unusually subdued all afternoon.

Ignoring Felicity, Louise pouted prettily at Ward. 'Although I'm sure you let me go once or twice when you could have saved me.'

He shrugged. 'You have to learn how to fall, or you never progress.'

'That sounds very philosophical,' Helen chuckled, leaning forward to take their plates. 'Are you talking about life or merely about skating?'

Ward smiled appreciatively. 'You're too clever to be an ambulance driver, Helen. You ought to be studying psychology at university.'

Louise frowned. She didn't like him flattering other girls. Particularly not on attributes she felt she didn't possess. She wondered if he would like her more if she was doing some kind of war work. It seemed to be the in thing nowadays.

'I'd love to drive an ambulance,' she said. 'But Daddy doesn't think it's proper for girls to drive.' If she had hoped to put Helen down, it didn't work.

'Really?' Felicity sneered slightly from across the rug. 'How provincial.'

As Louise, with some difficulty, resisted the temptation to ram Felicity's sandwich down her delicate throat, Ward stood up. 'Who's coming for a last skate?' he asked. 'The sun's dropping fast.'

Louise leaped to her feet. 'I will,' she said and couldn't resist a gloating glance at Felicity as Ward knelt to help her lace her skates.

They didn't stay on the ice long. It was getting colder by the moment and Louise was afraid that despite her copious scarves, her nose was getting unattractively red.

Wishing she could get out of the cold, but not wanting the afternoon to end, she was utterly delighted when Ward offered to drive her home. 'I want to call on my aunts,' he said.

But the others didn't know that. And Louise was aware of several jealous glances as, having packed up Helen's picnic and said their goodbyes, he led her across the meadow to his car.

'Where did you learn to skate so well?' she asked, blowing on her hands as they drew away.

'In Canada,' he said. 'I used to play ice hockey at one time. And in

Germany, we used to skate quite a bit there on the lakes.'

'In Germany?' Louise stared at him. 'When were you in Germany?'

He didn't answer at once and remembering a comment someone had made at the Veales' party several months before she added, 'Was it for the Olympic Games? Someone said you were in the Canadian rowing team.'

'I was until I got injured.' He was silent for a moment as he negotiated the turn outside the gates of Hampton Court Palace. Then he glanced across at her. 'But I went back the following year. To Berlin. As a journalist for a Canadian newspaper.'

'I didn't know that,' she said. 'How long were you there?'

He shrugged, his eyes turning back to the road. 'Less than a year.'

His voice was clipped, Louise nodded understandingly. 'I suppose, you had to leave because of the war and everything?'

His expression changed imperceptibly. 'Yes, because of the war and everything,' he agreed.

Studying his impassive profile, Louise suddenly felt awed by her companion. Being a journalist in Nazi Berlin was so far removed from her experience of life, she could hardly even think of an intelligent question to ask about it. In any case he seemed suddenly rather preoccupied.

'So do you speak German?' she managed finally as they swept up past Richmond Park and into the outskirts of London at Putney.

'Yes, I do.'

'Helen speaks German,' Louise said brightly. 'And French.' Then wished she had held her tongue as he smiled.

'Yes. Helen is a clever girl. She ought to be doing more for the war effort than sitting about at the Adelphi waiting to drive an ambulance.'

Louise frowned, wishing he was as impressed with her as he was with blasted Helen de Burrel. 'I wish I could think of something to do,' she said. 'I'd like to help with the war effort. But it would have to be something interesting.'

He glanced at her. 'I'm sure your turn will come,' he said dryly, changing gear as they climbed the hill out of Wandsworth. Then he smiled. 'In the meantime I think you ought to enjoy yourself as long as you can.'

Louise felt her heart bump. What did he mean? Enjoy herself with whom? With him? With some desperation she realised they were rapidly approaching Clapham Common and her parents' house. Already he was slowing down for the sharp turn in through the gates.

She was just about to ask Ward what he meant when she noticed he was looking out of the window and frowning. Following his gaze she saw Mrs d'Arcy Billière's refugee boys leaning against the wall.

'Who are they?' Ward asked as he swung the car past them into the driveway.

Mistaking his question for one of justifiable distaste, Louise grimaced. 'They're Jewish refugees. Daddy hates them hanging round our gates the whole time.'

Ward glanced at her in surprise. 'Poor kids,' he said. 'What else are they meant to do?'

Sensing his disapproval, Louise quickly softened her tone. 'I don't know,' she said. 'Of course they don't speak a word of English.'

Ward pulled into the drive. 'There's something you could usefully do, then,' he said lightly. 'Teach them English.'

Louise stared at him. She almost laughed but then realised just in time that he might be serious. 'I wouldn't know where to begin.'

He shrugged and then stopped the engine and smiled into her eyes. 'At the beginning. That's where I usually start.'

For a breathless moment Louise thought he was going to lean over and kiss her but then he merely touched her cheek.

'Don't look at me like that,' he murmured.

'Why not?' she asked coyly.

He sighed and ran a hand through his hair as he looked away. 'You're a very pretty girl, Louise, and it would be all too easy for me to take advantage of that.'

She flushed prettily, wishing she could say she wouldn't mind if he did. But knowing it would be forward she refrained and instead invited him to come in for tea.

She was disappointed when he politely refused on the grounds of an evening engagement elsewhere.

Louise frowned as he got out of the car to open her door.

Once more she feared that he might be preparing to leave her with no plans for a future liaison. If only there was a party or function she could mention to him. But there was nothing. Again Louise inwardly resented the onset of war, which far from providing endless jolly parties and an inexhaustible supply of eligible young officers as she had expected, had on the contrary proved a grave disappointment.

'Goodbye, Louise. Look after yourself. Be good.'

'How can I be anything but good when there's nothing to be naughty at?' she said crossly as he kissed her cheek politely. 'You say I must have fun but where, with whom? Everyone is away in blasted France. In a minute you'll drive away and that'll be the last I hear of you too.'

Ward laughed. 'The Canadian air force will be arriving in Croydon any day now,' he said. 'I'll take you down some time and introduce you, if you like. They're bound to hold a few parties.'

Louise brightened. 'Oh, yes please. When?'

He laughed. 'Patience, Cinderella. I'm afraid Mr Hitler has to take priority just now.'

'But you will come and see me,' she said with faint desperation. 'Or at least telephone.'

'Of course I will,' he said easily. 'As soon as I get a chance.'

And with that Louise had to be satisfied.

She watched him drive away, and was about to go inside when he stopped at the gate. At first, with a spurt of hope, she thought he was coming back, but then she realised he was talking to the Jewish boys.

To her astonishment she saw them step forward eagerly. When he finally drove away, the two younger ones waved and ran after him.

Louise sighed and opened the front door. What exactly was it about Ward Frazer, she wondered crossly, that had everyone running after him?

The night the river froze was the start of a very pleasant few weeks for Jen. Already, since Sean had come back from Ireland after Christmas, the tenor of their relationship had changed considerably. Her lonely Christmas had toughened Jen's attitude towards her lover. Gone were the days when she bit back her feelings for fear of annoying Sean. Now she said exactly what she thought when she thought it and to her surprise Sean seemed to like her all the more for it. Even when her comments were not entirely what he wanted to hear.

They had started doing all the things lovers do: gone boating on the freezing cold lake in Battersea Park, danced the night away at the Grand, Clapham Junction, sat in the gods at the theatre, laughed in the variety halls.

And, best of all, now that they had found a convenient if waterborne love-nest, Jen was finally able to relax in the physical side of their relationship. And her mother's home by ten thirty rule had gone out of the window.

Ten days later, at the end of January, the worst storm of the century swept across the country.

In the middle of Sean's most tender caress, as the wind howled around them and the little boat rocked alarmingly, Jen sat up abruptly. 'I think I'm going to be sick.'

'For goodness' sake ...' Sean lifted his head irritably.

In the past Jen would have bitten her lip, scared to annoy him, but now she pushed him away and swung her bare legs on to the cabin floor. 'Sean, honestly, I feel awful. If only the blasted boat would keep still.'

He stared at her. 'You're sea sick,' he said and started laughing. 'You can't be seasick moored at the edge of the River Thames.'

'It's not funny,' Jen said crossly, holding her stomach and groaning as the boat lurched again.

'Well, for heaven's sake don't be sick in the boat. Alan Nelson would surely guess what we are up to if he finds a pool of vomit in his cabin.'

'Don't be disgusting,' Jen muttered groping about for her clothes in the dim light of the little gas stove. 'Anyway, he must be blind not to have noticed already. I left my umbrella on the deck last time we were here.'

Sean frowned. 'You must be careful,' he said. 'It would be a crying shame to lose our bed.'

For a second Jen looked at him. He really minded. She felt a warm glow in her stomach.

Then the boat rocked again. 'I'll be crying if I don't get on deck in a minute,' she gasped, struggling out of the cabin as the warm glow turned into an ominous cramping pain.

'Mind nobody sees you,' Sean warned laughing. 'You're showing rather a lot of bosom.'

Thinking he would leave her to cope alone she was surprised and rather embarrassed when he came out after her and steadied her as she clung helplessly to the bouncing rail. The wind was wild. The way it whipped through the trees and crashed against the moored boats was alarming. Even as Jen was violently sick over the side a scatter of slates from a nearby roof crashed into the foaming water beside them.

One or two of the boats looked as though they might easily get damaged, already they were straining, their ropes when the wind caught them; if they broke free all hell would be let loose.

'I think we'd better get off here,' Sean shouted at Jen as she hung on his arm, her hair torn back in the gale. 'I'd better get you home.'

Ten minutes later they were back on dry land. The wind was no better but at least the ground wasn't moving under their feet although oddly it still seemed to.

Half laughing, half crying, Jen clung to Sean's arm. 'I'm sorry,' she shouted as they struggled up Putney High Street, her words getting whipped away in the wind. 'I'm sorry I wasn't much fun this evening.'

Sean stopped and glanced down at her. 'You're always fun, Jennifer Carter,' he said. 'Even when you're vomiting, you're fun.' He was smiling but his eyes were serious. He touched her cheek gently. 'That's what I love about you.'

Jen stared at him. Had she heard him right? He had been in an odd mood all evening. She had thought it might be the storm. But now it seemed he had been working up to some kind of declaration. A declaration she wasn't sure she wanted. Not just now. Not while she still felt sick.

'Don't Sean,' she said, smiling weakly at him. 'Don't say anything now. I'm not up to it.'

She winced as he jerked his eyes away, realising she had hurt him. 'To be sure, I won't say another word about it,' he said stiffly.

He didn't, and afterwards Jen wished she had allowed him to go on. But then the following Wednesday she made her weekly round of all the stage agents and Sean's words were pushed out of her mind.

'I was going to wash my hands of you when you turned down that job in Carlisle,' Nev Cooper said. 'But then this cropped up and I thought you might be interested.'

Interested. Jen was almost delirious with excitement. Had Nev Cooper not looked so stern and unapproachable she would have flung her arms round his neck there and then and kissed him full on the lips.

A job in a film. Well, not in a film exactly but in a film studio. As a camera stand-in for the actress Sylvia Robson, billed as the Vivien Leigh lookalike.

Jen could not believe her luck. And it was luck. It was because she vaguely resembled Vivien Leigh that Nev Cooper had thought of her.

She would be used as a model to sit it out under the hot studio lights while the sets were arranged and the cameras positioned so that Miss Robson could step out of her dressing-room and perform her part without endless lighting adjustments and without ruining her make-up by breaking into an unflattering sweat.

Being a stand-in was hard boring work, Nev Cooper warned her, but Jen didn't mind. Who knew what might come of a chance like that, rubbing shoulders with real stars, real professionals?

Sadly no chance came of it. And the only rubbing she did was of her eyes to keep awake. But every day as she struggled on slow crowded trains up to Welwyn Garden City to toil under the hot lights with the brisk unfriendly crew, she consoled herself that she was at least earning. The fact that nobody at the studio took the slightest notice of a young unknown stand-in, apart from yelling at her to turn her head or straighten her back or to hold some uncomfortable pose half in and half out of a chair for hours on end while some technical problem was overcome, was irrelevant. She was working and that was a start.

And even though she began to dread the hot lights, the endless unexplained delays and was treated as the lowest of the low, Jen enjoyed being part of the studio life. It was a new world, a new exciting technological world, with strange unidentifiable equipment and brisk rushed people. She particularly liked the sets, each one a fragile little replica of the real world, perfect down to the last detail. Somehow they seemed incongruous among the clutter of the great cavernous studio.

The whole film-making business fascinated her. But it also humbled her. For the first time she began to appreciate the professionalism of the real stars. And to realise just how much she had to learn.

'They are so slick,' she told Katy Parsons at the end of her first week. 'Especially Sylvia Robson. Even though it's obvious everyone thinks she is a first class bitch.'

But bitch or not, Sylvia Robson knew her job. And whenever she got a chance Jen watched in awe as the actress skilfully portrayed her character's emotions.

Even under the hot lights in the wobbly makeshift set of a society drawing-room, with all eyes and cameras on her, Sylvia Robson seemed to be able to switch from an utterly convincing smile of heartfelt love to tears of deepest despair at the drop of the hero's hat. She was also a perfectionist, refusing to allow a take until she was convinced that every word, every nuance, every pause was exactly as she wanted it.

For Jen it was a revelation, but it in no way reduced her desire to make it as an actress. On the contrary she was even more determined than ever. But perhaps for the first time she realised how far she still had to go to achieve her ambition.

But at least until the film was in the can, she had a job, she had some money coming in, admittedly not much, but some. Enough to pay Katy back for Sean's Christmas present, enough for the odd little extravagance, to have her hair trimmed, her nails manicured, a new shirt.

And she had a handsome boyfriend whom she very much liked and who was definitely quite keen on her. To her relief, even her family had stopped nagging her about him. And Sean had settled down. He no longer teased her about other girls. His blarney seemed more genuine these days, less mocking. He made fewer anti-British comments. Even though he still crossed the road when he saw a policeman coming, he was definitely more relaxed. Sometimes she almost forgot he was even Irish. Yes, things were definitely beginning to look up.

And then on the seventh of February, Peter Barnes and Frank Richards were sent to the gallows and hanged for the IRA bomb in Coventry.

That night she met Sean as usual on the boat, but it wasn't a success.

Sean got deeper and deeper into the whiskey and cigarettes, all the time ranting on about Barnes's innocence, about the bloody British legal system, about ending British tyranny.

When Jen tried to console him, his blue eyes glittered angrily. 'You don't understand.'

'I do understand,' Jen said. 'Nobody likes to see people hanged. But nobody likes to see people killed by bombs either.'

'It's war,' Sean said angrily. 'People are bound to die in war.'

Jen stared at him and shivered. Then she reached for her coat. 'I'm not staying if you talk like that,' she said. 'It gives me the creeps.'

In silence Sean watched her struggle into her coat in the confined space. Then suddenly he reached out for her. 'Don't go,' he said. 'Don't leave me, not tonight.'

Jen looked down at him. The anger seemed to have gone, leaving his handsome face pale and his eyes red. Suddenly she had felt sorry for him. Sorry that British injustice had killed his old school friend. So she stayed and they made love but for once Sean's heart wasn't in it and he left her unsatisfied.

Two weeks later a retaliatory bomb went off in a litter bin in Oxford Street injuring seven people, and Jen found herself torn all over again.

She could hardly bear to think that Sean might have been involved. But she knew he had been deeply upset about the hangings, and very angry.

But that evening, as people lay in hospital in the aftermath of the Oxford Street bomb, he was in a different mood altogether. He didn't want to go straight to the boat when they met; he wanted to walk along the river. He wanted to talk.

But for a while they walked in silence.

Then suddenly he stopped. 'Nobody was killed,' he said.

'I know,' Jen said stiffly. She felt sick. She was dreadfully tired, it had been a difficult day and the news of the bomb had not helped. She wished she was back in her room in Lavender Road instead of stumbling along the damp foggy river bank.

She stopped suddenly and turned to him. 'Look, Sean, I don't want to talk about it, all right?' She saw his expression and a cold hand ran down her spine.

'Aren't you going to ask if I was involved?' he said. 'You normally do.'

Jen sighed. 'I don't want to know whether you were involved in it or not,' she said bitterly.

Sean was silent and Jen glanced at him. It wasn't like him to take no for an answer. As their eyes met she realised he looked more worried than angry. Abruptly he looked away and kicked a stone on the towpath. 'Whether I was involved or not,' he said, 'I may need an alibi. You don't have to be involved these days for the police to find you guilty.'

Jen felt a cold hand clutch at her heart. 'Weren't you at work then today?'

'I was. But they'll probably think the bomb was planted sometime last night.' She stared at him. 'I wasn't with you last night.'

'I know. That's why I need an alibi,' Sean said patiently. 'I took a drink with some friends and I was late getting back. Mr and Mrs Nelson may not have heard me come in.' He lifted his shoulders. 'It would be easier if I could say I spent the night with you.'

Jen bit her lip, not deceived by that negligent shrug. She didn't want this. God only knew where it could lead. And yet she couldn't allow Sean to hang.

'Why should I?' she asked. 'Why should I lie for you?'

Sean smiled. 'Because you're my girl, Jennifer Carter. And I love you.'

Jen sighed. When he looked at her like that she was putty in his hands. He touched his thumb to her lips and a shudder of desire shook her slender frame. She wished she could ask where he'd really been the night before. But before she could, he touched her again and she felt the pulses begin to throb in her groin. She was too tired to resist him. Too tired to argue.

'All right,' she murmured helplessly as he drew her into his arms. 'If anyone asks I'll say you were with me.'

Sean's expression lightened as he lowered his lips to hers. 'You're a good girl, Jennifer Carter.'

Chapter Fifteeen

The last time Joyce had visited Stanley in Reading Jail she had thought he had looked rather better than usual. He'd lost a bit of weight and his eyes had seemed brighter than she remembered. Being off the booze helped, of course; not that she had mentioned that, as most of his conversation had revolved around his desperate craving for a pint.

But this time as she took her place at the visiting table she knew as soon as she clapped eyes on him that something was up. His badly shaved cheeks were puffy, and his eyes had gone narrow like they always did when he was annoyed.

'Where the hell have you been the last few weeks?' he said as greeting.

Joyce sighed. 'I can't come more than once a month, Stanley. That's what we agreed.'

'Who agreed?' He glared at her 'I never agreed nothing.'

'I told you,' she said patiently. 'I can't afford to come more than that. And it takes nearly a whole day to get all out here. It would be different if you were in London like Bob.'

He glanced round to check the whereabouts of the prison warders then leaned over the table, his voice grating. 'You're lucky I'm stuck out here, woman. If I had my way I'd be giving you a damn good thrashing.'

Joyce felt herself quiver and swallowed nervously. She could see the temper in him, the anger waiting to break out. More than anything she hoped he wouldn't cause a scene. 'What do you mean?'

He slapped the table. 'You know what I mean. You've disobeyed me and that's a dangerous thing to do.' His voice rose. 'You're working for them bleeding Rutherfords. That's why you haven't got time to come and see your husband.'

'Who told you that?' Joyce asked quickly, wondering if he was calling her bluff.

Stanley was gripping the table edge as though any minute he would overturn it and leap at her throat.

'Micky,' he said and saw her surprise. 'Yes, it comes to something, doesn't it, Joyce, when a man has to find out from his son what his wife is up to?'

Joyce felt a stab of anger. 'It comes to something when a child tells tales on its mother,' she retorted sourly.

'And his sister,' Stanley said, watching with grim satisfaction as Joyce blenched. He sat back in his chair, his icy control somehow more dangerous than straightforward anger. 'You've done badly wrong, Joyce, letting her make a fool of herself with that Irish fellow. He's no good. They say he's IRA.'

Joyce stared. 'Who says?'

'Micky says.'

Joyce snorted. 'What does Micky know?'

'He keeps his ear to the ground,' Stanley said, slightly taken aback by her scorn.

Joyce quickly followed up her advantage. 'He's up to no good, that boy,' she said. 'I'm worried about him, Stanley. Where did he find the money to come all down here? Tell me that. I never gave him any. Nor would Jen. She's got no time for him and he knows it.' She frowned. 'He's just trying to make trouble with this IRA business, Stanley. Trouble for Jen. To get back at her.' And at me, she thought. Bloody child.

'I'll give you trouble,' Stanley said. 'If you'd been in the house like any decent mother none of this would have happened.'

'And if you'd kept your nose clean and earned a bit of steady money like any decent husband I wouldn't have needed to work,' Joyce flashed back before she could stop herself. Before she could think of the consequences. 'But thanks to you I have needed to,' she went on. 'And what's more I enjoy it. I like it, do you hear me, Stanley? I like it. And you know what?' She stopped for a second, surprised at what she was about to say. 'Well, I don't mind that Mrs Rutherford. I'll admit the husband is a nasty piece of work, but she's all right. What's more, she treats me with respect, which is a damn sight more than you've ever done.'

Even as the words left her mouth she knew they were a mistake but somehow she hadn't been able to stop herself. He had provoked her. Now as Stanley's face reddened, she wished she had bitten her tongue. How could she have been so stupid as to hold up Mrs Rutherford over him. Even if it was true.

'You'll be sorry you said that,' he said, dangerously quiet. 'You'll be very sorry you said that. I'll be out of here before too long and we'll see about respect then.'

Joyce shivered. It suddenly occurred to her that she didn't want Stanley to come out. Especially not now. Not after today.

It was a shocking thought. He was her husband when all was said and done. For better or worse. And father of her children.

Then suddenly, unexpectedly, she felt her resentment bubble over. 'I'm not scared of you, Stanley. What I'm scared of is not meeting the rent and getting thrown out of the house. So you just bloody shut up about me working, all right? I'm doing my best for you and the kids and if you don't like it, you can lump it.'

For an astonished second they stared at each other, husband and wife, neither of them used to Joyce standing up for herself.

It was Stanley who dropped his eyes first and Joyce knew she had won a small victory. It was a heady moment, but she didn't know what to say next.

'If Mick comes again could you speak to him, Stanley?' she said at last. 'Tell him he ought to go back to the country.'

'Don't you tell me what to say to my children.' Stanley's jaw hardened. 'I'll say what I bloody like. And I'll do what I bloody like and all,' he added. 'I may be in the slammer but I still have influence, you know. And that business about Jen is a disgrace.'

Joyce stood up, knowing that any further discussion was pointless.

'I'll come next month, then,' she said inadequately.

He didn't reply.

Katy thought Ward Frazer's idea of Louise teaching English to the Jewish refugees was a marvellous one. To be honest she wished she had thought of it herself. Not that her parents would have let her. She knew they would be convinced she would pick up some awful disease if she associated with any foreigners, let alone refugees. It had been bad enough the day she had run out to protect them from Jen's brother and his nasty, bullying little friends. Her mother had watched her anxiously for days after that, expecting evidence of tuberculosis or some other emaciating condition.

Louise giggled when Katy admitted this, and then wrinkled her nose doubtfully. 'You don't think they have got anything, do you? They do look a bit mangy and thin.'

Katy frowned. 'You make them sound like dogs,' she said reproachfully. Then she smiled. 'Actually the older one is quite nice looking.'

Louise started at her. 'You're joking.'

Katy shook her head. She remembered the way the boy had held her eyes that day, his own eyes dark and surprisingly bold, the fierce pride in his voice as he thanked her. 'I saw him out of the window the other day in a new jacket,' she said now. 'He looked quite presentable. Anyway I'm sure Mrs d'Arcy Billière wouldn't have them there if they were diseased. Not with that Count still calling regularly and all.'

'Oh yes, the mysterious count,' Louise giggled. 'I suppose I might get to meet him now. Although I'm sure he'll be most disappointing. Middle aged and bald most likely. Anyway Mummy is going to fix this teaching thing up for me with Mrs d'Arcy do-da tomorrow.'

Katy sighed. 'You lucky thing. I wish I could think of something I could do.' Yesterday she had seen an advertisement for people to drive ambulances for the Red Cross in France. She would never in a million years have the guts to volunteer for something like that. Not that they'd take her. Not with her chest.

Louise shrugged. 'There doesn't seem much point until something starts happening.'

Katy felt a shudder of anxiety. It was already the middle of March. Spring was coming. The evenings were already getting lighter. The ghastly winter fogs had finally dispersed. Blossom was appearing on the trees up on the common and some blue tits were building a nest under the pub eaves.

Hitler would surely now begin looking towards the West. His planes were often over the Channel. Only yesterday the first civilian had been killed in Scotland in an unexpected air raid. It could only be a matter of time. And Russia was now in control of poor brave Finland.

And yet people's spirits were high. Two weeks ago Mr and Mrs Rutherford had taken Louise to see the triumphant homecoming of the victorious battleships HMS Ajax and Exeter, conquerors of the vicious German warship the Graf Spee, terror of the Atlantic. Apparently the atmosphere among the cheering crowds was fantastic. Katy wished she had been there.

But of course it hadn't occurred to Louise to invite her along. Nor had it occurred to her that Katy might have liked to go to the Canadian air force party last night.

It was that long-awaited event that Louise had come to tell her about this morning.

'There was music and dancing and food like you wouldn't believe. I don't think anyone's told the Canadians we've got rationing here.' Louise giggled. 'And then there were all these tall handsome officers.'

'Like Ward Frazer?' Katy asked.

Louise wrinkled her nose. 'Well, Ward was still by far the handsomest and the charmingest,' she said. 'But they all seemed very nice.'

Louise lapsed into silence then and Katy thought she looked a bit gloomy. Although how anyone could be gloomy after spending an evening with a gorgeous man like Ward Frazer she couldn't imagine. Katy would have given her life for ten minutes of his company.

'I don't know about Ward,' Louise said suddenly. 'He takes me out and everything but he never does anything.'

'What do you mean?' Katy asked bravely, colouring. 'Like kissing and things?'

Louise looked coy. 'We've kissed of course,' she said stiffly. Then she sighed heavily, the desire to unburden herself overcoming her desire to keep up the pretence of blissful happiness. 'But not ... you know, proper kissing. And nothing else. No touching. Nothing.'

'But you said you'd danced together,' Katy pointed out. 'He must touch you then.'

Louise tossed her head impatiently. 'Of course he does. He's a lovely dancer. But it's the other touching he doesn't do,' She looked at Katy and nodded with a grimace. 'You know sexy touching. He doesn't even try.'

'Oh.' Katy was scarlet. She didn't know. Or only what Jen told her. And she hadn't seen Jen much recently. What with the film job and Sean, Jen hadn't had much time for gossip. And now that the film job was over, Jen was busy looking for another job. Katy wished now she had questioned Jen more closely. Then she wouldn't have to show her ignorance in these matters to Louise.

But Louise was too deeply locked in her own thoughts to notice Katy's discomfort.

'I don't understand it,' she said. 'I'm sure he's taken other girls to bed. I'm certain he took my friend Felicity, even though he dropped her flat afterwards. And I know he fancies me, he's always saying how pretty I am. So why doesn't he do anything with me?'

Katy shook her head sympathetically. But her mind ran riot. It sounded like a minefield. The thought of a man like Ward Frazer even holding her for a dance made her feel faint, let alone anything else. And the thought of being dropped flat by him. That would just kill her.

'Maybe he respects you,' she suggested eventually. 'That's what happens in books. Maybe he doesn't respect your friend anymore because she let him go the whole way.'

Louise snorted. 'Well, I wish he didn't respect me. It's driving me mad. Honestly, Katy, it's not fair. He treats me more like a younger sister than a girlfriend.' She pouted. 'Not that I'd let him go the whole way of course. But it's not very flattering that he doesn't even try.'

'Perhaps it's because of his aunts being neighbours of yours and on the Parochial Council with your father and everything.'

'I'm sick of hearing about his blasted aunts,' Louise said crossly. 'He's always using them as an excuse. Saying he's got to spend time with them. Saying how amusing and clever they are. I wish they didn't live here then I'd see more of him.'

'I didn't know the Miss Taylors were amusing,' Katy said with interest. 'I always thought they were a bit odd. What with that terrible dog and everything.'

Louise rolled her eyes impatiently. 'Daddy thinks they're a nightmare,' she said. 'But Ward really likes them. He says they've had an interesting life. They used to be something to do with the theatre apparently. I can't imagine that, can you?'

Katy shook her head, astonished. 'No, I can't,' she said. 'But I must tell Jen.'

'Mrs Carter's daughter, you mean?' Louise said with a sniff.

Katy nodded. It was awkward that Louise looked down her nose at the Carters. She didn't like having torn loyalties. 'Jen wants to be an actress,' she said stoutly. 'She's just finished working on a film.'

Louise looked grudgingly impressed. 'My brother thinks she's quite pretty,' she said as though that might explain it.

Katy smiled proudly. 'Her boyfriend Sean says she looks like Vivien Leigh.'

'I think that's pushing it a bit far,' Louise said. 'Although I must say, I'm looking forward to seeing *Gone with the Wind* when it eventually opens here.'

'Oh, so am I,' Katy said eagerly. Like everyone else she had been delighted that English Vivien Leigh had recently won an American Academy Award for her Scarlett O'Hara. But it was really gorgeous Clark Gable she wanted to see. She hesitated. 'Maybe we could go together,' she added tentatively.

Louise shrugged. 'I'll probably go with Ward,' she said.

'Oh, of course,' Katy said quickly. 'I just meant if Ward was busy or away or anything.' Louise had frequently complained that he was often away. On military assignments. Or so he said.

Louise stood up and put on her gloves. 'I certainly hope he won't be away,' she said and giggled suddenly. 'A long, soppy, romantic film like that might be just what I need to get him going.'

The 77 bus was already packed when Pam got on in Whitehall. She didn't get a seat until it had trundled past Big Ben and the Houses of Parliament, along the river and across to Vauxhall, and even then she found herself next to an enormously fat woman who insisted on holding forth about Mussolini's decision to mobilise all boys over the age of fourteen.

'Fourteen,' the fat woman said loudly, turning slightly to include passengers at the rear of the bus. 'Can you credit that? Children, that's all they are. Children. I've never liked that Mussolini,' she added more confidentially to Pam. 'I saw him on the Pathé the other night. I reckon as he's up to no good. He's got a shifty look about him. Slimy, them Italians: I don't trust them, me. Any more than I trust the Irish.'

Pam smiled mildly as the bus picked up speed along Wandsworth Road. She didn't want to get into a discussion about the Irish. It was far too close to home. She didn't know what she thought any more. All she knew was that she was tired. Dead tired. Much as she enjoyed her job, it was taking its toll on her. She had been working longer and longer hours, reluctant to go home. Reluctant to face Sean Byrne's blue eyes, the look he gave her as he disappeared off for the evening, often, these days, for the night. God only knew where he went. But the dark rings under his eyes and the complacent smile on his sexy mouth made it more than clear what he got up to. And she couldn't help but envy Jennifer Carter.

'Do you have children?' the woman asked suddenly and Pam flinched.

'No,' she said stiffly, flushing, certain that everyone on the bus was looking at her, pitying her. 'No, I don't.'

The fat woman nodded. 'I didn't think so,' she said. 'If you had children you'd be more shocked about them fourteen year olds in Italy.'

Pam felt a flash of anger. She had enough to worry about without worrying about the age of Mussolini's conscripts. She stood up abruptly. 'Mr Chamberlain said today that Hitler had missed the boat. When the naval blockade on Norway takes effect, Germany will be strangled economically. Then with any luck nobody will have to fight. Not even Italian fourteen year olds. Now if you'll excuse me it's my stop.'

It wasn't her stop, but as she walked in the wake of the bus along Lavender Hill with its lining of second hand furniture shops and seedy tobacconists, she smiled grimly to herself. The woman had looked astonished at her outburst. Astonished and put out. But one or two of the other passengers had nodded encouragingly. Someone had even patted her on the shoulder.

'That's right, love. Hitler don't stand a chance. Not against our boys.'

But Pam's smile faded abruptly as she rounded the corner on to Lavender Road.

She could see Alan ahead of her, walking along with his head down. And stalking him was a group of young lads. Even from here Pam could hear their provocative taunting voices and their overloud laughter. She recognised the Carter boy, Mick, and knowing him for a troublemaker, quickened her step.

'What you doing for the war effort, then, Mr Nelson?' she heard one of them ask.

Alan didn't respond and another chipped in readily. 'Painting yer boat, ain't yer?' And they all broke into raucous laughter.

'Got a gun on it, have yer?' Mick Carter asked.

Alan shook his head. 'No, I haven't got a gun.'

'So what will you do if Hitler sails up the river? Ram him?'

The boys thought this was hilarious. Catching up on them, Pam saw Alan flush and felt an odd pang that she should be married to a man who couldn't stand up for himself.

'What about your lodger?' one of them asked roughly. 'Is he going to fight? Or is he lily livered too?'

'He's Irish,' Alan said, stopping at the gate. 'He's neutral.'

'Neutral?' the boy asked incredulously. 'Is that what you call people who bomb innocent people out shopping?'

Alan put his hand on the gate. He saw Pam approaching and smiled weakly. 'He's not involved in that.'

'Did you hear that, lads?' Mick Carter asked. 'He's not involved in that, he says. Well, we know different, don't we, lads?' He suddenly noticed Pam and backed off a pace, smiling ingratiatingly. 'Oh, hello Mrs Nelson. We was just chatting to your husband about his war work.'

Pam frowned. She didn't like these implications about Sean. Rumours flourished in tense times like these and these were dangerous rumours. Ignoring the boys she walked straight past Alan and opened the front door.

'Come on,' Alan,' she said impatiently as he seemed to hesitate, perhaps preparing to stand up for Sean Byrne. She stood aside to let him in then she glared at the boys who still stood expectantly at the gate.

'Haven't you got anything better to do than harassing innocent people?'

The boys looked at each other then one of them shrugged. 'No,' he said. And the rest giggled.

Pam felt her temper rise at their insolence. 'You're lucky you don't live in Italy or you'd be called up,' she snapped.

'We're not scared. We'd fight now if we could,' Mick Carter declared. He nodded at Alan who stood behind her. 'Not like him.'

Pam waited for Alan to speak. But he didn't. Biting her lip, Pam shut the door and rounded on him.

'Why don't you ever stand up for yourself?' she shouted at him furiously. 'Why don't you explain? Why do you let them get away with it?'

Helpless, frustrated, she stared at him, wishing she could shake some vigour into his defeated-looking body, wishing she could rouse some life into his gentle brown eyes.

For a long moment he stood there silently, accepting her angry gaze but giving nothing back. Then he quietly turned away and took off his coat.

'Alan, for God's sake say something.'

He gave her a brief, apologetic glance and then looked away. 'What can I say? They're right, I'm not helping the war effort.' He lifted his shoulders wearily. 'The council even turned down my request for an allotment on the common today. It seems they don't even want me to 'dig for victory'.'

Pam flinched at the gentle sarcasm. He knew her department had been involved in promoting the new Dig For Victory campaign. With the shipping convoys under increasing attack from the German submarines, the government was desperately trying to encourage the country to become self sufficient in the basic food stuffs. Already large chunks of the public parks were being ploughed up. And parsnips and broad beans were growing incongruously alongside the late bulbs and wallflowers in people's front gardens.

Suddenly she felt the temper go out of her. 'Well, it's not my fault,' she said. 'I may write the leaflets but I don't organise the allocation.' She sighed. If only Alan had more self respect. If only he had more go about him.

Alan touched her cheek briefly. For a second his eyes met hers and then he turned away quickly. 'No, it's not your fault,' he agreed quietly.

As he moved away to the kitchen, Pam had a sudden urge to go after him. To cheer him. To hold him. To comfort him. To talk to him. But before she could move, someone rapped sharply on the front door.

Alan turned back. 'Oh, that'll be Sheila, I expect,' he said. 'She wants me to go over and help her fix that leak.'

But it wasn't Sheila. It was a tall grim-looking policeman.

Pam stared at him in dismay.

'Mrs Nelson?'

She nodded blankly, all too aware of the boys still standing at the gate. A hundred horrors suddenly rushed through her mind.

The policeman glanced over her shoulder. 'I understand that someone of the name Sean Patrick Byrne resides at this address.'

Pam nodded again. 'Yes, he does,' she said. 'But I'm afraid he's not here at the moment. That's my husband, Alan, you're looking at.'

The policeman looked taken aback. 'In that case I'm afraid I will have to wait inside,' he said irritably. 'And I'll have to ask you and your husband to stay in the house until he comes home.'

Pam blinked. 'Why?' she asked stepping back: 'What's it about?' But deep inside her soul she already knew. And already her heart was grieving.

The policeman produced a typewritten document. 'I have here the warrant for his arrest,' he said.

Mick Carter caught sight of Jen before she noticed him. He had been annoyed to be shooed away from the Nelsons' gate by the police. He had badly wanted to see that Paddy bugger walking straight into the trap.

Mick had known it wasn't right, Jen seeing an Irishman. Even though his mum turned a blind eye. Well, what did women know? Nothing. That's what. So it had rested on him to do something about it. After all, how could he hold up his head on the street with everyone knowing his sister was dating a bloody Paddy? And on Alan Nelson's boat too. He'd followed them there one evening. Wished he'd had the guts to confront them. But he'd told his dad instead. Probably his dad had got word to one of his pals and they had told the police.

But if he couldn't gloat over Sean he could still gloat over Jen, and when he saw her strolling up the road he couldn't resist crossing over.

Jen was always running him down, treating him like he was a child. Well, this would show her that he had some influence. She'd be more careful what she said to him after this.

Jen frowned when she saw her brother approach. Her mum had let slip a couple of days ago that Mick had been down to the Reading nick and grassed on her and Sean. Since then she had hourly expected to find herself face to face with some bruiser. She had even warned Sean about it. Warned him to be careful. She didn't want him getting his beautiful blue eyes blacked or his teeth punched in.

'What's up with you?' she asked now as Mick stopped in front of her. 'You've got an ugly enough gob as it is without pulling faces.'

Mick glared at her. 'I'm not pulling faces,' he said crossly. 'I'm smiling.'

Jen sniffed. 'Smirking more like.' She didn't stop and he was forced to turn and walk beside her.

He shrugged resentfully, 'Well, I've got something to smirk about. Unlike you.'

As Jen glanced at him, a sudden shiver coursed down her spine. But she didn't let her unease show. 'What?' she asked sarcastically, 'Beaten up some poor old lady for sixpence, have you?'

'You think you're so clever, don't you?' Mick flashed back at her.

'Only compared to you,' Jen said.

He glared at her. 'Well, you're not as clever as you think.' The smirk crept back. 'You lost yer fancy film job, didn't yer?'

Jen gritted her teeth. 'I didn't lose it. It finished.'

But he wasn't listening. 'That's not the only thing you've lost and all.'

She stopped abruptly and jerked him round to face her. 'What's that supposed to mean?'

Surprised by her sudden show of strength, Mick found himself bluffing, 'Nothing. I didn't mean nothing.'

Jen wasn't fooled. She grabbed his ear and twisted it viciously. 'Tell me what else I've lost,' she said through gritted teeth.

Her face was close to his. Mick quailed from the glittering anger in her eyes. 'The Old Bill are on to your boyfriend,' he muttered as his ear began to throb. 'They're waiting for him at Mrs Nelson's.'

An ice-cold hand formed a fist round Jen's heart. But even as her skin chilled, even as sudden tears sprang to her eyes, her brain leaped into action. Could she warn him? Was she in time? And the box. He would need the things in the box. The escape box. If they were waiting to arrest him, it was sure to be too late for an alibi. She knew Sean wouldn't want to take the risk. She took a sharp breath and jabbed her nails into Mick's ear lobe.

'How long ago was this?'

Mick's eyes filled with tears of pain. 'Just now,' he gasped. 'Let me go. It wasn't my fault.'

Jen thought rapidly. It was six o'clock. Sean should be on his way home from work. If she was quick she might be able to intercept him at Clapham Junction. If they weren't watching for him there. If he hadn't got away early. If he hadn't caught an earlier train.

She dropped Mick's ear. 'If I find out this was your fault, you'll be for the high jump,' she hissed as he began rubbing it pitifully. 'Now sod off. And I should keep out of my way this evening if I was you.'

As soon as she had turned the corner into Lavender Road, she broke into a run. There was no sign of the police or anyone else outside the Nelsons' house. Either they were still waiting inside or she was too late. She prayed she wasn't too late. Whatever Sean had done, she couldn't bear the thought of him inside. He wasn't the sort of man to go inside. He was too clever, too attractive, too sexy to be locked up. He'd go mad in jail.

Running up the stairs she grabbed Sean's box and ran straight down again. There was no time to waste.

She was panting by the time she got back to Lavender Hill and sweating by the time she reached the traffic lights outside Arding & Hobbs.

And there was Sean. She caught sight of him between two trams, on the other side of the road by the Windsor Castle, waiting to cross.

As the lights changed Jen ran forward. They met in the middle of the road. Sean took one look at the expression on her flushed face and the box under her arm and his sudden smile died.

'The police are waiting for you at the Nelsons',' Jen panted out as he pulled her back to the kerb.

He swore, and for a second his shoulders sagged. Then he roused himself and shook his head. His eyes were very blue. He glanced at the box. 'I don't want to go away. Should I stay and risk the alibi?'

She stared at him. 'But the police … You said they never believe anyone's innocent.' She choked on a sob. 'I can't bear for you to go to prison, Sean. I can't bear it. Half my family is in prison. I can't bear for you to be locked up too.'

He closed his eyes briefly and when he opened them again they were full of tenderness. 'I don't want to leave you, Jennifer Carter,' he said.

She swallowed hard, fighting back the tears. 'You've got to go. It's the only way.' She thrust the box into his arms. 'Please go, Sean. They might come looking for you any minute.'

He touched her cheek. 'Would you not come with me?' Jen's heart lurched. Her brain spun. 'I can't, Sean. I can't.' He dropped his eyes. 'I know it. How could you? What would we live off?' Then he looked up eagerly. 'But when I've got myself set up in Ireland, I'll write for you then.' He stared questioningly into her eyes. 'You'll come then?'

'Oh, Sean,' Jen choked. 'Of course I will.'

Gently he touched his lips to hers. 'Goodbye, Jennifer Carter Leigh,' he murmured unsteadily. 'You're a good girl.' And then he turned away abruptly.

'Be careful,' she called after him. But he didn't hear. He had gone.

Chapter Sixteen

'Oh, there you are, Mrs Carter. Have you heard? Germany has invaded Norway and Denmark. I've just heard it on the wireless.'

Jerked out of her daydream, Joyce looked up from her polishing to see Celia Rutherford standing in the doorway with a bundle of fresh laundry in her arms.

It was the ninth of April. The first decent day they'd had in ages. The blossom on the trees in the garden looked like confetti in the bright sunshine. It seemed too nice for war. With an effort Joyce put on a suitable grimace of concern. 'Norway and Denmark?' she repeated. To be honest she was a bit hazy about the whereabouts of either country. Quite high up, weren't they? Miles away, right up in the North Sea somewhere?

'Yes, both,' Celia said coming into the room. 'Denmark was overrun with hardly a shot being fired.' She snorted. 'Can you believe it, the Germans are calling it protection? And they say it's because of our navy laying mines in Norwegian waters, which is obviously quite absurd. And now a huge naval battle is going on of the Norwegian coast.'

She deposited the laundry on the table. 'Do you know, Mrs Carter, the vicar told us on Sunday we must love Mr Hitler like any human being. I can't imagine what he was thinking of, Greville was most annoyed about it.'

'He's a menace, that Hitler,' Joyce agreed. 'But he'll have his work cut out if he thinks he's coming here. We're not going to lie down and let him walk all over us.'

'Certainly not,' Celia agreed warmly. 'I suppose we should be grateful that Belgium and Holland are neutral. At least that cuts down his options for launching an invasion on us.'

Joyce ran her duster lovingly over the gleaming surface of the walnut china cabinet. 'Well, if he does come here at least he'll find the place nice and clean,' she said with a short laugh.

'You're doing a marvellous job,' Celia said, glancing around at the spick and span dining-room.

Joyce smiled. 'Like I say, Mrs Rutherford, I get a real satisfaction from cleaning an elegant place like this. Not like my pig sty at home.' Actually she wished she could get round to giving her own house a good going-over. She had hardly lifted a finger upstairs for weeks. Not that the boys noticed. They most likely wouldn't notice even if she did start keeping a pig up there. Certainly not from the smell. They might notice the grunting of course but knowing how deeply they slept they probably wouldn't notice that either.

Celia Rutherford walked over to the window and surveyed her pretty garden with a frown. The daffodils under the cherry trees, having bravely weathered the storms, were now fading, like a tired army in the face of a spreading carpet of early bluebells.

'You know, Mrs Carter, I really think I ought to do something. Towards the war effort, I mean. It makes me feel guilty just sitting around here doing nothing.'

'You do your garden, vegetables and potatoes and whatever,' Joyce said. 'Digging For Victory and all that.'

Celia shook her head. 'It's not enough. Even Louise is getting involved now. She's going to start teaching English to Mrs d'Arcy Billière's Jewish refugees.'

Joyce was surprised. She wouldn't have thought that Miss Stuck-up Louise would have had it in her.

'I wish my Jen would do something useful,' she said. 'She's still hankering after being an actress.'

'Well, acting has its uses,' Celia said kindly. 'They say that ENSA is doing a marvellous job entertaining troops all around the country. And in France, I believe. And the London theatres are doing very well at the moment. Anything to take people's minds off the endless waiting and worry. We're taking Louise to Daphne du Maurier's *Rebecca* in a week or two. It's meant to be a marvellous production.'

Joyce had never heard of it. 'Well, I can't see Jen making a go of it,' she said. 'She made a great song and dance about a film job she'd got. But it only lasted five minutes. She says she needs training but I would have thought if she was any good at it they'd have offered her a proper job by now.' She shook her head. 'No, she'd be much better off down in the munitions factory. Or even in the services. Not that they'd have her, most likely, headstrong little madam as she is.'

As she spoke she glanced doubtfully at her employer. She could hardly imagine elegant Mrs Celia Rutherford stuffing shells in the munitions, nor manning one of those great searchlights out on the common like the WAAF girls did. 'What sort of war work was you thinking of, Mrs Rutherford?'

'I saw in the paper the Women's Voluntary Service are asking for volunteers,' Celia said lightly. 'I quite fancied doing a bit of canteen work.'

'Canteen work!' Joyce was shocked. 'That would never do. You're far too classy for a canteen.'

Celia smiled. 'Oh, come now, Mrs Carter. Things are different nowadays. Anyway,' she confided with a hint of self-consciousness. 'I've always had a dream of running a little café. Ever since I was a child.'

Joyce stared at her as old memories suddenly came flooding back. Childhood memories of a make-believe café, make-believe customers, make-believe cakes and sandwiches. Unrealised teenage dreams of being a Nippy in a Lyons Corner House. Wildly unlikely adult dreams of Stanley making good and setting her up in a cosy little snack bar on the south coast somewhere.

'So have I,' she said.

For a second they gazed at each other wistfully. Then they laughed.

'Greville wouldn't hear of it, of course,' Celia said and turned away from the window.

Joyce frowned. It was odd that Mrs Rutherford felt constrained by her husband's wishes just the same as she did. She was glad she had stood up to him over the job, though. She felt good about that.

She was about to say so, but Mrs Rutherford spoke first.

'I was sorry about that jewellery business back in December,' she said abruptly. 'The police never found the culprit, you know.'

'Well, it wasn't me,' Joyce said quickly.

Celia Rutherford looked stricken. 'Of course not. I never ...' she stopped and flushed slightly and started again. 'I'm afraid my husband was rather too hasty.' She blinked. 'But you know what men are.'

Joyce nodded. 'Bastards,' she said.

Celia's eyes widened. 'Well, I ...' She bit back a guilty giggle. 'Really, Mrs Carter, what will you say next?'

Joyce looked surprised. 'It's only the truth, Mrs Rutherford. You know, sometimes I reckon as we might be better off in the world without them.'

'Certainly we'd be better off without Adolf Hitler and his cronies.' Celia agreed, picking up her laundry. 'Oh, by the way, Mrs Carter,' she added cautiously from the door. 'Cook dug up far too many parsnips yesterday. I've asked her to put a couple out on the hall table in case you'd like them. You'd be doing me a favour actually. Otherwise we'll be eating them till the cows come home.'

The door closed before Joyce could reply and she shook her head with a wry smile. She wasn't a bad sort, that Mrs Rutherford. If she'd just let her hair down occasionally they could probably have quite a laugh.

For the first time in her life Katy felt deeply sorry for Jen. She had been so brave about Sean going. Declaring his innocence and accusing the police of trumping up charges when they questioned her. She'd told Katy privately that he had almost risked staying just for her. That he'd wanted her to go with him. That he wanted her to join him later.

But then he hadn't written. Not one line. Not one word in four weeks.

And Katy could see how much that upset her friend, however hard she tried to hide it.

And what made it worse was that since the film job Jen hadn't found any work.

A singing job seemed her best bet. But the agents said she didn't have enough repertoire and the producers said she needed voice training. Someone told her she could get a bit of piano practice at the music publishers where they'd play the songs through for you a couple of times if you bluffed that you were putting on a show. But even though she got some practice that way and a few sheets of music, you couldn't go every day. In any case, the publishers' pianists didn't help with voice technique or breathing, and at a guinea a time, she couldn't afford decent singing lessons.

The bright side was that they had been to several shows together. 'If I can't be in them we might at least go and see them,' Jen had said. 'Might as well spend what money I have got.'

So they'd been to see John Gielgud as King Lear at the Old Vic, and *The Beggar's Opera* at the Haymarket with Michael Redgrave as Captain Macheath. And then on Katy's birthday on the sixteenth of April, Jen had surprised her with tickets to *Gone with the Wind*, where to their mutual embarrassment, they had both wept buckets.

As they walked home together, still swooning for Clark Gable, Katy had almost begun to feel happy. The weather was improving, she was eighteen years old, and she hadn't coughed all day. Things were definitely looking up.

For a short while, even the war hadn't seemed too bad. At first everyone had said invading Norway was a major blunder by Ribbentrop. But now, reading through the lines of the meagre, uninformative news bulletins, it was becoming increasingly obvious that the Allies were fighting a losing battle.

The dreadful Norwegian weather, snow and freezing temperatures, was bad enough for the ill-equipped British troops without the vicious German tanks and artillery and endless aerial bombing. The casualty figures made grim reading.

In the House of Commons Mr Chamberlain was coming under pressure to resign. In the pub downstairs Katy could hear loud drunken voices making the same suggestion.

'He ought to go.'

'It's a right balls-up.'

'Fancy sending them without the kit.'

'More buggers dying of frostbite than being killed by Jerry.'

'Why don't they get the RAF up there to bomb the Jerry positions?'

'Who's running this war?'

'Not Mr bloody Chamberlain, that's for sure.'

Upstairs Katy bit her nails and wished she couldn't hear.

And then suddenly on the tenth of May, he did go. Handing over the shambles of a demoralised, frostbitten army and a worried, questioning nation to Winston Churchill.

And on the same day Hitler's troops invaded Holland and Belgium.

'But Holland and Belgium are meant to be neutral,' Katy whispered in horror when Jen came running in with the news. 'What else did they say?'

Jen shook her head. 'They're sending our troops up from France to help. But I reckon they'll be too late. Just like Norway.' She tossed back her head and smiled grimly. 'I wonder who'll get it next. Us? Or France?' She turned to Katy and grimaced. 'You'd better get out your gas mask again, just in case.'

Katy flinched. But Jen's words were not unfounded. That afternoon Reichsmarschal Hermann Goering's Luftwaffe, already bombing northern France, carried out a daring daylight air raid on Canterbury, for the first time dropping incendiary bombs on innocent civilian homes.

Suddenly there was too much news.

Katy listened in horror as the terrible loss of life was given out so calmly. One hundred German aircraft downed by the Dutch in one day. Thousands of soldiers killed every day. The dreadful treachery of Nazi sympathisers in Holland. But for Katy the RAF reports were the worst. The relief of hearing that 'all our aeroplanes returned safely' was immense. The news that 'one of our aeroplanes failed to return' made shivers run up her spine. And then the awful day when 'eleven of our aeroplanes failed to return.'

Katy couldn't help thinking of Ward Frazer in one of those aeroplanes. Wondering if he was safe. Wondering if he was scared. Wondering if he was dead. She knew Louise was worried too.

Everyone was worried. You could see it in their faces in the street. She could hear it in the subdued, irritable murmurings in the public bar.

And all Mr Churchill could offer was 'blood, toil, tears and sweat'.

Sheila Whitehead was in a terrible state. The last she had heard of Jo was that he was in Belgium, and now the Germans had invaded Belgium.

Listening to her panicked rantings, Pam bit her lip helplessly. For once the words of comfort just weren't there.

Even the King's brave broadcast on the wireless didn't help. 'We must all do our part with courage and endurance,' he said. 'And call on God most high.'

'What, on earth can God do to help?' Sheila had sobbed. 'God probably doesn't even know who my Jo is.'

'It's all right for you, Pam,' she added resentfully as Pam once again tried to reassure her. 'It's not as if your Alan's in any danger. You don't know what it's like.'

Pam was hurt. It was true, she didn't know the fear, but she was experiencing just the same feelings of loss and despair, Not that she could admit to it.

Sean's sudden disappearance had been a strain for Pam. She had guessed like everyone else that Jen Carter had warned him not to come home that day. And she wished it had been she who had had that privilege.

She knew the neighbours thought she and Alan had been duped. But she didn't care. All she cared was that he had gone. And that she hadn't said goodbye.

And she had an awful feeling that Alan knew how much she cared. Even though she had tried to brazen it out. To say good riddance. She couldn't help pining for that soft Irish voice, those appreciative blue eyes, those lazy smiling lips.

And when she packed up Sean's clothes into boxes, she couldn't bring herself to take them to the Red Cross as Alan had suggested. Instead she had stored them carefully in a dark corner of the attic. And her guilt made her even more irritable and dissatisfied with Alan.

One Saturday when she had been sitting at the kitchen table thinking about Sean, Alan came back unexpectedly. She had thought he was down on the river tinkering about with his boat as usual.

'What's up, Pam?' he asked, frowning in concern at her red eyes.

'The news is bad,' she said stiffly, deliberately misunderstanding him. 'The French have lost Amiens and Arras. The Germans are only sixty miles from Paris. There's a strategic withdrawal going on in Belgium.'

A strategic withdrawal. Nobody said the word retreat. The Dutch had surrendered. Belgium just had to hold out.

'I daresay we'll win through in the end,' Alan said calmly, and she stared at him.

'Thousands of people are dying every day over there,' she said angrily. 'Don't you care?'

'Of course I care,' he said.

'Well, you don't show it,' Pam snapped. 'I'm worried to death about Jo. Sheila hasn't heard for days.'

He came over and touched her cheek. 'You should try not to worry so much. Worrying doesn't help.'

Pam jerked away. 'Oh, yes it does. It keeps my mind off ...' She stopped abruptly. 'Off other things,' she finished lamely.

Off Sean, she'd wanted to say. Off us. Off our problems. She didn't say but he knew.

She stared at him, at his blank face, the hurt in his soft eyes.

'Pam, please ...'

Suddenly the whole thing was too much for her. The unspoken reproach was more than she could take.

Her shoulders sagged. 'It's not just worry,' she said flatly, turning away. 'If you must know, I feel guilty that so many men are fighting so hard in such terrible danger when you're sitting around at home or playing on your stupid boat.'

Louise couldn't believe her luck when Ward Frazer offered to drive her home after a party in Helen de Burrel's little Kensington flat.

Over the last month Louise had only seen him twice. And both those times had been with other friends. Even *Gone with the Wind* had been spoiled for her by the presence of Helen, Lucinda Veale and two hearty young naval officers on shore leave.

She had had no opportunity to try her campaign of seduction on him. But now, tonight, he seemed different, she knew he had drunk more than usual. Lucinda had whispered to her that she thought he had just come back from some dangerous mission. Certainly there was a hard glittering look to his eyes. But when she had asked him about it he had just smiled and pulled her closer towards him as they danced to Helen's new jitterbug records.

On the way home she told him proudly that it had been arranged for her to start teaching Mrs d'Arcy Billière's Jewish boys the following weekend.

'Hey, that's great news,' he said. 'I'm impressed.'

Encouraged by the warm look in his eyes as he turned to smile at her, she found the nerve to ask if he fancied a moonlight stroll on Clapham Common before dropping her off.

'It's such a lovely night,' she gabbled. 'So clear and everything. And I don't feel a bit tired.'

He nodded. 'Sure. I'll park by your parents' gate. We can go from there.'

So they did. And as they walked Louise racked her brains about how she could get Ward's hands out of his pockets and round her.

Eventually she spotted a bench and suggested they sit down for a moment.

'Look at the stars,' she said dreamily, leaning back, letting her shoulder brush his. 'I always think stars are so romantic, don't you?' She felt rather than, heard his soft chuckle and swung round to face him. 'What? What is it?'

He shook his head and stood up. 'It's you, Louise. You're cute.'

She flushed slightly. 'Stars are romantic,' she said crossly.

'Oh yes,' he agreed gravely, hands in his pockets again. 'Very.'

'Ward, please ...' She stood up too. Suddenly her heart was pounding.

His eyes narrowed. 'Please what?'

'Please don't treat me like a child.'

He sighed slightly. 'When you look at me like that with those big eyes I certainly don't want to treat you like a child, Louise. I want to treat you like the beautiful sexy woman you nearly are.' His eyes dropped to her slender figure then rose again to her flushed eager face. 'I want to touch you, to kiss you, to have you move against me like you did on the dance floor this evening.' He saw her responsive tremble and gave a wry grimace.' I know you want it too. But unfortunately we can't have everything we want. I'm sorry. It's a fact of life.'

Louise almost groaned. It was unbearable to hear his voice speak those soft caressing, seductive words and yet not be touching him. He was only a yard away but it felt like ten miles.

'But why not?' she whispered. 'If we both want it.'

'You don't know what you're saying,' he said suddenly impatient. 'You fancy you're falling in love with me, but you haven't the faintest idea what that means. You haven't thought it through. There's a war on, remember. Let's face it, I could be dead tomorrow.'

To her horror, Louise felt tears welling. 'I have thought it through,' she said, her voice catching pitifully in her throat.

He shook his head. 'I'm not the guy for you, Louise. I'm not the guy for anyone anymore.'

'Why not?'

He didn't answer for a moment then he sighed. 'It's a long story.' He took a hand out of his pocket then and touched her cheek gently. 'You don't want to get involved with me, Louise. It's not worth it.'

'Is there someone else?'

He withdrew his hand abruptly, his eyes staring away over the dark common. Then almost reluctantly he shook his head. 'No, there isn't anyone else.'

Louise pouted. 'Then why won't you have me?'

He smiled grimly. 'You don't know what you're saying.'

'I do know what I'm saying.' Louise bit her lip as her colour flared wildly. 'I'd go to bed with you. I'd do anything you asked, and ...'

Suddenly his hands were on her shoulders. 'Stop it, Louise. Don't say things you don't mean.'

'But I do mean it ...' And suddenly she was crying, uncontrollably sobbing out her agonising love for him and he was cradling her in his arms, swearing under his breath as he stroked her hair, his fingers lingering on her neck, sliding up to her chin, tipping her head back so he could gently kiss away her tears.

And then his fingers were on her face too, tracing the path of her lips. And suddenly she could hardly breathe.

She stood rigid, under the spell of his sensual caress, rigid with fear, rigid with excitement, wanting and waiting. Waiting for his lips to touch her mouth.

And when they did she thought she would melt, melt and explode at the same time as a sudden shudder rocked her body.

As her hands found his shoulders, slipped into his hair, she heard the soft groan in his throat, felt him pull her hard against him, the thunder of her heart, the painful craving desire that shot through her.

She couldn't believe what was happening. For weeks, for months, this had been her dearest wish and now it was happening. Handsome, wonderful Ward Frazer was kissing Louise Rutherford.

And then he wasn't kissing her any more. He wasn't doing anything. He was standing holding her tight in his arms, silent and still and she could feel the tension right through his strong body.

Her own body throbbed painfully, pulses hammered in places she didn't even know existed. Her breasts ached. Suddenly she felt sick.

When he spoke his voice was husky and low, quite unlike its normal self. 'Damn it. I'm sorry, Louise, I shouldn't have done that.'

He loosened his hold on her then, pushing her back so he could look down into her face. His dark brows were low over his eyes and his mouth was a hard straight line and when she smiled nervously he didn't respond.

Her heart sank. 'Don't you fancy me after all, then?'

His mouth twisted into a bitter smile and he raised a hand to her cheek, caressing her flushed skin with cool, confident fingers. 'Oh, I fancy you all right. Just now with the moonlight in your hair and love in your eyes and the taste of you on my lips, I could quite happily throw you to the ground and make love to you right here and now.'

'Then why don't you?' Louise asked softly.

'Because I'd be doing it for the wrong reasons.' He was silent for a moment then he sighed. 'So would you. You're too young, Louise. Too inexperienced.' He ran a hand through his hair and tried to smile. 'You need to learn patience, little one. You don't want to throw yourself at the first man you meet.'

A rush of agonising disappointment flooded through Louise as he took her hand and began to lead her back across the common.

'You're not the first man I've met,' she said sulkily.

He laughed then. Laughed. Louise felt the blood freeze inside her. How dare he laugh at her? She pulled her hand out of his.

He glanced at her. 'I told you, I'm no good for you, sweetheart,' he said seriously. 'I'm too old for you. And too bitter and twisted.'

'You're not that old,' Louise said crossly. 'And you don't seem a bit bitter and twisted.'

'Oh, I am,' he said and there was something hard and painful in his eyes as he slowly shook his head. 'Believe me, I am. But I do at least retain a shred of chivalry. And that tells me to leave innocent little virgins well alone.'

Louise blushed scarlet. But before she could speak they had crossed the road and he was marching her to the front door. 'I'm sorry, Louise. Very sorry. But I don't want to be responsible for breaking any hearts.'

But she knew it was too late. She knew he had already broken her heart. And she knew hers wasn't the only one he had broken. 'What about Felicity Rowe?' she asked suddenly.

For a moment he was silent. 'Felicity Rowe is somewhat different,' he said dryly. 'No way could Felicity Rowe be described as an innocent little virgin.'

Louise blinked.

Ward put out his hand and touched her cheek. 'Good night, Cinderella,' he murmured. Then he turned away. She watched him crunch back down the drive. And a moment later she heard him drive away at some speed.

On the twenty eighth of May, Belgium capitulated to the Germans.

Joyce heard the news as she cleaned her sons' bedroom. Mick had got hold of a smart little wireless from somewhere only last week and although the battery was already fading, it made a nice change to listen to it while she cleaned.

The general feeling was that Belgium's King Leopold had let the Allies down badly. If only he had called them in earlier to protect his country instead of leaving it until the Germans actually invaded. And then, just when they were beginning to make a bit of headway against the Wehrmacht, the blasted man surrendered, leaving the Allies badly in the lurch.

Crossly Joyce yanked the grubby sheets off Mick's bed and leaned over to turn the mattress. But before she did, her eye caught a jagged rip in the mattress covering. Some of the stuffing was already oozing out.

She poked it back irritably and frowned. There was something in there. Something other than wads of ancient horsehair. A small lumpy bundle tied carelessly with string.

As she pulled it out and began to unroll it, the news bulletin finished and the wireless began churning out the inevitable cinema organ music.

Vaguely assuming that the scruffy paper bag would contain some biscuits or even sweets, bulls' eyes or tigernuts, hidden away for Mick's private night-time eating, Joyce could not believe her eyes when she found herself staring at three or four bits of jewellery.

Blankly, heart thudding dully, she tipped the glittering pieces out on to the stained mattress. And at once the breath caught in her throat.

Numbly she put a hand to her eyes. And at the same moment she caught a small movement by the door.

Her head jerked round and she found herself staring straight at Mick.

She didn't know what to say. Words were beyond her. She recognised that jewellery. Recognised the crescent diamond brooch with the faulty clasp that

Mrs Rutherford used to wear on her lapel.

Disbelief and disgust vied for expression as she realised what must have taken place that night of the accident.

While everyone had been out seeing to little Ray Whitehead, lying half dead in the street, her son had been in Cedars House casually lifting the Rutherfords' jewellery.

Joyce felt her heart palpitate unnervingly.

Her voice was hoarse. 'Do you realise what would have happened if the police had found this jewellery here?'

Mick looked defiant. 'I knew they wouldn't find it,' he said. 'I kept it somewhere else until the heat was off. I'm not stupid.'

Joyce stood up and was horrified to discover her knees were trembling. 'Where's the rest of it?' she asked, dangerously quiet. 'Where are the rings and the pearls and the other brooch?'

'I didn't take no pearls,' he said sulkily. For a second she thought he was going to disclaim knowledge of the other pieces. Then he shrugged. 'One of the lads took the rest to Lorenz's.'

Joyce closed her eyes in despair. When she opened them again they were icy. 'And where's the money you got for it?' she asked.

When he didn't answer at once her voice rose. 'Where's the money?'

Mick bit his lip. 'We put it on the National,' he said grudgingly.

'And lost it, I presume?'

He nodded. 'It was a dead cert, Mum, honestly. I would have given you the winnings and that. I swear. But the stupid horse fell.'

Joyce had heard it all too often. Stanley's horses always fell too. They always had.

'It wasn't fair,' Mick went on, apparently unaware of his mother's terrible and mounting fury. 'A horse called Bogskar won and the only person who had money on him was bloody old Lorenz.'

Joyce suddenly felt like the empty kettle she had once left on the stove. When it finally exploded, little pieces of metal had embedded themselves all over the kitchen wall. She wanted to embed a piece of metal in Mick's head as she exploded now.

'I don't bloody care which bloody horse won the National,' she screamed. 'All I care about is you damn near lost me my job. The one thing in my life I've ever enjoyed.' She stabbed a finger at the jewellery on the bed. 'It may still happen if they ever discover about this.'

Unfortunately the BBC chose that moment to present Flotsam and Jetsam, the nation's favourite comic duo, and Mick made the mistake of laughing at their first joke.

It was too much for Joyce. Gritting her teeth she advanced across the room and slapped him hard on the face.

He backed away hastily before she could raise her arm for a second swipe. 'What was that for?'

'Get out,' she hissed. 'Just get out.'

He stared at her blankly, red eared, rubbing his cheek. 'What do you mean?'

'I mean, get out of my house,' she hissed. 'I didn't want you back here in the first place. You're a bloody nuisance. You always have been. You're a troublemaker, that's what you are. Well, I've had enough of you. Now you can just bugger off.'

Mick blinked, for the first time perhaps realising he had badly overstepped the mark. His chin hardened mutinously. 'Where would I go?'

She shrugged angrily. 'I don't bloody care,' she said. 'For all I care you can go and join the German army.' Her eyes narrowed. 'Not that you'd have the guts. But you listen here. If you come back to this house in a hurry, I'll hand you straight over to the police and you can go to Borstal.'

Jen stood in the semicircle of other hopefuls on the small stage and waited for the soprano introduction. Although how they expected anyone to sing well with two casting producers prowling along the line on red alert for a false start or a flat note, she didn't know. Her own heart was thumping in time with the music, she could feel her knees shaking and she was certain the other selectors would be able to see them from the auditorium.

As the soprano part started, Jen, to her horror, could hear that the girl next to her was singing terribly sharp. She groaned inwardly. It would be just her bloody luck for the producers to think the screeching belonged to her. Carefully she edged away and got a sharp nudge from the girl on her other side for her pains.

As the selectors hovered behind her a few moments later, Jen was convinced the dreaded hand of dismissal would fall on her shoulder. She could hardly concentrate on the music. Tried desperately to control her shaking limbs. But thankfully it was the screecher who got tapped and the off-key notes stopped abruptly as she burst into tears and was ushered off. Jen's sigh of guilty relief almost caused her own rejection, but then they passed on to another victim and she relaxed fractionally.

By the end of the piece there were only ten girls left. Jen didn't know how many they wanted. She wanted to ask but as she and the other nine girls stood in the wings waiting for the next stage of the audition, they suddenly heard a wireless somewhere backstage relaying the dreaded news that the British and French forces, retreating rapidly from Belgium, were now completely encircled on the French coast near Dunkirk.

One of the girls broke into noisy sobs. The other nine looked at each other in horror as the report went on to say that the exhausted soldiers were being pounded from all sides and from the air, even as they tried to embark on the few Royal Navy ships available to rescue them.

'They'll never get them away,' one of the girls whispered. 'How on earth many ships do you need to carry five hundred thousand men? More than we've got, surely.'

'They're calling for civilian boats to go over and help,' another girl said. 'I heard it this morning. They can't get them big warships close enough. The beaches are too shallow.'

Jen touched the shoulder of the girl who was sobbing. 'Are you all right?' she whispered.

'Her boyfriend Ralph was in Belgium,' a pretty brunette said when the weeping girl failed to respond. 'Gorgeous he is and all.' She shook her head. 'Poor kid. She needs a cup of tea.'

But before they could say any more, they were called back in to show off their tap steps.

Again Jen waited in trepidation for the hand of dismissal on her shoulder. She knew tap dancing was not her forté.

Miraculously, for once she got the steps right and the dreaded hand fell on other shoulders, not hers.

By the end of the number four girls still stood on the stage. Jen was one of them.

They were asked to wait while the selectors huddled together in the auditorium. 'I reckon as we've got it,' the pretty brunette whispered to Jen, and Jen felt her skin prickle.

'It'll be just my luck if Hitler invades on the first night,' she whispered back and the other girl giggled.

'If he invades anywhere near me he'll get a stiletto somewhere he won't like.'

All four girls were laughing when the producer beckoned them forward to the edge of the stage. Laughing and trying not to show it.

They soon stopped when he glared at them. 'Not so fast, girls, not so fast. We don't want gigglers. If you join this company you won't have time for giggling. Right.' He dropped his eyes to a piece of paper in his hand. 'This is it. Two pound ten a week. Three shows a day. Four on Saturday. Work starts twelve sharp. Last show comes down ten thirty.' He lowered the paper and looked up at them expectantly. 'Well, come on, ladies. I haven't got all day. Yes or no?'

To Jen's utter astonishment, the brunette tossed her head. 'Two pound ten isn't much.'

The producer shrugged indifferently. 'Take it or leave it, love.'

One of the other men spoke behind him, and he gave a sickly smile. 'There's extra money on the table for certain acts.' He leered at the brunette.

'If you're lucky, lovey, you might get picked for one of those.'

The brunette shook her head. 'No thanks,' she said rudely. 'I'm not that desperate.' And without further ado she turned on her heel and walked off.

Jen blinked. She was desperate. Completely desperate. Two pounds ten wasn't much, but it was a start. It was experience. And without training she desperately needed that experience. Her expectations had fallen over the last six months. Once she would have hoped for at least a walk-on at the Globe, now she was virtually on her knees for the offer of a chorus job in a backstreet revue.

'I'll do it,' she said quickly, before the producer could change his mind and one of the other girls nodded too. The third shook her head and followed the brunette off stage.

The producer looked peeved. 'Just two. Well, better than nothing. OK, girls. Twelve sharp Monday. All right?'

All right? Jen shrugged on her coat and stepped out on to the windy street in disbelief. It was more than all right. It was fantastic. For the first time since Sean had left Jen felt her spirits rise.

Bloody Sean! She missed him.

Damn him. If only she knew what he was up to. If only he had written, then she would know if she needed to worry or not. She didn't even know if he'd reached Ireland safely.

She had heard on the news about a big IRA explosion at Dublin Castle. A lot of suspects had been taken into custody.

Was Sean one of those suspects?

Or was he just having a good time and had forgotten all about her?

She shook her head crossly and lifted her chin. Well, she had a job now. Her first real paid acting job. So she would damn well forget about him. He could go and jump in the bloody Irish Sea.

For the hundredth time, Pam glanced irritably at the clock.

Where was Alan? She needed his help in dealing with Sheila. The news from Dunkirk was appalling. German planes were machine-gunning the exposed men on the beaches. German artillery was pounding the small town and the adjacent sand dunes where the shattered forces waited for their chance of rescue. Mercifully the brave rearguard of the Allied troops was still valiantly holding off the German tanks. But that small fragment of good news didn't help Sheila Whitehead.

She was convinced her Jo was dead, dying or about to die. She wouldn't or couldn't stop crying. She wouldn't or couldn't listen to reason.

She was impossible to cope with. She refused to eat or drink. She refused to leave the house. She refused to let little George leave the house. She barely let him sleep, hugging him constantly to her, clinging to him as the last living member of her family. The poor child was understandably upset. Upset and bemused. And exhausted.

In desperation Pam had called the doctor when she got back from work. But when he had eventually come, he had been typically unhelpful, saying carelessly that everyone was living through difficult times. There was nothing he could do.

If only Alan had been there. Doctors always took more notice of men. And Alan had a good way with people like that. Quiet but firm. Not all 'yes Doctor, no Doctor' and pathetically grateful like Pam had been brought up to be, even as she longed to yell at them to take some notice and treat her like a responsible human being. Not like some member of a second-class species who always made a fuss.

Mind you, that's probably what doctors did think, she thought, checking the clock again. Where was blasted Alan? She had promised to go over to Sheila's again in a few minutes and she didn't think she could face it alone.

When she heard the knock on the door she dimly assumed it must be Sheila and was astonished to find Mick Carter standing awkwardly on the step.

He looked odd. Flushed and unusually scruffy even for him. He was breathing hard.

Pam wondered for a second if he was ill but then she realised he had been running.

'What?' she asked harshly as the hairs on her arm began to prickle. 'What is it? What do you want?'

'I-it's your husband, Mrs Nelson,' he stammered out. 'It's Mr Nelson.'

Pam's mouth dried as she stared into the dirty, freckled face of Alan's former tormentor. 'What about him? What's happened to him? What have you done to him?'

'I haven't done nothing,' Mick said, momentarily aggrieved. 'He's done it. He's gone, and he wouldn't take me with 'im.'

Pam swallowed and tried to breathe normally. 'What do you mean he's gone? Gone where?'

Mick shuffled his feet. 'Gone to France.'

'To France?' Pam repeated blankly. 'To France?'

Mick nodded. 'On his boat. To rescue them soldiers what are trapped. He heard it on the radio they needed help getting them off, smaller boats and that.'

For a second Pam stared at him in disbelief. She couldn't take it in. Alan. Alan gone to France. To Dunkirk. In his little boat. The Merry Robin. He had never taken it further than Henley before. And that was years ago. One summer holiday for a week. Soon after they were married. It had been a kind of honeymoon. They'd made love every night in that little cabin.

Even as she quickly blocked that thought from her mind, it occurred to her that Mick Carter, of all people, was an unlikely recipient of Alan's plans. 'How do you know this?' she snapped at him. 'When did you see him?'

Mick shuffled his feet. 'I was on the boat,' he admitted.

Pam stared. 'On Alan's boat?' She felt her mind spin. Trying to breathe slowly, she steadied herself on the door frame. 'What were you doing on Alan's boat?'

'Mam threw me out the other night and I hadn't got anywhere else to go. It was cold.' He bit his lip. 'I knew Jen and that Sean Byrne had used it sometimes, so that's where I went. I had to sleep somewhere, didn't I?' He shrugged bravely even as his chin wobbled. 'Anyway I was still there this afternoon when Mr Nelson turned up.'

Pam was just trying to absorb the fact that Sean and Jen had used Alan's boat, when to her utter astonishment, Mick burst into tears.

'He wouldn't take me,' Mick sobbed. 'I wanted to go, Mrs Nelson. I could of helped. But he said I was too young.' He sniffed violently as the tears dripped unhindered off his nose and plopped on to the path. 'He said there would be much more useful things I could do for the war than getting myself killed crossing the Channel. But I don't know what they are, Mrs Nelson, them useful things. Nobody wants me to do anything.'

Pam was hardly listening. 'Alan said that?' she said tremulously, as tears threatened her own eyes.

Mick nodded and scrubbed at his eyes. 'And now the boat's gone, I've nowhere to go. I don't know what to do, Mrs Nelson. I can't go home because my mam won't have me.'

Pam found she was shaking all over. 'You'd better come in,' she said. 'You'd better come in. I think we both need a cup of tea.'

Dear Jennifer,

I have found a job and a small shack of a cottage just on the outside of Cork. It's not much of a place but it's enough. It's better than the boat at least. We can make a home of it. I want you to come over to me as soon as possible. I miss you. Every day I look at the photograph you gave me at Christmas.

There's no rationing, here. No shortages. You'd find work easy enough. In time we'll marry, my family will accept you. I've shown them the photo. I've told them I love you. I've told them how you helped me escape.

Thank you for that, Jennifer Carter Leigh. And thank you for all the wonderful nights and days we had together. You're the best girl.

I've put two ten pound notes in the envelope. I hope they're still there and that those post girls haven't been at them. It's for your journey. The ferry from Fishguard to Rosslare is the best way. Write me when you'll be coming and I'll borrow a van to meet you at the harbour. The address is on the envelope.

Come and see me at least. And then you can decide whether to stay.
With love always,
Sean

Chapter Seventeen

If Louise could have thought up a reason to withdraw her offer to teach Lael d'Arcy Billière's Jewish refugees she would have done. But now she was lumbered with it and it was all blasted Ward Frazer's fault. It served her right for trying to impress him. She might have known a man like that would prefer experienced girls.

Now, as she sat facing the three impassive, dark-eyed Jewish boys across Lael's exotic drawing-room and tried to smile confidently, all she could think about was seeing Ward Frazer at the theatre last night with another girl. A sexy, experienced-looking girl who seemed to lean closer to him than necessary to read the programme. A shapely blonde whom he introduced easily as Alice, when Louise bravely confronted them in the interval. Afterwards she wished she had avoided them. Wished she hadn't flushed so obviously when he politely kissed her cheek. And wished that Ward hadn't looked so tired.

She tried to convince herself that his weariness was caused by too much flying. She knew the RAF were heavily involved in protecting the desperate Dunkirk evacuation, but deep down she was sure that Alice and others of her ilk were responsible for the dark shadows under his eyes. He was quite obviously burning the candle at both ends. And as she stared at the dark head six rows in front of her all through the second act, she couldn't help wishing he was burning it with her.

'How much English do you understand already?' she asked the Jewish boys suddenly and was greeted with three blank stares.

'How, much, English, do, you, understand?' she repeated. This was hopeless. She glared at the oldest boy, the one Katy had said was good looking.

'My, name, is, Louise,' she said, pointing exaggeratedly at herself. 'Louise Rutherford. What, is, your, name?' It was all her parents' fault. They had brought her up to be restrained and well behaved. Brought her up to believe that you had to save yourself for your husband. And now she had lost the one and only man she wanted because she was too blasted restrained and hadn't got the experience he wanted. It wasn't fair.

'Aaref.' The oldest boy spoke for the first time. 'My name is Aaref Hoch.' A low voice, no smile. 'The name of my brother is Jacob,' he pronounced it Yackob, 'and Benjamin.'

Louise blinked. 'Benyameen? Yackob? Oh, you mean Benjamin. And Jacob.'

Aaref shrugged, and Louise quickly dropped her eyes to her papers. There was something unnerving about his unflinching black gaze. When she looked up it was Benjamin, the youngest one that she addressed.

'How old are you, Benjamin?'

Benjamin stared back at her helplessly as she repeated the question more slowly, then turned his gaze to his elder brother, who rattled off a quick phrase in German.

Benjamin still looked blank and Aaref answered for him. 'Benjamin has ten years old.'

Louise shook her head without looking at Aaref. 'He is ten years old,' she corrected. She nodded encouragingly at Benjamin. 'I, am, ten, years, old,' she said.

Benjamin again glanced questioningly at Aaref, and for the first time the older boy smiled. 'Then you are very young, Miss Louise,' he murmured. 'Perhaps we are needing a more older teacher.'

Louise was not in the mood for jokes. From Jacob's quickly stifled giggle she surmised that he understood more than he let on. Aaref certainly did. As for Benjamin, she could only think he was retarded.

'I am nineteen,' she said stiffly, flushing slightly over the lie. Well, what was a year or two here or there? She was sick of being eighteen. It did seem too young. Certainly too young for Ward Frazer. She wished now she had lied to him about her age. 'How old are you, Aaref?'

'I am seventeen years,' he said.

Louise stared at him. Seventeen? And yet he was so small. Well, not small exactly. He was quite tall actually. But slight. Slender and thin. Very thin. And gawky. Like a stick insect.

She couldn't imagine why Katy had thought he was attractive. Unless it was those odd dark eyes. And he had nice teeth. Even and white against his sallow skin.

Then, to her astonishment, even as she stared, she saw faint colour stain his cheeks and the long black lashes flicked down over his eyes.

So he was shy, was he? Louise laughed to herself. Or perhaps he fancied her. For a second she felt a flicker of interest, then she sighed moodily and looked away. It would be just her luck if the only man who fancied her was a seventeen year old stick insect.

'How old are you?' she asked Jacob abruptly.

But before he could reply, Lael d'Arcy Billière drifted in with a tray of tea and biscuits.

'How are you getting on?' she asked brightly, placing the tray on a circular brass table supported on carved wooden legs and engraved with pictures of small birds and strange inscriptions in an exotic indecipherable script.

'All right,' Louise said doubtfully. She would like to have said more, but there was something about Lael d'Arcy Billière's exuberant manner and her odd, unconventional house that made Louise feel distinctly ill at ease.

She had never been inside before. Her parents had never had much to do with their neighbours. And she knew that her father disapproved of Lael d'Arcy Billière. Louise had never really gathered why. Perhaps it had something to do with her having numerous parties to which they were never invited. Or the fact that she didn't seem to have a husband. Or that she wore rather flamboyant clothes and frequently had men to stay. Sometimes more than one at a time.

However, since he had discovered that one of Lael's visitors had proved to be of royal descent, her father had moderated his view somewhat.

In fact Louise secretly suspected that it was only because Count Stefan Pininski had acted so honourably and generously towards Sheila Whitehead over the accident, despite it not being his fault, that her father allowed her to embark on the English teaching idea at all. After the last half hour she wished he hadn't. All this foreignness gave her the creeps.

As her hostess now addressed the boys in their own tongue with apparent fluency, Louise studied her covertly. There was no doubt she was an odd woman. Today, she wore an exotic kind of gown that looked more like a Persian carpet than a dress, and on her shapely bare feet she wore strappy leather sandals. Her toenails were painted a fiery red and her fingers were weighed down with rings. Her long thick black hair was looped up in a wild bun and tied with a black silk scarf. Louise wondered how old she was. Late thirties? Forty? It was difficult to tell. But she was undoubtedly glamorous despite the odd attire. And when she smiled she was quite beautiful.

She was smiling now. 'The boys say you have been most helpful,' she said, handing Louise a cup of strong black tea. Louise stared at it dubiously, disconcerted by the piece of lemon bobbing about on the surface, and wished she had the guts to ask for milk instead.

But Lael was talking again. 'It is good for them to have company, particularly company as young and pretty as you. Aaref is quite taken with you. He says you are a wonderful teacher.'

'Does he?' In her confusion, Louise made the mistake of sipping her tea, discovering too late that it had clearly only very recently left the kettle.

As her eyes watered, and most of the tea slopped embarrassingly into the saucer to the evident amusement of the boys, she vowed silently she would never again set foot in Lael d'Arcy Billière's house.

'Oh, don't worry about that,' Lael laughed lightly as Louise tried to mop up the mess on the table with her handkerchief. 'Far too much alcohol gets spilled around this house for me to worry about a small tea stain.' She glanced out of the window as a car swirled up the short drive. 'Talking of which, here come Stefan and Adam. I must go and let them in. They'll have news from Paris.'

'I ought to go home,' Louise said, hastily gathering up her damp papers. The last thing she wanted was to be faced by more of these ghastly foreigners. Why did they make her feel so prudish and gauche? 'I promised Mummy I'd be back by five.'

'Oh, I do so hate deadlines.' Lael sighed as she moved to the door. 'Don't you? But you must come again soon, Louise. Very soon. Perhaps tomorrow?'

Louise gaped at her, appalled. 'Mummy said you'd arranged once a week,' she said.

'Did we?' Lael said vaguely, her thoughts clearly already on the new arrivals, who were even now ringing the doorbell. 'Well, whatever you like, my darling. Whatever you like.'

Assuming Lael would take her visitors into a different room, Louise was taken aback when she ushered them straight into the drawing-room. Despite longing to get away, Louise found herself being introduced to two tall distinguished-looking foreigners with dark, crisp curly hair and impeccable manners.

With charming smiles they both bowed and kissed her hand and murmured appreciation in lazy foreign accents.

'Count Stefan Pininski,' Lael introduced them. 'And his brother, Adam.'

'Enchanté,' Stefan Pininski drawled, his eyes resting on Louise's open mouth.

Flustered and flushing, Louise backed away, muttered her apologies, and fled.

Mick Carter slept in Sean Byrne's bedroom. Pam hadn't wanted him to stay. She had tried repeatedly to get him to go home but he adamantly refused. He said he'd rather kip down on the common than go home. In the end she had written a short note to Joyce Carter saying that Mick was going to be staying with her for a couple of nights and she hoped Joyce didn't mind.

She walked down to deliver it while Mick had a bath. She didn't want the boy staying with her, but just now it seemed she had little choice. She could hardly turn him out on the street.

She was curious about what it was he had done to make Joyce Carter throw him out. After all that Joyce had been through with that awful husband and older boy, it was hard to imagine what crime Mick could have committed to incur Joyce's wrath so badly.

Mick hadn't said and Pam hadn't asked. She didn't really want to know. Oddly, despite his surly manner and his bullying mentality, she felt sorry for him. He was only fourteen, after all, and his tears earlier had been genuine and quite heart rending. Alan's refusal to take him to France had rattled him, dented his cocksure complacency. It might even have done him good.

Quickly, furtively, she shoved the note through the Carters' letterbox and retreated. Sometime soon she would have to talk to Joyce, but just now she had other things on her mind. Alan.

Alan in that tiny little boat, tossing about in pitch darkness somewhere in the English Channel. Alan being machine-gunned by the Luftwaffe. Alan being sunk. Alan being rammed by other bigger boats manoeuvring in the darkness off the French coast.

As she fed Mick Carter that evening with boiled potatoes and battered Spam, and watched in horrified amazement as he consumed about three loaves of bread and butter and cleaned her out of milk, already reports were coming in on the wireless from the first lucky British troops to arrive home from Dunkirk.

Reports of incessant waves of German bombs and machine-gun fire raking the beaches and harbours where the tired soldiers waited for ships. Reports of the heroic rearguard who were risking everything in their attempts to keep the Germans back long enough to enable those on the beaches to get away. Reports of the scores of ships blown up or sunk as they waited to take on men from the shallow beaches.

Pam didn't sleep a wink that night. Nor the next. By Sunday morning, mainly thanks to Mick Carter, news had spread about Alan's dramatic departure, and at church Pam was overcome by the sympathy, hope and encouragement that everyone expressed on Alan's behalf.

'Any news?' Katy Parsons whispered as they went in and bit her lip when Pam shook her head.

'Do let us know when you hear, won't you?' Mary Parsons murmured. 'We're so worried about dear Alan.'

'He's such a nice man, your husband,' the younger Miss Taylor called across from her pew. And the older one nodded. 'Always willing to help. He did a marvellous job replanting our cherry tree after the gales in January.'

'It's covered in blossom now,' her sister agreed. 'Better than ever.'

Even the vicar did his bit. 'Today we pray especially for all those risking their lives for the protection of their country. Especially we pray for your faithful servant, Alan Nelson, member of this church, that he may return safely from his brave mission, to continue his worthy life among the people of this parish.'

Pam had forgotten how many people Alan knew. She had forgotten how fond everyone was of him. She had forgotten how fond she was of him. She had forgotten how much he meant to her and she felt terrible that it had taken this, this daring dangerous escapade, to make her remember.

What was worse, she knew she had goaded him into it with her cruel words. Her and Mick Carter and his nasty, taunting little friends.

'You must be so proud,' Celia Rutherford said to her after the service, 'It's a wonderful thing he is doing.'

'Didn't know he had it in him,' Greville Rutherford said heartily. 'Jolly good show. Fine man your husband, Mrs Nelson. The brewery would be lost without him.'

'Ever since the war started he's been wanting to do something,' Pam said. 'Something to help. But I didn't know he was going to do this.'

Celia touched her arm. 'I do so hope he comes home safely. I hope they all do.'

'So do I,' Pam said weakly, biting back tears. 'So do I.'

She wasn't the only person waiting for news of course. There were many families waiting to hear whether sons and husbands had managed to get away from those bloodstained beaches.

Some had heard already. Good news and bad. Mrs Potter at the bakery had had a telegram from her son who was safely back in Dover. And rumour had it that dopey Tom who used to help on the Rutherford & Berry beer wagon had died in the sand dunes at La Panne.

Others hadn't heard. Poor Sheila Whitehead was still waiting for news of Jo.

And now, suddenly and quite unexpectedly, Pam joined the ranks of those living in fear of a War Office telegram.

Oddly, having Mick Carter in the house gave Pam some relief. It took the loneliness out of the wait. And the boy was so moody and awkward and so incredibly hungry that in her efforts to cheer him up and to keep food on the table, she found her mind being taken from her own immediate worries.

Keeping busy was definitely the answer. And she wanted to keep Mick busy too. It was no wonder he got into mischief and fell into bad company. With no school to go to and no job, he was bored and restless and looking for excitement. Well, she hadn't got excitement to offer him but she had got plenty of tasks to keep him occupied.

'I'll be going to work tomorrow,' she told him on Sunday evening. 'So I'd like you to do the shopping for me.'

His eyes widened in horror. 'I can't do the shopping.'

She raised her eyebrows. 'Why not? Can't you add up?'

He shook his head, flushing. 'Of course I can. It's not that, Mrs Nelson. It's just that doing the shopping, well … that's woman's work.'

Pam looked at him steadily. 'If we want to eat, then we have to do shopping. It's just one of those things, Mick. And if I'm busy at work and my husband is busy rescuing our soldiers from the Germans, then the only person available in this household to do the shopping is you. Think of it as war work.'

'But I can't queue up with all those housewives, Mrs Nelson. They'll laugh at me.'

Pam stood firm. 'Then you'd better go home and let your poor mother shop and cook for you like she used to.'

He thrust his hands into his pockets and frowned. 'I'm not going home.'

Pam shrugged. 'You can't stay here for ever, Mick. For one thing I won't be able to afford to feed you for long. For now, we can use Alan's ration book and eat his food, but when he comes back,' she paused and swallowed hard. 'If he comes back ...' She stopped and looked away. If he comes back? He must come back.

As she blinked back the threatening tears, Pam felt a sudden stab of resentment against the surly boy in front of her. If only Mick Carter hadn't mocked Alan's courage and taunted him about his boat, Alan might be here now.

She put her hands to her face, pressing her fingers to her eyebrows.

Because it wasn't only Mick's fault. If only she hadn't said she felt guilty about Jo serving when Alan wasn't. If only she had been more supportive of his search for war work. If only she had appreciated him more. If only she had stayed at home, looked after him better. If only she hadn't been so besotted with Sean Byrne.

The tears were flowing now. Dripping through her fingers on to her knees. Staining her fawn skirt.

Through her silent agony, she heard Mick shuffling his feet awkwardly. 'If you make me a list, I'll do the shopping,' he muttered suddenly. 'And I promise if Mr Nelson comes home, I'll come up to town to tell you straight away.'

Joyce Carter stared at the glittering jewellery in Mr Lorenz's shapely hand.

'That's it,' she said, nodding dully. She braced herself. 'OK. So how much is it worth, then?'

Mr Lorenz blinked once or twice and then to her surprise, smiled thinly. 'Do you really want to know its value, Mrs Carter?' he asked. 'Or merely what it would cost you to buy it back?'

She frowned. 'What's the difference?'

He coughed and laid the jewellery carefully back on the counter. 'In a business such as mine, Mrs Carter, I'm sure you appreciate that what I offer for a piece may bear little relation to its true value. There are risks involved related to the source of the goods. And, of course, to a certain extent it depends on what I think the customer will accept.'

Of course. No wonder the tight bastard made so much money, Joyce thought sourly, wondering just how often over the years he had ripped her off. Not that it showed. He wasn't a spender, Lorenz. But word had it that he owned quite a bit of property. And he gambled, of course. She remembered Mick saying that Lorenz was the only one locally to win on the National this year.

She gritted her teeth. Bloody Mick. If he hadn't caused her enough grief already. She was already indebted to Pam Nelson for taking him in. God only knew what she was going to do about that. What with Alan Nelson taking his life into his hands and going off to rescue those poor trapped soldiers and all. And now she was going to have to get down on her knees to Lorenz of all people.

'What I want to know is how much I would have to pay you for it,' she said stiffly, meeting his dark eyes. 'I can't redeem it because I haven't got the papers.'

He glanced down at the jewellery and then back up at her. 'Without the papers, I'm afraid it won't be redeemable until June.'

Joyce flinched. Of course. The six month delay. She had forgotten that. Her shoulders slumped. It was hopeless. The whole idea was hopeless. Where was she ever going to find money to buy back fancy jewellery like this? She had enough experience of Stanley's shady offerings to know that it wasn't going to be cheap. Even if Lorenz did let her have it for what he'd paid for it. And why on earth should he? Let's face it, he was in business to make money, wasn't he? Not to do favours.

She took a last look at the jewellery and shook her head wearily. Then she bent down to pick up her basket. 'Oh, forget it,' she said. 'I'll never be able to afford it anyway. I'm sorry for wasting your time.'

To her surprise he leaned over the counter and touched her arm gently as she turned away. 'No, Mrs Carter, don't go,' he said. 'I'm sure we can come to some agreement.'

She looked back at him. For once he had some colour in his cheeks. As their eyes met he blinked. The sweep of the long thick lashes made him look oddly shy. 'This jewellery is obviously very important to you, Mrs Carter.'

She nodded, wondering whether to confide in him. Wondering whether to trust him. 'My son stole it,' she said abruptly, astonishing herself. She stared straight into his dark, oddly gentle eyes. 'I ... I want to return it to its rightful owner.'

He looked away abruptly and her heart sank. She had made a mistake. He'd bubble Mick to the police now and then she'd be done for.

It was a long moment before Lorenz spoke. 'I see,' he said simply at last. 'That is very creditable of you, Mrs Carter. But are you sure your generosity is worth the cost?'

Joyce considered his question and nodded slowly. It would be worth anything, she realised, to feel at ease with Mrs Rutherford again. They had made tentative progress towards mutual respect and even friendship over the last few months, but the question of the missing jewellery was always lurking between them, festering on one or other of their minds like a sore ready to break open if overstretched. This was the best and probably only chance that Joyce would ever have to heal that wound.

'It is important to me,' she said. 'I think it will be worth the cost.'

'Then I will endeavour to make it easy for you,' Lorenz said. 'I will let you have it back for the price I paid.' He sucked his lip for a moment with his eyes on the jewellery, and then looked up at her. 'Ten pounds would cover it, Mrs Carter.'

Joyce gaped at him. 'Ten pounds.'

Ten pounds. It was absurd. She dropped her gaze to the jewellery lying on the counter. The rings alone must be worth ten times that that. Unless they were fake. No, of course they weren't fake. Mrs Rutherford wouldn't dream of wearing fake jewellery. So what game was Lorenz playing? Surely he had given the boys more than that. Or would he? Was this what he had meant by it depending on what the customer would accept. Had he well and truly pulled the wool over the boys' eyes? Good old Lorenz. In other circumstances she might have laughed.

Nevertheless ten pounds was currently beyond her. It would take time to save that amount. Time and sacrifice.

Lorenz was looking at her. She felt herself flush faintly. 'That's very reasonable, Mr Lorenz,' she said reluctantly. 'Of course I haven't got that on me just now. But in a week or two perhaps …' She sighed. It would be more like a year or two, realistically. Then she remembered that Jen had got work at last. Or so she said.

Joyce reckoned she could expect a bit of Jen's wages towards the housekeeping. That would help. But ten pounds. She'd never get that together. Not all at once. Lorenz would never wait that long for his money. Not when he could most likely sell that jewellery tomorrow for three times that amount. Or more. She shrugged despondently. 'Things are a bit difficult at the moment.'

'These are difficult times for all of us,' Lorenz smiled briefly. 'If Hitler invades this country, no amount of jewellery will save us.'

Joyce frowned. As a Jew, Lorenz had more to fear than most. The horrors of Hitler's Jewish camps had been all over the papers recently. And Joyce had heard that traitorous Lord Haw-Haw on the radio only yesterday asking if Britain was really prepared to die for the Jews. And yet Lorenz was smiling. She had rarely seen him smile. It made quite a difference to his face. To her surprise she found herself smiling back.

'Would it be easier for you to pay by instalments, Mrs Carter?' he suggested. 'A pound or two each week perhaps?'

Chapter Eighteen

Dear Sean,

Thank you for your letter. I am glad you got home safely. I was worried about you before when I didn't hear. I thought something must have happened to you. You should have written sooner.

I am not going to come to Ireland. Not yet. I miss you very much. More than I can say. But I have just got a part in Fox's Review (like the Windmill, but not quite so famous) which might be just the break I've been waiting for. Rehearsals start tomorrow. It's only a chorus job but with experience there I might be able to move on into one of the ENSA concert parties or even to the Windmill itself. I'm going to try to get acting lessons on Sundays.

I'm sure you'll understand, Sean. You were always so enthusiastic about my acting. The only person who is.

There have been big excitements here since you left. Can you believe it, your old landlord Alan Nelson has sailed our little love-boat away to France to rescue the soldiers trapped on the beaches at Dunkirk. I hope he'll be all right. And Mrs Nelson has taken in my brother Mick, who was apparently living on the boat after my mum threw him out. Mum won't tell me why but I think it was him who stole the jewellery from that Mrs Rutherford up in the big house on the common. Stupid little bugger. Anyway he's been at Mrs N's two nights now, staying in your old room.

I'll stop now because we're not meant to use too much paper. We even have to save bones and rags nowadays. Apparently they make weapons out of them! I can't imagine us winning the war with weapons made out of bones, can you?

I'm sorry not to be coming, Sean. It was a hard decision.

I won't ask you to wait for me. I know that's not fair. Not for a lovely handsome (sexy) man like you. But I'll wait for you anyway. And one day perhaps when this beastly war is over, you may be able to come back for me.

With all my love always.

Jen xxx

P.S. I was tempted to keep the money, I'll admit. Just in case. But I didn't think that was fair, so here it is.

Pam found it hard to concentrate at work on Monday. It was understandable and Mr Shaw understood. He had listened in sympathetic silence as Pam had explained that her husband with no word to anybody had taken it into his head to set sail for France to help with the evacuation in a boat far too small, Pam thought, to undertake such a journey.

'How long would it take?' she asked Mr Shaw who always seemed to know the answer to everything. 'How long would it take to get over there and back?'

Her boss frowned. 'A small river cruiser? From Putney? To Dunkirk? What's that? About a hundred and twenty miles at say five knots? Well, depending on tides and winds, roughly twenty four hours each way.'

Pam nodded bravely. 'So why isn't he back, Mr Shaw?'

Mr Shaw sucked his lips. 'I don't think they'd use a small boat like that to go back and forth. How many could he take safely? Ten? Fifteen at a pinch? They'd be more likely to use it to ferry men from the beaches to the bigger boats offshore. That's why they were calling for the smaller boats.'

So he might still be alive, Pam thought, with a flicker of renewed hope. Still there, risking his life minute by minute to save others. She prayed that the RAF were keeping the beastly Luftwaffe at bay. Prayed that the German guns would miss a very small river boat in the general melée, prayed that Alan would not stay a moment longer than necessary. Prayed that the little boat was not already holed and sunk. Already the news bulletins were talking of seven French destroyers and scores of other ships sunk as they tried to load the escaping troops. Despite the heavy losses, the general mood was high. *Bloody Marvellous* was the Express headline. *So many men saved. A truly heroic British effort. One in the eye for Hitler. Our boys home and dry. And ready to fight again.*

Crowds of well wishers lined the railways from the south coast ports, waving Union Jacks and cheering the evacuated troops as they were sped away from the crowded ports to barracks and hospitals, or home to thankful, delighted families, for whom the long anxious wait was over.

But for Pam it was a very long morning. A very long lunch break and then at two o'clock the office telephone suddenly rang,

'Mrs Nelson?' A polite, well-spoken male voice. A military voice. An officer's voice. A tired voice. Pam's heart jumped once and then began to race.

'Yes.'

'My name is James Wilcox. Captain James Wilcox. Your husband asked me to call. I'm afraid it's been a devil of a job getting through.'

Suddenly Pam couldn't breathe. She could see Mr Shaw watching her from behind his desk. Feel his steady compassionate gaze on her face.

'Where is he?' she asked. 'Is he all right?'

A second's crackling pause made her blood freeze, then Captain Wilcox spoke again. More hesitant now, more careful. 'He was fine when I left him. He brought a group of us back to Dover from Dunkirk in the early hours of this morning. He wanted you to know he was safe.'

Pam swallowed. Something was not quite right here. Why wasn't Alan calling himself? 'What do you mean he was fine?' she asked. She sat down and leaned on her desk. 'Please tell me everything, Captain Wilcox. I need to know.'

'Your husband is a very brave man, Mrs Nelson,' her caller prevaricated. 'Very brave indeed. He spent two nights and two days off the French beaches ferrying men out to the larger vessels under terrible conditions, constant bombardment, constant aerial attack. He seemed impervious to it. Quite impervious. Last night the navy ordered the rescue vessels withdrawn before dawn. The danger was too great in daylight. So reluctantly your husband loaded me and my troop and sailed us to Dover. Twenty of us. It was a marvel we didn't go down. We came under fire but only lost one man. Your husband was slightly wounded in the arm, nothing too serious. Just a small bullet wound.'

Pam's fingernails were digging into her palms. Slightly wounded. 'So where is he now?' she asked. 'In hospital somewhere?'

The line crackled again.

James Wilcox coughed awkwardly. 'I'm afraid he went back, Mrs Nelson. Against all advice.'

Pam closed her eyes. 'He went back?'

'I'm afraid so. He said he couldn't bear to leave so many men to their fate. It was a bloodbath over there, Mrs Nelson. Men were drowning in their efforts to get to the ships.'

James Wilcox was trying valiantly to explain. Trying to make her understand why her husband had sailed off again to his almost certain death.

'The Germans were quite ruthless,' he said. 'And there were still an awful lot of men on the beaches when we left. Whatever the papers here say about a victorious withdrawal, up our end of the line the whole thing was a shambles. A right military shambles. Right from the start. We've lost thousands of men, Mrs Nelson. Thousands.'

James Wilcox sounded bitter now. 'And if it wasn't for men like your husband, ordinary civilians, we would have lost thousands more.'

'Thank you,' Pam said quickly stemming the morbid flow. 'Thank you for calling, Captain Wilcox. I'm very grateful to you.'

'It's my pleasure,' he said, recovering himself. 'I do hope your husband gets home safely, Mrs Nelson. I'd be so pleased if you would let me know. I'd like to come and shake his hand.'

Swallowing hard, Pam promised to let him know and took down the number. Thanking him again, she carefully replaced the receiver, then she glanced across at Mr Shaw and burst into tears.

Louise's second English lesson didn't go any better than the first. After several false starts, a series of misunderstandings and an unsatisfactory conclusion, she decided that she hated her three pupils and would be quite happy never to see them again in her life. In fact she wished she could get out of further lessons. But now Lael d'Arcy Billière had gone and invited her to an evening do and she had been so taken aback that she had failed to think up an excuse in time.

So now she was lumbered with that too. A party full of glamorous, supercilious foreigners who seemed to have the knack of making her feel about three and a half and very uninteresting.

'I don't want to go,' she said to Katy. 'Do you think I should pretend to be ill?'

'But what about the count?' Katy asked, excitedly. 'He might be there.'

'I've met the count,' Louise admitted. 'I met him last time I was there.'

Katy giggled. 'What was he like? Foreign, fat and balding?'

Louise hesitated. 'Foreign,' she said at last. 'Quite old, but very handsome and sophisticated.'

Katy blinked. 'So why don't you want to see him again?'

'I don't know,' Louise said. She flushed slightly. 'I think he was too sophisticated, too foreign. He made me feel like a rag someone had used to clean the car.'

Katy laughed. 'That's how Ward Frazer makes me feel.'

Louise looked at her sharply. 'Ward Frazer has been here?'

'Oh no,' Katy shook her head hastily. 'I meant at the accident before Christmas. I haven't seen him since then. Not to talk to, at least.'

Louise stood up abruptly and looked out of the window at the bright sunlit street. 'I know he doesn't want to go out with me anymore,' she said crossly. 'But I wish he'd telephone me sometimes. I hate not knowing if he's all right. The RAF have lost a lot of planes recently.'

'He was all right yesterday,' Katy said helpfully. 'He called to see the Miss Taylors. I saw his car out of the window.' She didn't say that she had sat patiently by the window for two hours hoping to see him emerge again, only to miss him when she finally, in desperate need, took five minutes to go to the lavatory.

She was glad she had held her breath when Louise swung round incredulously.

'You mean Ward was here and he didn't bother to call on me?' She glared at Katy. 'You might have told me.' Her eyes filled with tears.

She picked up her coat and gloves and turned angrily for the door. 'Ward Frazer is a beastly pig,' she said. 'It would serve him right if I did run off with a glamorous Polish count.'

*

Jen was elated. Her first day's rehearsal had gone well. It was a brand new show that Fox's were putting on, so the experienced chorus girls were involved as well as the newly recruited ones. They had a week to put the show together. A week of intensive rehearsals.

It was exhilarating stuff. First of all they had sung through all the music, all clustered round a piano, and then they'd worked on the opening, a dramatic song and dance piece that would launch the show as the curtain went up and the stage lights came on.

As part of the chorus, Jen would be on stage right from the start. Then one by one, the solo performers would come on, sing a few lines of their own introduction and then join in the dance until everyone was on stage and the show proper would begin.

Jen was thrilled to be picked to lead on one of the stars, the conjuror. It would make her stand out, she thought, having a tiny separate moment of her own, and perhaps someone would spot her and know that she was destined for better things. There was no way she was going to be a backstreet chorus girl all her life.

But Fox's Review was a start and as she walked home from the Underground that first evening she was glad that she had had the courage to refuse Sean's offer. It had been hard writing to him. She hated to disappoint him. But much as she missed him, much as she loved him, and she had had a physical ache in her heart ever since he left, she had to give herself a chance. She couldn't settle for a quiet life in Ireland. Not yet.

'How much are you earning at this acting lark, then?' Joyce asked suddenly, interrupting Jen's excited account of her day. Pete was sitting there listening with his mouth open in awe of his sister's glamorous new job. But Joyce wasn't interested in how many costume changes Jen was going to have. Nor in hearing about the producer who'd been so pleased with how quickly Jen had picked up the dance steps of one number, he'd asked her to show the other girls.

What Joyce was interested in was how much money she was going to be able to get out of Jen towards the housekeeping. And then she could work out how long it would take to pay off old Lorenz for the Rutherfords' jewellery.

Jen hesitated. 'Two pound ten a week,' she said, with a certain defiance. Joyce guessed she wished she could have named a higher wage. She was proud as they come, her daughter. Never wanted anyone to laugh at her. Not that two pound ten was to be sniffed at. Not really. Not that she'd let Jen know that. She didn't want her getting big headed.

Jen was looking at her suspiciously. 'Why do you want to know?'

Joyce shrugged as she sliced the Spam. 'For the housekeeping. I reckon as now you've got yourself a proper job you can contribute, same as Pete does.' She put down the knife and checked the potatoes. 'I reckon as ten bob a week would be fair.'

Jen's mouth fell open. 'Ten bob?' she gasped. 'But that leaves me two pound a week. Less after insurance has been taken off. And I've got to pay my fares up to town every day and I've got to provide my own stockings and shoes.' She looked up at Joyce pleadingly. 'Mum, I can't afford to give you ten bob.'

Joyce sniffed as she began to mash the potatoes. 'Then you should get a better-paid job.'

Jen's colour rose. 'I will get a better job,' she said angrily. 'In time I'll be one of the principals. But just now this is the best I can get.' She bit her lip, trying to control her temper, 'Mum, please. To get a better part I need training. I was going to put a pound a week into training. One of the girls in the show knows someone who offers twelve singing lessons for nine guineas.'

'I thought you could sing already,' Pete chipped in. 'I thought that's how you got this job.'

Jen glared at him. 'Do none of you ever listen to what I say? I can sing. But I need to sing better to get a solo part. Or I need to dance better. Or I need to act better. Everyone needs training. Peggy Ashcroft had training. Vivien Leigh had training. That Joyce Grenfell you like on the wireless had training. Alec Guinness had training. John Gielgud had training. Even blasted Laurence Olivier had training. It's just that most of them had money and could afford it. I bet they didn't have to pay ten bob for a few lousy pieces of Spam and some lumpy mashed potato.'

That did it. Joyce had been wondering whether ten bob had been a bit steep. Wondering whether she might drop it to eight, even five. Wondering if she mightn't get another day's cleaning off Mrs Rutherford instead. The Rutherford boys would be home for the summer holidays soon. Surely they would make extra work.

But now Jen had complained about her food she was damned if she would budge an inch. The spoilt little madam could pay up or move out.

She slammed the saucepan of mashed potato on the table. 'It's ten shillings, Jen, and that's my last word.'

Jen stared at her plate in disgust as Joyce dished out the food. Then she laughed sourly. 'Lucky old Mick. He's got more sense than I thought. I bet he's wolfing down poor Alan Nelson's meat ration even as we speak.'

Joyce clenched her fists under the table. She knew Jen was trying to rile her. 'More fool Pam Nelson,' she said. 'I didn't ask her to have him. And if he thinks I'll pay her for his keep he's got another think coming.'

'Donny Smith said he saw Mick in Dove's today,' Pete said suddenly with a giggle. 'He was doing Mrs Nelson's shopping. Had a list and a basket on his arm and all.'

Joyce and Jen gaped at him. 'Micky?' Joyce almost choked on her Spam. 'Doing Pam Nelson's shopping?'

Pete nodded, smiling broadly, pleased to have the attention for once. 'He was queuing up for the bacon ration with all the women. Donny and the boys gave him right stick for it. Donny said they laughed all the way to the pub.'

Jen was smiling despite herself. 'I wish I'd seen him,' she said gleefully.

Pete grinned broadly. 'Me too.'

Good old Pam Nelson, Joyce thought. That would serve the little bugger right.

It was Katy Parsons who saw Alan Nelson come home. She saw him out of the window. Walking up the road from Lavender Hill at eight o'clock on Wednesday evening. His left arm was thickly bandaged and in a sling. Over the other shoulder was slung a heavy-looking canvas bag.

But despite the bandage, the dark shadows under his eyes, the lines of weariness or pain on his face, there was a spring in his step. A lightness to his stride that Katy hadn't seen for a long time. Ever, in fact. Although she'd heard them downstairs saying that he had been over the moon, pleased as punch, and happy as a sandboy, whatever that was, when he'd brought home pretty Pam Riley from Islington five and a half years ago.

They'd talked about Alan Nelson a lot over the last few days. Talked about him with wry affection, talked about the odd things he'd done, the funny things he'd said, almost as though he was already dead.

And now here he was. Alive. A local hero by all accounts.

Katy felt a bubble of emotion form in her chest. Shabby little Alan Nelson. Who would have thought it possible?

Tears prickled Katy's eyes as she thought how relieved Pam Nelson would be. The poor woman had looked like death for the last few days, what with Alan in danger and that awful sulky Mick Carter to cope with. Katy wondered why she had put up with him. Mind you, she was making good use of him it seemed.

She'd heard them laughing themselves sick downstairs at lunchtime over him doing her shopping. She wondered what would happen now Alan was back. Mick Carter and his pals had been known to have a go at Alan, taunting him about his cushy job, his lack of war service, his little boat.

Well, they'd be eating their words now all right, Katy thought with some pleasure. It was sad that it took a war to let people show their true colours.

She glanced out of the window again and was surprised to see Alan stop halfway up the street. For a second he stood still, braced rigid as though burdened suddenly with heavy thoughts, then abruptly he turned back and walked briskly away from his own front door and into the pub downstairs.

Katy blinked.

Then even as the sudden clamour broke out beneath her, she frowned.

Why hadn't he gone home? It wasn't as though he was a great drinker. One of the jokes about Alan Nelson was that he preferred to buy someone else a pint than drink his own.

She could hear the excitement below. Questions. Jokes. Loud voices. Laughter.

Men were odd, she thought. They showed their emotion in hearty back-slapping, in crude jokes, in the offer of a pint. They little knew that upstairs she was crying her eyes out because a man she barely knew had shown unexpected courage and had come home safely.

He didn't stay in the pub long and he didn't say much. Creeping halfway down the stairs Katy heard him saying in his usual self-deprecating way that he had only done what he could, what anyone else would have done, that the injury was only a flesh wound that the nurses at Dover had got over-excited about. Then he downed a whisky and headed back into the street.

As he approached his own front gate, his steps slowed again. Back at the window, Katy found she was wringing her hands together, willing him to go in. What on earth was the matter with him?

And then just as he put his hand on the gate-catch, the front door opened unexpectedly and there was Pam.

Even then he didn't move. Nor did she.

Katy felt her stomach clench.

Then slowly Alan pushed the gate open and went in. Carefully he lowered the canvas bag to the ground and almost shyly he held out his hand to her.

Katy's eyes were streaming again. It was like a film. Like a real weepy with a happy ending. She felt she shouldn't be watching. But she couldn't help herself. It was so odd. Surely if her husband had come home safely she would be crying her eyes out, hugging him to death.

And then just as Pam was about to take Alan's hand, Mick Carter appeared behind her and Alan jerked back. Katy could have killed Mick Carter then. Strangled him to death right there on the Nelsons' front path.

But then she saw Mick Carter was crying. Crying. It was unbelievable. And Pam was crying too. And suddenly she was in Alan's arms, and presumably he was crying too.

Katy certainly was. If this went on much longer she'd be flooding out the bar downstairs.

And then Alan drew back from Pam, patted Mick awkwardly on the shoulder, picked up his bag and ushered them all back inside.

And the show was over.

Katy blew her nose violently. Then she stood up and squared her shoulders.

If Alan Nelson could do it, so could she. She would tell her mother tomorrow that she was going to enrol on one of the Red Cross courses they were running on Lavender Hill.

Chapter Nineteen

Lael d'Arcy Billière's party was on the 14th of June. The day the Germans marched into Paris.

'And not one shot fired in its defence.' Greville Rutherford spoke with disgust as he switched off the wireless and took his seat at the head of breakfast table. 'Those damn Frogs have been a dead loss right from the start.'

'I suppose they didn't want their beautiful buildings ruined,' Celia said mildly, spreading her toast. 'It's understandable.'

'Understandable!'

Louise jumped as her father's fist came down heavily on the table.

'The only thing that's understandable is that the French are cowards,' he said bitingly. 'They always have been. My goodness, Celia, you won't see Mr Churchill surrendering London just because Germany threatens to bomb a few buildings. Oh no, it'll take more than that. Mr Hitler is not facing lily-livered Europeans here, you know.'

Louise smirked. 'Don't forget we're Europeans too, Daddy.'

But her father was not amused. He had recently been elected on to the Clapham Committee for Moral Re-armament, and had taken its message of patriotic pride very much to heart. 'We're British, Louise,' he said sternly. 'British through and through. And don't you ever forget it.'

But ten hours later as she stood awkwardly among a seething mass of foreigners at Lael's party, Louise wished she could forget it. She dearly wished she could be something more exotic than British. Something more interesting than an eighteen year old, tongue-tied English girl. Even her rather daring strapless dress seemed dull and dated among the extraordinary selection of garments that the guests wore.

The talk was all of Paris of course. Everyone seemed to have lived there at one time or another, to own property there, or at least to know someone who did.

Louise who had never been there in her life and knew nobody who had, apart from possibly Ward Frazer, whom she didn't want to think about, felt at a distinct disadvantage.

Bored to death and feeling like Cinderella caught at completely the wrong ball, she quickly drank two glasses of champagne and longed for the moment when it might not be too rude to go home. It was a hot evening. The room, shrouded with the inevitable blackout curtains, was stifling.

It was ironic, Louise thought sourly, that when she usually had to fight tooth and nail to be allowed to go to parties, on the one occasion when she didn't want to go she was told that it would be bad manners to refuse.

'It's very kind of her to ask you, Louise.'

'But Mummy,' Louise had moaned. 'It will be full of sweaty, middle-aged foreigners, all clicking their heels and kissing each other all over the place and smelling of garlic.'

Her mother had merely smiled. 'Then just be thankful that Daddy hasn't been invited,' she said wryly.

In fact Louise's description was not far wrong. Most of Lael's guests were indeed foreign. And there was a lot of kissing and greeting. Many of them had only recently arrived in England, intellectuals, aristocrats, artists and wealthy Jews, fleeing ahead of Hitler's armies, and were delighted to find old friends safe and sound at the party.

Considering that Hitler was now virtually knocking at the door to England, everyone seemed in remarkably high spirits, Louise thought, feeling a bead of sweat form under her breast and run uncomfortably down her stomach. The noise level was high, an impromptu string quartet was running through a repertoire of frantic middle European music, and the drink flowed abundantly. A group of people were performing an extraordinary stamping dance by the heavily curtained French windows.

It was quite unlike the stiff little drinks parties her parents sometimes held at which two glasses of sherry and some derogatory remarks about Adolf Hitler seemed to be all anyone expected. It was certainly all her father provided.

At this party there were bottles everywhere and people seemed expected to help themselves. Lael herself was deep in conversation with a bearded man on the sofa and seemed entirely unaware of new arrivals coming in at the front door. It was all very odd.

It was almost a relief when Louise saw Aaref Hoch approaching her. She had noticed him earlier, when she had first arrived, and had ignored him then, unwilling to embark upon yet another stilted conversation about the names of his brothers, or the state of the weather. But now she was resigned to anything. Anything was better than standing conspicuously alone in a crowd of chattering people.

'Hello Aaref,' she said as he stopped in front of her.

'Good evening, Miss Louise,' he replied formally with a slight click of his heels.

He offered his hand and she shook it, withdrawing her own as quickly as she could. There was something about Aaref Hoch which gave her the creeps. He was so thin, his face was so gaunt, and his skin was so pale.

Although to give him his due, he wasn't quite as pale as he had been when she first saw him. Hanging about endlessly on the common in the recent hot weather had tanned him a bit. But she didn't like the way he looked at her, that dark, moody stare, as though he was assessing her, analysing her and finding her wanting.

'Where are your brothers tonight?' she asked. 'I haven't seen them.'

'Upstairs,' he said. 'They do not come. We do not like the party.'

Louise grimaced inwardly: Nor did she.

'But you have come,' she said, wishing that she had not. Wishing she had stood up to her mother for once.

Aaref hesitated. 'I come because you come,' he said seriously. A shy smile flickered briefly on his lips then faded.

Louise didn't return the smile. 'You shouldn't have bothered,' she said ungraciously. 'I'm going to go home in a minute. I don't feel very well.' She did in fact feel rather sick suddenly and wondered if she had overdone the champagne.

She was just about to ask Aaref to go and find her evening wrap, just about to interrupt Lael's tête-à-tête to make her apologies, when she realised the room had suddenly hushed.

At first she thought somebody was about to make a speech, but then she saw Lael moving towards the door. It seemed some important latecomer had arrived.

Louise stared across towards the door. She wondered who all the fuss was about. And then as the heads shifted, the question became superfluous.

There was only one member of the group by the door who drew a second glance, and that was a tall, tanned man with crisp, curly hair and a lazy, sophisticated smile. Count Stefan Pininski.

He was dressed in a dinner jacket of impeccable cut, yet under the smoothly urbane veneer lurked a distinct aura of restless vitality, a hint of danger, that made Louise's fingers curl nervously in her damp palms. She wondered how old he was. Forty perhaps, although he looked younger.

'Oh, the wonderful count,' Aaref murmured sarcastically beside her and she glanced at him in surprise.

'Why do you say it like that?' she asked.

Aaref shrugged. 'I believe this man is too good for the truth,' he said.

'Too good to be true,' Louise corrected automatically.

Aaref shook his head. 'So charming, so handsome, so rich.' He nodded scornfully to the door where Stefan Pininski was already surrounded by an admiring group of women. 'I think he makes the slave of the ladies.'

Louise giggled. 'I believe you are jealous, Aaref.'

He frowned. 'What is this word jealous?'

Louise groaned. How on earth did you explain jealousy? She glanced irritably back towards the door, thinking about Ward Frazer, and thought how extremely pleasant it would be to turn the tables and make him jealous.

Then even as she chided herself for the thought, she saw Stefan Pininski laugh at something Lael said, and without warning his eyes flicked restlessly round the room.

Louise felt the impact of that gaze like a bolt of electricity and for a moment her head spun.

Taking a quick breath she downed the remains of her champagne and tried to remember what she had been saying. She put down her empty glass and shook her head slightly, trying to clear her whirling brain. It was surely absurd to imagine that those humorous, dark eyes had rested on her for a moment. That she had glimpsed a flicker of desire under the heavy brows.

So why did she feel so strange? So peculiarly light headed. It must be the wine. She could feel it now, stirring her blood, pumping in her veins. She felt suddenly curiously detached, floating in an unreal world of glittering jewellery, exotic costumes and tinkling laughter. If she wasn't careful, she would fall over and make a fool of herself.

Aaref was looking for a fresh bottle. Quickly, while his back was turned, she slipped over to the French doors and pushed through the blackout curtains. She needed some fresh air.

But the air in Lael's garden wasn't fresh. It was muggy and hot, heavy with the scent of jasmine and honeysuckle. And very dark.

Stumbling down a stone path it was a moment before Louise's eyes acclimatised. Ahead of her seemed to be some kind of pagoda and she headed for it with wavering but dogged steps.

It seemed an odd thing for anyone to have in a London garden. Another example of foreign taste, Louise supposed. Nevertheless she was pleased to find a wooden seat inside and sat down gratefully. She really did feel very peculiar. Leaning forward she rested her elbows on the balustrade and her head on her hands. As soon as she closed her eyes strange blurred images spun in her head. Lights, drinks, men. Mostly men.

A noise behind her jerked her out of her daydream. A noise and the sudden, sweet, rich scent of expensive tobacco.

She swung round blinking rapidly and saw a tall figure leaning against one of the pagoda's supporting pillars. She knew at once who it was because the hairs on the back of her neck prickled.

Louise stood up and swayed. The figure detached itself from the pillar and bowed courteously. At the same moment a small crescent moon floated out from the clouds, throwing a thin watery light over the pagoda.

Stefan Pininski's cigar shone red as he inhaled. 'I'm sorry. I didn't mean to disturb you,' he drawled in that rich, seductive voice. 'I thought you were sleeping.'

Louise shook her head. He had disturbed her. Very much.

'No,' she said, and wished her own voice sounded less like that of a strangled mouse. 'I wasn't asleep. I just wanted some fresh air. It was so hot inside. It's cooler in here.' Actually she was sweating again now. But for different reasons.

He inclined his head. 'May I join you?'

'Of course,' she gulped nervously. 'It's a free world.'

His black eyebrows rose as he stepped under the wooden arch. 'Some might disagree with you there,' he said dryly.

Louise felt stupid. What an utterly idiotic thing to say when virtually the whole of Europe was now in Nazi control. Count Stefan Pininski was himself presumably in exile from the country of his birth.

'I'm sorry,' she mumbled. 'That was a tactless thing to say.'

He waved his cigar tolerantly. 'I know you didn't mean it like that. In any case I am more lucky than most. After all, I am here. If it was not for the war I would not be standing here in the scented moonlight talking to the prettiest girl I have seen in many years.'

Louise stared at him and he leaned back casually against the balustrade and drew on his cigar. Had he meant it? Did he really think she was pretty? She saw the speculative glint in his eyes and swallowed hard. She waited breathlessly for him to flatter her some more, but he didn't and she was searching her fuddled brain for a suitable response, when Aaref's voice floated down the garden.

'Louise, where are you? Are you all right?'

Heart hammering, Louise frowned but didn't respond. Blasted Aaref was going to spoil everything.

But to her relief Stefan Pininski remained silent too, a small smile curling his sensual lips, and after a moment they saw the chink of light through the curtains as Aaref went back inside.

Louise felt herself flushing. She knew by not responding to Aaref's call she had taken a dangerous step. 'You have an admirer,' Stefan Pininski murmured.

Louise rolled her eyes. 'Hardly,' she said scornfully.

'Oh yes, I think so. I think young Aaref has fallen in love with his teacher.'

'He is too young for me,' Louise said bravely. 'I like older men.'

'Very wise.' Stefan nodded gravely. 'Young men rarely know how to please a woman. They seek only their own pleasure.' His eyes narrowed slightly and Louise shivered. Suddenly she felt very nervous. She knew nothing about this man, except that he was rich and drove too fast.

As though reading her thoughts, he smiled faintly. 'You look afraid, Miss Rutherford. I am flattered you will talk to me at all. I was afraid I had been branded as a heartless murderer in these parts.'

Louise swallowed. 'Oh no, not at all,' she said shocked. 'Everyone knows that the accident wasn't your fault. And how generous you were afterwards.'

Stefan Pininski grimaced. 'It was the least I could do,' he said simply. He sighed and looked away. 'But no amount of money can compensate for the loss of a child. I still feel very bad about it.'

Louise stared at hm. 'You mustn't feel bad,' she said. There was something so appealing about his admission. 'There was nothing you could have done. I was there. I saw it all.'

For a second he looked surprised. Then suddenly he clicked his fingers, 'Now I remember. I thought I recognised you when I came to Lael's the other day.'

Louise's eyes widened.

He nodded. 'You were with another girl running down the street. That's a pretty girl, I said to myself. As I turned my head to look at you again, the child fell under my wheel.'

Louise gaped at him, half horrified, half flattered. 'And I was right,' he continued softly. 'You are a very pretty girl.' He leaned back lazily to flick ash off the end of his cigar. 'Pretty, and also untouched, I think.'

He smiled faintly as she blushed scarlet. 'I thought so. The best combination.'

'What do you mean?' Louise stammered.

He blew out smoke. 'Beauty in purity. The most priceless fragile jewel. Once it is gone, it can never be regained. I am a rich man, Miss Rutherford. I can buy jewellery and paintings and medical expertise. But physical purity is very much harder to find.'

As his pensive gaze lingered on her, Louise didn't feel at all pure. She felt completely terrified. Nervously she moved away slightly and found herself in a thin shaft of moonlight.

He laughed softly. 'Yes, that is better. Now I can see the perfection of your skin. The enticing curve of your breast. The fear in your eyes.'

Louise gulped. 'There isn't any fear in my eyes.'

'Oh, I think so, Miss Rutherford. I think you are afraid almost to death.' He raised his dark eyebrows quizzically.

Louise shook her head. But she was afraid. She was terrified of Stefan Pininski. She thought suddenly of Ward Frazer and felt sick.

But Stefan's voice was gentle, reassuring. 'Then perhaps we might have lunch one day?'

She stared at him in relief. Lunch, that was safe. Nothing could happen over lunch. Lunch with a real live Count. It sounded so glamorous. Excitement fizzled in her veins. She couldn't wait to tell Katy.

He took her hand then and pulled her to him. He was lean and hard and smelt faintly, oddly, of lime. A heady, expensive, male blend of lime and cigar tobacco and Louise suddenly felt pulses hammering all over her body.

For a second he looked into her eyes and smiled then he lowered his head.

His lips were cool. Everything in her upbringing urged Louise to pull back, she was shocked by such an intimacy from a man she hardly knew, but the alcohol had lowered her resistance and she found herself welcoming his embrace.

It didn't last long. Then he was releasing her, laughing softly.

'Yes, I think lunch next week would be most pleasant,' he said. 'I am staying at the Savoy. Shall we say Thursday? In the foyer? One o'clock?'

Louise nodded.

He touched her lips with a cool finger as he led her back up the garden path. 'It will be our little secret, yes? We don't want to make Aaref jealous.'

'All right,' Louise nodded obediently. Keeping it secret made it even more daring. A clandestine lunch. It was too exciting, too dangerous to be true. She hoped to God Hitler didn't invade in the meantime.

'I'll come in by the other way,' he murmured. 'Or people will be suspicious.' He lifted her hand to his lips in the darkness and clicked his heels. 'Good night, Louise. Until next week.'

Inside the party was in full swing. Louise blinked mole-like against the lights.

'There you are.' Aaref looked aggrieved. 'Where were you? I am calling in the garden.'

Louise shrugged. 'I didn't hear you,' she said. On the other side of the room she saw Stefan Pininski calmly rejoin the party. He really was extraordinarily handsome. Definitely the best looking man in the room. Even if he was a bit older than she would like. Already women were crowding round him.

'I've got a headache,' she said to Aaref. 'I'm going to have to go home. Please will you get my wrap?'

Lael was sorry to see her go. 'But I wanted to introduce you to so many people,' she said. 'Such a pretty girl as you. All the men want to meet you.'

Louise shook her head, blushing prettily. She thought she could feel his eyes on her. 'No, I really do to have to go,' she said. 'I don't feel very well. Oh, there's Aaref now with my wrap.'

Aaref draped the silk tasselled shawl around her shoulders with surprising skill.

Louise glanced back into the room and caught Stefan's eye. He was smiling at her over the rim of his glass, a thoughtful, tender expression in his eyes. Louise felt her stomach turn over. Nervously she glanced around to make sure nobody was looking, then flashed a quick smile back. His smile widened and as she turned away she saw one dark fringed eye drop in the briefest wink.

She turned back to Aaref. 'Thank you so much,' she said warmly. She could afford to be generous now. She touched his hand briefly. 'Good night, Aaref. See you next week.'

Aaref clicked his heels politely. 'I look forwards to it,' he said and she could feel his eager gaze burning into her back as she crossed the road. Stupid boy. Little did he know.

Jen was shocked to discover that there were nude tableaux in Fox's Review. She knew it had a bit of a racy reputation, like the Windmill, but she hadn't known that anyone actually took off their clothes.

Not that she had to, of course. Not as part of the chorus. And the girls who did pose nude weren't allowed to move, the producers were very strict about that. When one of the girls told her it was against the law to have nudes moving in a show, Jen couldn't help remembering the awful evening when Sean had taken her to the strip show in the Kilburn pub. They had moved in that show all right. No wonder the doors had been locked and bolted against the police.

It was much more discreet in the Fox's show. The nude models took up their tableaux positions in wrap gowns which stage hands whipped off moments before the curtain rose.

Often they weren't completely nude. It depended on the scene. For example Fiona who posed as a nymph in the 'Beneath the Deep' scene had a piece of flimsy gauze seaweed concealing one breast and her pubic triangle. The men in the audience loved that. The whistles and catcalls were often so loud you could hear them backstage.

But it was Brenda who everyone said pulled the crowds. She was revealed in all her glory in the 'Olympian Delights' scene, balancing on a Grecian plinth. She had to stand stock still for seven minutes.

Jen was on stage as chorus in that scene, dressed demurely like the others in a long white gown with a wreath of laurel leaves draped over her shoulder. But nobody had eyes for the chorus. It was Brenda they stared at. Every night you could feel the audience collectively willing Brenda to lose her balance.

She never did, but at the end of each show when the men in the front rows left, their places were rapidly filled with men who'd been sitting further back and everyone knew it was big busty Brenda they climbed forward to see.

Jen didn't mind. She was getting her stage experience and that was all that mattered. She knew Mr Boyle, the producer, liked her. He was pleased with her performance. He'd said she was quick on the uptake. He often smiled at her. Once he even asked if she was happy with her chorus role.

'What about the money?' he asked. 'It's not great pay, chorus work, you know.'

'Well, obviously I'd like to earn more,' Jen had said bravely, flattered to be picked out.

In truth her wage was a sad disappointment to her. What with giving so much to her mother and all, she certainly wasn't saving. The prospect of acting lessons receded further into the future. But maybe now she wouldn't need them. If only the producer would give her a chance to shine. It was impossible to stand out in the chorus.

'I can sing and dance and act,' she had said eagerly. 'I can make people laugh.' She smiled winningly, envisaging a solo role in one of the dramatic scenes or comic skits. You got more money for taking on a small part. 'I'd obviously like to earn a bit more if I could.'

Somebody pushed past them then and the producer had drawn away from her. 'I'll bear that in mind, Jennifer,' he said with a conspiratorial wink. 'I think you show potential, so I'll certainly bear that in mind.'

Jen glowed. She longed to tell someone, but she didn't want to crow in front of the other chorus girls. Some of them already resented her for getting picked out so often.

If only she could tell Sean. He would have been so proud. He'd written such a sweet letter in reply to hers. She had it in her pocket now. He was disappointed she wasn't coming to Ireland, he said. But in the meantime he wished her every success with her new role and was sure it would lead on to greater things. And one day they would be together again to celebrate her success. One day. Some of Jen's excitement evaporated. One day seemed a long way off. She wanted him here now, tonight. She sighed deeply and shook her head sadly. Never mind. She would have to tell Katy Parsons instead.

Pam glanced at Sheila Whitehead's bloodshot eyes and wondered how many women around the country were still waiting for news of their husbands and loved ones after the debacle of Dunkirk.

All they knew was that Jo had not made it back to England. His regiment had been unable to throw any light on his whereabouts. Jo's platoon had been cut off in the retreat. A counter attack had failed to find them. Nobody knew whether they were dead or prisoners of war. There were still a large number of men unaccounted for.

Pam had heard in the Ministry that the Germans were being very slow releasing the names of the prisoners of war. The Red Cross were involved now. Already there was a system for registering prisoners of war to receive Red Cross relief parcels. There was a system for everything these days it seemed. Except apparently for finding out who was dead.

Pam thanked God daily that Alan had returned safely. And yet his homecoming had not been quite what she had expected. Even as Alan had walked up the path that day, she knew things had changed between them.

It had been awkward to say anything much in front of Mick. But later that night when she tried to let him know how much she had missed him, he detached her fingers gently from his arm.

'Don't, Pam,' he said. 'Don't feel you've got to just for my sake.'

Pam had felt rebuffed. It's not just for your sake, she thought crossly. Didn't he realise how worried she had been?

He shook his head in the darkness. 'It's better to wait until we are ready,' he murmured drowsily. 'These things don't change overnight.'

But they do, she wanted to cry, and I am ready. But he had fallen asleep and she bit it back. Perhaps he no longer wanted her. For so long now she hadn't wanted him, it hadn't occurred to her that he might feel the same about her.

Tears trickled out of her eyes and soaked silently on to the pillow. Why was marriage so difficult? Why was Alan so difficult? So different from how he used to be?

Because he was different. His Dunkirk experience had changed him. He walked much taller. Talked more. Laughed more. With everyone else. Not with her. He didn't seem to want to talk to her at all.

Not even about what had happened to the boat. She knew he had left it at Dover. But it was only from Mick that she discovered that it had been too badly damaged on the second Channel crossing to bring it home. It had barely made Dover.

'They was bailing the whole way back, Mrs Nelson. Can you imagine? And Mr Nelson with two bullets in his arm and all. I bet as you're ever so proud of him.'

Pam nodded, but inside she sighed. She was proud, but what was the point of being proud if your husband didn't talk to you anymore?

A couple of the men he had rescued came to see him and after the briefest of introductions Alan took them off to the pub. Pam resented it. She was Alan's wife after all. Now, once again she had to hear it second hand from Mick who had slid into the pub with them unobserved.

'The army boys had made this sort of pier, Mrs Nelson, by driving their vehicles into the sea,' he told her eagerly. 'And everyone had to climb along it to reach the ships because the beach was too shallow and then the Germans dive bombed the pier and suddenly all the soldiers were in the sea and injured and drowning and all, and Mr Nelson took his little boat right in all among the wreckage and hauled them aboard and saved hundreds of them like that. Corporal James says he was ever so brave. Quiet like, you know, on the side. So Mr Nelson didn't hear.'

Mick hero-worshipped Alan.

At first Pam thought it was quite touching. When Alan's arm had needed stitches and had started to go septic, it was Mick who had accompanied him to the Wilhelmina Hospital.

But then she began to feel excluded. It was Alan who discussed Mick's future with Joyce Carter, Alan who came home with his ration book, Alan who fixed up for Mick to work on the Rutherford & Berry delivery dray in place of poor half-witted Tom, who had died in France less than a month after volunteering for military service.

It was Alan who decreed that six shillings of Mick's wages would go to Pam for his bed and board. Two shillings would be pocket money and the rest would go to his mother to repay money he apparently owed her.

Pam shook her head. She could hardly believe this was the same half-hearted, ineffective man she had been living with before Dunkirk.

Two days after his arrival home, Alan was invited to join the new Local Defence Volunteers. Everyone was talking about the LDV. It was a precaution against Hitler's imminent invasion.

And although some people laughed at the motley selection of uniforms and weapons they displayed in their drill session in the school hall, most were seriously concerned that their future lay in the hands of these amateur soldiers.

Pam began to resent the amount of time he put into it. It was like his boat all over again. He was out most evenings. Mick didn't like it either. He nagged Alan endlessly to be allowed to join the LDV.

He'd been at it again last night as Alan pulled on his khaki beret and armband. 'Why can't I join?'

Pam had marvelled at Alan's patience. But Alan had merely smiled tolerantly, 'You're too young. I've told you a hundred times, the age limit is seventeen.'

'I'm nearly fifteen. That's only two years short. Oh please, Mr Nelson. Nobody would know.'

Alan smiled. 'Everyone would know. You're notorious in these parts, don't forget.'

Pam could see from his lowered eyes that Mick was genuinely disappointed and secretly thought it served him right. But then to her surprise Alan relented.

'OK, OK. I'll put in a word for you.' He picked up the rusty old Lee Enfield he'd been issued in the absence of better weaponry. 'I fancy we might need messengers, or something of that sort.'

Mick's face glowed briefly then fell again. 'But I haven't got a motorcycle,' he said pitifully. 'Military messengers have motorcycles. I've seen them.'

Alan shook his head. 'I reckon a motorcycle might be beyond the resources of the LDV. But I could lend you my pushbike. Providing you look after it, mind. It's the only form of transport I've got now the boat's gone.'

'I'll guard it with my life,' Mick promised with a big grin.

'You may have to,' Alan had laughed grimly as he opened the front door. 'I certainly don't want Adolf bloody Hitler to get his thieving hands on it.'

Chapter Twenty

'Jennifer Carter?' One of the stage hands popped his head round the chorus dressing-room door. 'Mr Boyle wants to see you.'

Jen looked up. 'What, now?' It was very late. The curtain had just come down on the last show of the evening. Everyone was exhausted. Nineteen shows a week were taking their toll.

The stage hand shrugged. 'So he said.'

As he closed the door again one of the girls in the room sniggered. 'Must be your lucky night.'

'How are the mighty chosen,' someone else murmured.

Jen ignored them. She knew the other girls were jealous of her. She didn't care about that. What she cared about was what Mr Boyle was going to say.

As she pulled on her skirt and blouse, she quickly ran her mind back through the day. Had she done something wrong? Or was he going to offer her something? A part?

Nervously she ran down the passage to the producer's office.

He opened the door to her knock and nodded briskly.

'Good. I'm glad I caught you. I've got something to offer you.'

Jen's heart jolted. 'You have?'

He smiled. 'I told you I'd keep you in mind. Well, I have. You can't say Fred Boyle doesn't look after his girls. And it will bring you in another pound a week.'

'What is it?' Jen asked eagerly. 'What do you want me to do?'

An extra pound a week. She could hardly believe it. That would buy her a singing lesson every Sunday. Or a dancing lesson. Or an acting lesson. Something, anyway. Something to enhance her career.

Mr Boyle ran his eyes over her in a quick professional appraisal.

'I want you to do one of the nudes,' he said. 'Brenda wants out. I need a replacement.'

Jen stared at him. One of the nudes? Brenda?

She could hardly take it in. Mr Boyle wanted her, Jennifer Carter, to replace big busty Brenda on her wobbly pedestal.

A slight frown creased Fred Boyle's sweaty forehead. 'Nothing the matter with you, is there?' he asked bluntly. 'No scars or blemishes?'

Numbly in shock, Jen shook her head. For a horrified second she thought he might ask her to prove it.

But he merely smiled. 'That's all right, then. Well? What do you think? Pleased, eh?'

Jen didn't know what to say. 'I didn't think ... I imagined ...' She stopped in despair.

Imagined what? A small part in one of the dramatic scenes? A few bars of music on her own? A few solo dance steps? But not a nude. A pound a week to take off her clothes and have all the soldiers in London leering at her naked body. Climbing over the seats to get a closer look. It was unthinkable. Her whole body burnt in mortification. She was an actress not a stripper.

She lifted her chin bravely. 'I'm sorry, Mr Boyle, I don't think ...'

His smile faded abruptly. 'It's not a matter of choice, Jennifer.' He folded his arms over his chest. 'You're one of the prettiest girls we've got here at the moment. I need you to do it. You do this, and I'll see you all right in the future. You never know, something else might come up.'

Jen swallowed, 'And if I don't?' she asked bravely. He shrugged. 'Then you're out. You signed the contract. You read the terms.'

But she hadn't. She had been so thrilled to have a job at all she had signed blindly. Ecstatically. Terrified they would jerk the paper away before she'd got her signature down on it.

She looked up pitifully now at the man she had thought was to be her saviour. He unfolded his arms and patted her on the shoulder. 'You'll be all right, love. Think of that extra quid.' He winked. 'You've got a good body. Might as well make money out of it, eh?'

Somewhat to Louise's relief, Stefan Pininski did not intend to eat at the Savoy. She had eaten there once or twice with her parents and it had occurred to her that it might be awkward to bump into somebody who knew her. Instead he took her to a small French restaurant in an alley just off St Martin's Lane where he ordered champagne and told her how much he had looked forward to seeing her again.

Louise had told her mother that she was lunching with Lady Helen de Burrel, who luckily worked quite near the Savoy, in the Strand, or rather under the Strand because Helen's ARP post turned out to be an enormous underground, smoke-filled cavern right below the Adelphi theatre.

When Louise had finally managed to gain admittance in order to corroborate her lie, she discovered that the Adelphi ARP post involved a huge number of people keeping themselves and their equipment and ambulances in readiness for the daily expected bombing, under the command of a few terrifyingly bossy women with stentorian voices.

As the crisis deepened so, according to Helen, did the noise, the revving engines, the endless piped music, the shouted orders. And she joked with

Louise that the type of women who ended up in senior positions seemed to think they had to act like men.

'They call all that shouting and cursing leadership,' she shouted over the racket. 'They don't seem to realise that women have a lot to offer in their own right. Oh no, they have to model themselves on the worst kind of men. Officious and insensitive and brash and trampling on everyone's feelings.'

'It sounds ghastly,' Louise said, hardly able to hear herself think. 'Why on earth do you do it?'

Helen laughed. 'I quite like it actually. And you have to do your bit, don't you?'

'Ward always said you ought to be doing something more important,' Louise remarked airily. 'What with your languages and everything.' She hadn't told Helen about her Ward Frazer debacle. Now she watched the other girl's reaction carefully, wondering if he had told her. Wondering if Helen had had a similar experience with him. After all, he had always seemed quite interested in her.

But her ruse failed. Helen just smiled. 'I think Ward Frazer has a rather unrealistic view of other people's abilities and courage,' she said. 'Just because he's happy to risk his life behind enemy lines, doesn't mean that anyone else particularly wants to deliberately put themselves in danger.'

Louise stared at her. 'Behind enemy lines? What on earth do you mean? I thought he was in the air force.'

Helen jerked her hand to her mouth. 'Oh God. Hasn't he told you?' She shook her head with a guilty grimace. 'I'm sorry, Louise. I know it's not public knowledge, but I assumed he would have told you.'

'Told me what?' Louise asked crossly. She was meant to be the expert on Ward Frazer. She certainly didn't like Helen de Burrel knowing his secrets.

Helen lowered her voice and Louise found herself straining to hear her. 'Officially he's in the RAF, but mostly he works for the government, the War Office I think. A couple of times since the war started he's been parachuted secretly into Germany to find out what's going on there. The atmosphere and things. The attitude of the people. You know the sort of thing.'

Louise didn't know. All she knew was that she was furious. Furious that Ward had pulled the wool over her eyes. Furious that she'd been shown up in front of one of her friends.

Why hadn't he told her? Why did he let her believe he was in the RAF? Why didn't he tell her he was running about all over Europe as some kind of stupid spy?

She was jerked out of her silent fury by Helen touching her on the arm.

'I'm sorry,' Helen said gently. 'I've upset you. I shouldn't have said. I didn't mean to worry you. I know you are keen on him.'

Louise gritted her teeth. The last thing she wanted now was Helen's sympathy. 'Oh no, not at all,' she said dismissively. 'In any case, I'm seeing someone else now.' She lifted her chin. 'Someone rather gorgeous.'

'Really?' Helen raised her eyebrows. 'Who? Someone in Clapham?'

'Oh no,' Louise said, shocked. 'Much grander than that. He's a member of the Polish nobility. A Count actually.' With some satisfaction she saw Helen's eyes widen. Helen was only a Lady. She smiled sweetly. 'Very sophisticated. Very attractive. Very rich.' She glanced at her watch. 'In fact I must run. He's expecting me at the Savoy and I'm late already.'

A quarter of an hour later, as he led her past the countless theatres and concert halls that lined the narrow streets between the Strand and St Martin's Lane, Louise realised that Count Stefan Pininski was in fact even more sophisticated and attractive than she had remembered. The way his eyes lit up when he saw her hovering nervously in the ornate gilded foyer of the Savoy had caused a spurt of excitement to course through her.

'Louise,' he murmured as he kissed her hand. 'All morning I have been worried you would not come.'

His ability to charm extended even to the waiters in the chic little restaurant, who were delighted with his effortless French and almost came to blows over which of them should present the menu.

Louise stared at him across the table and couldn't believe her luck. He was everything she had always dreamed of. Handsome beyond belief, courteous, charming, amusing, rich, thoroughly debonair and just a tiny bit scary. Because even the deprecating charm, the smart Savile Row suit and impeccable manners couldn't disguise the seductive tone of his beautiful voice as he complimented her on her choice of clothes, the colour of her hair, the light tan on her skin.

The only thing about her he didn't apparently approve of was her choice of jewellery.

'Pearls are too old for you,' he said reaching over the red and white chequered tablecloth to lift the string at her neck. As he let them fall again, the backs of his fingers brushed across her bare collarbone.

He smiled as the skin on her neck and chest rapidly infused with colour. 'I would prefer to see you in gold or even perhaps a jewel, amethyst or emerald, something young, fresh like you. Jewellery should always reflect a lady's personality.'

'I don't like pearls very much either,' Louise said breathlessly. 'But all my jewellery was stolen just before Christmas and I haven't got anything else.'

'Then after lunch we will go shopping,' he said. 'And I will buy you a little gift.'

He was intending to buy her jewellery. How glamorous. How flattering. Louise blinked. No man had ever bought her anything. Certainly Ward Frazer hadn't.

She frowned, suddenly remembering her mother's childhood exhortations not to take sweets from strangers. Quickly she shook her head. 'Oh no, you mustn't buy me anything,' she said, rather flustered. After all, what would he expect in return?

'You have those scared eyes again,' Stefan Pininski murmured. 'Don't look at me like that, Louise. I will not make you do anything you don't want to do. An unwilling lover is worse than no lover at all.'

Louise blushed scarlet. Lover? She swallowed and nearly choked on her last mouthful of lemon sole.

When she recovered, he was charmingly contrite. 'I am sorry to shock you. Where I come from these things are out in the open. Not hidden away under the covers like in England. I would like to take you to bed. I want to make love to you, Louise. Does that shock you so much?'

'No, no,' Louise lied valiantly. 'I'm not shocked. It's just that I haven't ...' She broke off thankfully as the waiter came for their plates. Stefan calmly ordered mousse au chocolat for them both then resumed where they had left off as though there had been no interruption.

'No?' He smiled. He took her hand and lifted it to his mouth, slowly brushing his lips to her skin. 'Good. Then I will teach you. I think we will have very happy times ahead.'

'It's just that my parents are a bit old fashioned,' Louise stammered. 'They don't like me being out with people they haven't met. I ... I had to pretend to be seeing a girlfriend today.'

Stefan's dark eyes held hers steadily. 'Then I hope you will be seeing this girlfriend quite a lot, Louise,' he murmured, his voice as thrilling as a physical caress. 'Because I want to know you, Louise, to love you, and, if you permit, to make love to you. And we do not want your parents breathing on our necks.'

Louise fiddled with her napkin nervously. This was going rather more quickly than she had intended.

And yet when he lifted her fingers to his mouth as he was doing now, she felt her blood heating up in the most extraordinary way. He kissed her knuckles again then straightened her little finger and dipped it in his champagne.

Louise could hardly breathe as he sucked it dry. He released it and chuckled at her expression. 'Oh yes, we will have very much fun together I think, little one. But not today, I think. Today we will just do a little shopping.'

Katy pinned the bandage neatly at the elbow and leaned back to admire her handiwork.

'How does that feel?' she asked, squinting against the high late June sun.

She and Jen had brought a rug up to the common to take advantage of the beautiful day while Katy practised her newfound bandaging skills.

Jen flexed her arm and winced. 'It's a bit tight,' she said cautiously,

Katy frowned. 'Last time you complained it was too loose.'

'It was too loose,' Jen said. 'It fell off when I stood up.' She poked her finger doubtfully under the top of the bandage. 'This one's more likely to make my arm fall off.'

Katy giggled. 'It's meant to be firm. And look, I've got a lovely criss-cross pattern on it. Just like the picture in the book.' She pointed eagerly to the open copy of Red Cross Home Nursing that lay on the rug beside them.

Jen grimaced. 'It's my arm I'm worried about, not the stupid pattern. You know who you ought to practise on, Alan Nelson. He'd tell you if you'd got it right.'

Katy looked appalled. 'Oh, I couldn't do that. He's got a real wound. I'd be scared to death.'

'But surely that's the whole point of the course,' Jen said, reaching over to pick some daisies. 'To prepare you for the real thing. When the Wehrmacht march up Lavender Hill we'll all be running to you to bandage our arms.'

Katy paled. 'Don't, Jen. Stop it. It gives me the creeps.' She frowned, watching Jen piercing the daisy stems with her thumbnail. 'Anyway you can get had up for saying things like that.'

Threading the delicate daisies into a chain, Jen almost wished she would get had up. Almost wished Hitler would march into London that very night. Anything to avoid what awaited her at Fox's on Monday.

She wondered briefly what advice Katy would give if she consulted her. And quickly quashed the temptation. It wasn't Katy's problem, it was hers.

Instead she dropped the daisies on the rug and stood up abruptly, puffing out her chest. 'Combat defeatism with all your might,' she said portentously, imitating the Moral Re-armament speaker they had heard earlier on the wireless. She rolled her eyes at Katy's obvious disapproval and rubbed her bandaged arm. 'Honestly, Katy, I don't want Hitler here anymore than you do. But now France has fallen, there's not much we can do about it. I reckon if he comes, he comes.'

Katy shaded her eyes to look up at her. 'But you are doing something, Jen. You are entertaining people, keeping their morale up, raising their fighting spirit. And if you get a solo part and maybe get into ENSA, entertaining the fighting troops and factory workers, then you'd be doing something really important.'

Jen sat down again, heavily. If only Katy knew. She wouldn't be talking about ENSA then. ENSA didn't have nudes on stage. Despite the sunshine, Jen shivered and hugged her arms round her knees. Because she knew she was going to have to do it. There really was no decision to make. She couldn't afford to lose the job at Fox's. Without the job she had nothing. No money. No credentials. No future. No, she would grit her teeth and do it. And she would tell nobody. Not even Katy.

The only alternative was to write to Sean and say she had changed her mind. And she was too proud to do that. Not after her last letter in which she had written excitedly about a possible break at Fox's, about Mr Boyle saying she was quick on the uptake, that she had potential. God, if only she had realised what he had meant.

'You're lucky, Jen. You've got a vocation,' Katy said now, unaware of her friend's private agony. She nodded across the common to the gun emplacement where a small troop of uniformed women were doing physical jerks outside one of the Nissen huts. 'So have they presumably.' She grimaced. 'All I'm doing is rolling stupid bandages.'

Jen looked at her, surprised. 'I thought you liked it.'

'I do.' Katy said. 'But it's not much, is it? A piddly Red Cross first aid qualification. Not when you think what Alan Nelson did. What the men in the services are doing every day. Risking their lives.'

'Risking lives or saving lives,' Jen said thoughtfully, rubbing her fingers. For the first time she felt humbled by Katy's patriotic concern. By her sensitivity. By her loyalty. She looked up. 'Seriously, Katy, if that bastard Hitler does invade, you may find you're asked to do more than you expect. We all may.'

She grinned suddenly and raised her arm. 'But before you start panicking, I think you'd better take this blasted bandage off. I can't feel my fingers any more. I'm sure you've cut off my circulation.'

Mick Carter had taken to Alan's bicycle in a big way. Each evening when he got back from the brewery, he took it out, riding for miles through Surrey, Sussex and Middlesex and coming back with tales of trenches and tanks, barbed wire and barricades.

He described the fields dotted with anti-aircraft spikes. Talked eagerly of a squadron of new planes at Croydon aerodrome, of pilots sunning themselves on the grass alongside Purley Way, while they waited for orders.

He had even claimed to have exchanged words with some Canadian soldiers camping in Richmond Park.

He was equally enthusiastic about his new role as Lavender District LDV messenger. What he was not enthusiastic about was his job on the brewery dray.

'He's scared of the horses,' Alan told Pam one evening as he polished his boots on a piece of newspaper on the kitchen table. 'He says it's a relief to get to the end of each day without being bitten or kicked or run away with.'

He laughed. 'And what with old Cyril mouthing off about his laziness the whole time, I reckon it's doing him good.'

Pam shook her head. 'It's you that's doing him good,' she said, looking up from the washing-up. 'I can hardly believe it's the same boy who only a few months ago was taunting you about your boat.' Or the same man, she thought to herself.

Alan didn't answer for a moment and she wondered if she had upset him reminding him of those awful traumatic days before Dunkirk. How angry she had been with him then. How despairing. It was different now. Now she was despairing for different reasons. Alan seemed to have lost interest in her. And now she had lost him she wanted him badly.

Alan moved suddenly on his chair, making it scrape on the concrete floor. 'I'm sorry about all that,' he said, and she looked at him in surprise.

He shook his head. 'I always thought when war came I'd be up there with the rest. Fighting for King and country. Fighting for you. But when I found I couldn't, I lost my nerve. I lost my direction.' He dropped his eyes. 'I lost you.'

It was true. He had lost her to Sean Byrne. She dearly hoped he hadn't realised that.

'And now I've lost you,' she said. She dug her nails into her palms behind her back and added softly, 'And I don't know how to get you back.'

It was a courageous admission. A complete departure from their recent reticence. A cry for help. She thought he would reach over and draw her on to his knee. But he didn't.

Instead he got up and turned away.

She bit her lip painfully and watched him anxiously from the sink. Two months ago she would have laughed at the sight of him in his cobbled-together LDV uniform and stockinged feet. Now she just wished he would come over and take her in his arms.

'It would be easy to say let's start again,' he said. 'But I don't know if that's the answer. Perhaps it's too late.'

Pam felt her heart jolt painfully. 'It's not too late for me,' she whispered.

He swung round to face her. For a moment he stared at her silently, a muscle working in his cheek, then he swore angrily.

'Damn it, Pam,' he said, jerking his boots off the table and dropping them to the floor. He crumpled the newspaper angrily. 'I don't understand you. One minute you're saying I'm the most pathetic individual that ever graced God's earth and won't touch me with a barge pole. And the next you're all over me.'

He sat down on the chair and pulled the boots on roughly. 'OK, so I went to Dunkirk. I had to go. And now everybody thinks I'm a hero. But I'm not. I went because I had to get away. I didn't care whether I died. Just then I

243

would almost rather have died than see my life and my marriage fade into insignificance.'

Suddenly he stopped struggling with the boots and lifted a hand to push the hair off his forehead. 'Or so I thought. But when it came down to it, I was scared, Pam. Scared as hell. And when we came under fire, I found I didn't want to die after all.'

Pam leaned over the sink and closed her eyes to hold back the sudden threatening tears. When she turned back again Alan had finished lacing his boots and was standing by the kitchen door. He adjusted his LDV armband and straightened the threadbare khaki jacket he'd borrowed from Malcolm Parsons at the Flag and Garter. Uniform wasn't yet a priority in the hastily formed citizens' army. Pam realised he was about to go out and reached forward desperately.

'Alan, don't go. Please. We haven't sorted anything out.' She said helplessly. 'You going to Dunkirk has made a difference. It made me realise ...' She stopped, balking at the final confession.

He looked round but he didn't move towards her. 'Made you realise what?' His voice was unusually crisp, almost harsh. Something in his face told her he didn't want any declarations of love.

She dropped her hand. 'It made me realise what we had lost,' she amended sadly. She looked at him pleadingly, close to tears again. 'Is it gone forever, Alan?'

He shook his head and sighed. 'I don't know. Maybe in time we can build it up again.' He grimaced. 'But it takes a certain courage to walk the gangplank of love a second time. I don't know if I have that courage.'

'You went to France a second time,' Pam pointed out crossly. Wasn't he even prepared to try? Was saving a few soldiers really more important to him than saving their marriage?

For a moment he looked surprised. 'I had to go back,' he said simply. 'There were already too many men lying dead on those beaches.'

Pam frowned as he walked away up the passage to the front door. 'Well, it took courage, whatever you may say,' she called after him irritably.

He turned at the door and nodded slowly. 'To an extent, yes, I suppose going over a second time did take a certain amount of courage.' Then he shook his head and for the first time he smiled, his old dry smile. 'But to be perfectly honest, Pam, my sweet, the prospect of falling in love with you all over again makes facing up to a few Jerry Messerschmidts look like child's play.'

Jen hardly spoke during her brief rehearsal on Monday morning. Fred Boyle did all the talking, while she stood self consciously beside him in a wraparound gown, underneath which she still wore her bra and knickers.

Thankfully he hadn't asked her to remove those.

'Save that for the show,' he said with a wink. 'Don't want anyone getting a preview, do we? People pay to see this show. I'm not having the wings full of gawpers seeing it free.'

Just a theatreful, Jen thought bitterly, suddenly hating this sweaty man who pretended to be so concerned about her welfare when all he cared about was his beastly third-rate little show.

'Right,' he said now. 'Climb up, then. Let's see you balance. That's the trick. Not losing the balance. They want you to fall. And we don't want you giving them that satisfaction. Not allowed anyway. Moving. Case they see something they oughtn't.' He winked and Jen felt herself blushing furiously.

The female stage hand looked at her with faint sympathy as she reluctantly removed the gown and stepped up on to the pedestal.

Standing on a box, Fred Boyle positioned her carefully. His hands clammy and far too familiar on her bare skin. Jen had a terrible desire to push him away. She longed to see him topple backwards off his box. And then, reaching for her left hand, his fingers inadvertently brushed her groin.

'Keep your eyes on the top of the curtain,' the stage hand murmured as a sudden wave of nausea made Jen wobble. 'Don't, whatever you do, look into the audience.'

'That's the ticket.' Fred Boyle got off his box and stood back, eyeing her up and down with a satisfied smile. 'You'll get up, hand the gown to Marj here and that's all there is to it. The curtain will rise. Don't take any notice of the audience. Just keep the smile on. That's it, nice and wide. Look as if you're enjoying yourself, love. Then you will.'

No chance, Jen thought as she hurried back to the dressing-room to get ready for the opening number of the first show of the day. The Grecian scene didn't come until near the end of the show. She had all the normal chorus numbers to do before it.

Even as she blandly met the curious eyes of the other girls, she could feel her whole body rebelling from what she was going to have to do. If she could have got on a train to Ireland there and then she would have.

Chapter Twenty One

Joyce put down the letter from Angie in Devon and sighed heavily. Angie's letters had been becoming increasingly skimpy over the nine months she had been evacuated. Young Paul's had stopped altogether.

Joyce regretted sending them away. She had almost forgotten what they looked like after all this time. It was odd to think of them growing up without her. But there was no point in getting them back now, just as it finally seemed certain that Hitler had his sights on London.

He'd already issued his troops with English phrase books, they said, ready for the invasion, and he was already bombing the south coast. Military targets admittedly, but a couple of civilians had been killed too.

The government weren't giving out weather forecasts on the wireless any more in case it helped the Luftwaffe, and people had been told to clear out their attics because of the threat of incendiary bombs. Even the King was nervous. It was in the paper that he'd been practising his pistol shooting in the gardens of Buckingham Palace.

No, the kids were better off in Devon, it was just a shame that Angie suddenly seemed homesick again. It seemed she'd got her first curse and had thought she was dying until Mrs Baxter had found out what was wrong and tried to explain it was normal.

Mrs Baxter had given her some bunnies to put in her knickers. But even then it seemed Angie hadn't entirely believed her. None of her friends had it. And she was sure Jen had never had it. And she wanted to know if it was something you only caught in the country because one of Mrs Baxter's dogs had it too. And if so she wanted to come home.

Joyce shook her head. Perhaps she should make the effort to go down there and see them. But the trip would cost her both time and money. And now she was so close to getting that jewellery back off Lorenz. It was already late June and the six-month pledge was up now, so he could sell it if he wanted to. He'd said he would keep it for her into July. But what if she delayed too long?

Ten pounds. Another week or two and she'd have it. By scrimping and saving and with money coming in from Jen and Pete, and Mick, thanks to Alan Nelson, her deposit with Lorenz had grown steadily.

She wanted to have that jewellery back in Mrs Rutherford's hands before Hitler invaded. Because God only knew what would happen to everyone then. It hadn't passed her notice that Lorenz was the most likely to be affected. The papers were full of the terrible things, that bugger Hitler was doing to the Jews, not only in Germany but in all the countries he had invaded too.

Joyce frowned. Stanley used to say the Jews deserved what they got, but there was nothing wrong with Lorenz really. He was a bit of a twister, but that was his job after all and he'd been decent enough over her redeeming the jewellery. Letting her have it at a bit of a knocked-down price and that, although why he'd done that for her, she couldn't imagine.

Joyce sighed again and picked up her pen. She would write back to Angie to tell her that the curse was just one of those many things that women had to put up with in life wherever you lived. Tell her that it was a sign of growing up, like bosoms. Tell her she would come down to visit just as soon as she could get away.

Louise was surprised to find that Aaref was absent when she arrived at Lael's on Monday morning to give the boys one of her twice-weekly lessons.

'He's been interned,' Lael said angrily. It's quite absurd. The police came for him early this morning. Just because he's over seventeen and was born in Austria, they've got him down as an enemy alien.' She glanced at Benjamin and Jacob who were sitting in silence side by side on the sofa, blank eyed and shivering. 'My God, you would think these poor boys had been through enough without this.'

She took a scarlet shawl from the back of a chair and draped it round her shoulders. 'Of course they think that's the last they've seen of him. They've seen too many people disappear over the last few years not to believe that, whatever I say to the contrary.' She shook her head. 'Anyway, thank God you're here. I didn't want to leave them alone. Now I can go down to the Town Hall and see what I can do about it.'

Louise's heart sank. It was bad enough trying to get Benjamin and Jacob to respond when Aaref was there to interpret, but without him she knew it would be completely hopeless. Particularly as both boys looked as though they were about to throw up.

After Lael had gone, Louise sat on a chair opposite them and smiled tentatively.

'Hello,' she said. 'How are you today?' There was no reaction.

'Mrs d'Arcy Billière has gone to find Aaref,' she said slowly. 'She will bring him home.'

Still no reaction. Although it was quite possible they didn't understand. Aaref was the only one of the three who showed any ability in English. In fact it had irritated her over the few weeks she had been teaching them, how Aaref had quite clearly picked up a lot more from her lessons than he let on.

He sometimes asked her to repeat a phrase or explain a meaning half a dozen times and then said it himself as though he'd known it all along.

She had wished on a number of occasions that she could open up his head and see just what was in there. She knew he was attracted to her from the way he jerked his eyes away quickly and flushed as she glanced in his direction. The way he sulked if she ignored his sudden smiles, which she invariably did. She wasn't interested in a scrawny seventeen year old Jew.

She had bigger fish to fry. She nervously fingered the delicate gold chain at her neck.

When, outside Tessiers Ltd, she had thanked Stefan shyly for the valuable present, he had smiled. 'The next gift I give you, my little one, will be when I make you mine.'

But that hadn't happened yet. Although she knew she couldn't hold off much longer.

On Saturday Stefan had taken a box at the Albert Hall, to hear Sir John Barbirolli and the Halle Orchestra play Tchaikovsky. One or two people had waved at him as they took their seats, and smiled questioningly at her. She had smiled back hoping he might introduce her but he didn't. He said he wanted to keep her to himself. 'The little time you allow me of your company, Louise, is too precious to share with anyone else. One lunch, one afternoon tea and two short evenings is not enough for me, my darling. I want to see you every day, every night.'

Louise wished she could see him more, but it was so hard thinking up excuses to escape from Cedars House without arousing the suspicions of her parents. And in truth she was a little bit nervous of being alone with him for too long. Particularly at night.

That Albert Hall night she had once again told her parents she was seeing Helen de Burrel and had promised to be back by eleven. Stefan had been flatteringly unhappy about the early deadline. In the taxi he had touched her breast through her blouse, smiling as she nearly jumped out of her skin. 'I think you are ready for me, Louise,' he had murmured. 'Next time I will take you to bed.'

'Don't you think we should wait a little bit longer?' Louise had said nervously. Stefan's outspoken desire for her scared her a little bit. After all she had been brought up to see sex before marriage as a complete taboo and if her parents found out they would be simply appalled. Not that they would find out of course, she never told them anything these days. Not after the way her mother had treated her over Ward. Nevertheless she had only met Stefan four times and despite her body's dramatic reaction to his smallest touch, she would have preferred to wait a little bit longer before taking the plunge.

'But Stefan has shaken his head. 'Sometimes in life you must wait. If you are not sure. But between you and me, Louise, is something powerful, something wonderful, something exciting. What I feel for you, I have felt for no other woman.'

Louise stared at him. 'Perhaps it's love?' she suggested breathlessly. He smiled and kissed her fingertips. 'It is more than love. It is a power. A destiny. Do you believe in destiny, Louise?'

'I don't know.'

He shook his head seriously, 'When I make love to you, you will believe. Sometimes two people are meant for each other.' He smiled suddenly: 'It is the only thing I would thank Adolf Hitler for, that he has brought us together.'

It was certainly very powerful. Louise was impressed, flattered by his attention, by his charm, by the warmth and tenderness she saw in his eyes.

Now battling doggedly through simple sentences with her two silent pupils, replaying his words in her head, she felt the stirring of excitement. At first she had gone along with Stefan Pininski because she thought he would be a good person to make Ward Frazer jealous. A glamorous older man, a Count no less. She had vaguely hoped he would somehow impart to her the experience and sophistication she lacked.

But now it was coming to the crunch, she found she was feeling rather differently about it. Despite being a lot older than her, Stefan Pininski was gorgeous, there were no two ways about it. He was courteous, charming and extremely attractive. Increasingly Louise felt her body heat up whenever she was near him. And she knew he felt the same. Somehow the age difference didn't matter anymore. She liked his maturity, his worldly smile, his confidence. Day by day she longed for the moment when she would see him again.

Because gaining experience and getting back at Ward Frazer suddenly didn't seem quite as important as getting Stefan Pininski. How jealous her friends would be about that. And her parents would be astounded.

She imagined Stefan arriving at Cedars House in one of his exquisite Savile Row suits to ask her father for her hand in marriage. Imagined her father's shock, his grovelling acceptance, his anxious enquiries about the size of the wedding.

Even better, she imagined her mother's surprise when she realised that the daughter, who she only recently accused of being a schoolgirl, actually had the maturity to land a Count.

The noise of a car pulling up outside brought her back abruptly to Lael's sitting-room. She realised that almost an hour had elapsed. And so far neither of the boys had uttered a single word. Now she felt a moment's panic that it might be Stefan and got to her feet nervously.

But in fact it was Lael, seething with fury after battling with bureaucracy at Battersea Town Hall.

'It's quite monstrous,' she said. 'The poor boy has got to go in front of some sort of tribunal before they'll let him out.'

'Where is he?' Louise asked, imagining Aaref languishing in some hideous jail and feeling a bit sorry for him despite herself.

'They've put him in the Royal Victoria Patriotic Asylum on Wandsworth Common.'

Louise stared. 'I thought that was a girls' school.'

'It is,' Lael smiled. 'But the girls have been evacuated. They're using the building for refugees and internees now apparently.' She glanced at Aaref's brothers and spoke to them in rapid German. Then she turned back to Louise. 'I've told them I'll take them down to see him later on. Perhaps you would like to come with us? He'd be so pleased to see you. He holds you in high regard.' She smiled. 'I believe he is a little bit in love with you.'

Louise cringed inwardly. The last thing in the world she wanted to do was go to see Aaref locked away in some awful school dormitory.

'I promised Mummy I'd help her clear out the attic this afternoon,' she lied. Actually Mrs Carter had helped her mother with it on Friday. Louise had heard them chit-chatting up there all afternoon. Although what they found to talk about she couldn't imagine.

'Well, perhaps tomorrow, then?' Lael said easily. 'He really would be so pleased.'

I bet he would, Louise thought sourly. But I wouldn't. She had better things to do. Like dreaming about Stefan Pininski for example. Gorgeous, sophisticated Stefan, with his immaculate taste and lazy admiring eyes.

Wow, she thought dreamily as she strolled back to Cedars House. I'm falling in love.

Jen had expected the catcalls, the whistles, but she hadn't anticipated the howls of derision as the curtain drew back on her naked figure and the audience, an especially rowdy one on this particular afternoon, realised they were being cheated out of Big Brenda.

As she stood on the pedestal, her whole body quivering with humiliation as the chorus tried to project their voices over the noise, she made herself think only of the money.

If she thought of all those eyes fixed on her nakedness she knew she would be sick. Sean Byrne was the only man who had ever seen her private parts before. That had been hard enough, she had only done it because she loved him, and yet now here she was showing them off to the whole of London.

And London clearly didn't like them. The men in the audience had come to see big busty Brenda. And they didn't think Jennifer Carter was a satisfactory substitute at all.

In the chorus dressing room that Monday evening, the other girls seemed to take delight in Jen's discomfiture. 'You want to watch out, darling,' someone said. 'They'll be bringing rotten eggs in tomorrow.'

Jen bit her lip. But in fact by Tuesday afternoon, five humiliating shows later, the situation had improved a bit. There had been no sign of any rotten eggs. The jeers and catcalls were not so angry. And Jen had perfected a technique of blanking her mind to her surroundings, even as she displayed her most personal and private wares to the leering, eagle-eyed audience.

Nevertheless she was certain that the poor reception she had received would cause Mr Boyle to replace her. So she wasn't particularly surprised when she was summoned to his office after the early evening show on Tuesday. She just prayed he wouldn't fire her altogether.

'They don't like you,' he said baldly.

Jen nodded. 'I know,' she said miserably. 'They want Brenda.'

'It's not that.' Fred Boyle shook his head. 'They can tell your heart's not in it.'

'What do you mean?'

His eyes narrowed. 'You're cold,' he said. 'You just stand there. They want you sexy. Do you know what I mean?'

Jen shook her head uncomfortably. 'No.'

He looked at her. 'Then I'll have to show you.' He pulled a wooden chair forward for her to stand on. 'Slip your things off, love.'

Jen stared at him aghast. 'What, now? Here?'

He pushed the door closed behind her and shrugged. 'I'm trying to help you. You want the job, don't you? I told you before, you do this for me and I'll see you all right in the future.'

Silently Jen stripped down to her bra and panties and swung round to face him self-consciously.

He nodded briskly. 'Leave the panties on if you want,' he said running his eyes thoughtfully over her slender frame, 'But we'll need the top off.'

His professional appraisal reassured her slightly. Reluctantly Jen reached round to unbuckle the bra.

'Now up on the chair,' he commanded. 'Up's a daisy. That's it. Now get into your position. Good. That's nice.' Jen flinched as he ran his hand up her leg, twisting the knee slightly, pushing out the other thigh a fraction. 'Got a boyfriend, love?' he asked casually.

Jen blinked. 'Yes,' she said firmly. It wasn't a lie. She was waiting for Sean.

Fred Boyle nodded. 'Thought so, pretty girl like you.'

Jen gritted her teeth as his hand travelled on up her thigh, certain that any moment he would withdraw it. But he didn't.

Instead, to her utter astonishment, he quite blatantly rubbed her between the legs. She could feel the warmth of his fingers through her thin panties, and after a moment of paralysed horror, almost overbalancing, she swung round angrily pushing his hand away.

He laughed and she stared at him uncertainly, hoping she hadn't over reacted. 'W-what are you doing?'

He smiled. 'Just warming you up a bit, darling. I told you, you're too cold.' He patted her bottom and reached a hand up to her breast. 'A bit of arousal,' he added, squeezing one of her bosoms casually. 'That's what they want.'

Before she realised what she was doing Jen lashed out, catching him between the legs with her bare foot. As he doubled over with a shriek, she scrambled off the stool and grabbed her clothes off the chair.

But he was between her and the door. And he was recovering rapidly.

As she tried to dodge past him, he lunged at her and pinned her against the wall.

'Oh no you don't,' he gasped out. 'You don't kick Fred Boyle and get away with it.'

'Don't you dare touch me,' Jen hissed, trying desperately to twist out of his painful grip.

He laughed suddenly, obviously enjoying the struggle. 'Calm down now, love, calm down. I like a bit of spirit, but you don't want to hurt yourself. We don't want bruises.'

'I want to bruise you,' Jen muttered through gritted teeth. She could feel his hands gripping her arms, feel his knee forcing up between her bare legs, pinning her against the wall as he rubbed himself against her. She could see the sweat on his brow and the lust in his eyes and she suddenly felt sick with fear.

'Oh, come now,' he panted. 'I thought you wanted a solo part in the show. This isn't the way to go about getting one.' Carefully he transferred her two small wrists into his one hand and used the other to touch her naked breasts, his hands hot and clammy on her delicate skin. She tried to bite his hand and he just laughed delightedly.

At that moment if Jen could have killed him she would have. Tears of fury sprang into her eyes as her ambitions crumbled. Had it really come to this? That she would have to give her body to get a decent part?

He mistook her tears. 'Oh, don't cry, darling. It's not that bad. Uncle Fred will see you all right. One favour for another, eh? That's the way of the world, isn't it?'

As he tried to lower her to the ground, Jen took her chance. She hadn't grown up with four brothers in the back streets of Clapham without learning a few street-fighting tips. Jerking a hand free she lashed out at his face.

A moment later she was free, and Fred Boyle had blood oozing from three deep welts in his cheek.

Before he could move she had picked up the chair and slammed it hard into his body.

As he crashed into the wall, she struggled into her blouse and dragged on her skirt.

'You little bitch.' He stood up and swore at her from the corner of the room but made no attempt to get any nearer. 'You vicious little bitch.'

His face was bleeding copiously. He dabbed it painfully with a handkerchief. 'I was going to give you a break next week in one of the comedy skits,' he said. 'But you've missed your chance of it now.'

Jen stared at him through glittering, dangerous eyes. 'I wouldn't do a part in one of your miserable shows if you paid me a million pounds,' she said. 'I'm an actress not a prostitute.'

'Actress?' He laughed bitterly. 'I wouldn't pay you two and six for your so-called acting ability, love. I only took you on in the first place because of your pretty face. You'll never get a better job, you know, not here or anywhere. Not without me behind you.'

His words were like a kick in the stomach. Shaking all over, Jen picked up her bag and opened the door, 'Goodbye, Mr Boyle,' she said. 'I'm leaving now and I'm not coming back.'

'Hey,' he called after her. 'What about the last show? You've got to do that.'

She looked back at him incredulously. 'You can stuff your last show,' she said. Then she slammed the door and ran out of the theatre.

It was a warm, clear night. The trees on the common made dark, rustling silhouettes against the midsummer sky. From time to time the breeze caught the long curving wires of the two barrage balloons, making them sing like some weird primeval instrument. The balloons, high above, gleamed silver in the thin moonlight. Towards London the smoke from Battersea Power Station hung in the night like a yellow cloud.

It would have been a perfect night for Hitler's invasion. Or for the long awaited aerial bombardment. But there was little sign of activity in the gun emplacement on the north side of the common, the long-muzzled anti-aircraft guns stood as silent as they had for the last nine months. The nearby Nissen huts were dark too, only a couple of sentries patrolling the fence gave any sign of life.

Jen was sitting on the edge of the bandstand where the paths met at the centre of the common.

She looked up as some geese honked to each other as they flew heavily overhead and landed a moment later, splashing noisily on the pond behind her.

She didn't know how long she had been there. She had cried

intermittently. But her misery was interspersed with anger, anger mainly with herself for being so naïve, so gullible, so stupid as to kid herself that Fred Boyle could have seen any latent talent in her chorus performance.

Perhaps she had no latent talent. Perhaps she had no talent at all. Latent or not. She should never have lashed out at him like that. Surely she could have talked her way out of it.

She suddenly remembered the beastly hawk-faced woman at Croydon Theatre School all those months ago telling her that if she wanted to be an actress she would have to learn to control her feelings. Mrs Frost, she was called. She had been right.

She should have laughed off Fred Boyle's repulsive advances. Instead she had lost her temper and her job. And her self-confidence.

Jen swallowed painfully. Perhaps she would end up working in a white hat in the Croydon munitions factory after all.

Without a job, without some form of training, it would seem that she had little choice.

It was either that or going to Ireland. And much as she longed to see Sean again, much as she still missed him, deep down she knew she couldn't go. Not until she had something to show for herself, something to be proud of. She loved Sean and she knew he loved her, but she wanted him to respect her too. She couldn't ask him to take on a failure. It wouldn't work.

She pulled up her knees despondently and was about to drop her head into her hands again when she became aware of an odd, wheezing noise somewhere nearby.

After a moment's alarm, Jen realised that some kind of animal was snuffling against the base of the bandstand.

Swinging her legs down and leaning over to look, she identified an ancient, rough coated dachshund. Even as she watched, it manoeuvred itself fussily into a position whereby it could lift its leg against the wall of the bandstand.

Jen frowned. Surely that was the Miss Taylors' mangy dog. But what on earth was it doing out alone so late at night?

She stared at it, wondering suddenly if it was some kind of omen. Hadn't Katy told her once that the Miss Taylors had been in the theatre? Was this her chance to meet them? To request their help? Maybe she would return their precious dog and find some famous film producer staying the night with them?

She glanced at the dog again, then, just as she was toying with the unappealing idea of attempting to capture it, she realised it was not alone after all. Over in the trees a shadowy figure was emitting a low commanding whistle. In vain.

The dachshund was either deaf or disobedient, or both. Either way it took no notice of the whistle and continued to relieve itself copiously at Jen's feet.

As the shadowy figure moved further away into the trees, Jen felt obliged to call out.

But her voice had suffered from the recent racking sobs and her first attempt came out more like a husky cry.

She cleared her throat and tried again. 'It's here,' she called. 'If you're looking for a dog, it's over here.'

At once the figure began to walk in her direction. It certainly wasn't either of the Miss Taylors. Neither of them moved with such brisk masculinity, nor did they have such broad shoulders, nor did either of them ever wear trousers

It must be that Canadian nephew of theirs that Katy was always going on about, Jen thought to herself, as the figure approached.

'Thanks,' he said easily, crouching down to clip a leash on to the dog, as though it was the most natural thing in the world to meet a strange girl sitting quite alone on the Clapham Common bandstand at dead of night.

He straightened up and smiled. 'It's my aunts' dog. They would have killed me if I'd lost him.'

It obviously wasn't an omen at all. She could see him quite clearly now in the thin moonlight and she had the uneasy feeling that if he could see her as clearly he would see she had been crying. She must look a complete fright.

Sure enough he frowned. 'Are you OK?' he asked. 'Can I do anything to help?'

She shook her head. 'Only if you can get me a job in the theatre,' she said bitterly. 'Because I've just lost mine.'

She wished he would go away again and leave her to her misery. She wished she had never drawn attention to the blasted dog. She also wished she hadn't been quite so rude. It wasn't his fault after all.

But he didn't seem to hold it against her.

'You should talk to my aunts,' he said mildly 'They know all sorts of people in the theatre.'

She smiled thinly and turned her head away dismissively.

But just as he turned to go, a telephone rang shrilly on the gun emplacement.

'I wonder what's going on over there,' he said, as a number of dark figures emerged from the Nissen huts and started running towards the guns.

'Oh God,' Jen said following his gaze. 'I hope blasted Hitler isn't going to choose tonight to invade. That's all I need.'

Ward shook his head. 'If they are manning the guns, it's more likely to be an air raid,' he said.

And even as he said the words, the sirens began to wail.

It was the first time the sirens had sounded in Clapham since the beginning of the war. Jen didn't move and he glanced at her in surprise.

'Aren't you going to take shelter?'

She shook her head. 'I'm staying here. There's no law that says I have to go underground. It's probably a false alarm anyway.'

She looked at him defiantly. If she wanted to die it was none of his business. She would rather die than spend the night crouching with her mother and brothers under that bit of corrugated iron in the garden.

He returned her look steadily for a moment, then shrugged. 'I guess it's your choice.'

'Yes, it is,' Jen agreed stiffly. She wanted to be alone. She wanted to cry again.

He turned away then hesitated and turned back. 'Just promise me one thing.'

Jen frowned. 'What?'

'That if any planes come over, you'll take cover. 'He nodded towards the guns. 'When those guys fire, the flak will be lethal. And once Jerry knows the guns are here, this won't be a good place to be.'

Jen found she was touched by his concern. 'OK,' she said grudgingly. She nodded towards Battersea Rise. 'There's a public shelter on the common over there. I'll go there.'

'Thanks.' He nodded and smiled briefly. 'If you hear a plane, run for it like hell. It would be a shame to give Hitler the pleasure of an unnecessary civilian casualty.' Then he picked up the dog, tucked it under his arm and set off himself at a steady effortless jog across the common towards Lavender Road,

But Jen didn't need to run for it. No planes came anywhere near London that night. She didn't run, but nor did she cry any more.

For some reason her brief encounter with Ward Frazer had cheered her. Made her feel more positive. Perhaps it was an omen after all. It was almost as though by making her promise to save her skin he had persuaded her not to give in.

She lifted her chin. Maybe it was worth one last try. Maybe she call on the stupid old Miss Taylors. They might at least have a piano.

When the all-clear came three hours later, she went home and slept the sleep of the dead.

Pam leaned out of her office window and laughed at the sight of two portly French officers chasing a young boy up the street.

'He's got their berets,' she giggled over her shoulder to Mr Shaw. 'He must have snatched them straight off their heads. But he's going to get away with it. He's much faster than them.'

'Serves them right,' Mr Shaw replied. 'They should have stayed and fought, instead of prancing about over here in their fancy uniforms.'

Pam smiled. Mr Shaw's opinion of the French had dropped even lower since the French government had agreed terms with Hitler last week. She was about to tease him about his prejudice when she saw a familiar ginger haired figure in the street below, swerving through the traffic on a familiar bicycle, his foxy face tense with concentration.

Mick Carter.

Pam's heart leaped. What was Mick doing here? Had something happened to Alan? She prayed not. Not just as he was beginning to smile at her again. Last night in bed he had even kissed her good night. Not a deep kiss, just a peck, a brush on the cheek, but it was better than nothing. Better than rejection. She couldn't bear it if something went wrong now.

Numbly she watched Mick prop the bicycle against the wall and disappear into the entrance below her. He was too far away to call to. He'd never hear her over the noise in the street anyway.

Quickly she withdrew her head and shut the window.

'I've got to go down,' she told her boss. 'There's somebody I know just arrived downstairs.'

When she reached the lobby, Mick was still at the entrance arguing with the guard on the door.

'But I've got to see her,' he was shouting. 'She works here.'

Pam flew across the hall. 'What is it, Mick? What's happened?'

His face was white. 'You've got to come, Mrs Nelson. That Mrs Whitehead has had a telegram. Her Jo's dead and she's gone berserk.'

Chapter Twenty Two

When Celia Rutherford asked Joyce over elevenses one morning in early July, if she would like to go with her to the WI Summer Fayre, Joyce was astonished.

'Oh, but I'm not a WI sort of person,' she said. 'They wouldn't let me in.'

'What on earth do you mean?' Celia seemed surprised. 'It's open to anyone.'

'But I don't make jams and chutneys like you do, Mrs R.' Joyce was squirming. What she wanted to say was that she would feel completely out of place among Mrs Rutherford's posh WI friends. She had no money to buy their produce, nor had she anything to wear. She'd lost so much weight recently for a start. Not that she'd had anything smart in the first place. Not to a smart, outdoor function. Not to any sort of function, come to that. The invitation was meant kindly she knew. But there was no way she could accept.

But Celia was impervious to her reservations. 'Oh, do come, Mrs Carter,' she said. 'I'm sure you would enjoy it. You work so hard, a day off would do you good.'

That was certainly true. Joyce could hardly remember the last time she had a proper day off. What with three and a half days a week at Cedars House, her own house to see to, and with all the queuing and waiting involved with shopping nowadays, she had no time for herself.

And she had to have a meal on the table for Pete every night. And for that damn Jen, even though she'd lost her precious acting job. She said someone touched her up but that might have been an excuse. Maybe she just wasn't up to it. Maybe now at last she'd knuckle down and get a decent job.

Joyce frowned. Jen losing her job was a nuisance. It meant a delay in getting the jewellery back from Lorenz. She could have hit Jen when she told her yesterday. She was so close to having the money. But Pete had gone through the sole of his boot last week and a pound had had to go on a new pair, they'd been resoled too many times before. And that damn Mick would soon need shoes too and clothes, she'd seen him yesterday queuing up at Dove's for Mrs Nelson looking like nothing on earth.

And now Jo Whitehead was a goner and Sheila screaming the place down, Joyce guessed Pam Nelson would ask her to take Mick back and all. Pam Nelson was bound to offer to have Sheila and her son in with her and Alan. And then there'd be no room at the Nelsons for Mick.

Joyce glanced at Celia Rutherford's elegant but ringless fingers as she stirred her tea and wondered suddenly if Lorenz might let her have the stuff back early, if she promised to pay the rest when she could.

In the meantime she had to change the subject, get Celia Rutherford off the idea of this blasted WI business.

Luckily at that moment the telephone rang, and a second later Louise came in.

'There's some Women's Voluntary Service lady on the phone for you, Mummy,' she said.

'Oh really?' Celia said, getting to her feet, 'I wonder who that could be.'

Her casualness did not fool Joyce for a moment. She had been astonished when Celia had told her she had offered to help out at the WVS. She was equally astonished now to discover that Celia had clearly not told her daughter of her intentions.

But Louise seemed oblivious to any undercurrent. She seemed to be in a daze as she stared dreamily out of the window. Her mind was quite clearly elsewhere.

Her mind often seemed to be elsewhere, come to think of it. In the past, Joyce had sometimes wondered if she was all there. Either that or in love. Both states seemed to give people that moody vacant look.

Still, it was none of her business what Miss la-di-da Louise got up to. She could be knocking off Adolf Hitler himself for all she cared.

She was still smiling at the thought as Celia came back into the room.

At once Louise turned away from the window, 'I'm going out now to visit Aaref Hoch, Mummy. He's been interned.'

Celia frowned. 'That's kind of you, darling. But do you think it's safe to go on your own?'

Louise rolled her eyes. 'Of course it's safe,' Mummy. What on earth do you think can happen to me between here and Wandsworth Common?'

'Well, take your gas mask.'

Louise groaned. 'Mummy honestly ...'

But Celia interrupted. 'You do as you're told, Louise,' she said sharply. 'Or Daddy won't give you permission to go out with Helen again on Saturday.'

She grimaced apologetically at Joyce as Louise closed the door behind her with the hint of a slam. 'I do wish she would grow up a little bit. She doesn't seem to take the war seriously.' She sighed. 'She wants to spend the whole time gadding about with her friends in town. Luckily this Helen de Burrel is a very nice, respectable girl, otherwise Greville would never give her permission to go up to town alone.'

For a second Joyce smiled to herself, wondering what Jen would say if she had to ask permission to go up to town alone. It certainly wouldn't be the sort of language Celia Rutherford was used to hearing. But then Jen Carter and Louise Rutherford were poles apart. At opposite ends of the social and moral scale. Louise Rutherford certainly wouldn't have given herself to a disreputable Irish rogue. She would be saving herself for a nice classy boy, who would treat her like a lady.

Although it seemed incongruous that her ladylike mother was even now thinking of joining the WVS as a tea lady.

'You probably gathered I haven't told Louise,' she said. 'And nor have I told Greville. I thought it was best to see what the WVS offered me and then present it as a fait accompli.' She grimaced slightly. 'He can be so stuffy about things like that.'

Joyce nodded. As far as she was concerned Greville Rutherford was stuffy about everything. It was no surprise to find he was stuffy about the WVS. 'But he does the ARP,' she said mildly. 'What's the difference?'

'Oh, but the ARP is Important,' Celia said sarcastically. 'Especially now that it looks as though Hitler really is going to start bombing. But serving in a WVS canteen isn't going to win the war, is it?'

'It might,' Joyce said stoutly. 'Who can tell? One portion of bangers and mash to the right person might make all the difference. Even Winston Churchill presumably has to eat. And quite a bit too, I should think, with a figure like that.'

Celia laughed. 'You're a tonic, Mrs Carter.' She glanced at her watch and frowned. 'They want me to go down to see them this morning.'

Joyce stood up and picked up her duster. 'Then you'd better go. Don't want to get pipped at the post.' She shook her head from the door. 'Although frankly I can't see you in a mob-cap and pinny behind a tea trolley.'

Celia smiled. 'You may have to come and help me, Mrs Carter. Oh, and do think about the WI Fayre on Saturday. I'd like you to come. They're going to have a display on hen-keeping.'

Outside the door Joyce stopped in the hall and shook her head. Hen-keeping? Why on earth would Mrs Rutherford think she might be interested in that? The only hens that interested her were ones that lay dead and plucked in her roasting tray. And she hadn't seen one of those in months.

It occurred to Louise that she ought to take Aaref something, like her mother always took things to people in hospital and to Bertie and Douglas on her twice a term school visits. Mainly, admittedly, because they complained constantly about the Bradley College food. But then the Royal Patriotic Building where Aaref was being held usually housed a school, so the food was probably awful there too.

Aaref certainly seemed pleased with the half-pound bag of mixed biscuits she handed him when she finally gained admittance.

'Thank you, Louise,' he said. 'I am happy that you make a visit. Come with me outside. We will sit in the sun and eat biscuits, yes?'

Louise wished she could say no, but it had been such a rigmarole getting in at all that she could hardly turn tail and leave straight away.

Aaref led her through the dark austere chateau-style building and out on to a sloping tiered lawn where a large number of internees equipped with deckchairs were apparently taking advantage of their enforced idleness to take in a bit of sun.

Blinking against the midday glare and uncomfortably aware of the interest her bright, fashionably nip-waisted sundress was causing, Louise followed Aaref to a couple of empty chairs under an enormous horse-chestnut tree.

Aaref seemed surprisingly at home in his new environment. Several of the other internees smiled as they passed, and once or twice Aaref introduced her to bearded men with unpronounceable names. Each time there was a lot of heel-clicking and bowing over her hand and Louise was glad to reach the safety of the deckchairs.

'I can bring tea if you wish,' Aaref said as Louise sat down rather awkwardly in the deckchair, trying not to show too much leg.

Louise shook her head hastily. 'Oh no. Honestly, Aaref, I can't stay long. I only called to see how you were.'

He shrugged. 'I am very good. Better now my teacher is here.' He smiled briefly then frowned. 'But my brothers are not so good, I think. They fear I will die in the camp like many of our family.'

Louise stared at him in horror. She didn't know what to say. She couldn't believe he had said something so awful, so crass. They had only just sat down, for goodness' sake. 'But this is England,' she stammered eventually. 'That sort of thing doesn't happen here.'

Aaref smiled thinly. 'Not yet. But if the Nazis come here then I don't know …' He glanced to the high perimeter fence where two or three soldiers were patrolling lazily with rifles slung over their shoulders. 'How you say, we are sitting hens?'

Louise couldn't help a giggle. 'Sitting ducks. Aaref, I know you get things wrong on purpose.' She frowned. 'But seriously, I'm sure the Nazis won't come. And if they do, it won't be like Holland and Belgium and France. We will fight them every inch of the way. There would be plenty of time for you to escape.'

Aaref smiled suddenly. 'You are an optimist, Louise. I hope you are right. Perhaps you and I can escape together from the Nazis. This would be romantic, yes?'

Louise stared at him. Could he possibly be serious? Romantic? He must be joking. She laughed grimly. 'I don't think we'd get very far with half a pound of biscuits between us.'

Taking the hint, Aaref offered her the bag. Louise took one and leaned back in her chair, closing her eyes while she bit into it. The only person she wanted to escape with just now was Stefan Pininski. He had enough money to flee. And to flee in style. If Hitler did invade, perhaps Stefan would take her to America. That would be romantic. She imagined the notice in the paper. 'Family and friends will be pleased to know that Count Stefan Pininski and his new bride Louise Elizabeth Rutherford have arrived safely in New York and will be staying at the Carlyle on Madison Avenue.'

'You joke, Louise,' Aaref said suddenly, jolting her back unpleasantly to the present. 'But I am very serious. I like that you are my teacher but I would prefer that you are my girlfriend.'

Louise was appalled. Her eyes flew open. 'I couldn't possibly be your girlfriend, Aaref. You are far too young for me. Anyway,' she added, 'I'm seeing someone else at the moment.'

Aaref looked taken aback. 'Who?' He asked crossly. 'Who is this man you see?'

Louise shook her head and stood up. 'I don't think we should talk about this. It's embarrassing. I think I'd better go.'

Aaref grabbed her hand as she went to move away. 'Who is it, Louise? Not the man you were with before, the German speaker?'

'Ward Frazer?' Louise frowned and jerked her hand back out of his grip. 'No, it's not him. It's someone else. Someone older, more distinguished.' She flushed suddenly. 'I'm not going to tell you, Aaref. But you might as well know it's serious. We're thinking of getting engaged.'

Aaref's face fell. 'But you are so young,' he said as he escorted her back up the sloping lawn. 'You do not want an old man. You have so much life.'

Louise glared at him. 'I said older, not old. And he's also very rich.' As they reached the door, Aaref shook his head. 'The money cannot buy the loving.'

'Money can't buy love,' Louise corrected him automatically, then frowned. 'That's not what I meant, Aaref. I just meant that somebody like you is out of the question for somebody like me.'

'Then you should go now, Louise,' Aaref said sadly. 'Or I will perhaps cry. But I will wait. Hoping you are changing the mind.'

Louise lifted her chin. 'I won't change my mind,'

He shrugged. 'If you do, you know I am here.' He threw a wry glance at the perimeter fence. I cannot go very far.' He smiled bravely as he clicked his heels. 'Goodbye, Louise. And thank you for the very nice biscuits.'

Pam and Alan Nelson did decide to move Sheila Whitehead and little George in with them. They agreed that there was no way they could be left alone in their own house on the other side of the road. Sheila was quite distraught.

Understandably.

She had been hoping that no news was good news for so long, and yet it turned out that Jo had in fact been killed six weeks ago in the retreat from Belgium. He and a dozen other men in his unit had got cut off. His regiment had assumed they had been captured by the Germans. Now it seemed more likely that they had either fought to the death or had been massacred as they tried to surrender. Either way, all their identity discs had now been returned to the Red Cross.

Everyone agreed it was incredibly bad luck to lose both a son and a husband in such a short space of time. Jo had been such a nice young man. And he and Sheila had been so deeply in love.

It was tragic, completely tragic, but it was war, and there was really nothing else that could be said about it. No further explanation was forthcoming from the Germans, nor was one expected. Sheila would come to terms with her loss sooner or later. But until then Pam and Alan would look after her. And little George.

Which meant that Mick Carter had to go back to his own home up the street, which he was reluctant to do.

'Please, Mrs Nelson, don't make me go. I like it here. What with Mr Nelson letting me use his bike and that.'

'I'm sure he'll still let you use his bike,' Pam said. 'But we need the bed, Mick. As it is, little George will have to sleep on cushions on the floor.'

'Why can't they stay in their own house?' Mick asked sulkily.

'Mrs Whitehead can't cope on her own,' Pam said. 'She's too upset even to sleep.'

'If she's too upset to sleep, why does she need my bed?' Mick muttered crossly.

In the end it was Alan who persuaded him he really would have to go. Pam listened in amazement as Alan promised Mick that he could come round for tea every day.

'What on earth did you say that for?' she asked him when Mick had finally gone upstairs to collect up his things. She didn't want Mick Carter hanging round all the time. Alan gave the boy so much of his time already. Time that she wanted for herself, for their marriage, what there was left of it. Admittedly they still shared a bed. But all they did in it was sleep.

Alan shrugged. 'Poor kid. He's not going to get much of a life back at home.'

Pam frowned. 'It's wartime,' she said peevishly. 'None of us are getting much of a life.'

Alan looked, at her. 'That's not always the fault of the war,' he said steadily.

Pam blinked. There was something in his eyes that suddenly unnerved her. 'What do you mean?'

He smiled. 'I mean, my love, that I think it might be time to start touching again.'

'Touching?' Pam stared at him.

He nodded and held out his hand. 'Come here, Pam. I want to touch you. I can't bear you skirting round me as though I have leprosy.'

Tentatively Pam advanced and put her hand in his. She had forgotten how much she liked the feel of him. 'I thought it was you who didn't want to touch me,' she said.

Alan looked down at their joined hands. 'I didn't,' he admitted. 'But now I do.' He raised his eyes suddenly and smiled. 'I don't want to rush it, but do you think a small kiss might be in order?'

He was smiling at her. Smiling into her eyes just like he used to. Pam felt a weight ease off her heart. She giggled and smiled back. 'Oh, all right then, but only a small one mind.'

It was only a small one, but infinitely tender and Pam closed her eyes suddenly fearing she might cry.

When she opened them again. Mick Carter was standing at the bottom of the stairs staring down the passage with his mouth open. Even as she met his horrified eyes he turned the colour of an over-ripe tomato.

'Oh … I …' Words were clearly beyond him.

Alan grinned at him as he loosened his hold on Pam. 'She is my wife, Mick. You needn't look so shocked.'

Even as he said the words, Pam remembered that other incident, when it was Sean Byrne's arms she was in and little Ray had stared at her with a similar expression.

At once all the old guilt flooded back and she pulled quickly away from Alan.

'Are you all packed up, Mick?' she asked briskly.

He nodded dumbly and she picked up the linen off the kitchen table. 'Then I'd better get Sheila's bed made up.'

She could feel Alan's eyes on her, puzzled and hurt, as she marched stiff backed up the passage. But she couldn't help it. The guilt was too strong.

Chapter Twenty Three

Jen was surprised to discover that the Miss Taylors were not at all what she had expected. She had often imitated their fussy old-fashioned little ways and their awful dog to amuse Katy Parsons. Now she realised her impersonations were way off.

For a start the two old ladies were far more on the ball than she had ever realised.

When she had knocked tentatively on their front door, she had envisaged lengthy and awkward explanations and was steeling herself for a completely hopeless quest.

But they seemed to know at once who she was, and furthermore what she had most likely come about. Nor did they waste any time getting to the point. Having got over her initial embarrassment at nearly sitting in an armchair that already contained the awful dachshund, Jen was only halfway through her carefully prepared opening speech, when the younger Miss Taylor interrupted her.

'Ward said he'd seen a pretty girl crying up on the common the other night,' she remarked, bringing a tea tray in from the kitchen. 'We guessed it was you.'

'Lost your job, have you?' the other one chipped in, lifting the sleeping dachshund tenderly out of his chair and sitting down with him on her lap. 'Fox's, wasn't it? What happened? Boyle put his hand up your skirt? Or worse?'

Jen stared from one to the other in utter amazement. Speechless. She hadn't even realised the Miss Taylors would know who she was. Let alone what she did. Or what had happened. She had told nobody the full details of Mr Boyle's assault, nobody.

'Mrs Parsons mentioned you'd been taken on at Fox's,' the younger Miss Taylor said by way of explanation. 'That interested us, having been in the business ourselves. Not on the stage of course. Wardrobe. Costume design and repair. That was our thing.'

Jen blinked. 'But you were right, Mr Boyle did try to …' She stopped and bit her lip. Somewhere deep inside her she still thought it might have been her fault. Or certainly that she might have avoided what had happened. In any case she didn't want to shock the old ladies. Already she could feel herself blushing.

But they didn't seem particularly shockable. 'Dreadful man, Boyle,' the older Miss Taylor said implacably, petting the comatose dog. 'He's always at it. Ought to be shot.'

'Ought to have been shot years ago when he was senior stage hand at the Bradford Alhambra,' her sister put in, pouring tea into unmatching china cups and offering one to Jen. 'Don't you remember, Esme, he made an awful nuisance of himself with that little soubrette in *Aladdin*. She was a pretty girl too. I forget her name.'

'Pansy.' Esme Taylor supplied the name effortlessly. 'Pansy Dale. Not her real name of course. Never did much after that. Put her off, I suppose.'

Her sister shook her head. 'Somebody ought to teach him a lesson.'

'I scratched his face quite badly,' Jen said suddenly. It was hard to get a word in edgeways with these two, 'And I kneed him quite hard between the legs.'

'Did you?' The sisters looked at her with new respect. 'How splendid.'

'But I lost my job in the process,' Jen added, putting down her tea cup. It might be splendid for them, but it wasn't so good for her. It still made her feel sick to think about it. 'And now I don't know what to do. It was difficult enough getting in at Fox's.'

'You should have come to us earlier,' Esme Taylor said.

'Too busy with that nice-looking Irish boy, I expect,' her sister remarked.

Jen stared. Was there anything they didn't know? 'But how did …?'

'We've got ears,' Esme Taylor said.

'And eyes,' her sister added, nodding obliquely to the bay window from where, Jen suddenly realised, to her horror, you could see straight across the street into the Nelsons' front room. Furious colour stained her cheeks as she remembered what she had got up to with Sean in that very room.

'We thought you'd go back to Ireland with him,' Esme said, munching through a sweet biscuit. 'Didn't we, Thelma?'

'Yes, we were quite surprised you stayed behind,' the younger Miss Taylor said. 'We thought you were smitten. And him with you.'

'He was.' Jen was still blushing, 'So was I. I still am. He wanted me to go. But I didn't want to give up my career.' She shook her head. 'What there was of it. Which wasn't much. But I had high hopes then.'

'Had?' Thelma Taylor asked gently. 'Then?'

Jen hesitated. She hated to admit weakness. But the Miss Taylors were looking at her quite kindly. She shook her head: 'I don't know if I'm any good anymore,' she admitted finally on a sigh, 'I thought I was. But now I'm not sure.'

'Well, there's only one way to find out,' Esme said crisply. 'We'll have to get someone to see you.'

'But who?' Jen asked helplessly. 'Nobody would be interested in me. I haven't had any training. Just a tap class, that's all. And I wasn't very good at that.'

But the Miss Taylors weren't listening. They were firing off names as rapidly and forcefully as one of Hitler's Panzer divisions.

'What about Harry?'

'Oh no, not at all suitable. What about Eleanor?'

'Oh no, not at all suitable. What about Margot?'

'Margot? Now there's a thought.' Thelma Taylor nodded. 'Oh yes. Just the person. She needs something to do.'

Esme Taylor smiled in satisfaction at Jen. 'There you are. The perfect person. Used to teach drama. Used to youngsters like you. Knows all the theatre people.'

'And she only lives in Purley,' Thelma put in. 'Just by Croydon airport.'

Jen blinked. This was all happening rather fast. 'It's very kind of you, but …'

Thelma shook her head. 'No buts. We'll fix it all up for you. You just practise a couple of pieces, songs, dances, whatever, ready to show her. And she'll say if you've got potential.'

Esme nodded eagerly. 'And if you have, she might take you on, give you a bit of help. You never know.'

Even the dog seemed excited. Having slept soundly throughout the entire conversation it now suddenly leaped off Esme's lap, belly flopped on to the floor, hunkered back on its absurdly short hind legs and started barking ferociously at Jen.

Wondering what she had done to invite such hostility, Jen eyed it dubiously. It seemed to have very large teeth for such a small dog.

Thelma Taylor giggled. 'Winston wants you to give him a biscuit,' she explained.

Winston? Jen blinked. The geriatric, moth-eaten animal was called Winston.

He likes the sweet ones best,' Esme added helpfully.

Desperately biting her lip to hold back her sudden mirth, Jen leaned over to take a biscuit off the plate. At once the barking subsided. The dog watched her beadily as she broke it in two.

As the biscuit and most of Jen's fingers disappeared into Winston's cavernous mouth, both the Miss Taylors sat back in their chairs and sighed happily. 'Aah. He'll be your friend for life now.'

Katy stared at Louise. 'Let me get this right. You've been secretly dating Mrs d'Arcy Billière's Count and now he wants you to go to bed with him?'

Louise nodded. 'He says if Hitler invades, we may not get another chance for ages. What do you think? Do you think I should, or not?'

'What do I think?' Katy's eyes widened. 'You're seriously asking me, who has never even dated anyone, let alone gone to bed with them, what I think?'

Louise shrugged. 'There's nobody else I can ask. Nobody else I can trust. Stefan said I must keep it a secret, but you don't really count.'

Katy wondered whether to be flattered or not. And decided she was pleased at least to be considered trustworthy. 'It seems very soon,' she said doubtfully. 'It's a bit risky. You don't really know much about him. And what about Ward Frazer?' she asked suddenly: 'I thought you were still in love with him.'

'I don't know if I am or not,' Louise admitted. 'I hate the thought of him being with anyone else, but then I wouldn't want to marry a spy. You'd never know what he was up to ...'

Katy leaned forward so quickly, she nearly fell off her chair. 'A spy? Ward Frazer?'

'Didn't I tell you?' Louise sniffed. 'It turns out he's a blasted spy. For our side, I mean. He keeps going underground, or undercover or whatever spies do. In Germany. That's why he was always disappearing off the face of the earth and never telephoned. All that RAF business was hogwash.'

'But he took you to that Canadian air force party,' Katy stammered.

'Well, I suppose he still knows people in the air force,' Louise said, 'He probably knows how to fly.' She tossed her head peevishly. 'I don't know. Anyway I have a nasty feeling that he only took me to that party to try and push me off on to somebody else.'

Katy was speechless. Ward Frazer was a spy. All this time she had been worrying about him flying missions for the RAF, and all the time he had been doing something even more dangerous, even more isolated, even more brave. And now she would worry even more.

She felt her chest tighten and took a sharp breath. She couldn't bear it if she had an asthma attack now. 'When did he tell you this?'

Louise snorted. 'He didn't tell me, that's the whole point. Someone else did. Another girl. That's not very flattering, is it?'

'He probably didn't want to worry you,' Katy said loyally. 'Anyway spies don't usually go around telling everyone they're spies, do they? Goodness, I wonder if the Miss Taylors know.'

But Louise wasn't interested in speculating about the Miss Taylors. She had much more important things on her mind. Decisions to make.

'But what about Stefan?' she said. 'I need to make up my mind. I'm seeing him again on Saturday.' She fiddled with her sleeve for a moment. 'What did your friend Jen say about it, you know, sex? She did it, didn't she? With that Irish chap the police were after.'

But Katy couldn't stop thinking about Ward Frazer alone in enemy Germany.

She coughed and shook her head, trying to breathe slowly, trying to concentrate. 'She said it was kind of embarrassing at first, but that you soon get the hang of it. Mind you, she was in love with Sean. Maybe that makes a difference. And he was very sexy.'

'Stefan's sexy too,' Louise said, piqued. 'Very sexy.'

'Surely not sexier than Ward?'

Louise frowned. 'Completely different. Much more keen. Much more in love.' She leaned forward. 'You know, I think he's almost on the verge of proposing.'

She hugged herself excitedly then caught sight of the clock and stood up abruptly. 'Goodness, I'd better go, or Mummy will think I've been locked up with the enemy aliens.' She grimaced suddenly. 'Can you believe it, Katy? That ghastly little creep Aaref declared undying love for me in the garden of the internment camp. I didn't know where to look. It was perfectly frightful.'

Katy winced. She'd guessed from other things Louise had said about her pupil that Aaref had fallen for her. 'What did you say?'

'I told him it was out of the question, of course,' Louise said irritably. 'What else could I say?'

'Poor Aaref,' Katy said.

Louise groaned. 'Poor me. It was so embarrassing.' She opened the door and glanced downstairs. Katy's mother was moving about downstairs getting ready for opening time. 'Don't forget it's a secret about Stefan and me,' she whispered.

Katy shook her head. 'I won't tell anyone. Good luck. Oh, and be careful, Louise. If you do decide to do it, don't forget you have to make him use those things.'

'What things?'

Katy flushed. 'You know. Those things that stop you having babies. French letters.' She knew Jen and Sean had been meticulous about that. Even though Sean said it went against his religion.

'Oh.' Louise nodded blankly. 'Oh yes. Stefan will know all about that.'

I hope he does, Katy thought, after Louise had gone. Or God knows what will happen. Maybe she should have advised Louise more strongly not to do it. Not that she would have taken any notice. In any case, everyone seemed to be doing it these days. Except her of course.

She thought again of Ward Frazer, and chided herself for being a fool. Someone like that would never give someone like her a second glance. She stifled a cough crossly and pulled her Red Cross books towards her. Her final test was on Friday and she was determined to pass with flying colours. It somehow seemed the least she could do.

'What are we going to do about her?' Pam whispered to Alan in the kitchen, as Sheila Whitehead sat sobbing in their sitting room with little George clasped in her arms. 'She can't go on like this. And it must be so bad for George.'

Alan pushed the kitchen door to. 'What did the doctor say?'

Pam sniffed. 'What does the doctor ever say? It'll pass. A time of grieving is natural.' She scrubbed at a saucepan angrily, 'I honestly think the medical profession should be lined up and shot.'

Alan smiled mildly. 'You're getting very reactionary in your old age.'

Pam grimaced. 'She needs help. But more than anything, she needs to sleep.'

'Pity we can't get a couple of pints of Rutherford & Berry down her,' Alan said, picking up a tea towel. 'That knocks me out like a light.'

Pam stared at him. 'What about whisky?' she whispered. 'That might do the trick. If she won't drink it, I could always put it in a trifle.'

'In a trifle?' Alan grinned. 'It would have to be a damn strong one. Goodness knows what it would do to George. Let alone to me.'

Pam giggled. 'Go up to Malcolm Parsons and get a bottle, Alan, It might do us all good.'

As it turned out Sheila Whitehead did accept a small glass of whisky after George had been put to bed, and by dint of swigging it back themselves, they eventually got two more glasses down her, and her demeanour improved dramatically.

She even laughed once at something Alan said. And then just as Pam was beginning to feel a bit tipsy herself, Sheila announced that she suddenly felt sleepy.

Twenty minutes later Pam and Alan were lying in bed congratulating themselves.

'You're a genius,' Alan said, reaching to turn out the light. 'Mind you, I'm going to have a hangover tomorrow.'

Pam chuckled as the light clicked off, 'So will I. But it'll be worth it, won't it? Even if she only sleeps a couple of hours.'

'Unfortunately it's had the rather opposite effect on me,' Alan murmured in the darkness.

Suddenly Pam was very aware of him lying next to her. She kept very still. She realised it was the first time in months that they had gone to bed at the same time. The first time in ages that they had talked after lights out.

'What do you mean?' she asked softly. 'D-don't you feel sleepy?'

It was a game they used to play. A silly code. Pam had almost forgotten the words.

Now she sensed his smile as he replied. 'Not sleepy as such. No, not really.'

Pam took a careful breath. 'Do you think a cuddle might help?'

'It might,' Alan said mock doubtfully. 'I suppose we could try it.'

Pam sighed slightly as he rolled over and took her in his arms. She had longed for this for the last few weeks. Longed for the feel of his arms round her, for the feel of his kisses, the feel of his touch in her skin, his caresses, his strokes, his tender arousal.

As her nightdress bunched up round her waist, he stopped and groaned. 'I'm sure you didn't used to wear so many clothes in bed.'

Pam giggled. 'Nor did you.'

He touched her face. 'I'll take mine off if you'll take yours off.' Quickly, before she could change her mind, he disentangled himself from her and got out of bed.

He stripped off his pyjamas and opened the blackout curtain slightly to let in a little moonlight. As he turned back to the bed he stopped, staring at Pam, naked on the bed.

He smiled. 'If those bloody air-raid sirens go off again just now, I'll personally go and garrotte Adolf bloody Hitler myself.'

But it wasn't the sirens that disturbed them, it was a scream: A child's scream. George's scream.

Alan lifted his lips from Pam's collarbone and groaned. 'I don't believe it.'

But he got off the bed quickly, and wrapping a towel round his waist, headed for the door.

Struggling back into her nightdress, Pam followed him.

'Mummy's dead.' George was standing in the spare room doorway. 'Mummy's dead, I can't wake her up.'

Quickly Pam gathered the child up into her arms as Alan went to check on Sheila.

He came back after a moment. 'She's asleep, George,' he whispered and then to Pam, 'She's flat out.'

'I want Mummy,' George wept noisily into Pam's shoulder and she grimaced at Alan. 'I don't want Mummy to be dead.'

'Mummy isn't dead,' Pam said firmly. 'Mummy's asleep and we mustn't wake her.' She glanced at Alan. 'I think he'd better come in with us.'

Alan nodded resignedly and later when little George had finally, reluctantly dropped off to sleep in the bed between them, he glanced across the little boy's tousled head at Pam and rolled his eyes comically. 'Why did we ever think we wanted children?'

Louise bought herself some new underwear in the Harrods six day July sale. She didn't want Stefan peeling off her sophisticated outer garments only to discover her old school bra and knickers underneath. He was always so particular about how she looked, what she wore.

As Saturday lunchtime approached, she became increasingly terrified about what lay ahead. She could hardly speak when they met as usual in the lobby of the Savoy.

Stefan was as charming as ever as he led her across the Strand to the same little French restaurant he'd taken her to on their first date.

It was another hot July day and already, as they walked through the dusty side streets, Louise could feel the sweat trickling down her back. She was relieved they were going out but in one way she would have liked to get the sex part over with.

As they sat down, he looked at her, his eyes warm and speculative under the thick continental lashes. 'So, my Louise, have you made up your mind? Is today going to be my lucky day?'

She swallowed. When he looked at her like that she could do nothing but nod.

Stefan touched her arm gently, 'Relax, my sweet. It is to me, Stefan Pininski, that you will give your body, not to the lions.'

'I'm scared,' she muttered, flushing.

He smiled tenderly. 'Then I will order some very good wine. That will relax you.' He leaned forward and took her hand. 'Trust me, Louise. You have nothing to fear. Making love to someone you love is the most wonderful thing in the world.'

A new fear suddenly assailed her. 'Have you loved lots of women, then, Stefan?'

He looked surprised. 'A man can hardly reach my age without a little experience,' he murmured, lifting her fingers to his lips. 'But this time it is going to be very special for me.' He tasted the wine he had ordered, waited for the waiter to pour it then raised his glass in a silent toast. 'I hope also for you.'

Louise felt sick. What if it wasn't with her? What if she couldn't do it? She barely touched her food. To her relief, Stefan talked easily throughout, mainly about the war, about the Germans' shocking invasion of the Channel Islands, about the British navy destroying the French fleet in Algeria. It had to be done, he said, even though over a thousand French sailors were killed. Those ships couldn't be allowed to fall into German hands. The Germans were already having far too much success against British shipping.

He talked a little about her too, how adorable he found her, and a little about himself, how he had lost so much in Poland, his various homes, his material possessions, his horses, his dogs. How desperately sad he had been to leave them behind when he fled in the face of Hitler's advancing army.

There was something so touching about a grown man grieving for his dogs and horses. Moved almost to tears, Louise wished she could somehow console him for his loss. But all she could do was smile sympathetically as he refilled her glass and promise herself that one day she would buy him a puppy.

By the end of the meal they had consumed between them two bottles of wine. Louise didn't know if it was the wine that made her so light headed, or what lay ahead.

As they left the restaurant, Stefan took her arm. 'Come now and let me make you happy. You will feel different afterwards. No longer will you be a nervous young girl. You will be a woman, a beautiful, grown up woman. My woman.'

Chapter Twenty Four

Joyce did go to the WI fête with Mrs Rutherford. And she felt like Lady Muck sitting in the back of the Rutherford & Berry car. The chauffeur, Mr Wallace, whom she'd never liked, had even held the door for her and all. And not a sneer in sight.

It was wearing Jen's suit that made the difference of course. That was what gave her the courage to go, the fact that she'd lost so much weight since the war broke out that she could just squeeze into Jen's suit. Not that Jen had wanted to lend it to her, they'd had a right old humdinger about it, truth be told. But Joyce had got her way. After all, it had been bought with the money from that diamond ring Jen had pinched from the flour jar all those months ago, so Joyce didn't see why she shouldn't borrow it. In her view the outfit was as good as hers.

Jen said she looked like mutton dressed as lamb. Well, Joyce didn't care. At least she didn't look like some drab old sheep that needed a good shearing like usual. At least she felt she could show her face in public. And even though she watched them carefully, nobody gave the impression she was out of place at the WI. Some of those la-di-da women looked shabby as anything anyway in their awful old tweedy skirts and baggy stockings.

It was a hot afternoon, so luckily she could have the jacket open with the shirt showing underneath. Luckily, because even though she had lost weight she was still bustier than Jen and she could hardly breathe if it was done up.

It was young Mick of all people who had suggested leaving it open. 'Mrs Nelson sometimes wears hers like that,' he had said. 'I think it looks quite nice.' He'd then, to her astonishment, offered to do a bit of shopping while she was out.

Mr and Mrs Nelson certainly done a good job on him, Joyce thought as she wrote out a list for him. Shame that they didn't have any children of their own. Still, at least it meant they could help out with Sheila Whitehead and her little boy. Quiet as a mouse nowadays, that child, Mick said. Poor little mite. Used to be such a sunny child too.

Joyce and Celia Rutherford walked around the fête together. The ladies of the WI had put on a good show. Celia wanted to see if she'd won any prizes with her jams and chutneys. She hadn't, but she had won a red ribbon for the best set of vegetables. She was thrilled about that and when they found themselves a moment later at the homemade wine stall they decided to have a taste of a couple of bottles to celebrate.

After three glasses Celia got quite tipsy, and Joyce didn't feel too steady on her feet herself.

By the time they got to the poultry display that Celia so wanted to see, they had become rather incoherent.

'What do you think, Mrs Carter? Do you think I could manage it?'

Joyce dragged her gaze from an extremely large red hen that had fixed her rather unnervingly with a beady eye from the other side of its wire-mesh run. 'Manage what?'

'Chickens,' Celia said. 'I'm thinking of keeping a few chickens in the garden. For the war effort.'

Joyce tried not to laugh. The thought of Celia Rutherford cleaning out a hen house was quite absurd. She must be joking. But she looked quite serious, as serious as anyone could look with three glasses of elderflower wine inside them. And it was true, you could hardly get your hands on a fresh egg these days for love or money.

'But what about all that crowing they do in the mornings,' Joyce said. 'Wouldn't it drive you mad?'

'Chickens don't crow,' the hen-keeper said. 'It's cocks that crow. Cocks aren't allowed in London.'

'Quite right too,' another woman chipped in briskly. 'Cocks are a damn nuisance in my opinion.'

Joyce looked at her. 'A woman after my own heart,' she said dryly. 'All they do is disturb a good night's sleep.' And was surprised when Celia gave a kind of agonised snort and beat a hasty retreat.

She found her a few minutes later, convulsed with laughter behind the dried-flower tent.

'Oh, Mrs Carter, you are naughty,' she said dabbing her eyes with a dainty handkerchief. 'What on earth would your husband say if he heard you?'

'He won't hear me,' Joyce said. 'Because he took a swing at one of the screws last week, and now he's had his sentence extended until the autumn.'

Celia looked upset. 'Oh, I'm sorry.'

'I'm not,' Joyce said. And she wasn't. Oddly, she was pleased. It had been tough on her own for the last ten months. But she'd made it. And tomorrow she was getting the jewellery back from Lorenz. Not that Celia Rutherford would ever know it was her who'd returned it of course. She couldn't risk that. But at least she would have done it. Her conscience would finally be clear.

'I'm going to talk to Greville about the WVS tonight,' Celia said. 'I'm afraid he's not going to like it that I've already joined.'

'What do you think he'll say?' Joyce asked, watching a couple of children unsuccessfully throwing tennis balls at two cans of corned beef at the so-called coconut shy. Presumably there were no coconuts available any more.

'I don't know,' Celia replied thoughtfully. 'I'm rather hoping he loves me enough to understand I need to do my bit. However mundane.'

Joyce shrugged. 'Short of locking you up, he can hardly stop you, can he?'

Celia sighed. 'Men seem to have a talent for making life very unpleasant,' she said. 'If you cross them.'

Joyce snorted. 'You can say that again.' She chuckled. 'Pity, men aren't banned from London. Same as cocks.'

Celia laughed and then sobered. 'My eldest son leaves school at the end of the month,' she said, shaking her head. 'I'm afraid we may be in for rather a trying summer. He's picked up a lot of tiresome liberal ideas which of course are like a red rag to a bull to his father.'

'Will he join up, do you think?' Joyce asked. Young Bob would be out of the nick in September and she had a feeling he would join up. If they'd have him.

Celia frowned. 'I'm hoping he'll go up to university before trying for a commission.'

'You won't have to worry, then,' Joyce said. 'About Hitler getting him and that. That's if he doesn't get us first.'

Celia grimaced. 'They say he may invade tonight,' she said as they approached two ladies with buckets collecting for the Mayor of Battersea's Spitfire Fund, 'I heard on the wireless that his stars are right for it. But Greville says if he's got any sense, he'll try to knock out the RAF first.' She opened her handbag, nodding to the ladies with the buckets. 'I'd better give something to the Spitfire Fund. They're hoping to raise enough for two planes. Greville is on the committee.'

Joyce felt like asking if there was a committee in South London that Greville Rutherford wasn't on, what with the ARP and the church and the Conservatives and all. But she bit her lip. She'd enjoyed the fête. She'd enjoyed having a giggle with Celia Rutherford. It wouldn't do to put her back up now.

And she was glad she hadn't, because a moment later Celia took a jar of jam out of her basket.

'Please have this, Mrs Carter,' she said. 'I had to buy it because I gave Mrs Trewgarth the recipe but I have so much at home, I really don't need it.'

She put it so nicely Joyce could hardly refuse. Anyway she loved strawberry jam. And she wasn't as touchy about accepting things from Celia as she used to be. Not now she knew her better. She wasn't a bad stick, Celia Rutherford, what with her vegetables and her chutneys and all. Although where she got these mad ideas about serving in the WVS canteen and keeping chickens was anybody's guess.

On the way home in the back of the car, Celia patted her arm awkwardly.

'Thank you for coming, Mrs Carter. I do hope you enjoyed it.'

Joyce nodded. 'I did. Very much.' She smiled at her employer, surprised at the sudden warmth she felt for her. It was nice knowing someone you could have a bit of a chat with. It was almost like having a friend. 'Thank you for asking me.' She hesitated for a second. 'And if you do, you know, get them hens, I don't mind helping out a bit and that.'

Stefan Pininski was an accomplished lover, and Louise benefited both from his easy confidence and his considerable skill.

As he ushered her into his room at the Savoy and lowered his head to kiss the back of her neck, her vision blurred and she swayed against him.

Through a hazy glow she sensed his fingers on the fastening of her dress and she felt a twinge of fear.

But with gentle fingers he slid the dress down over her hips, effortlessly unclipping her bra and efficiently removing her panties and stockings as well. Obediently she stepped out of her shoes.

Then as she stood stark naked, trembling before him, feeling unusually small and vulnerable, he drew his hands slowly back up over her smooth flanks, the curve of her hips, the narrow waist. She felt his fingers on the hard bones of her ribcage and then he was cupping the soft mounds of her breast.

Unable to watch, unable to think, she closed her eyes.

'I want you, Louise,' he murmured. His questing thumbs brushed over her nipples and she gasped as a shockwave of sensation rocked her entire body.

Her eyes flew open to find him staring down at her with an adoring smile on his lips. 'You are beautiful, my little darling.'

In one easy movement he lowered her on to the bed, and quickly stripped off his own clothes.

Louise felt his weight on the bed and tensed. She was utterly terrified, but the alcohol was dulling her senses. She started to speak nervously, but then she felt his warm hands on her, drawing her close to him, stroking her, kissing her, entwining her in his naked limbs.

And suddenly nothing existed for her but the feel of his body against hers, the cool smooth flesh of his back, the touch of his hands, the warmth of his mouth.

At first her heart seemed to stop as her bones liquefied under his gentle caresses, then it began to accelerate wildly.

'No, Stefan, no!' She yelped as, with shocking familiarity, his fingers and tongue sought out her most secret and sensual places.

'Oh, yes, Louise, I think so,' he murmured softly pushing away her restraining hands, smiling slightly as she moaned in horrified pleasure.

Utterly mortified, she tried to squirm away as his tongue drove her rapidly to an excitement beyond anything she had imagined.

Then suddenly, just as she was about to cry out, he lifted his head, not allowing her the release she craved. Kneeling back he looked down at her flushed, restless body.

'Now, little one, you will be mine,' he murmured.

Carefully he pinned her arms above her head and, with a groan of satisfaction, thrust hard into her.

She shrieked in pain and her eyes flew open in alarm as he clamped a hand over her mouth.

'Shh, Louise, I'm sorry but it's the only way,' he said, with a glittering smile as she struggled against his bruising thrusts. 'The pain is over now.'

He removed his hand and kissed her tears away. 'Now you can start to enjoy yourself, my sweet, as a woman. As my woman.'

And as the pain and fear and tears abated, to her astonishment she did.

And when it was over and she descended slowly from a frantic, exploding peak of desire, she was gratified to find Stefan was still smiling. He was pleased with her. Delighted. Even though it was her first time.

His pleasure took away some of the flatness she suddenly felt. The sudden emptiness. The unease about what she had done. The embarrassment. The soreness.

But then he drew out a small velvet box from the bedside table and she forgot even the soreness.

'This is for you, Louise,' he said. 'A little gift from your lover.'

Opening it eagerly she discovered a small but exquisite diamond brooch in the shape of an S.

'S for Stefan,' she murmured, fingering it carefully. 'How lovely.' She had hoped it would be an engagement ring but his initial was almost as good. It meant she was his. He was hers.

'Thank you for the brooch, Stefan,' she said, kissing him shyly on the chin. 'I love it.'

He raised his dark eyebrows. 'You kiss me only for the brooch?'

She blushed. 'For everything.'

He laughed complacently and drew her to him again. 'Now we will sleep for a while and then I suppose you will tell me you have to go home.'

He slept but she didn't. She lay beside him under the crisp Savoy sheets wondering how she was going to face her parents.

But when she finally got home, her parents were far too busy arguing about whether her mother should or should not join the WVS even to notice how late she was.

At least, her father was arguing. Her mother was quietly sewing a WVS armband on her navy blue cardigan.

'I don't care what you want,' her father was saying angrily. 'A woman's place is in the home. It always has been and it always will be.'

As Louise edged warily into the room, he broke off abruptly.

'Oh, there you are, Louise,' he said with false heartiness. 'Did you have a nice time with Lady Helen?'

'Yes thanks,' Louise replied, crossing her fingers behind her back. She couldn't believe that they wouldn't notice the change in her. She had done it. She had had sex.

But her mother didn't even glance up from her sewing. Louise looked from one to the other. There was definitely an odd atmosphere in the room. Her mother's stitches were jerky and her father looked ominously red in the face.

As he suddenly got out his watch, Louise cringed, certain his anger would now fall on her. But he merely muttered something about the ARP and strode out of the room.

Louise looked at her mother's bowed head. 'How was the WI fête?' she asked with an effort. 'I bet old Mrs Carter looked a fright.'

Celia's head jerked up. 'She looked very nice,' she snapped. 'We had a very pleasant afternoon.'

'No need to bite my head off,' Louise said sulkily. She didn't approve of her mother's budding friendship with Mrs Carter any more than she approved of her joining the WVS. But worse than that, she suddenly felt very close to tears. Absurdly she wanted to confess everything to her mother. She couldn't, of course, and she hated wanting to. She was grown up now. A woman. A woman in love. She lifted her chin.

'I'm going to have a bath.'

Celia shrugged. 'Remember not to use too much water.'

After her bath, Louise put her head round the door again. Her mother had turned on the wireless. Winston Churchill was speaking. Louise recognised his rich, eloquent voice at once.

He was talking about the deprivations people were beginning to suffer, the threat of invasion and bombing. 'While we toil through the dark valley, we can see the sunlight on the uplands ahead.'

It was a moving speech. As he finished, Louise coughed, and as her mother looked up, to her surprise Louise saw that her eyes were brimming with tears.

'I'm rather tired, Mummy,' she said awkwardly, pretending she hadn't noticed. 'I think I'll have an early night.'

Jen couldn't help remembering that the last time she had taken the bus to Croydon was the day she had first met Sean Byrne. That had been right at the beginning of the war. It seemed so long ago. That had been the day her hopes were dashed by that sour faced old dragon at Croydon Rep Theatre School. Mrs Frost. Sean had been amused by Jen's fury. Told her she had fiery eyes. That was also the day he had told her she looked like Vivien Leigh.

Jen sighed deeply. Vivien Leigh was now a Hollywood star, married to Laurence Olivier with an Oscar behind her for her portrayal of Scarlett O'Hara. Whereas Jen Carter was on a bus to Croydon to ask some old lady whether it was worth her struggling any longer to become an actress.

Jen looked out of the window and wondered if she would ever again feel the audience hanging on her words as they had in the school play this time last year. To be honest she could hardly even remember what it felt like. It was odd, she thought, the way you could forget things that seemed so unforgettable at the time. It was the same with Sean. When she'd been with him, particularly on Alan Nelson's little boat, she had thought she would never forget how she was feeling, the excitement, the thrill, the craving desire for his body. And yet now even that seemed like a dream. She could hardly believe it had happened. She certainly couldn't believe it would ever happen again.

Not since she had seen the picture in the paper three days before, and read the short caption alongside it.

She could hardly bear to think about it.

Once again, as she had done a hundred times, she pulled the tatty newspaper cutting out of her purse. Every time she looked at it, she felt sick. But that didn't stop her looking.

She had caught sight of the picture over someone's shoulder in the Tube and had hardly been able to believe her eyes. There was no mistaking it. It was Sean. A bit fuzzy, but Sean none the less, handsome as ever, with a defiant smile on his face and a girl in his arms, standing next to an older man in a crowd of people on the steps of a tall Dublin building.

Unable to control herself, Jen had virtually snatched the paper out of her fellow passenger's hands. 'Excuse me, could I just see?'

The man had shrugged and given her an odd look, 'Keep it,' he said in a broad Irish accent. 'I'll be getting off here anyway.'

The picture was bad enough but the words that went with it were even worse:

Emotional scenes outside Dublin courthouse today as Sean Byrne and Jerry Gallagher walked free after being brought to trial on charges of suspected terrorism. One of the witnesses for the defence, local beauty Miss Aisling O'Donnell, had sworn to hunger strike if the men were convicted.

When asked afterwards if she would have carried out her threat, she said, 'As an Irishwoman, I would have been proud to die for the freedom of my country and the man I love. I am glad justice has been done.'

For two days Jen felt numb. She told nobody about the article. Nor would she. She couldn't bear their pity. And she knew if anyone said 'I told you so', she would punch them in the face. Luckily it was an Irish newspaper, so the chances of anyone else seeing it were remote.

Now as she looked at it again, she felt a surge of furious anger. Bloody Sean. No wonder he hadn't replied to her last letter. Suddenly Jen tore up the cutting and dropped it on the floor. She was astonished how much that simple act hurt.

'Wasn't it Purley Way you wanted, love?' the conductress suddenly shouted from the back of the bus and Jen jerked out of her mournful thoughts.

'Yes, yes it was,' she said, picking up her bag. 'By the aerodrome.'

The conductress winked as Jen swayed down the aisle. She pressed the bell. 'Lovely boys in the RAF, ain't they? Got a boyfriend there, have yer? Pilot, is he?'

Jen shook her head. 'No,' she said shortly. 'I'm just visiting someone who lives nearby.'

The conductress looked disappointed. 'Not a feller, then?'

'No. A woman.' Jen said, stepping down as the bus pulled up. 'I'm hoping she's going to find me a job.'

As the bus pulled away, the conductress waved. 'Best of luck then, love,' she called from the back platform. 'Don't forget, there's always room on the buses if she doesn't. It's not a bad life. Get to meet lots of people.'

Maybe it would come to that, Jen thought wearily, as she looked about for the scent factory and the row of neat terraced houses the Miss Taylors had described. Then she straightened her suit, checked for the hundredth time that the speck of strawberry jam her blasted mother had spilt on it had completely gone, took a deep breath, lifted her chin and crossed the road, ducking absurdly as two Spitfires roared low overhead as they came in one behind the other to land at the aerodrome.

The war seemed closer here. Probably it was closer. Mick had told her last night that the Luftwaffe had dropped a couple of bombs somewhere near Esher.

He also claimed to have seen a Messerschmidt caught briefly in the beam of a searchlight over Streatham, but Jen didn't believe that. Mick's sojourn at the Nelsons hadn't stopped him telling fibs. Nevertheless she shivered now, and clasped the shabby box containing her gas mask closer as she hurried down the pavement.

Number five Purley Row had brown paper in the windows and vegetables growing in the flowerbeds. The Miss Taylors' friend Margot Rose was obviously well into the war effort. Banishing all thoughts of Sean and putting on a bright, professional smile, Jen knocked confidently on the door.

But as the door opened, the smile dropped from her lips and she recoiled in horror halfway down the garden path.

The woman in the doorway was no anonymous Mrs Margot Rose. It was the ghastly hawk-faced woman from Croydon Rep whom she had insulted so badly all those months ago.

Jen's mind spun as she gaped in amazement. She would have recognised that beaky nose, those painted lips, anywhere. But she hadn't expected to find them here. There must be some dreadful mistake. Surely that woman had been called Mrs Frost.

It was like some awful dream. A nightmare.

But sadly she wasn't asleep.

Nor was the drama teacher. The red lips twisted into something resembling a smile.

'Won't you come in, Miss Carter? Or do you wish to hurl abuse at me from the garden?' She nodded towards the direction of the aerodrome. 'If so I'm afraid you'll have to compete with the planes.'

Jen didn't move. 'You knew it was me?' She suddenly felt sick.

The pencilled eyebrows rose slightly. 'I was hardly likely to forget your name, was I, Miss Carter? It's not every day of the week I get sworn at by prospective students. You, on the other hand, had clearly not made the connection. I confess I was mildly surprised when I heard you wished to see me.'

Jen began to wonder if she had been tricked. 'I didn't know it was you,' she said rudely. 'The Miss Taylors said I was to see a Margot Rose.'

'Ah.' Margot Frost seemed amused. 'That explains it. Rose was my maiden name. I used it professionally for some time. Some of my older theatre friends still use it.'

So it hadn't been a trick. Not a deliberate one anyway.

Mrs Frost was watching her with faint interest in her beady eyes. 'Now do come inside, for goodness' sake. I'm not going to eat you.'

'I'm not scared of you,' Jen muttered crossly, following her reluctantly into the terraced house.

'Well, you should be,' Mrs Frost said briskly, leading her into an unexpectedly cluttered back room and turning to face her. 'You were intolerably rude to me last time we met. If you had any manners, which you clearly don't, I would have thought an apology was in order.'

Jen felt her temper rise. 'I was cross that you had closed the drama school, that's all,' she said stiffly. She was damned if she was going to apologise.

Mrs Frost's eyes narrowed. 'If you must know, I fought tooth and nail to keep the school open. But the principal was adamant that it should close for the duration of the war,' She glanced coldly at Jen. 'I was as upset as you were about it. You only lost a chance to audition. I lost my job.'

Jen bit her lip. She felt embarrassed now. How on earth could she have got herself into such an awful situation? Why on earth had she allowed the blasted Miss Taylors to interfere?

'Well, I'm sorry,' she said grudgingly. 'But I didn't know that.' She lifted her chin. 'Anyway, if you thought I was so rude, why did you agree to see me today?'

Mrs Frost shrugged. 'Esme and Thelma Taylor are very old friends. I could hardly turn them down. In any case they said they thought you might have potential.'

'Did they?' Jen gulped. The only acting they had ever seen her do were love scenes with Sean in Pam Nelson's front room. She flushed again at the thought. Bloody Sean.

'You're surprised?' Mrs Frost's brows rose again. 'I must confess I find it somewhat hard to believe too. Histrionics and temper are all very well for established film stars. But they are not things I look for in drama students.'

Jen stared at her. She was a dragon. There was no doubt about it. She ought to be kept in a cage at the zoo. She ought to have been destroyed with all the other poisonous reptiles at the beginning of the war. For a second the thought amused her, then she glanced at Mrs Frost again and her smile faded rapidly.

The drama teacher was standing with her hands folded across her chest. 'So what pieces have you brought to show me?' she asked briskly.

Surely she didn't expect her to launch forth there and then in this poky little room. There was hardly room to swing a cat. Jen swallowed. She was quite clearly trying to unnerve her. Well, she was damned if she was going to be unnerved.

But before she had thought of a suitably chilling response, Mrs Frost had smiled grimly. 'Or do you want to leave it and go home? I daresay you could persuade the Miss Taylors to find you a more acceptable teacher.'

Jen gritted her teeth. 'I've got a piece from *Romeo and Juliet*, and one of Anne Boleyn's speeches from *Henry VIII*,' she said stiffly, 'And a tap dance piece, and a song, *A Nightingale sang in Berkeley Square.*'

Mrs Frost nodded. 'I suppose you want me to play for you?'

Surprised, Jen glanced around for a piano and realised there was indeed one in the room against the wall behind her, virtually buried under a mound of books and papers. She clicked her fingers and sighed in mock exasperation. 'Damn. I knew I'd forgotten something. My accompanist. I must have left him on the bus.'

Mrs Frost smiled grimly: 'Very funny, Miss Carter.' She held out her hand. 'If you'll give me the music, we'll start with that. We haven't got all day.'

'What, here?' Jen gaped, looking around appalled. There was only about three square feet of floor space unoccupied by books or play sheets or piles of music scores. It suddenly occurred to her that Mrs Frost had brought the entire drama school repertoire back to store in her tiny little house.

'How much space do you need?' Mrs Frost asked sarcastically from the piano. 'Perhaps we'd better get some of the RAF boys to move the piano out on to one of their runways.'

Jen glared at her and surreptitiously pushed a pile of *Showboat* scores to one side with her foot. 'I'm ready when you are,' she said sweetly, handing over the sheet music she'd only last week bluffed out of Peter Maurice Music Publishers.

The audition was not a great success.

Jen felt desperately self conscious about being in such close proximity to her assessor. Particularly one as grim and unresponsive as Margot Frost.

At the end of each piece, Jen waited for a comment, for some sort of reaction, but none was forthcoming. So she ploughed on gamely, longing for the moment when this would all be over and she could go and get a straightforward, boring job on the buses instead.

When she finally ground to the end of her prepared Juliet speech, the room seemed suddenly very silent. Jen could hear her heart beating. And then a plane roared overhead.

Mrs Frost waited for the engine noise to die away then frowned.

Jen felt suddenly sick. If Romeo had heard that Juliet, he would most probably have fetched a rope and hanged himself off her balcony. Why on earth had she ever thought she could act?

As for the songs, despite running through it three times at the publishers, the nightingale had sounded more as though it was squawking in Berkeley Square than singing. And she had nearly hit the deck when she slipped on a sheet of music trying to do the beastly time step.

Dully she watched Mrs Frost rummaging in a pile of paper by the stool. Why couldn't the beastly woman say something? At least put her out of her misery? But no, like the hawk she resembled, she was clearly waiting for the kill.

Wondering suddenly whether to pick up her bag and walk out, Jen cringed as the drama teacher looked up sharply.

'Take this,' Mrs Frost said briskly. 'It's a song and dance called *Ma, He's Making Eyes at Me*. And pick up one of those *Pygmalion* scripts. Choose one of Eliza's speeches and learn it for next time. And there's a copy of *The Importance of Being Earnest* around here somewhere. Take one of Miss Prism's speeches from that.' Her expression was fierce as she met Jen's startled eyes. 'I expect you to be word perfect by this time next week. And practise your scales. We need to improve your breathing and your range and resonance if you're intending to sing professionally.'

Jen couldn't believe her ears. Suddenly she felt quite differently about the audition. It couldn't have been quite as bad as she thought.

'So you do think I've got talent?' she asked eagerly as she took the offered papers.

Mrs Frost leaned back against the piano and regarded her thinly. 'You've certainly got something. I'm not sure what to call it. Gall, I think, might be the best description at this stage.'

Jen flinched. 'But you want to see me again?'

The drama teacher smiled grimly. 'I don't *want* to see you again, Miss Carter. But I am *willing* to see you. The two things are entirely different.'

Chapter Twenty Five

The Miss Taylors were worried about Ward Frazer. They had known he was going away and they knew enough about what he did to know what that meant. But previously he had always reappeared when he said he would. This time he hadn't. He had told them he would be back in July, and it was now the fourth of August and they still hadn't heard anything.

'The poor old things are worried to death,' Jen said to Katy. 'I tried to cheer them up, but it was hopeless.'

'Sometimes no news is good news,' Katy said hopefully. But then she thought of poor Sheila Whitehead. No news hadn't been good news for her.

'All they wanted to do was talk about him,' Jen went on. 'They told me this really sad story about him.' She shook her head. 'Apparently he used to be a foreign correspondent for a Canadian newspaper in Berlin. Before the war.'

Katy nodded. 'Louise said something about it. Something to do with going there first of all for the Olympics.'

'That's right,' Jen said. 'Well, while he was there, he met this girl and fell madly in love with her. He wanted to marry her and take her back to Canada and everything, but he couldn't.'

Katy swallowed. 'Why not?'

Jen made a face. 'She was Jewish. She couldn't get a passport, and anyway she was worried about leaving her family.' She sipped the cup of tea Katy's mother had made her. 'The Nazis were already getting nasty then apparently.'

Katy lifted her own cup and found her hand was shaking. She put it down quickly before Jen noticed. 'So what happened?' she asked.

For a second Jen was silent. 'You remember that Kristallnacht business they had in Germany a couple of years ago when they beat up the Jews and smashed their shops and everything?'

Katy nodded silently, her nails digging into her palms in the anticipation of horror.

Jen frowned. 'Well, it seems this girl was killed while trying to protect her parents' business.' She glanced at Katy's white face. 'Awful, isn't it?'

Something froze inside Katy, 'How can he go back?' she whispered. 'How can he set foot in that beastly country?'

Jen shrugged. 'I suppose he sees it as the best way of getting rid of the Nazis. Although the Miss Taylors think he's got a bit of a death wish. That's why they're so worried.'

Katy looked at her in horror. Suddenly she remembered the tone of Ward Frazer's voice that night of the crash. That private, bitter anger when he had said it was Adolf Hitler's fault.

'What about the girl's family?' Katy asked suddenly, thinking of the terrible Jewish purges that Germany had seen since the war began. There was even talk of death camps for Jews. 'What happened to them?'

'Apparently he managed to help get her parents out before the war started,' Jen said. 'And a sister, I think. They lost everything. They're living up in North London somewhere. And the worst thing of all is that his own parents have cut him off completely. They wanted him to take over the family business and marry some society girl in Canada. And they made a dreadful fuss when he took off to Germany.'

Katy looked out of the window. 'Poor Ward Frazer,' she said quietly. With a history like that it was no wonder he was reluctant to fall in love again. 'I bet that's why he didn't want to get involved with Louise.'

Jen shook her head. 'He told the Miss Taylors that Louise reminded him of the girl in Germany.' She grinned suddenly, wickedly. 'I'd have thought he'd have better taste, wouldn't you?'

'Jen, don't be naughty,' Katy said indignantly. 'Louise is very pretty. And she's got a lovely figure.'

Jen shrugged. 'Well, I've only met Ward Frazer once, but I wouldn't have thought he was the sort to choose someone just for their figure.' She grimaced. 'Not unless he just wanted sex or something.'

'Ward didn't want sex with Louise, that was the problem,' Katy said. 'He said she was too inexperienced for him.'

Jen sniffed. 'Too spoilt and hoity-toity for him, more like.' She suddenly leaned forward confidentially. 'Did you know that the Miss Taylors can't bear Mr Rutherford?' She glanced at Katy with a gleam in her eye. 'I know he's your dad's boss and that, but they reckon he's a pompous old bigot. That's why they put on all that High Church stuff, especially to annoy him. And the vicar too.' She giggled. 'They don't like him either. Don't you think that's hilarious?'

It was funny, but Katy was still too concerned about Ward Frazer to laugh. She watched Jen drain her tea and nearly did laugh at Jen's revolted expression.

'That was completely disgusting, if you don't mind me saying so,' Jen said. 'What has your mum put in it? Sawdust?'

Katy smiled. 'She said it was some kind of herb. It's meant to make the ration last longer.'

'By making it undrinkable?' Jen raised her eyebrows. 'Yes, I can see that might work.' She laughed and glanced teasingly at Katy. 'Anyway we'll probably all be drinking German tea in a day or two. They say Hitler's bound to invade tonight because it's the anniversary of the outbreak of the last war and he's meant to love anniversaries.'

Katy frowned. Every day the papers came up with a new reason why that day would be the day for invasion. It was driving her mad. 'Well, I wish he'd stop talking about it and blasted well get on with it,' she said crossly, then blushed as Jen nearly fell off her chair.

Jen stared at her. 'Katy Parsons, I can't believe I'm hearing you say that. A year ago you would have fainted clean away at the thought of invasion.'

Katy made a face. 'Well, I'm sick to death of all this waiting around and worrying. And sandbags and stirrup pumps and everything. At least if he got on with it we'd know how bad it was going to be.'

Jen stood up. 'All I know is it couldn't be any worse than five minutes with Mrs Margot bloody Frost.' She rolled her eyes. 'Margot, I ask you. What a name. Maggot, more like.'

Katy smiled sympathetically. She knew Mrs Frost had become the bugbear of Jen's life. Their first meeting had sounded bad enough, but the second one had apparently been even worse. Mrs Frost had pulled Jen to pieces to such an extent that Jen had come home almost in tears. Tears of fury, that was. Jen was certain Mrs Frost was doing it on purpose to teach her a lesson. And there was nothing she could do about it. Except try to impress her, which she seemed entirely incapable of doing.

According to the Maggot, everything about Jen was wrong; her breathing, her posture, her elocution. So, to the hilarity of her brothers, Jen had spent the last week making the most absurd noises as she doggedly practised the ridiculous breathing exercises the Maggot had given her.

'Are you all right? You sounded like a stuck pig up there,' Mick had remarked when she came downstairs after one particularly gruelling session of scales.

'At least I don't look like one, like you,' Jen had retorted and had removed herself up to the common for her exhalation practice. It was only hard work that kept her mind off Sean. She hadn't heard from him for weeks now. Admittedly she hadn't written either. But having secretly prayed for an explanation, for a believable excuse, Jen was disappointed. She had had no idea how much his silence would hurt.

'When's the next lesson?' Katy asked now.

Jerked back to the present, Jen groaned. 'Next Thursday. And she's given me about a hundred things to learn for it. She says I need to build up my repertoire. As well as my lung capacity.' She sighed, deeply. 'I wish I could get out of it. She is so utterly ghastly. But I don't want to hurt the Miss Taylors' feelings. They're so pleased with themselves for setting it all up.'

Katy nodded. But actually she was surprised. Jen had changed over the last year. The old Jen wouldn't have cared two hoots about hurting the feelings of a couple of cranky old ladies. Nor would she have put up with being bossed about by a middle aged, unemployed drama teacher. As she watched Jen carry their cups through to the kitchen, Katy wondered secretly if Mrs Frost might not just be the making of Jen Carter.

But Jen obviously didn't see it like that. She grimaced at Katy from the top of the stairs. 'You know, I hope that bloody Hitler does invade. And I hope he heads straight for Croydon. He's the one person in the world who might be a match for the Maggot.'

Louise lay on her back and stared up at the bedroom ceiling. By now she knew all the little cracks and blemishes where the elegant gold and white paper didn't quite meet the cornices. She had spent quite a lot of time staring at this particular ceiling.

Stefan always slept for half an hour after they had made love. Normally she wished he wouldn't because that was the time she most wanted to talk to him, when the passion was over, before it began to creep into her again, making her want nothing but his hands on her body, his beautiful tender caresses which gave her such previously unimaginable pleasure. But today she was happy for him to sleep because it gave her time to think.

She had to decide how to tell him she'd got to go away. For three weeks. She glared at the ceiling rose as irritation flooded over her again. It was her stupid brother's fault. Bertie's fault. He had come back from school at the end of term wearing a pair of cream corduroys and sandals, and saying he was going to register as a conscientious objector.

There had been one hell of a row.

Her father had lost his temper completely and at one point had hit Bertie rather hard on the side of the head.

Her mother had cried.

Douglas had made things a hundred times worse by saying that he wanted to leave school and join up there and then.

Bertie had quite calmly pointed out that now he had left school he was entitled to make his own decisions. Greville Rutherford had said it was an absolute disgrace and if he didn't pull himself together he would be disinherited. He wouldn't tolerate a coward in the family.

Bertie said he didn't want to run a brewery anyway. Louise had screamed at him to shut up and her father had blown his top again and said they were all a disgrace to the Rutherford name and he didn't want to see any of them again until they'd grown up.

And the long and short of it was that they were all being packed off to Aunt Delia in Shropshire for the rest of the holidays.

Shropshire. Louise was furious. So were the boys. And so, oddly, was her mother.

Louise had overheard her pleading with her father to change his mind. Or at least to send the three children on their own. But she had got her head bitten off for her pains. He was adamant. And adamant that she should go too.

'I've had enough, Celia. You'll take the children up there, and that's all I want to hear about it. I'm damned if I'll have that boy in the house another minute.'

'But what about the WVS?' Celia had murmured. 'I've only just joined. I haven't done anything yet.'

Greville Rutherford's voice rose. 'I've told you before I didn't want you getting caught up in all that. It's a complete waste of time. Quite absurd. Not at all suitable for someone in your position. Hobnobbing with all and sundry. In any case, the ARP wardens are perfectly in control. In a crisis, women will only panic and get in the way.'

To Louise's surprise her mother had retaliated bravely. 'The WVS is not a waste of time, Greville. And I don't think they will panic. They are doing very useful work. In an air raid we would be providing sustenance to people in difficulties. After all, the Prime Minister has asked us all to do our duty. Women and men.'

His response had been swift and vicious. 'And your duty is in the home, Celia. I don't like to criticise but if you'd been doing your duty by the children, none of this nonsense with Bertram would have happened.'

That was so blatantly untrue that when her mother didn't respond, Louise almost burst into the room to take issue with him about it. But she had more sense. When her father got on his high horse anything could happen. And she didn't want to get gated. She was due to see Stefan on Thursday evening, under the pretence of a theatre outing with Helen de Burrel, and she was damned if she was going to run the risk of missing it just to back up her mother.

In any case she didn't feel her mother merited her support. She had been so uninterested lately. She rarely asked what Louise had been up to. Not that Louise would have told her of course, God forbid. But nevertheless she was her mother and she might have made a bit of effort to communicate with her daughter instead of nitter-nattering with that ghastly Mrs Carter all the time.

Louise turned her head to glance at her bedfellow. His jaw slackened slightly in sleep but he wasn't any less handsome for that, and the silver in the hair around his ears gave him a distinguished look. He was distinguished. Very distinguished, and Louise couldn't wait for the moment when she would present him to her parents as her prospective husband.

They would die.

She hugged herself gleefully then jumped as Stefan's finger touched her curving lips.

'What has made you so happy?' he asked, levering himself up on to one arm.

Louise blushed. 'You,' she said. 'You make me very happy, Stefan.' She hesitated. 'Do I make you happy?'

He looked at her for a moment, then frowned. 'You would make me more happy if I could see you more often.' He reached for a cigarette and lay back on the bed, inhaling deeply. 'Twice a week is not enough, my darling. And always we have our eyes on the clock.'

Louise's face fell. 'It's because we have to be secret,' she said. She bit her lip and glanced at him warily. 'If we didn't have to be so secret then we could spend more time together. We could go out more. Meet people.' She smiled winningly. 'I haven't met any of your friends. Or your brother.' She pouted. 'Sometimes I think you must be ashamed of me.'

He laughed softly and holding the cigarette in his teeth he leaned over and jerked the sheet off her, exposing her naked body.

She screamed in surprise and tried to cover herself. 'Stefan! What are you doing?'

'I am looking at you,' he said, holding her still by one arm. 'And if you look too, you will see why I want to keep you to myself.' Removing the cigarette, he leaned forward and kissed her. 'You are mine, Louise. Mine to do with as I want.' His eyes glittered as he drew his hand slowly down over her stomach, pausing before running on between her legs, easing them apart.

Louise gasped.

He laughed. 'What I want, when I want,' he murmured, pushing away her restraining hand: 'Don't move, my sweet, I want to teach you something new.'

'Stefan, there's something I've got to tell you,' she said nervously as he reached over to the bedside table to stub out the cigarette.

For a moment he stilled. Then his eyes narrowed in a slight frown. 'Which is?'

She bit her lip. He wasn't going to like it.

'I've got to go away for a few weeks. With my family.' She looked at him, dreading his reaction. She loved him so much, she couldn't bear for anything to go wrong.

'Oh Louise, no.' He sounded upset. He stubbed out the cigarette and turned back to her. 'How long? How many weeks?'

She bit her lip. 'Three, I think.'

He closed his eyes briefly. 'You can't go, my love. You'll have to get out of it.'

She shook her head. 'I can't get out of it, Stefan. Not without telling my parents about you. That we are, well, you know, serious.'

He looked at her. 'I am very serious, Louise. But I am afraid you are not so serious about me.' He hesitated for a second.' I am always afraid you will tell me I am too old for you. That you have found a younger man.'

'But Stefan, I am serious about you,' she said sitting up eagerly. 'Completely serious. I don't even look at anyone else anymore.' She stroked his arm with a deep sigh. 'I wish I didn't have to go to beastly Aunt Delia but I honestly can't see any way of getting out of it.' She looked at him pleadingly, hoping he would understand. 'I promise I'll come and see you as soon as I get back.'

He shook his head. 'You will have forgotten me by then.'

Louise stared at him in amazement. 'Of course I won't.' She eyed him doubtfully. 'Will you have forgotten me?'

'My darling, I could never forget you.' He shut his eyes and ran his hands through his hair. 'Three weeks,' he groaned. 'How will I survive without you for three weeks?' Suddenly he looked up. 'Stay with me. Stay with me here now. Damn your family.'

Louise's eyes widened as a wave of excitement coursed through her. Then reality reasserted itself. 'Stefan, I can't. I-I'd love to stay more than anything in the world. But I can't, Daddy would kill me. And you.' She clung to his arm as he tried to withdraw it. 'Stefan, when I get back I will introduce you to them? Then it will all be OK.'

For a moment Stefan was silent then he leaned forward and kissed her gently on the lips. He stared into her eyes. 'Do you really love me, Louise?'

She nodded.

'Then will you show me? Will you prove it to me before you go?'

She frowned at him. 'What do you mean?'

He released her then and lay back on the bed. 'I want you to make love to me, my sweet. I have, shown you how much I love you so many times. Now it is your turn to show me.'

Louise stared at his impassive face, appalled. He always took the lead, manoeuvring her body to suit his purpose, seducing her with his knowing caresses, dulling her inhibitions with his murmured endearments. She glanced down at the outline of his body under the cotton sheet. 'Stefan, I can't,' she said, blushing furiously. 'I don't know how to.'

His eyes opened slightly, enough for her to see the smiling challenge in their smoky depths. 'Oh, please don't disappoint me, Louise. I am going to miss you so much. And his mouth curved into a wicked grin. 'You should know by now what will please me.'

Louise bit her lip. She didn't want to disappoint him. More than anything she wanted to please him. She didn't want him to go off her now. She had to keep him, had to make him love her. Holding her breath, squirming with embarrassment, she leaned forward and drew her breast across his closed lips.

'The most extraordinary thing happened yesterday.' Celia Rutherford looked up from the suitcase she was packing and glanced at Joyce who was cleaning the windows. 'The police turned up with all that jewellery we'd had stolen before Christmas.'

'Really?' Joyce tried to sound surprised. 'How extraordinary. The whole lot?'

Celia nodded slowly. 'The whole lot,' she said. 'All in a paper bag. The police said it was virtually unheard of to get stolen property back after such a long time.'

'Really?' Joyce said again. She saw her reflection in the window and quickly banished the smile.

'Somebody handed it in,' Celia went on, carefully folding a skirt before smoothing it into the leather suitcase. 'A woman. Down at the police station in Battersea. Just after the all-clear sounded. She didn't give her name.'

Joyce breathed on the window. 'I wonder who that was, then,' she murmured.

'I wonder,' Celia Rutherford agreed mildly. 'Whoever it was I'm very grateful.'

Joyce felt herself colouring She scrubbed determinedly at the window. 'Well, it's only right as you should get it back, isn't it?' she said gruffly.

Celia paused for a minute. When she spoke again her voice sounded rather tentative. 'You know, Mrs Carter, when the jewellery was stolen I wanted to offer a reward. I was so upset about losing my mother's brooch. But Greville was against it. He said rewards encourage crime.' She hesitated. 'But now we've got it back, I would so like to give a little something to the person who handed it in. Do you think I'd ever be able to find out who she was?'

'Oh no, I shouldn't think so,' Joyce said quickly. 'If she wanted it known who she was, she'd have said, wouldn't she?'

Celia Rutherford sighed. 'I suppose so.'

Joyce heard the other woman move behind her and when she spoke again she could tell she was smiling. 'That window is looking very clean, Mrs Carter,' she said gently. 'Perhaps you might move on to the next one now?'

Joyce blinked. She had been rubbing the window for about five minutes. She was lucky she hadn't made a hole in the glass. She flushed. 'Best to get them nice and clean, she muttered.

Celia nodded gravely. 'Absolutely.' She fiddled with the clasp on the suitcase. 'Mrs Carter, I'm afraid my husband doesn't think we'll need any cleaning done while I'm away. With just him here he doesn't think it's necessary. He'll be out checking on the ARP posts most evenings now it looks as though the Luftwaffe are starting to engage the RAF in earnest.'

Joyce swallowed. She didn't care particularly about the Luftwaffe. But she did care about being laid off. Even though she had expected it ever since Celia had told her she was going away. But it didn't make it any easier. For a fleeting second she wished she had delayed returning the jewellery. She had promised Lorenz another two pounds next week. With no cleaning money coming in, if she gave it to him she and the kids would have nothing to eat.

Celia was watching her. 'Did I tell you that Cook is taking a couple of weeks off while we are away?'

Joyce looked up in surprise. 'No, you never mentioned that. Who is going to look after Mr Rutherford, then? Cooking and that?'

Celia closed the suitcase and slanted Joyce a coy look. 'Well, I was rather hoping you might agree to do it, Mrs Carter. Of course it would involve a bit of work in the evenings and at weekends but I'd give you a little bit extra for that. It's only fair.'

Joyce stared at her. Somewhere along the line she smelt a rat. That tight-lipped old cook hadn't said anything about going away. She'd had a holiday in January, after all. And there was something else too. Joyce frowned. Mrs Rutherford was looking a bit devious. Joyce knew she hadn't wanted to go to Shropshire. That she and Mr Rutherford had had a bit of a tiff about it. That she was upset about having to delay getting her chickens. About leaving the garden at its best. And most of all about abandoning the WVS just as it looked as though Hitler might be going to make his move.

Joyce eyed her carefully. 'But would Mr Rutherford mind me doing for him?' she asked. She didn't like to say she knew he disapproved of her. Or that she hated his guts in return. Cold, dismissive bastard as he was. Twice recently she had found Mrs Rutherford almost in tears because he had upset her so badly.

'He'll be delighted,' Celia said firmly. Her mouth curved. 'After all, he won't have much choice, will he? Not if he wants to eat.'

It was the fifteenth of August and the talk on the bus to Croydon was of the aerial fighting between the Luftwaffe and the RAF. The day before yesterday, according to the papers, seventy eight Nazi planes had been brought down over the south coast. And the day before that, fifty seven. Although painful, the RAF losses were small in comparison. They were calling it the Battle of Britain.

The sirens had sounded frequently in London the last few days but although some German reconnaissance planes had been seen, so far no bombers had made an attempt on the capital. Despite the damage to the south coast ports, particularly Portsmouth and Southampton, and the odd stray bomb in Surrey and Sussex, the RAF successes proved that the Germans were failing to gain air superiority. And until they managed that, everyone said, an invasion was doomed to failure.

'That blighter Lord Haw-Haw says it'll come this weekend,' one of the passengers remarked and was immediately shouted down vociferously by the others for listening to German propaganda.

Jen glanced over her shoulder and smiled to herself. She did rather a good imitation of Lord Haw-Haw. She wondered what the reaction on the bus would be if she launched into it now. But then she yawned and decided against it. The sirens had gone off again last night, keeping her awake far too long. She hadn't gone down to the shelter, even though her mother and the boys had, but she hadn't slept either. At least not until the all-clear had sounded. And now the last thing on earth that she wanted to do in this muggy early evening heat was to try and impress the Maggot.

Automatically she began to do the deep breathing exercises Mrs Frost had taught her as she ran silently through one of the speeches she had been set to learn. But fatigue overcame her. It was too late now anyway. She either knew her pieces or she didn't. And if she didn't, she'd feel the rough side of the Maggot's tongue. The scornful look that penetrated to her very soul, the cutting inquiry as to her commitment, the brutal request not to waste her teacher's time.

Jen yawned again. She craved sleep. For once she didn't care if she could reach top G or not. Or whether her resonance had improved.

But just as she had leant her head against the window and closed her eyes, the driver of the bus, with no warning at all, stamped hard and dramatically on the brake and the vehicle jerked to a sudden, shuddering halt.

After a momentary confusion in which two or three dislodged passengers struggled back into their seats, complaining about bruised knees and dropped parcels, people started peering through the blacked-out bus windows and asking each other irritably what was going on.

Then suddenly over the sound of other traffic, quite clearly there came the noise of aircraft.

But not the aircraft noise they were used to, the steady drone of the RAF planes, but a heavier sound with an odd irregular beat, a dull, threatening roar, interspersed with deep, resonating thuds, which made the bus vibrate, and lifted the hairs on the back of Jen's neck.

Someone on the top deck started shouting, 'It's the Hun!'

And someone else, 'By God, the bastard's bombing Croydon.'

The driver was shouting for everyone to get out, to take cover. A moment later the conductor took up the refrain. But the passengers had different ideas. To a man they herded up the narrow twisting bus stairs, forcing the conductor to retreat ahead of them onto the top deck.

Even Jen found herself pressing her nose against the badly painted glass. The bus had stopped on a slight rise. Some way ahead and slightly to the right of them, a grim looking phalanx of fat-bellied black planes were droning low across the rooftops. Even as she watched, they emptied their deadly cargo, the bombs looking small and strangely insignificant as they dropped away through the haze.

The resulting explosions weren't insignificant though, but even before the noise of them had reached the stranded bus, the planes had banked steeply away.

'Must be the aerodrome,' someone murmured in awe as something exploded in a ball of flame.

And then suddenly with a tremendous volley, the anti-aircraft fire began. The crowd on the bus cheered as the Luftwaffe formation broke. The air round the enemy planes was suddenly full of black smoke balls, unfolding and dispersing quickly on the light breeze.

And then, even better, half a dozen Spitfires and Hurricanes roared into view, swooping down through the haze.

At once the battle began in earnest. It seemed the German bombers had a fighter escort and it was these smaller planes that engaged with the RAF, even as the bombers emptied yet another load of death and destruction on unsuspecting Croydon.

'Why the hell aren't the bloody sirens going?' someone muttered. 'I pity them poor buggers living down there.'

Jen blinked. The whole thing had been like a dream. Like a film. Exciting and dramatic. Now suddenly, with a dreadful shock, she realised it was real. That people were probably dying down there. Pilots definitely were. She saw one of the German fighters peel away, spinning badly with smoke pouring out of its wing. There was no parachute. A Spitfire, machine-guns rattling, pursued it out of sight.

The passengers cheered again. Three cheers for the boys in blue.

But Jen felt sick. She had got her bearings now. It was the airport that was getting it. Through the smoky haze she could just about make out the aircraft hangars and the scent factory. Even as she watched, a flicker of flame shot up into the dark air.

And then suddenly it was over. The Germans, damaged and struggling, had turned away in an untidy formation, heading back towards the coast, followed and harried by the darting British planes.

And then, just as the last smoking German plane disappeared into the haze, the sirens finally went off, the fluctuating whine starting at some distant point, rising to a deafening local crescendo.

'Bloody hell,' one of the passengers complained. 'They left that a bit bleeding late for the poor sods living there. Hopefully most of 'em were out at work.'

Jen felt numb. Ten minutes later and she would have been there herself.

Walking towards Mrs Frost's house. The neat little terrace between the scent factory and the aerodrome. Exactly where those bombs had been falling.

Suddenly her blood ran cold. Mrs Frost. The Maggot? What of her? She wouldn't have been out at work. She would have been in her shambolic little house. Waiting for her pupil.

Chapter Twenty Six

It took Jen only a few seconds to decide what to do. She turned and accosted the Conductor who was still trying to get people off his vehicle. 'Is the bus going on?'

He shook his head. 'Not bloody likely. Once the sirens go we're at a standstill.' He looked at her. 'You better take cover, love. Pretty little thing like you. That's what you'd better do. Don't want to get caught out in a raid, do you?'

'The raid's over,' Jen snapped. 'There's no point in taking cover now.'

But astonishingly down on the street, people were hurrying to the shelters and she realised that they didn't know the raid was over. Perhaps they didn't even know there had been a raid at all. It was only from the vantage point of the top deck that you could see out over the Croydon plain. At street level, among the traffic, they probably hadn't been able to hear the noise of the bombs.

Ignoring an ARP warden beckoning her to his shelter, Jen began to run down the rapidly emptying street.

She had no idea what she was going to do when she got there. She had no idea why she was going. But she knew she had to. It was one of those things. If nothing else, she owed it to the Miss Taylors. She could hardly tell them she had witnessed a raid on Croydon without bringing them news of their friend.

As she panted towards the smoke, several police cars roared past her. Two clanging fire engines lumbered past in their wake. They, in turn were followed by four grey-painted ambulances.

Jen grimaced and stopped to regain her breath for a moment. Catching sight of a bicycle leaning against a lamppost, she glanced round quickly to make sure nobody was looking, then hitched up her skirt and mounted it. It wasn't so much theft, she told herself as she wobbled off, as an emergency requisition.

Either way, it took a moment for her to get her balance, it was a long time since she had ridden a bike, not since Bob had pinched one from outside the Morgan Crucible factory in Battersea. But soon she was pedalling energetically and it wasn't long before she began to smell the fires. A pungent, sulphurous aroma that got into her sinuses and made her sneeze.

And then suddenly her way was barred.

'You can't go in there, love.' A policeman waved her down, 'Purley Way is closed.'

Breathing deeply, Jen put one foot to the ground and grinned at him disarmingly. 'Just watch me,' she said and accelerated past him.

Men in helmets and armbands kept shouting at her, but she ignored them. Mostly they were busy manning pumps and manoeuvring vehicles and shouting orders at each other. The smell was almost unbearable now.

Slowing up as she turned off Purley Way, Jen began to breathe through her mouth, coughing on the thick black smoke that hung in the warm air. She passed two or three policemen holding handkerchiefs to their noses. Ironically it seemed to be the scent factory that was giving off the dreadful odour. It had been badly hit. Already stretcher parties were at work. The road was badly pitted now so Jen dumped the bike and went on by foot, averting her eyes as she passed a number of bodies being laid out carefully on the pavement and covered in grey blankets.

As she turned the last corner, once again her way was barred, this time by a small man in the belted uniform of the Auxiliary Fire Brigade. 'Oi, where are you going?' he shouted, grabbing her arm. 'It's emergency services only in here.'

Jen stopped and stared over his shoulder. One of the houses in the terrace had been hit. The roof had caved in and the walls were leaning drunkenly. Three firemen were playing water over the smoking ruin from a pump hitched to the back of a taxi. Her heart sank. And then she realised it was the house next door to Mrs Frost's.

'I've got to go over there,' she said urgently to the man holding her. 'My teacher lives there.'

He shook his head. 'Oh no, you don't. We reckon as all those houses are going to collapse any minute.'

Jen stared at him, then back at the terrace. 'Have they cleared them?' she asked. 'Have they got everyone out, then?'

He shrugged. 'We've knocked on the doors. Nobody in any of them, love. All out at work, most likely.'

Jen shook her head. 'She's not out at work. She must still be there.' Mrs Frost wasn't the kind of woman to abandon her home with no argument. Jen smiled sweetly at the fireman and then as he relaxed, jerked her arm free and sped across the street.

'Oi, you, come back. Get that girl.'

Something had happened to Mrs Frost's front door. It seemed to have come away from its hinges. Jen pushed hard on it and jumped back as it fell into the hall in a cloud of dust.

After the hubbub outside, the house seemed very quiet. Dust danced in the evening light streaming through the back windows. Behind her Jen heard running feet and quickly clambered over the twisted door into the narrow hall. Something creaked ominously above her as she hurried down the passage.

Mrs Frost was in the rehearsal room.

She had pulled a wheelbarrow in from the garden through the kitchen door and was calmly loading it with all her scripts and scores.

Jen stared at her in amazement. And then at the wide, gaping crack in the back wall. A light powder of white dust covered all the surfaces. Mrs Frost herself, her hair and clothes cobwebbed with the same white dust, looked like something out of a horror movie, like someone risen from the grave.

'You've got to come out,' Jen said, coughing. 'Didn't you hear them knocking? The house is going to fall down.'

Mrs Frost looked at her blankly. 'I can't leave without my things,' she said.

Jen noticed a dark stain on Mrs Frost's sleeve. 'Mrs Frost, for goodness' sake. You're injured.'

Her teacher shook her head. 'Only a flesh wound,' she said, continuing to load her wheelbarrow.

The house creaked again and Jen heard renewed shouting outside, 'You've got to come out,' she said urgently. 'Or it'll be a damn sight more than a flesh wound.'

Grabbing the wheelbarrow she manoeuvred it through the doorway. There in the passage she came face to face with a burly fireman. The look on his face as he caught sight of the wheelbarrow almost made her laugh. 'Take this,' Jen said to him abruptly, 'I'll bring the lady out.'

But Mrs Frost didn't want to move.

'You're bloody well coming with me,' Jen swore at her, taking her good arm and jerking her to her feet. 'I know you don't like me,' she muttered through gritted teeth, 'but I need you and I'm damned if I'm going to let you die. I'm going to make it on the stage whether you like it or not, and I want you to be there when I do.'

Later, back at the Miss Taylors', as she sipped a reviving cup of tea and watched Katy Parsons carefully bandaging Mrs Frost's arm with shaking fingers, Jen could hardly believe how lucky they had been.

They had scarcely reached Mrs Frost's garden gate when the front wall of her house had given way behind them and fallen forward in a cracking, grinding moan in a cloud of thick white dust. At once an avalanche of beds and chairs and cupboards had come sliding out of the gaping upstairs rooms towards them and if was only by virtually pulling Mrs Frost's arm out of its socket, that Jen got her clear of the flying furniture in time.

Coughing and choking from the dust, they had stood in the middle of the street, stunned to silence by their miraculous escape, and the devastation they had left behind them.

Events after that had merged into a hazy blur. Mrs Frost had refused to be taken to hospital, insisting there were more needy cases than hers. And hearing the screaming and sobbing coming from the direction of the wrecked scent factory, it seemed she was right.

Somewhere along the line a Civil Defence Force officer had promised to have her property roped off and her surviving furniture and effects removed to storage.

And then even as the dust began to settle, the sirens had wailed out the all-clear.

'There,' Katy said suddenly as she neatly pinned the end of the bandage and leaned back to admire her handy work. 'How does that feel?'

Jen grinned, 'You want to watch out, Mrs Frost. Last time she bandaged my arm, she cut off my blood supply.'

Mrs Frost smiled at Katy. 'Don't listen to her. You've done it beautifully. You ought to be down in Croydon Hospital helping out there.'

Katy flushed. 'I'd like to train as a nurse, but I'm not sure if my parents would let me.'

Suddenly Jen felt pleased she had managed to persuade Katy to come and bandage the drama teacher. It was good for her morale to feel useful and Mrs Frost's crisp matter-of-fact manner hadn't intimidated her as much as Jen had feared it would. On the contrary, it seemed to be bringing out the best in her.

Mrs Frost was looking at her carefully. 'If today was anything to go by, they'll soon be needing all the nurses they can get, I dread to think how many casualties there were down there today. And all because they didn't sound the sirens in time.'

Jen saw Katy's shudder and wondered, for the hundredth time why someone who found pain and suffering so distressing should ever want to be a nurse. It was like someone who was scared of heights suddenly deciding to become a trapeze artist. Jen shook her head and glanced fondly at her friend. She was a funny, sickly thing, Katy Parsons, but you had to admire her for wanting to do something with her life. And she seemed to be getting on like a house on fire with the Maggot.

She was asking how they had got back from Croydon now and Mrs Frost was smiling slightly. 'Your friend here chatted up a policeman,' she said, nodding at Jen. 'Didn't take her long to get the offer of a lift out of him. He thought he was getting her on her own of course. He wasn't quite so pleased when she produced me and the wheelbarrow.'

Jen giggled. 'I don't mind the old lady, love,' she said in a comical policeman's voice. 'But I'm not takin' a friggin' wheelbarrow.'

Mrs Frost's brows rose. 'I didn't know you were such a good mimic.'

Katy looked from one to the other. 'Jen's the best mimic there is,' she said, surprised.

Feeling suddenly self-conscious under Mrs Frost's thoughtful gaze, Jen dropped her eyes. It was odd, but since their dramatic escape from Mrs Frost's house she had felt strange affection for the other woman. A grudging respect. She'd got guts, the old Maggot, you had to give her that. To her surprise Jen felt oddly humbled by her teacher's stoicism. She herself still felt dazed and faintly sick. The after effects of adrenalin, Katy said.

But even though she had lost virtually everything she owned, Margot Frost had still retained her crisp matter-of-fact manner, her caustic tongue. She'd certainly had the poor old Miss Taylors scurrying around like mad things ever since she'd knocked peremptorily at their door.

Poor old things. They were upstairs now, making up a bed for their visitor.

It had done them good actually, Jen thought, to worry about something other than Ward Frazer. He was nearly a month overdue now, and still there had been no word.

As for Winston, he'd retreated upstairs after being sharply reprimanded by Mrs Frost for attacking the policeman's ankles as he obligingly carried in her papers.

Jen smiled to herself as she remembered what Mrs Frost had said in the police car after they had emptied the wheelbarrow into the boot.

'You probably saved my life back there, Jennifer Carter. And I'm very grateful. But if you think I'm going to let you get away with sloppy performances and bad manners because of it, you've got another think coming.'

Jen had grinned. Somehow the sharp words didn't seem quite as vicious coming from a bedraggled, homeless old lady with dust-white hair and clotting blood on her sleeve.

'I promise to be as well mannered as the Princess Elizabeth herself if you promise you'll get me on to the stage,' she had retorted.

Mrs Frost had snorted in amusement. 'Oh, we'll get you on the stage all right. You see if we don't. But I don't think we need to involve the Royal Family. You're far too big for your boots as it is.'

Two days after the Croydon raid, the guns on Clapham Common fired for the first time.

The noise was unbelievable, a deafening, thunking roar that made the whole street vibrate. The Nelsons' house trembled to such an extent that three cups fell off Pam's drying rack and smashed on the kitchen floor.

At first the presence of the big guns up on the common had given everyone a sense of security. But now, as the Luftwaffe became daily more daring, people began to realise that the guns might become a target in themselves, and suddenly they seemed uncomfortably close.

The Luftwaffe raids were definitely getting more frequent and it seemed they were no longer directed just at military targets.

The newspapers, operating under strict censorship, were vague about where bombs had fallen, letting 'South London suburbs' cover a multitude of sins. The RAF was battling valiantly, they said. On average seventy German planes were being brought down each night. They quoted Winston Churchill's recent words: 'Never in the field of human conflict has so much been owed by so many to so few.'

But bad news travelled fast, as did Mick Carter on Alan's bicycle, and soon everyone in the street knew that South Wimbledon Underground Station had been hit, that a train had been dive bombed near Morden and that at New Malden, the devastation had been such that bits of the corpses had to be collected up in sacks.

Unfortunately Mick had imparted this last piece of information to Pam in the presence of Sheila Whitehead and little George, and Pam had had to spend the rest of the evening sitting with them in the Anderson shelter trying to divert Sheila's mind from Mick's gruesome report.

Sheila virtually lived in the shelter these days. Alan, worried about the chill in there at night, had rigged up a couple of plank bunks, enough for her and George, and a paraffin lamp, and Pam had brought blankets down. Each night her two visitors tucked themselves up in there whether the sirens had sounded or not.

Little George had developed a passion for jigsaws and spent hour upon hour poring over a farmyard puzzle that Pam had found on a market stall round the corner from her office. Unfortunately the picture had turned out to be larger than Pam had realised and even though Alan had made George a special tray to put the pieces on, it still took up far too much room. Nobody wanted to banish it from the shelter, though, because it was such a relief to see George smiling again.

If she heard planes, or if the Clapham Common guns fired, then Pam would go down to the shelter, squeezing into the confined space. But otherwise, despite Sheila's anxious protests, sirens or not, she stayed indoors. She needed her sleep, and if Alan was home she wanted to be with him. She had hardly seen him alone in weeks.

Little George had slept in their bed for three weeks after the night when he had thought Sheila was dead. In the end it was Alan who had put his foot down and insisted that the child return to his own bed. He and Pam had had a bit of a row about that. But Alan had stood firm.

'I never see you,' he said. 'If you're not at work, you're morale-boosting Sheila or playing with George, or asleep. We need some time together, Pam. Some time alone together.'

But then the raids had started and Pam often found herself trapped north of the river, unable to get home from work because they closed the floodgates on the Underground during raids. In any case Alan was more often than not out on the streets in his capacity as newly promoted sergeant in the Home Guard, as the LDV was now called, searching for German parachutists, or training for invasion.

It wasn't until the twenty fourth of August, the night the Luftwaffe made their first real bid for London, that Pam and Alan found themselves alone, and awake.

'Can you believe it's nearly a year since war was declared?' Pam said, putting down her book. She knew the sirens would sound any minute. There was little point in trying to sleep. Alan had told her the ARP were on purple alert.

Alan shrugged stiffly. 'It hasn't been one of our best years, has it?'

She shook her head, disconcerted. 'No.' She looked at him. She knew he had something on his mind. Something more than the prospect of yet another sleepless night.

She touched his hand. 'What is it, Alan? What's the matter?'

He looked at her for a moment and then turned his head away. She saw him swallow and he moved his hand out of her reach.

'There's something I have to ask you,' he said finally. 'Something I have to know. I've tried not to think about it. Not to let it worry me, but I find I can't.'

Pam frowned. 'What is it?'

A muscle moved in his jaw. Then he took a deep breath. 'I have to know if you went to bed with Sean Byrne,' he said.

He saw her flush and groaned. There was an agonised look in his eyes. 'I'm sorry, Pam. I'm sorry. But I have to know. It's like a cancer gnawing at me. I've tried to shake it off, but every time I look at you, every time I touch you ...'

'Stop it. Alan, please stop it.' She was shaking. 'I wish you'd said. I didn't know ...' She felt tears spring to her eyes. 'It's me that should be sorry, not you.' She saw his expression and added quickly, 'I never went to bed with Sean Byrne. I promise. Never.'

Alan was silent for a moment. 'But you wanted to.'

Pam bit her lip. 'Yes. I wanted to.' she admitted. 'And once I let him kiss me. But that was all.' She closed her eyes, feeling the old guilt, still somehow linked to the death of little Ray. 'I didn't realise you'd noticed. Why didn't you say something to me, Alan? Why didn't you boot him out?'

He shook his head. 'I thought you wanted him here. He seemed to make you happy. I wanted you to be happy. You were so unhappy about not having a baby.'

Pam looked away. 'Having Sean here made me more unhappy than I've ever been,' she said quietly. She hesitated, then glanced shyly at Alan. 'There's only one man that can make me truly happy. And that's you, Alan. And I don't care about the baby any more. It's you I want more than anything.'

Faint colour stained his cheeks. 'You don't have to say that.'

'I know I don't have to,' Pam said angrily. 'But I can if I want to.' She steadied herself, trying to explain. 'What made me so unhappy was you being so down. It all got so awkward between us. I thought you cared more about trying to have a baby than about me.'

'I did care.' He sighed. 'I felt inadequate. I couldn't get war work. I couldn't get a promotion at the brewery. I couldn't even get my wife pregnant.' He looked away. 'I couldn't even arouse her any more. And it seemed another man could.'

Pam bit her lip. 'We were in a rut,' she said quickly. Then she shook her head. 'But I think we are out of it now.'

Something in her voice made him turn back to her. For a long moment they stared into each other's eyes. Pam had forgotten what nice eyes he had. The way the irises darkened towards the outer rim, the way the pupils dilated as he looked at her. The way the lids lowered slightly to hide his desire.

She wasn't surprised when his hand touched her cheek. Turning her head, she kissed his fingers and smiled as he drew her into his arms.

Very gently, very cautiously, like a man finding a mirage of water after weeks in the desert, Alan stroked her face, her hair, her neck.

'Will you forgive me for fancying Sean Byrne?' Pam asked eventually.

'No. I won't,' he said, peeling back her nightgown to kiss her neck. 'But I'm going to make damn sure you start fancying me again.'

She smiled to herself as something stirred inside her. The old excitement. The sudden stab of desire that heated her blood and sensitised her skin.

'Alan?'

He looked up. 'What?'

Her voice was slightly breathless. 'Do you think we could be quite quick? I couldn't bear it if we get interrupted by an air raid.'

He laughed. 'Damn the siren. If we get bombed tonight I can't think of a better way to go.'

And sure enough, when the sirens went off a few minutes later they hardly faltered in their languorous caresses, and by the time the guns on Clapham Common started pounding, their mutual excitement was such that the blasts of the guns and the associated shuddering vibrations seemed more like an accompaniment to their own explosive reactions than a reason to hurry to the shelter.

It was only as they gradually came down to earth, sweating and panting, that Pam fully realised what was going on outside.

Through the open window she could see the searchlights raking the sky, and distant thunderous explosions reverberated on the still air. The drone of planes seemed ominously near. As the guns fired again, she could see the smoke explosions against the luminous night sky.

'Alan,' she murmured, 'I think we are under attack. I think it's worse than usual.'

He groaned. 'Do you want to go to the shelter?'

'Well, not particularly,' she said. 'But on the other hand, I don't really want to die either.'

He smiled lazily. 'I think I have just died and gone to heaven. But now you come to mention it, it would be a shame if that was our last lovemaking ever, wouldn't it?' He leaned over and kissed her gently on the lips. 'I love you, Pam Nelson. That's why that Sean Byrne thing hurt so much.'

She looked at him and her heart twisted. 'Oh, Alan. I love you too. I always have. I just faltered a bit, that's all.'

He lowered his lips to her breast. 'Well, from now on I'm going to make damn sure you don't falter again,' he growled. 'Oh my God, Pam,' he added, lifting his head in some dismay as her body arched provocatively. 'I hope you're not expecting me to go through all that again. I'm not as young as I was, you know.'

She opened her eyes and smiled up at him, pleadingly. 'I feel as though I've got to make up for lost time.'

'What about the bombs?'

She giggled. 'What about under the stairs? They say that's quite a safe place.'

Joyce was surprised when Mr Lorenz offered her a cup of tea when she took him in the last two pounds she owed him. It took him ages to make it. At one point she almost offered to go round the back and pour it herself.

But he produced it in the end, and some Nice biscuits and as she leaned on the counter, she thought how odd things were. This time last year she never would have dreamed that she would be partaking of tea and biscuits with Lorenz before walking up to Cedars House to prepare a tasty dinner for Mr Rutherford.

She was doing him a steak and kidney pudding today. Nice and succulent, with thick brown gravy, boiled potatoes and peas out of the garden straight from the pod, and plums and custard to follow. She had forgotten how much she liked cooking. She was going to do him an apple pie tomorrow with a thick pastry crust. He'd like that. Not that he'd complained about her cooking yet. Just about the only thing you could say in Greville Rutherford's favour was that he liked his food.

Joyce glanced at Lorenz. He looked as though he could do with a bit of feeding up and all. She suddenly heard herself asking him if he liked apple pie.

He looked as surprised by the question as she was.

'Well, yes, I do,' he mumbled awkwardly. 'Very much. Although it's not something I often have.'

She wondered briefly what Jews did eat. Some sort of foreign muck, most likely. And with no one to cook for him it wasn't surprising he looked so thin and peaky. 'Then I'll send you one over tomorrow,' she said decisively.

As he lifted his eyes she noticed, not for the first time, how very thick and long his lashes were behind the steel-rimmed spectacles.

He looked quite embarrassed. 'Oh no, Mrs Carter, you needn't worry about that.'

She smiled. 'I'd like to do something for you, Mr Lorenz.' It was her turn to blush. 'I know you did me a good deal on the jewellery, and in my book one good turn deserves another.'

She'd make a pie for the kids and all, she decided. They hadn't had much in the food line recently what with the air raids and that. And they hadn't complained too badly considering.

Even Jen's temper had improved recently. Especially since she had pulled that odd hawk-faced woman out of her house in Croydon. Quite brave she'd been by all accounts. Funny how war changed people. Like Alan Nelson, he was another one who seemed on top of the world these days.

She looked back at Lorenz. He hadn't changed. Or if he had, it was for the worse. Of course he had even more to worry about than most, being Jewish and that.

She fiddled with the handle of her cup. 'Have you had any news of your friends, Mr Lorenz?' she asked abruptly. 'Those ones in Poland?'

He looked startled. 'Fancy you remembering that, Mrs Carter,' he said. Then he shook his head. 'I believe one or two may have made it as far as Paris, but there has been no word since Hitler invaded France. And for those left behind in Warsaw, I'm afraid we can only fear the worst. There is talk of special Jewish areas, camps,' he shrugged. 'But with no employment or money to speak of I fear they are only places where people wait to die.'

Joyce shook her head. Nobody liked the Jews much, but she couldn't see why anyone would want to treat them so badly.

'Do they look like you?' she asked suddenly. 'Those people in Poland? Or is there something odd about them? Something, you know, like different?'

'People come in all shapes and sizes,' he said. 'My Jewish friends are mostly indistinguishable from the local population. But they are Jews, Mrs Carter, that is what is different.'

Joyce nodded seriously. 'Have you made any plans, Mr Lorenz?' she asked. 'If there was an invasion or whatever?'

He shrugged and glanced around his shop. 'I am in the lucky position of having a certain amount of transportable wealth. I have thought of trying for America.' He hesitated and looked at her almost shyly. 'But I find I don't want to run away, Mrs Carter. Something inside me urges me to stand and face what comes.'

Joyce stared at him. If she was him she would be on the first ship to New York. Particularly now it looked as if the Germans were set on bombing the guts out of London. She didn't say anything then, but as she left the shop a few minutes later she turned in the doorway.

'If the worst happens maybe you should come over to us,' she said awkwardly. 'We could hide you up in the attic or something.'

Lorenz didn't answer for a moment. Then he blinked suddenly and shook his head. 'I appreciate your concern, Mrs Carter,' he said, and it showed in his voice that he was deeply touched. 'But I would hate to put you, of all people, in any danger.'

Joyce frowned. 'Well, we'll see,' she said. Then she brightened. 'I'll send you over that pie in any case.'

Margot Frost was a good influence on the Miss Taylors. Her brisk no-nonsense attitude kept them going. After a week of sirens, gunfire and sleepless nights, tired and irritable, it would have been easy for them to get depressed about the lack of news about Ward. To give up hope. But Mrs Frost's stoic confidence and positive outlook forced them to keep their chins up.

Jen too benefited from her drive, and her ruthless adherence to 'practice makes perfect'. She was still suffering from Sean's defection. Time and again she found herself wishing she had gone to Ireland. If only she had gone when he asked, then Aisling O'Donnell wouldn't have had a chance to get her claws into him. She hadn't had a letter since early July, but that didn't stop Jen thinking about him in every spare moment of the day. Nor did it stop her dreaming about him at night.

Thankfully, due to the Luftwaffe's activities overhead, there was not much opportunity to sleep at night these days, let alone to dream, and Mrs Frost kept her busy most of every day.

At first Jen had felt awkward at having to work on her scales and voice exercises within earshot of the Miss Taylors. But after a couple of sessions, she had discovered that they were genuinely interested in her progress. And under Margot Frost's strict, uncompromising tuition she definitely was progressing. Having discovered her talent for imitation, Margot Frost encouraged her to copy the tone and phraseology of the stars, and gradually even Jen began to hear the difference in her projection and resonance.

But as her ability grew, so did her embarrassment that Margot Frost's dedication, and the Miss Taylors' encouragement, was going entirely unrewarded. However, there was nothing she could do about it. Just now she hadn't got a penny to her name.

Margot Frost brushed off her concern when she mentioned it. 'You can pay me back if and when you get a job,' she said gruffly. 'As for Thelma and Esme, they're getting a lot of pleasure from seeing you improve. And it's keeping their minds off that damned nephew of theirs.' She suddenly gave one of her rare smiles. 'The best way you can repay them is to stay to tea and keep them chatting.'

It was no hardship. Having both worked as wardrobe mistresses in the London theatres, the Miss Taylors were full of stories and Jen was fascinated to hear about all the famous people they had met. At one time or another they'd dressed all the famous names; the Gibson Girls Isadora Duncan, and even Mrs Patrick Campbell in her famous role as Eliza Doolittle in *Pygmalion*.

Getting into the nostalgic mood one afternoon, Margot Frost had started to play some of the old classics on the piano, like *My Old Man said follow the Van, Daisy, Daisy*, and *Keep the Home Fires Burning*. They finished with a rousing chorus led by Mrs Frost of *It's a long way to Tipperary*, which, to Jen's complete embarrassment, had caused uncontrollable tears to pour down her face. Luckily nobody had thought to question the true cause of her emotion.

The tears notwithstanding, Jen found it astonishing how much she enjoyed her afternoons over at the Taylors' house. Even though they were increasingly frequently interrupted by the blasted sirens.

Since Berlin had been bombed a few days ago, Hitler now seemed to be dead set on London. The City of London had copped it again last night and Katy Parsons heard in the pub that some of the warehouses down by the East End docks were still on fire.

Everyone knew that it was only a matter of time until a bomb fell locally, there had already been near misses, but nevertheless an extraordinary air of nonchalance prevailed.

Mrs Frost was a typical example of the British bulldog spirit. Even though she had been awake half the night trying to calm Winston who apparently howled the house down every time the guns fired, she had refused to give in to fatigue and instead had marched the Miss Taylors, Jen and Katy Parsons out on to the sunlit common to listen to the Friday lunch time concert.

'I'm taking you all to the cinema tomorrow night,' she said as the band of the Royal Marines finished a rousing rendition of *Land of Hope and Glory*. 'We need to celebrate surviving a year of war.'

'Tuesday is the anniversary of the start of the war,' Katy remarked, feeding a bit of her sandwich to Winston. The Miss Taylors had prepared Marmite sandwiches and lemonade, and had insisted that Jen and Katy share their picnic.

'Exactly,' Margot Frost nodded. 'I reckon that's the day Hitler will invade. He loves anniversaries. So we need to have our night out before he comes.'

Thelma Taylor looked uneasily at her sister. 'I don't think we'll feel like celebrating anything until we hear from Ward,' she said.

'Nonsense,' Margot Frost replied crisply. 'No good crying over milk that may not yet have been spilt. And whatever's happened to him, Ward Frazer wouldn't want you to miss seeing Shirley Temple in *The Blue Bird*.'

'And it's in glorious Technicolor,' Jen chipped in eagerly.

'But what about Winston?' Esme said anxiously. 'We can't leave him alone in the house. What if there was a raid?'

Margot Frost frowned and Jen smiled to herself. It wasn't often that the drama teacher was flummoxed. But Katy came to her rescue.

'What about your brother, Jen?'

Jen blinked. 'What, Pete?' she said incredulously. 'I wouldn't leave Pete in charge of a goldfish.'

Katy giggled. 'I was thinking of Mick actually.'

Jen frowned doubtfully. 'I suppose Mick might do it. He owes me a few favours.' Not that looking after Winston was any recompense for bubbling Sean Byrne, Jen thought sourly as she stood up with the others for the *National Anthem*. But it wouldn't hurt to pull in a few favours.

But when she put the request to her brother that afternoon, having spotted him rolling beer barrels off the Rutherford & Berry dray into the Flag and Garter, he was extremely reluctant.

'Come off it, Jen,' he said, straightening up and wiping sweat off his forehead, 'I'm no good with animals, you know that.'

Jen frowned. 'Well, you'd better be good with this one or I'll have your guts for garters.' She eyed him grimly as he went to protest. 'You owe me one, Micky. More than one. And you owe Mum one too. Don't think I don't know why she's been scrimping and saving. To buy back that jewellery you nicked from the Rutherfords.'

Mick blanched. But his nervous glance up the street gave him away. Jen laughed harshly. 'Don't worry, I won't bubble you.' Her eyes narrowed dangerously. 'Unlike some people round here, I'm no grass.'

For once Mick had the grace to look ashamed. 'I'm sorry about that Sean Byrne business,' he mumbled, kicking the ground with his toe. 'I didn't realise as you was so keen on him.'

It was as much as Jen could do to hide her astonishment. 'Yes, well,' she floundered. She turned away before he could see the tears in her eyes. 'Well, you see to it you look after that dog for me Saturday night and if anything happens to it, you're dead.'

*

Celia Rutherford was hating Shropshire. Bertie's conchie arrogance and Douglas's absurd enthusiasm to fight were getting badly on her nerves. And Greville's sister Aunt Delia was so heartily unbearable that after a brisk exchange of telegrams with her husband, Celia announced that she would be leaving for London the following morning.

By dint of some impressive pleading, Louise had persuaded her that she should be allowed back to London too. But the boys were to be left behind. Douglas had discovered a school friend who lived in Aunt Delia's village. And Louise wasn't sure, but she guessed her father had refused to have Bertie back in the house.

Louise was delighted to be home. It was the last day of August, a beautiful Saturday afternoon. And she lost no time in going to visit Stefan Pininski.

She dressed carefully, glad there was nobody there to see her leave. Her father was doing some ARP duty, and her mother had rushed off to some WVS meeting as soon as he had left the house after lunch. They hadn't wanted her to go out. But on the pretext of going to the cinema with Katy Parsons she had persuaded them.

They were worried about her getting caught in a raid. The raids had been worse in London, it seemed, than up in Shropshire. But there was no sign of any damage on her way into town on the Underground although the barrage balloons were flying high on the common. A bad sign, Katy had said.

Katy had also told her with a long face that Ward Frazer was missing, had been for the last month, and, somewhat to her surprise, Louise found that she rather cared about that.

She also cared that Jen Carter had been some kind of heroine and had saved some woman from a bomb in Croydon.

Katy had been full of admiration for her friend. Just as Louise's father had been full of grudging admiration for Jen's mother.

'Excellent cook,' he had said when Celia asked him about her. 'Best shepherd's pie I've ever tasted. Can't think why you put up with that other cook. Food's always cold and tastes of cabbage.'

Louise had noticed that her mother had seemed pleased with this response. It was almost as if her mother had sent Cook away for a few weeks on purpose to give Mrs Carter a chance.

Anyway Louise was sick of hearing about the Carters. She wanted some admiration herself. And Stefan was just the person to give it to her. She had missed him. And there was no way she was going to put off seeing him, just to join Katy and Jen Carter at the cinema. Particularly as the world and his dog seemed to be going, the Miss Taylors, this Mrs Frost woman Katy kept going on about, even Mrs Carter had apparently been invited. Louise couldn't imagine anything worse than sitting next to Mrs Carter in the cinema.

'I don't like Shirley Temple,' she had said rather haughtily. 'Anyway I'm seeing Stefan tonight.'

Katy had leaned forward eagerly. 'I bet he's thrilled you're back.'

Louise made an excited face. 'He doesn't know yet. I thought I'd make it a surprise.'

And now here she was, in the lobby of the Savoy. And suddenly she didn't feel quite so certain. Suddenly she wished she'd telephoned. What if he was busy? What if he was out?

Nervously she glanced in one of the gilded mirrors, adjusted the S brooch and straightened her thin dress. He would like this dress. She had bought it especially with him in mind, but hadn't had time to wear it for him before her precipitous departure. Short sleeved and scooped, it showed off her neck and arms, with just a delicate hint of cleavage. She carried a matching handbag and her smart air-force blue, gas-mask holder was slung discreetly over her shoulder.

The liftboy glanced at her appreciatively as he asked her which floor she wanted.

Pleased, she checked her appearance surreptitiously once more in the lift mirror. As well as the S brooch, she was wearing the pretty necklace Stefan had bought her on their first date. The gold looked rather nice against her lightly tanned skin. The only good thing about Shropshire had been the weather.

Quivering with expectation, she stepped out of the lift, walked along the corridor and knocked tentatively at the door.

It opened almost at once. But it wasn't Stefan looking out with his usual lazy smile, it was a rather fierce-looking, middle-aged woman with smooth dark hair pulled straight back in a tight bun.

Thin black brows rose in enquiry, as the eager smile froze on Louise's face.

She must have knocked on the wrong door. Quickly she glanced at the number. Perhaps he had moved rooms. She kicked herself for not checking at reception.

'I'm so sorry, I must have got the wrong room,' she muttered, backing away.

'Who was it you wanted?' The voice was guttural and faintly accented, and seemed to be delivered down the woman's elegant nose.

'Stefan Pininski,' Louise replied stiffly. 'Count Stefan Pininski. I am a ... friend of his.'

A thin, humourless smile found its way on to the painted lips of the woman. 'And your name is?'

Louise frowned. 'Louise Rutherford.'

'I see,' she said, looking her up and down with a certain amount of interest. 'Well, Miss Rutherford, I'm afraid my husband is not here just at the moment.'

The words took a moment to sink in. Then Louise felt the floor shift under her feet. 'Your husband?' She stared at the woman in gaping disbelief. 'But ...'

The woman laughed dryly. 'But he never said he had a wife. No, my dear, he seldom does. But he has, and I am she. And despite the efforts of Mr Hitler, I am now here, so Stefan will no longer need you in his bed.' She smiled faintly as Louise's shocked pallor turned suddenly to a vivid blush. 'Yes, you are his type, I can see. He likes pretty, virginal little girls. And boys too, sometimes. He says it is the youth that attracts him, the innocence, the seduction.'

The casual words were like nails in Louise's heart. Stefan Pininski was married. She had given herself to a married man. A man who had just used her body while his wife was away.

His wife. Louise felt her heart crack in two as his wife shrugged negligently. The Countess Pininski was clearly used to her husband's indiscretions. They were obviously frequent and meaningless.

'You are disappointed,' she said now, as tears filled Louise's eyes. 'But I am sure he has rewarded you well. A little jewellery perhaps?' She smiled again as Louise's hand went involuntarily to the necklace at her throat, 'I thought so. My husband is a generous man.'

'Stop it,' Louise screamed. 'Stop it. I can't bear it.'

The woman looked surprised. 'My dear, you'll get over it. Everyone does.'

'I'll never get over it,' Louise cried out as wracking sobs overtook her. 'Never.'

Chapter Twenty Seven

Shirley Temple and the Blue Bird had only got as far as the Haunted Forest when the cinema lights came up suddenly and the front of house manager climbed up on to the stage.

'I am obliged to let you know that the air raid sirens on Lavender Hill have just sounded,' he announced, reading from a piece of paper that shook slightly in his hand. 'Anyone who wishes to leave is welcome to do so. However, for those that wish to stay we are obliged to keep the cinema open for the duration of the raid.'

One or two people in the audience stood up, but most people stayed in their seats, perhaps reluctant to miss the end of the film. In any case the cinema was a far more comfortable place to sit out a raid than the public shelters on Lavender Hill.

Jen glanced along the row. 'We'll stay, won't we?' she whispered.

Mrs Frost nodded but Esme Taylor looked anxious. 'What about Winston?' she murmured.

'Mick's with him,' Jen said. 'He promised on pain of death to look after him.'

Katy nervously fingered the gas mask on her lap. She felt her chest tightening already. It was the first time she had been out during a raid. She glanced surreptitiously up at the gilded ceiling high above her and wondered what their chances of survival were if it came crashing down on top of them. Then she wondered why the thought didn't make her feel more scared. Perhaps she was getting braver. She certainly hoped she was. Carefully she relaxed her chest and tried to breathe normally.

'In any case,' Mrs Frost was saying, 'it would take us at least ten minutes to get home and I wouldn't want to risk being outside when those guns fire. The shrapnel goes everywhere. The vicar had a piece straight through his greenhouse on Friday night.'

Thelma Taylor nodded in agreement. 'Quite ruined his tomato plants,' she said. 'I do hope we don't lose ours.'

Katy smiled to herself. What was it about Londoners, she wondered, that made them more concerned about their pets and their plants than themselves? Or perhaps it wasn't just Londoners. Maybe it was a British trait. If so, dear old Hitler was going to have quite a problem on his hands.

As the lights dimmed again, to a small cheer from the audience, she leaned over and touched Esme Taylor's arm. 'I'm sure Winston will be all right,' she whispered. 'Jen and I gave him a good run on the common this afternoon. He'll probably sleep straight through it.'

Having taken the Underground back across the river, but unable to face going home, Louise was sitting on the Clapham Common bandstand, crying, when the sirens went off.

Almost at once she heard the grumble of distant planes.

Her father had remarked countless times what a hindrance the guns were to the German planes as they came over Balham and Battersea on their final run in towards central London. Everyone knew it was only a matter of time before Goering tried to take them out, and the Battersea Power Station too, if he had any sense, and the gas works, and of course Clapham Junction, the busiest station in England.

As the drone of planes got louder, Louise knew she was in a dangerous place, but suddenly safety seemed a long way away. Beyond the trees around the bandstand, the smooth open grass stretched dark and very exposed between her and the distant houses.

The searchlights had been waving gently in the sky all evening, but now as she stared nervously across the common, they suddenly seemed more purposeful.

And then even as she watched, one of them caught a small formation of approaching planes in its beam. At once the searchlight switched to full power and, squinting against the sudden glare, Louise saw the formation break and spread across the dark sky.

But still they came on. She could hear the erratic, grating beat of their engines and see the silver glint of their wings. The searchlight still had one gripped in its yellow dancing swathe like a cornered rabbit, as it ducked and dived, trying to escape.

And then suddenly, above the drone of the other planes, Louise heard a different noise, a lighter, rattling beat, approaching rapidly, and she knew instinctively, with a flash of cold panic, that one plane had escaped the searchlights and was swooping in on the common unhindered.

She knew at once she was going to die. But fear had somehow paralysed her legs.

In any case, before she could even think of escape, the noise became deafening. The ground vibrated as the heavy, dark shadow roared low overhead and something like hail rattled against the roof of the bandstand. Screaming, Louise ran out through the trees.

She could hear shouting over at the gun emplacement. She could hear the clatter of light guns, she could smell cordite, and a line of smoke hung over the ground ahead of her.

And then just as she reached the open grass, the big guns fired and her whole world spun. As the shockwave hit her, it lifted her into the air, the ground disappeared from under her feet and she fell heavily, winded, face down in the grass.

As she lay there, gradually acknowledging that she was still alive, even as the shrapnel thumped, hissing, to the ground around her, she couldn't help thinking of all the dogs that relieved themselves out here and she gradually eased her head off the ground to spit the grass out of her mouth.

And then there was someone pulling her arm.

'Come into the shelter. It's dangerous here.' Aaref was crouching beside her. His voice urgent. Concerned.

'What are you doing here?' Louise mumbled, struggling to her knees. 'I thought you were still locked up.'

'I had tribunal,' he said. 'I am free again.'

Louise stood up and winced, still dazed, 'I've hurt my ankle.'

The searchlights were all on full power now, crisscrossing the sky, the smoke from the guns spiralling eerily in the beams. The air smelt of sulphur like a struck match.

Ignoring the drumming roar of approaching planes, Aaref peered at Louise as she spat out grass and wiped her mouth. 'Are you all right, Louise?' he asked awkwardly. 'You look like you are crying.'

Suddenly the events of the evening flooded back into Louise's numbed brain and a sob rose in her throat. She lifted her hands to her face in silent despair.

She felt Aaref's fingers on her arm and shook him off irritably. 'Leave me alone.'

'Let me take you home.'

She glared at him with red eyes. 'I don't want to go home,' she said angrily, her voice raised over the sudden crash of the ack-ack barrage.

Aaref looked at her, bewildered. 'Then we must go to the shelter,' he said urgently, as bright white magnesium flares began to cascade down, lighting the common like daylight. 'We will die if we stay here.'

'I want to die,' Louise shouted at him. 'I want to stay here.'

For a second Aaref stared at her, then he glanced over her shoulder and suddenly, to her astonishment, with surprising strength, he grabbed her arm and yanked her back against a tree.

Furiously she struggled against him, kicking and scratching, but he refused to release her, trapping her between him and the tree.

'Let me go,' she yelled at him. 'Why should you care if I live or die?'

Suddenly a plane thundered above them and bullets tore through the thick foliage. Louise screamed and Aaref shouted in German as something exploded violently nearby. For a second they stared at each other, rigid with fear, then Aaref leaned forward and kissed her clumsily on the lips.

'Now you understand me,' he shouted with a certain desperate bravado, as he raised his head. He saw her shocked expression. 'Now you will hate me. But I cannot stand by and watch you die.'

He closed his eyes for a moment as another plane screamed overhead. When he opened them, there were tears on his lashes. Seeing she was crying too, he pulled on her arm again. 'Please come to the shelter with me, Louise. I can't leave you, and my brothers will be so unhappy if I die.'

Joyce sat in the kitchen alone. Jen was out at the flicks. Mick was over at the Taylors', looking after that absurd dog of theirs, Pete was up in the West End with some pals.

The windows rattled as the Clapham Common guns fired off another massive salvo. The sirens had gone off a few minutes ago.

Joyce frowned. She could hear planes, the occasional distant crump of bombs, and she knew she ought to go to the shelter. But she didn't fancy sitting out there alone all night.

It was bad enough with the kids there. But at least their bickering took your mind off the uncomfortable splintering benches and the chill of corrugated iron.

Momentarily she wished she'd agreed to go to the cinema when Jen had asked her yesterday. But she knew as Jen didn't want her really. It was probably the Miss Taylors who had insisted she was asked. Out of politeness. In any case, Joyce knew she would feel left out with all that acting talk.

But now she found she didn't want to be in the house on her own. For the first time in ages she felt lonely with nobody there. But she could hardly go calling in the middle of an air raid. Everyone would be in their shelters, for a start, and wouldn't hear her knocking.

Anyway, who would she visit? Lorenz? She smiled suddenly as she remembered how pleased he'd been with the apple pie. He'd brought the plate back all nice and clean too. She liked that in a man. Cleanliness.

She clenched her fists as a plane roared directly overhead. She couldn't tell if it was one of ours or one of theirs. She wasn't as good as the boys in making the distinction. All she knew was it was bloody loud. At the same time she heard a tremendous clattering from up on the common and then the big guns fired again.

In the distance she could hear a dreadful repeated roaring noise, like gigantic rolling claps of thunder. She winced and waited nervously. Was this the invasion? Would the church bells ring out any moment? Or would she hear the clack of the ARP rattles indicating gas?

Then, not too far away at all, she heard the violent thump of an explosion and, without any further thought, she did what she had secretly intended to do all along.

Pulling on her cardigan, she grabbed her gas mask and ran down the street to the school, where Mrs Rutherford and another WVS lady were preparing the new mobile emergency canteen.

'Mrs Carter, thank God,' Celia Rutherford greeted her eagerly. 'I so hoped you'd come along. We need you. Mrs Walker hasn't turned up and I'm making a pig's ear of these sandwiches.'

'But I'm not a WVS member,' Joyce protested weakly as the other woman introduced herself as Penelope Trewgarth and shook hands briskly.

'Who cares,' Penelope Trewgarth shouted excitedly over the noise of the guns. 'We've word that Brixton has been hit so we're going down there. I'm driving. Climb aboard.'

At the cinema the film had come to an end and to keep the audience amused the management had replayed last week's Fred Astaire film. And the cartoons. And the news.

And still there was no sign of the raid abating. On the contrary it seemed rather worse than usual.

When the newsreel ended, the organist played a few numbers and then, in some desperation, the manager got up on the stage to ask if anyone in the audience would like to do a few turns.

'We may still have a while to wait,' he announced apologetically. 'The ARP warden has just notified us that they are not expecting the all clear for some time yet.'

Esme Taylor leaned round Katy Parsons to prod Jen's arm. 'How about it?' she whispered. 'There's a piano up there. Margot would play for you.'

Heart pounding, Jen shook her head. There was no way she was going to go up on stage to entertain a restless cinema audience. At least not yet. She would sit tight and see who else went up first. See what sort of reception they got.

Half of her wanted to do it, it would be good practice after all, but the other half balked, terrified she would lose her nerve or be a flop.

And she couldn't bear that. Not in front of the Miss Taylors who hoped for so much of her. Or Katy whose open admiration and unquestioning faith in her ability had kept her going through thick and thin for so long.

In rigid silence Jen listened to the audience applauding a young man as he took the stage and invited the audience to throw up their gas mask boxes, three of which, to their delight, he began to juggle with considerable skill. It was only when he added a fourth and then a fifth that he began to get into difficulties, and when the sixth went flying rather painfully into the audience he decided he had gone far enough and retired.

He was followed by a moustached man who cracked a few quite funny jokes about Hitler and his Nazi cronies, but he soon ran out of material and was replaced by a young girl pushed forward by her mother to sing an excruciating rendering of *Lovely to look at*, which, as she herself wasn't at all lovely to look at, fell almost as flat as her voice.

The audience applauded good naturedly but they were getting bored now and Jen could feel her heart pumping. She felt as though she was sitting under a huge great big sign saying 'This Girl Wants To Be A Performer But Is Too Scared To Try'.

Suddenly she knew she was going to do it and she began to breathe slowly and calmly, flexing her facial muscles, preparing herself for the moment just as Mrs Frost had taught her.

Two men got up on the stage then and performed an excellent run through of the Two Gendarmes from one of Offenbach's operas and a Gilbert and Sullivan piece from the *Mikado*, but sadly that seemed to be the sum total of their repertoire and they were followed by a young girl pianist who played a brisk no-nonsense rendition from *Peter and the Wolf*.

Then there was a pause.

Hardly daring to breathe, Jen crossed her fingers and glanced cautiously along the row at Mrs Frost.

In the chilly, dank trench shelter on Clapham Common, Aaref held Louise's hand tightly. It was very scary. Bombs were falling. They could hear the crump of them landing, feel the vibration in the duck-boards under their feet, but not judge how close.

Louise had stopped crying. Sitting in a dark corner, well away from the other occupants, shaking with fear, she had finally told Aaref her painful story, stumbling over the words, saying a million times she wished she was dead. To her surprise Aaref had listened with attentive sympathy.

'Don't wish you were dead,' he said now, 'That would be too sad. You are alive and young. And pretty and clever.'

Louise shook her head dully. 'I might as well be old and dead for all Stefan will care.'

'Stefan Pininski is a stupid dumb-head,' Aaref said dismissively. 'But I care. I care so much, Louise. And your friends. And your family too. I'm sure they care. Doesn't that count for something?'

Tears sprang into Louise's eyes again. 'My family doesn't care. My mother just thinks I'm a nuisance. She doesn't know about Stefan anyway, I haven't told her. I haven't told her anything for weeks.' She gulped. 'And now she's probably being bombed and I won't have a chance to say goodbye.'

She suddenly looked up and clutched his hand urgently. 'Aaref, I've got to go home. Poor Mummy. She'll be so worried.'

He shook his head. 'You can't. Not in the middle of a bombing raid. The

319

ARP man at entrance would never let you out.'

She stared at him. 'But they might die,' she said desperately. 'They might be dying now. Mummy and Daddy and everyone. And Ward Frazer has been missing for weeks. He's probably dead already.'

As she began to cry again, Aaref put his arm round her shoulders. 'I'm sure your mother will be safe in a shelter. And your friends too.'

Louise was suddenly overcome by self-pity. It hadn't slipped her notice that she was invited less and less often these days to the Lucie Clayton lot's parties and outings. She was hardly even one of the gang any more. Maybe she never really had been. She had always thought it was because they were jealous of her looks or snooty because she lived south of the river, but perhaps the truth was that they just didn't like her.

'My friends will think I've got my just desserts over Stefan,' she said miserably, remembering how she had gloated about his title to Helen de Burrel.

'No. I'm sure not the nice girl at the pub,' Aaref said, surprised. 'I don't think she will give you bad desserts.'

Louise tried to smile but for once Aaref's mistakes didn't amuse her. 'No,' she admitted grudgingly, 'Katy Parsons is all right. She won't gloat.' She wished suddenly she had gone to the cinema after all. It had been kind of Katy to ask her.

'And I?' he asked, squeezing her hand gently. 'I do not gloat. Am I all right?'

She looked at him. In the dim light his gaunt face didn't seem quite as angular as it used to. Perhaps he had put on weight in the internment camp. Certainly he had got some colour in his skin at last. And there was a new confidence about him. And it was true he didn't gloat. Even though he had indirectly warned her about Stefan Pininski several months ago, he hadn't once said 'I told you so.' Nor had he shown any disgust at what she had done. He had taken her confession in his stride. As far as he was concerned the whole thing was Stefan's fault.

Suddenly, Louise realised she was grateful for Aaref's presence. She had always thought he was only a boy, too young for her to take seriously. Outside on the common, as bullets rained down on them he had kissed her like a boy, clumsily and crossly. But now, in the horrible smelly shelter, he was different, reassuring and sympathetic. And suddenly she found his uncritical appreciation of her humbling.

What he had been through, losing his parents and his home, and being forced to flee his country with his two young brothers in tow, was so much worse than anything she had ever experienced. So much worse than finding Stefan Pininski was married to someone else. It simply didn't compare. And yet she had been so horrid to Aaref. So unkind about him.

And he had done nothing to hurt her. Nothing at all. All he had done was admire her, and now he was standing by her in her hour of need.

She felt tears in her eyes again, tears of remorse this time, and wished she was a nicer person. Someone who might deserve the affection of good, kind, genuine people like Aaref Hoch and Katy Parsons. Even Jen Carter. She thought of Jen and Katy going to the cinema with those old women. She closed her eyes and promised herself that if they survived the air raid she would make an effort to be nicer. To do something kind for somebody else.

'You're all right, Aaref,' she whispered through her tears. 'But I'm not. I've been so beastly to everyone. It's no wonder nobody really likes me.'

'How can you say that?' Aaref said crossly. 'When I am liking you so much my heart is going to explode like one of Hitler's bombs.'

'That's lust,' Louise said sadly. 'It's my body you like, not me. The same as Stefan.' She stopped as a lump rose in her throat. She could hardly bear to think of the absurd ease with which Stefan Pininski had pulled the wool over her eyes. Two pieces of fancy jewellery and a few flattering words had efficiently blinded her to his deceit. And yet even now, even in this dingy, dank air-raid shelter, under attack from the Luftwaffe, she longed for his touch, his provocative caresses.

'Aaref?' She swung round to him suddenly, desperately, clutching his cold hands. 'Please will you kiss me? Like you did before under the tree.'

To her surprise he flushed slightly and shook his head. 'No,' he said steadily, disengaging his hands. 'I don't want to kiss you when you are thinking of another man. I will be your friend, Louise. But that is all. Until you can tell me you want me for myself and not so to make you forget of someone else.'

Taken aback, Louise stared at him aghast. For a moment she was angry. How dare he turn her down, when for so long he had been saying he wanted her?

But then she thought again, and realised he was right. It wouldn't be fair. She needed time to get over Stefan. To be honest she still wasn't sure she had got over Ward Frazer. And it might be nice to have a friend in the meantime. And Katy Parsons would approve.

Slowly she nodded. 'OK. So we'll just be friends,' she said. Then she frowned. 'So what do friends do during an air raid?'

Aaref grinned and drew a pack of cards out of his pocket. 'They play with cards,' he said. 'But first I will perform to you a very clever trick that Benjamin showed to me this morning.'

For a second Louise thought of correcting his English, then she decided against it. There was plenty of time after all. And in any case, there was something rather charming in the way he got it wrong.

*

321

Katy Parsons felt sick as Jen and Mrs Frost walked down the aisle. Her heart was pounding so hard she was certain everyone in the row must hear it. She had had no idea she would feel so anxious for her friend. She almost thought she would rather be going up there herself than having to sit here, watching helplessly. And then she felt Thelma Taylor's hand creep into hers to give it a nervous squeeze, and she realised that the old ladies were feeling the same choking apprehension as she was. After all, Jen was their protégée.

As Mrs Frost calmly took her seat at the piano and Jen stepped up on to the stage, Katy found herself praying. Praying to a God whose beneficence she had recently begun to doubt. Now she hoped that even if he didn't seem able or willing to prevent his subjects killing each other, he might at least give a moment's thought to a budding young actress. Katy hadn't seen Jen perform since *Romeo and Juliet* at school. Jen had been great in that. But acting out a part in a play was quite different to standing up and holding the audience single handed.

Katy crossed her fingers. She dearly hoped Jen was up to it.

They started with *A Nightingale Sang in Berkeley Square*.

For the first few bars, Jen's voice seemed very small and uncertain, and Katy felt her nails digging painfully into her palms.

Closing her eyes, she willed Jen to relax, willed her to raise her voice, to sing out to the back rows, who were already muttering about not being able to hear.

And then suddenly she did.

On the higher notes her voice swelled and grew. As the muttering behind her stopped abruptly, Katy opened her eyes and breathed again.

Jen was smiling now, her tawny eyes raking the audience for a reaction as the last notes echoed away into the auditorium. She received the applause gracefully.

But Mrs Frost didn't allow her to stop. Stiff-backed and stern, she went straight into the introduction to another number, a musical comedy which Jen performed with considerable panache. And then she was into *Ma, He's Making Eyes at Me*, one of her favourites, and Katy found herself laughing along with everyone else at Jen's exaggerated facial expression and coy hand movements.

They were applauding before Jen had even reached the end.

Suddenly there were tears running down Katy's face.

Jen was good.

Slowly Katy eased her nails out of her palms to applaud. She found herself crying and smiling both at once. In relief and in admiration. Jen was good. Very good. And very brave.

Reaching into her pocket for a handkerchief to blow her nose, Katy's fingers closed on the envelope hidden there. Mrs Frost had helped her write it. A letter of application to St Thomas's Hospital, Westminster Bridge.

It had sat in her pocket for a week. But if Jen could go out on a limb, so could she. She would take it to the post office on Lavender Hill tomorrow. And she would only tell her parents what she had done when it was safely in the post.

The police had cordoned off the area where the bombs had fallen, and, weren't allowing anyone through.

In the back of the WVS canteen van, Joyce and, Celia Rutherford heard Mrs Trewgarth arguing vociferously with a policeman. 'She'll get us in,' Celia murmured. 'You wait and see.'

'What's the point of having an emergency canteen van if we're not allowed near the emergency?' Mrs Trewgarth was asking the policeman heatedly. 'Answer me that, young man, if you can.'

Joyce peered out of the hatch and giggled. 'He's fifty if he's a day, that policeman.'

'I hope my husband isn't here,' Celia said, wincing as a plane flew overhead and everyone started shouting outside. 'You can't see him anywhere, can you, Mrs Carter? He told me quite expressly this morning that I wasn't to come out in a raid. But Louise was out and I couldn't face sitting in the cellar worrying all on my own.'

'I can't see him,' Joyce said, coughing. 'Mind you, there's so much smoke everywhere it's hard to see who's who.' She withdrew her head and closed the hatch. 'He's not going to be too pleased when he gets home and finds nobody there, is he?'

Celia shrugged. He's so angry about me coming back from Shropshire, I doubt it will make any difference.' She looked at Joyce. 'What would your husband say if he knew you were here?'

Joyce grinned. 'He'd say I was bloody stupid.'

Celia smiled. 'But would you take any notice?'

Joyce was about to shake her head, when she stopped and thought. Would she take any notice? She frowned. That was a good question. She had used to take notice. Mainly because Stanley had thumped her if she didn't. She shivered. It was a long time since she had thought about that. That awful gripping fear. The painful sting of the back of his hand. The bruises. The shame.

She wouldn't put up with that again when Stanley came out. She was her own person now, not some cowed old punch-bag for Stanley to vent his anger on.

She could see Mrs Rutherford looking at her, waiting for her answer. 'I used to take notice,' Joyce admitted at last. 'But now I reckon I'd try to stand up to him. Of course that's easy for me to say, what with Stanley inside and that.'

Celia nodded. 'It's easier when they're not there. If Greville had been at home tonight, I wouldn't have dared come out.'

Joyce shook her head with new respect. 'I reckon as you've more guts than me, Mrs Rutherford. To go against his word and that.' Mind you, she added silently to herself, Greville Rutherford probably didn't hit her. That made a difference.

'Oh no, Mrs Carter,' Celia said, surprised. 'You're far more gutsy than me. I've learnt a lot from you over the last year.'

Joyce blinked at her in astonishment. 'I can't imagine what, apart from a bit of bad language.'

Celia smiled. 'I've learned to stand up for myself more. I've learned to laugh at things that don't matter. I've learned to be a bit more tactful. Oh, and best of all I've learned to worry about the children less. Particularly Louise. I used to baby her too much. Since I've stopped paying so much attention to where she's going and who she's meeting, she's improved. I almost feel I can trust her now not to do anything stupid.'

Joyce thought about the suppressed excitement she had noticed on Louise's pretty face that morning and hoped that paying less attention to her children hadn't been a bad lesson for Celia to learn from her. After all, her own children weren't much to write home about.

Although come to think of it, even they had improved lately. Jen behaved less like a cornered tiger these days. And even Mick had grown up a bit. Mind you, she had Pam and Alan Nelson to thank for that. Throwing him out that time, over the jewellery, had been the best thing she had ever done.

'I've also learned how to have fun,' Celia added. 'Fun on my own. Without my family. And definitely without my husband.'

Joyce looked at her, surprised. 'So have I.'

Suddenly they both began to smile. Celia reached for the WVS biscuit tin and offered it to Joyce with a giggle. 'Who needs men when you can have biscuits?' she asked.

And Joyce was just about to reply when a great shout of triumph came from Mrs Trewgarth at the front of the van.

'Get the kettles on, Mrs Rutherford, we're going in.'

Jen wanted to leave the stage, she knew it was best to leave the audience wanting more, but they wouldn't let her go. Even the lads in the cheap seats at the front had loved her absurd take-off of the tap number, *In the Mood*, and she'd had the whole theatre singing along with her to some of the old classics

As the applause went on and on, she glanced at Mrs Frost still sitting staunchly at the piano and smiled. Who would ever have thought she and the brisk, beaky drama teacher would be entertaining a cinema audience together? Jen could hardly remember now why she had hated Margot Frost so much at first. It was partly her looks, the hawk nose, the thin lips and eyebrows. But when Mrs Frost smiled as she was suddenly doing now, it warmed your heart.

Jen squinted over the footlights into the auditorium and saw Katy Parsons and the Miss Taylors all applauding like mad with beaming smiles. Jen felt sudden tears in her eyes and blinked them back rapidly. She wished suddenly her mother had agreed to come. Or even one of the boys. But once again, just as in the school play, her entire family was absent. And for a second she felt a stab of desolation. A stab of loneliness. But it didn't last long.

'*She Had to Go and Lose It at the Astor*,' Mrs Frost muttered, preparing to launch forth again.

But before she could touch the keys, there was a deafening crash outside and the whole cinema shook. The lights flickered briefly and the applause stopped abruptly.

'Keep your seats, keep your seats, no damage done,' someone shouted frantically from the back.

Jen glanced at Mrs Frost and nodded. And at once they swung into the racy number.

And as she played with their reactions, dancing about across the stage to amuse them, seducing them away from their anxiety, taking their minds off whatever was happening outside, for the first time in months Jen was glad she had stayed in England and hadn't gone with Sean. This was worth anything.

As the audience laughed again she felt a kick of pleasure.

This is it, she thought to herself. I don't care about my family. I don't care about Sean. I don't care about anything except this. This is power. This is me.

But gradually, despite Mrs Frost's efforts, she was running out of repertoire and out of breath. She was beginning to have problems with the high notes.

And then suddenly there was someone calling up at her from the front row.

Jen couldn't believe her eyes. It couldn't be. But it was. Gillian Price. The girl who had played Romeo to Jen's Juliet in the Lavender Road School production over a year ago. Jen hadn't seen her for ages but she had heard that Gillian was not only married but pregnant. Sure enough, as her former schoolmate giggled beyond the footlights, Jen could see the massive bulge under her summer frock.

'Why don't we do the balcony scene?' Gillian shouted. 'I can still remember the words.'

Jen gaped at her appalled and then at Mrs Frost who was shaking her head.

But laughing, beyond caring now, Jen beckoned Gillian up on to the stage and dragged a chair from the wings into the middle of the stage.

'We will now perform an excerpt from William Shakespeare's *Romeo and Juliet*,' she announced in perfect imitation of John Gielgud, that most famous of Shakespearean actors. 'We would be grateful if you would excuse Romeo's somewhat er ... delicate condition.'

And then, to the complete hilarity of the audience, they acted out theatre's most famous love scene.

The chair made a makeshift balcony, and Jen, balancing precariously, deliberately hammed the whole thing to such an extent that even Mrs Frost was wiping her eyes by the end. Jen, herself, could hardly stop laughing as she declared undying love to a Romeo who was quite clearly bursting at the seams. One impassioned plea too many, she thought, and Gillian Price would have the blasted thing on the stage.

The applause was tumultuous.

As Gillian Price clambered off the stage, Jen put on her best Joyce Grenfell voice. 'Is there a midwife in the house?' she asked and then hearing the distant wail of the all-clear switched seamlessly to Neville Chamberlain.

'Ladies and gentlemen,' she announced in the familiar clipped tones. 'There may not be peace in our time, but it sounds as if we might get a bit of peace tonight.'

The audience roared as Jen took her curtsey. She indicated to Mrs Frost to stand up to take her bow and the applause lifted again.

It was a heady moment. She could see the tears in her teacher's eyes and she ran over and hugged her there and then right by the piano.

'Thank you,' she whispered, almost sobbing into the bony neck. 'Oh, thank you for helping me so much,' Then, cautiously, conscious of several bad mistakes she had had to gloss over, she added, 'I know it wasn't perfect but it wasn't too awful, was it?'

Margot Frost sniffed. 'Shakespeare would turn in his grave,' she said. 'Otherwise not too bad.'

Jen gazed at her teacher in delight. A 'not too bad' from the Maggot was praise indeed. Worth more than any amount of applause.

As they climbed off the stage, Jen felt as though she was walking on air. Ignoring the all-clear, the audience clapped her all the way back to her seat.

But as they approached, she realised her seat was taken, and so was Mrs Frost's. As the Miss Taylors, muttering incoherently, struggled out of the row to hug her almost to death, two men stood up politely.

Still partially blinded by the stage lights, Jen peered at them. For a strange, tense second she thought it was Sean Byrne, and was surprised to feel her heart sink.

Then her eyes widened.

It wasn't Sean Byrne. It was Ward Frazer, with another man, a stranger.

A smile spread on her lips. No wonder the Miss Taylors were so excited.

Disentangling herself from Thelma's clutching fingers, Jen turned to face the handsome Canadian. 'You're back.'

'I'm back,' he said gravely. 'Just in time to see your act.' He inclined his head. 'You were great.'

Jen glowed. 'How did you know we were here?'

Ward Frazer smiled his beautiful smile. 'Your brother told me. He was at my aunts' house. It was rather cute. He was singing lullabies to Winston in the cellar. Rocking him in his arms. Trying to soothe him, he said.' He chuckled. 'I guess he was doing a good job because Winston was fast asleep.'

Jen bit her lip. Tears were pouring down her face.

Everything was suddenly all right. She was over Sean Byrne. She hadn't been a flop. Mrs Frost was beaming. The Miss Taylors were happy. Ward Frazer was safely home. They'd survived a year of war.

Admittedly, at the other end of the row, Katy Parsons looked as though she was about to be sick or faint, or both. But that was fairly normal for Katy. She was probably scared of the bombing.

'It's Jennifer, isn't it?' Ward was saying. 'I'd like you to meet a friend of mine, Henry Keller. He's in the theatre too. A producer.'

Blankly Jen offered her hand and found it taken in a firm grip.

'Delighted to meet you, Miss Carter.'

Henry Keller's voice was cultured and warm. 'I enjoyed your performance tremendously. I don't know what your plans are, but I'd like to talk to you about auditioning for ENSA. We're always on the look-out for talented, versatile young performers like you.'

But before she could answer, before she could even glance at Mrs Frost, the organist began thumping out the sonorous strains of the *National Anthem*. And suddenly everyone was standing to rigid, patriotic attention.

Author's note:

The idea for the Lavender Road series came to me when I met a neighbour at a bus stop on Clapham Common in South London. We fell into conversation and she pointed out the sites of the old gun emplacements, and the air-raid shelters on the common. She had lived in Clapham all through the war and had some amazing stories to tell. As I listened to her I thought what an interesting project it would be to write a series of novels following the lives of the people in one particular street all the way through the war. And so the Lavender Road idea was born.

Readers often ask how true to life the Lavender Road books are. My aim is to make them as 'real' as possible. But although the historical events are accurate, and most of the places I mention actually exist (or existed then), the 'Lavender Road' of the story is a figment of my imagination and the people who live in it are fictional.

Finally I would like to thank all the people who have helped me in so many different ways with creating this book. I am especially grateful to the four wonderful South London ladies who gave me such unstinting access to their memories, Laura Boorman, Ethel Smith, Murial and last but not least, the magical Mary Morland; may she sing and dance for ever.

Helen Carey
www.helencareybooks.co.uk

Next in the Lavender Road Series

HELEN CAREY

Some Sunny Day

It is 1940, a year into the Second World War. London is now a very dangerous place. But despite the bombing and the privations, living and loving must go on.

Shy Katy Parsons from the pub summons the courage to enroll as a nurse, but quickly discovers that the rigours of hospital life are hard to bear, although not quite as hard as falling in love with an unobtainable man.

Away on an ENSA tour, Jen Carter finds herself unexpectedly homesick. While her mother, Joyce, prefers to face the terror of the burning streets on the WVS van than suffer her husband's violence at home.

Following on from LAVENDER ROAD, SOME SUNNY DAY vividly depicts the courage, the resilience, and the defiant laughter of war-torn London, when, as friends and neighbours, men and women, rich and poor, the inhabitants of Lavender Road face up the the trials and tribulations of the London Blitz.

'Funny, poignant, emotional and un-putdownable, SOME SUNNY DAY rips along, taking you with it into wartime London and the lives of these engaging and incredibly varied characters.' **London Evening Standard**

'Will keep you turning pages long into the night.' **Natalie Meg Evans**

Also by Helen Carey:

Lavender Road
Some Sunny Day
On a Wing and a Prayer
London Calling
The Other Side of the Street
Victory Girls

Slick Deals

The Art of Loving

http://www.helencareybooks.co.uk

CPSIA information can be obtained
at www.ICGtesting.com
Printed in the USA
BVHW05s2336280518
517560BV00023B/1536/P